THE WANDERINGS OF WUNTVOR

THE
WANDERINGS
OF WUNTVOR

A Difficulty with Dwarves
An Excess of Enchantments
A Disagreement with Death

CRAIG SHAW GARDNER

Nelson Doubleday, Inc.
Garden City, New York

CONTENTS

A
DIFFICULTY
WITH DWARVES

This one's for
Anne
a.k.a. Supersister

ONE

"*Even wizards sometimes have bad days. I shall give you an all-too-common example:*

"*The magician, about to begin a spell of great importance, discovers that all his duckwort has gone bad and he is completely out of eye of newt. And it gets no better! The sorcerer quickly dons his walking robes and strolls down to the corner alchemist, only to discover they've had duckwort back ordered for months, and what newt eyes they have in stock are far too small and altogether of the wrong color.*

"*Well, the good magician is far too resourceful to let a couple of missing ingredients spoil a perfectly good spell. The mage quickly returns to his eyrie, and attempts some prudent substitutions, say batwing and dried salamander's blood, with perhaps some chives tossed in to give the whole thing color. And the potion looks correct at last! The sorcerer begins to chant the spell that will bring his day's work to fruition. But wait! The pot is burbling when it should be boiling! What could be wrong?* (See footnote)

"*The mage quickly checks a nearby reference work, perhaps the forty-six volume* Universal Guide to Magic, *or my own much more concise* When Bad Spells Happen to Good Wizards. *There, to his horror, the magician sees that, through an almost infinitesimal error, he has transformed a simple weather-predicting spell into a conjuration that will destroy himself, his loved ones, and every other living thing in this hemisphere!*

"*The wizard somehow manages to stop the spell in time, but ruins a perfectly good pair of boots in the process. By now the wise magician will have faced up to one inevitable conclusion: That this day will be one of misfortune, not only for the wizard, but for all those with whom he comes in contact.*

Footnote: The apt student would have known instantly that our sorcerer should have used parsley instead of chives for coloration.

"But the resourceful mage should not despair that the fates conspire against him! Rather, the prudent sorcerer should take what small advantage of the situation still remains available, and spend the remainder of the day visiting one's mother-in-law or insisting upon an immediate audit by the royal tax collectors."

—Ebenezum, greatest magician in all the
Western Kingdoms,
MAGIC FOR THE MILLIONS:
A HOME STUDY COURSE
(fourth edition), General Introduction

It seemed like everybody was sneezing.

"Oh, Wuntvor," Norei whispered. Her beautiful green eyes looked deep into mine. "Isn't it terrible?"

The sound echoed through the Great Hall in which we stood, perhaps a hundred different wizards sneezing as one; high sneezes, low sneezes, short little shushing sounds, and huge, long nasal blasts. As difficult as it was to tear my eyes away from the beautiful young witch by my side, this true love that I had found at last, the nasal avalanche was far too overwhelming. With great trepidation I turned away from my beloved and looked down to the far end of the hall.

My worst fears were confirmed. The great oak door, behind which the wizards had conferred in order to find a cure for my master Ebenezum, had been flung open. The sorcerers, so noble and grand when they had entered that room some hours before, now staggered out of it one by one, their once-fine robes askew and torn.

But wait! One man strode through the wizard's ragged ranks, a look of grim determination on his dark-skinned face. Two arms clad in brilliant silver rose above the sneezing mass as this magnificent wizard, this mage among mages, cried "Enough!"

The wizards nearby held their noses and turned to watch their fellow.

"This will happen no more!" The silver-clad wizard cried in a voice as deep as the farthest depths of the Inland Sea. "I will banish this curse, as I call upon the spirits!"

His hands wove a pattern through the air too fast for the eye to see. "Come forth, oh mighty waa . . ." He paused. "Come forth, oh mighty waa . . . waa . . . WAAAA . . ." His voice seemed to rise with every word. He stopped and swallowed, his dark brows furrowed in concentration.

"Enough!" he began again. "This will happen no . . . WAAAACHOOO!"

His sneeze tore his silver robes in half as the multitude of mages about him answered in kind. The entirety of the Great Hall trembled with their distress. The silver wizard was soon lost beneath the sneezing mass.

Something must have gone horribly wrong. My master and I had traveled here, to far and fabled Vushta, the city of a thousand forbidden delights, in hopes of ending our quest—a quest that began when my master was forced into battle with the dread rhyming demon Guxx Unfufadoo! My master won that first battle, but discovered that he suffered from a sinister aftereffect. From that moment onwards, whenever the wizard Ebenezum was even in the presence of magic, he would begin to sneeze uncontrollably!

Now, a malady of this sort might have driven a lesser magician to despair, but not my master! Ebenezum set out to find a cure, even if it meant traveling to far and fabled Vushta, seat of wizardly learning for all the Western and Central Kingdoms!

So travel to Vushta we did, learning on our way of a sinister plot by the forces of the Netherhells led by the dread rhyming Guxx! We redoubled our efforts to reach our destination, only to discover that the demons had spirited away the very city that was our goal and hidden it deep within their dwelling place beneath the earth, the dreaded Netherhells!

Well, there was nothing to do then but rescue Vushta as well. Since there was no legitimate hero handy, I was sent in the hero's stead, and with the help of good luck and noble companions, Vushta was rescued at last. In return for my service, the greatest wizards of the greatest city on the face of the globe had gathered together, all for the sake of Ebenezum. Now my master's malady would be cured, and all set right with the world.

Or would it?

Wizards were still emerging from the room at the far end of the hall, climbing over the bodies of their fallen comrades, the latter now convulsed with sneezing fits. It was a gruesome sight. I swallowed hard and turned back to my beloved.

"Yes," I replied, looking once again deep into Norei's eyes. "It is truly—"

"Terrible!" The old wizard Snorphosio called as he approached us, carefully stepping around or over the prone wizards in his path. "Instead of curing Ebenezum's malady, he has given it to all of them. I knew this would happen!" He coughed nervously into a thin, almost birdlike hand.

"They took too direct an approach! I knew it! Something of this magnitude needs to be studied for weeks at least. Sometimes even years!" Snorphosio mopped his brow with a gray scholar's sleeve. "Everyone knows that sorcery is an elusive art. Well"—he paused and took a breath—"perhaps everyone doesn't know that, but at least wizards do . . . well, good wizards know the truth of what I'm saying." He glanced distractedly at the roomful of sneezing sorcerers. "Well, good wizards *should* know the truth I speak. But then again, what is the nature of truth? And how do wizards approach that nature? For that matter, how does nature approach wizards? In fact, is there truth in natural wizardry, or is there rather—"

"Indeed," I replied in an attempt to cut short the learned sorcerer's musings. At least Snorphosio seemed to be calming down. Before, he had been so upset that he had actually managed to talk in short, coherent sentences. Now, however, the never-ending theorist deep in his soul seemed to be reasserting itself.

"Yes, you are quite right," Snorphosio replied to my surprise. "This is no time for theory. It is time for action. I say there!" His voice rose above the collective sneezing. "Fellow wizards! Can any of you catch your breath long enough to tell me what happened in the other room?"

Half a dozen wizards tried to speak at once. None of them uttered more than a phrase before they rejoined their sneezing comrades.

"This is even more serious than I imagined!" Snorphosio exclaimed. "But then, who is to say how truly serious a situation can be? And who can put a limit on imagination? And exactly how serious is imagination, anyway? Or how imaginary is the limit of seriousness—"

The theoretical wizard's body shook with an effort of will. "No! I have no time for these musings. It is time to act!" He paused. "But, is not musing in itself an action? And what if you act on musing? Is that not—"

Snorphosio shook himself again, clenching his fists. "Action!" He looked again at the mass of ailing wizards. "Colleagues!" he called. "Please, hold your breath for but a moment. I will perform a short magic eradication spell, after which we may talk in peace."

The noise level dropped considerably as the sorcerers attempted to comply. Snorphosio got halfway through his spell before he, too, began to sneeze.

"Hold!" came a clear voice from the room in which the wizards had conferred. "Go no further!"

Norei and I turned to look across the disabled wizards, at the meeting room where this had all begun.

One more wizard strode boldly from the room, also seemingly unaffected by the magical malady. The large mass of sneezing wizards filling the hallway about us had raised a great deal of dust. It was difficult to see clearly. Still, there was something familiar about the way the man carried himself, his long, white beard, and dark blue robes.

The mage paused at the edge of the sneezing mass of sorcerers. "Indeed," he intoned.

With that word, I knew. It was my master, the greatest wizard in all the Western Kingdoms, Ebenezum!

"Master!" I called, delighted to see him so self-possessed in the midst of this chaos. "Did the wizards succeed? Are you cured?"

The mage frowned at the mass of magicians before him. He pulled absently at his beard, then turned his gaze from the shuddering mass to look at me.

"Alas, no." He sniffed delicately into a sleeve threaded with silver. "I have but had the malady somewhat longer than these others, and thus have learned to control it better." He shook his head. " 'Tis a sorry sight, to see the amassed wisdom of Vushta brought to such a pass."

"Pardon me, good wizard," Norei interjected, "but how could such a thing have happened?"

"Indeed," Ebenezum replied as he wove through the disabled mages. "Perhaps if I got a bit closer, we would no longer need to shout." He moved as quickly as he could through the sneeze-wracked horde. The very sight of the tastefully inlaid silver moons and stars on his wizard's robe seemed to send those crouched nearby into redoubled nasal attacks. Finally he reached the end of the hallway in which we stood, the flagstones here still relatively free of incapacitated sorcerers.

Ebenezum looked back over the trembling sea of wizard flesh. "It seems that we face new difficulties. It appears that the machinations of the Netherhells were even more insidious than we first thought. By

dragging the city of Vushta down within their noxious domain, the
demons have somehow subtly changed it. I fear this change may affect
everything within the city. We have already seen how it affects the use
of magic."

"This is all the doing of demons?" Norei asked. "Then that means
we haven't defeated them as thoroughly as we thought!"

"Alas, no." My master scratched absently at the thick white hair
beneath his wizard's cap. "I fear that our victory celebrations are
premature. It appears that we have won but the first battle. Vushta
and the Netherhells are still at war."

"But this is terrible!" I shuddered at the very thought of these
underhanded Netherhells schemes. "What can we do?"

"The first thing is not to panic." He nodded at the still sneezing
mass. "The enemy has, temporarily, taken us by surprise. They have a
slight advantage over us now, but it will not last for long. Already the
wizards around us are learning to control their disability."

It was true. There were far fewer sneezes than there had been but a
moment before. Perhaps my master was right. There was cause for
hope after all.

"Indeed," my master continued, "we must now plan for the long
run. As long as we can keep our heads—"

There was an explosion in the middle of the room.

"Hi, guys!" a tiny voice exclaimed. "I'm back!"

I knew who it was even before the smoke had cleared. Only one
creature I knew had a voice as squeakily high and relentlessly cheerful
as that.

"Talk about Brownie Power!" the voice added.

There was no doubting it now. A small, brown figure jumped merrily up and down on a pile of sneezing wizards. It had to be Tap the
Brownie.

"Boy, is it great to be back!" Tap continued. "I had a hard time
leaving you before, let me tell you. I mean, who wants to go back to
making shoes when you could visit Vushta, the city of a thousand
forbidden delights! But now I can do all the visiting I want. That is,
once I deliver my message!"

Tap unfolded a piece of brown parchment which had been stuck in
his belt. "This is an official proclamation from his Brownieship," he
began.

Tap paused to clear his throat, then spoke in a clear, high voice
above the constant sneezing: "Three hundred twenty pairs of laces;

two thousand two hundred four buckles; four hundred twelve yards of—"

His tiny voice died in his throat. "This appears to be an inventory list," he remarked as he rapidly searched beneath the rest of his belt. "Oh, dear, I must have left the proclamation in my other suit. Well, never mind. We'll get it later. Let me just say that, from what our superior Brownie Intelligence has gathered, you folks are in a lot of trouble. Yes, even more than before!"

Only now did he seem to notice the roomful of sneezing wizards. The Brownie whistled. "Looks like I didn't get here a moment too early! With what's going to happen, you're going to need all the Brownie Power you can get!"

What did this all mean? I turned to my master, to ask him what to do. But the Brownie's arrival had been too much for his malady. Now Ebenezum, like all the dozens of other wizards in this great hallway, was sneezing uncontrollably.

TWO

"The sages say that 'You cannot have too many friends,' and for a change, the sages are largely correct in their sagacity. Anyone can see, for example, that the friendlier a crowd, the better a wizard's chances for survival after his spell has gone seriously awry.

"However, there are some circumstances when even friends can become burdensome to the working sorcerer. Wizards, after all, need their privacy, especially when involved in extremely complicated and delicate conjurations of powerful magical forces, or when dealing in spells concerning the concealment of large sums of money.

"But friends do form a very important part of a wizard's life, especially when said mage must go on a fearsome quest far from his native land and thus needs someone at home to take care of his cat."

—THE TEACHINGS OF EBENEZUM,
Volume XXVII

The door that led from the Great Hall outside crashed inwards, then smashed against the floor, its hinges ripped from the wall with the force of its opening.

"Doom!" the immense warrior Hendrek intoned. His bulk filled the large doorway, a huge shadow that blotted out the late summer sun. He held the doomed warclub Headbasher in one immense hand, the club no man could own, but could only rent. The winged helmet atop his head turned as he surveyed the room.

"Doom!" Hendrek repeated. "Something is amiss!"

"That's what I like about you, big fellow," a higher, infinitely more grating voice replied. "You're always able to point out any problem, no matter how obvious it is to those around you." The truth-telling demon Snarks poked his small, green head around the warrior's belly. "What have we here? It looks like an influenza convention."

"It's terrible!" I explained. "Ebenezum's malady has spread to every other wizard in Vushta!"

"Doom!" the warrior responded with instant understanding. " 'Tis another foul plot by the Netherhells!"

Snarks whistled. "It looks like they've come up with a winner this time." The demon flinched as the warrior growled above him. "Okay, okay, maybe it's inappropriate to compliment the Netherhells at a time like this." Snarks got a far away look in his eye. "Still, one has to have some feelings about the place one was born. I still remember it all: The smell of the slime pits, the gooey feel of fungus on the walls of my nursery, the special way those swamp gases would get into your eyes." The demon sighed. "It gave one a real sense of revulsion, let me tell you."

Allowances had to be made for Snarks. His mother had been frightened by demon politicians shortly before he was born, a misfortune that led to Snarks growing into a demon that could tell nothing but the truth, especially the unpleasant truth, the more unpleasant the better. This truth-telling tendency had gotten him banished from the Netherhells, but that same extreme honesty had made him a trustworthy companion in our battles with his former home.

"Doom," Hendrek said again as the sneezing continued unabated.

"What have we been thinking of?" Norei demanded. "We have to get these wizards out in the open, away from this sorcery-tainted air!"

My beloved was right! I fought down a momentary pang of guilt for not thinking of rescuing the wizards myself, after all the times I had had to come to the aid of my master. There was just something overwhelming about being in the midst of two score sneezing wizards, something—perhaps the noise level—that made it difficult to think at all. A chill ran through my frame. Could this be yet another facet of the Netherhells' plot?

"Doom," Hendrek muttered as he began to drag bunches of wizards outside the hall. Norei and Snarks turned to aid those few sorcerers still able to walk.

"That's not what I think it is," Snarks whispered, his voice tinged with fear.

"Hi, there!" The Brownie waved from where he had been wandering among the prostrate mages. "How are those shoes I made for you holding out? Talk about Brownie Power!"

Snarks groaned, his normal, sickly green face turned a sickly gray. "No," he moaned softly. "What have I done to deserve this? I am banished from the Netherhells. This I accept. I am forced to wander through a strange world, and even battle my own kind whenever I should meet them. This, too, I accept. My human companions don't heed the helpful advice I give them that would so much improve their lives. Even this I accept. But the Brownie, again?" The demon drew a ragged breath, and fell to his knees. "Is there no justice?"

"Why the sad face, friend demon?" Tap jumped merrily to Snarks' side. "You have nothing to worry about. Now that I'm back, I've decided to take the time to show you the Brownie Way."

"The Brownie—" Snarks began.

"Oh, there is no need to thank me," Tap interjected before the demon could finish his sentence. "I know it will take great patience, but making shoes teaches great patience. And if my efforts aren't enough to show you the light, fear not, there are a thousand of my fellows ready to take my place. You are in good hands with Browniedom. Soon you will know that there is justice—Brownie Justice!" The little man did an impromptu jig on the corner of Snarks' robe.

The demon stared back at the Brownie. Snarks opened his mouth repeatedly, and shut it as many times. No sound issued forth.

"Yes, it is all a bit overwhelming, isn't it?" Tap laughed infectiously. "Come, what better time than now to begin our first lesson?"

The Brownie looked dreamily off into the middle distance. "Lesson One: The Selection of Shoe Leather. All good things must begin somewhere. Shoes are no exception, and proper raw materials are essential. . . ."

Snarks rose unsteadily and staggered from the room. Tap paused at last and looked around, realizing that his audience had fled. "Oh, how right you are!" he cried. "How much better to conduct our lessons outside, in the warm summer air! I am coming, friend demon!"

Tap romped merrily from the room.

I stopped before a sneezing mass covered in royal blue.

"Master?"

Ebenezum looked up and nodded. "Too much," he managed. "Outside—"

I helped the mighty wizard out onto the lawn that fronted the building. The grass was already crowded with prostrate mages. We had to walk some distance before we could find a place Ebenezum might sit undisturbed. He slid onto the grass with a groan. At least, I reflected, it wasn't a sneeze. In fact, the air out here on the lawn was remarkably sneeze-free.

"Thank you, 'prentice,'" my master said after he had regained his breath. " 'Twas an unhealthy situation in there. Too many magicians per square foot. The residual sorcery alone was enough to trigger the malady in all of us. And then, with the arrival of the Brownie, not to mention Snarks, and Hendrek's warclub . . ." Ebenezum shook his head. "We will have to make plans"—the wizard stroked his beard contemplatively—"but never again in such a large group."

I did not say aloud what I thought; that the Netherhells had won a considerable victory if they could prevent the wizards of Vushta from ever using their collective magic against demonkind. The situation looked grimmer with every passing moment.

"Indeed," Ebenezum replied to my glum expression. "This proliferation of my malady is a serious setback. But we have faced other trials before, and triumphed."

Snarks walked rapidly past us, a haunted look in his eyes. Tap was right on his heels. "Now that we know all about the leather," he called after the fleeing demon, "just what do we do with it? This brings us to the second part of our lesson: Rudimentary Shoe Design!"

Ebenezum stroked his mustache as the Brownie also disappeared into the crowd of slowly recovering wizards. "In fact," he added, "methinks I see the beginning of a plan." He turned to me, an edge of excitement to his voice. "Wunt! Gather all our compatriots together and tell them to meet us at yon willow tree an hour hence."

I glanced at the tree my master had indicated, a huge weeping willow at the far end of the courtyard from the Great Hall.

"All our compatriots?" I inquired.

The wizard nodded. "Every single one. Meanwhile, I need to confer with one or two of my fellow wizards. By the time we meet, I will have put the final touches on our counterstrategy."

I nodded and rushed away. We had made quite a few allies in our numerous adventures; I imagined them scattered all over Vushta by now. I somehow had to find all our compatriots in under an hour.

I found Snarks busily conversing with Hendrek directly around the corner of the building. The Brownie stood a few feet away, discoursing to no one in particular about the proper space one should put between eyelets. Here were three of these whom I sought. Perhaps this wouldn't be as difficult as I first had thought.

"Doom," Hendrek remarked.

"Please!" Snarks pleaded. "For the sake of all we've been through together! Only one tiny little blow from your warclub, and we'll never have to hear about eyelets again!"

"Doom!" Hendrek insisted. "The Brownie has done nothing wrong!"

"Nothing wrong?" The demon groaned. "The Brownie's very existence is an affront to demonkind! Just look at that little fellow, bopping up and down, talking about shoes as if they were the most important thing in the world. How can something that—that *cute* be allowed to live!"

Tap was indeed jumping up and down at this very moment, waving his hands and shouting at the top of his voice: "You put one here, and you put one there! Shoe eyelets, shoe eyelets, everywhere!"

I had to admit that Snarks was at least partially right. Even lecturing about shoe eyelet placement, Tap the Brownie was adorable.

"Give me an S!" Tap continued. "Give me an H! Give me an O! Give me—"

"Doom." The large warrior shook his head. "I couldn't do it. Violence is not always the answer, friend demon. Have you tried reasoning with the little fellow?" He turned to the Brownie, who was now leaping about in circles.

"What's that spell?" Tap cried. "Shoe! What's that spell? Shoe! What's that spell? Shoe!"

"Doom," Hendrek repeated. Snarks began to shiver.

"Hold, friends!" I called to the three of them. I had seen enough. If I was to accomplish my master's wishes, I would have to speak to them quickly and be on my way. "Does there seem to be some problem?"

"No problem at all!" the Brownie piped up. "We're talking about Brownie Power!"

"Whether we want to or not," Snarks added quickly. He tugged nervously at my sleeve. "You'll talk to him, won't you? My mother didn't raise me to be Brownie fodder."

"Brownie fodder?" Tap replied. "Brownie fodder? Sir, I want you to know that, to my knowledge, Brownies have never eaten demons for dinner. Or for lunch or breakfast either. Actually, we prefer to eat tiny cakes, baked to resemble boots, and even smaller sandal-shaped sugar cookies. Of course, when we are really hungry—"

"Doom," Hendrek interjected. "I believe the demon was speaking metaphorically."

"Really?" Tap seemed taken aback. "You'll have to excuse me. We in the shoe trade were never very good at metaphors. Similes are more our style! You know, like: 'As industrious as a Brownie' or 'As well made as a Brownie shoe.' Now those are comparisons that mean something!"

The Brownie hesitated, doubt creeping into his enthusiasm. "But metaphorical Brownie fodder? I had no idea you felt that way about the lessons. Perhaps His Brownieship is right. I do have a tendency to be too direct. Go for the gold, you know. That's a saying we wee folk have. I apologize if I have shocked you, friend demon."

"Shocked?" Snarks replied, obviously startled by Tap's abrupt about-face. "Someone who grew up in the Netherhells cannot be shocked. Being stunned by an excess of Brownie prattle, however, is another matter." The demon took a deep breath, warming to his subject. "And yet, you have apologized. Perhaps there is some hope for you little people after all. I could give you some advice on proper deportment. I'm sure if we worked on it long enough, we might find something for you to do that might even make a Brownie's life worthwhile!"

The Brownie nodded. "It's obvious where I have gone wrong. I was too direct, too overwhelmed by Brownie Power! I must take a much more subtle approach, working by this deluded demon's side, showing him the truth in little ways every day, even though it may take weeks or months—"

"Months?" Snarks wailed, his rebuilt confidence evaporating at the very suggestion. "Months?"

Tap nodded again. "Perhaps even years. We Brownies have time. That's the joy of Brownie Power!"

"Joy?" Snarks' mouth began to work in a manner unnatural even for a demon. "I'll give you joy!"

I restrained the demon's lunge with my stout oak staff and turned to Tap.

"Pardon me, but didn't you have a message to deliver?" I inquired.

The Brownie slapped his forehead. "That's what happens when you start talking about shoes! I mean, the excitement just drives everything else out of your mind." He hastily patted Snarks' footwear. "Sorry, friend demon, but I have to go. Oh, what will His Brownieship think of me? I'll be demoted to buckles and laces!"

He waved hastily in my direction. "I shall be back within the hour!"

"Meet us at the willow by the Great Hall—" I called after him.

A modest explosion, a small cloud of dust, and the Brownie disappeared.

"Gone?" Snarks asked, a slight quaver in his voice. "Gone?"

"Doom," Hendrek murmured, an immense, yet comforting hand on the demon's shoulder. "Calm yourself. I have never seen you so undone before."

"Yeah," Snarks retorted. "And I've never heard you use the word metaphor, either. Better watch out. High-flung language like that will get you kicked out of the Warriors Guild."

"Doom," Hendrek glowered. "There is no such thing as a Warriors Guild. We mercenaries are all alone, forced to ply our trade without kith or kin. I am but a lone man, with a lone enchanted warclub. Is it any wonder that we take refuge in symbolism?"

The demon whistled. "I didn't know anything was large enough for you to take refuge in."

Hendrek raised his club.

"Now, now!" Snarks hastily took a few steps away. "If you are not going to abide by some of those handy diet and exercise plans I have so helpfully given you, you have to expect comments like that! You should follow the apprentice's example here. Does he go on a rampage every time I show him how he might clear up his frightful complexion? I should say not! And I actually think my hints about his posture are having some positive effect!"

"Indeed!" I remarked neutrally. I had too much to do for my master to get into an argument now. I quickly explained how we needed both of them to meet the rest of our band by the great willow tree in under an hour.

"Doom," Hendrek agreed.

"That means the Brownie will be there, too," Snarks mused. "He took me by surprise this last time, wouldn't let me gather my demonic wit. But that won't happen again." A smile spread slowly over Snarks' bright green face. "I'll be ready for him next time." He turned to Hendrek. "Are you sure I couldn't borrow your club for just a few minutes?"

"Doom!"

I decided to let the two of them continue their discussion without me. I still had to seek out the rest of our fellows. Most could be found close by the Wizards College, I knew, but there was a pair I would have to fetch from Vushta proper, where they were currently appearing under their professional names, "Damsel and Dragon." Perhaps it would be most economical to go after them first.

"Wuntvor!" a woman's voice called after me. "Where are you running to?"

I turned to see Norei, my beloved, her hands upon her hips, her perfect mouth turned down to a perfect frown.

"I must fetch the rest of our compatriots to meet with Ebenezum!" I called to her. "Pardon me, but is something wrong?"

"Well, it was awfully nice of you to tell me about it!" She sighed loudly and threw her arms open in a gesture of hopelessness. "Wuntvor, one minute you are looking deep into my eyes, saying you will never leave my side. Then we go to help the sneezing wizards, and you vanish without a word of explanation! I swear, do you ever think about your actions at all?"

"Um, er . . ." I began. Everything she said was, unfortunately, true. When my master gave me this emergency task, I had quite forgotten that I was in the midst of a deep discussion with my beloved.

"Oh, I know you might tell me I'm being petty," she continued. "Here I am, thinking of my own concerns when we have another emergency at hand. But it seems like there's been nothing but one emergency after another since I've met you!"

"Um, er . . ." I tried to explain.

"Maybe it's because I've done nothing but rescue you from one bad situation after another. You seem properly grateful for a moment or two, and then—zip!—off you go again on some new adventure!"

"Um, er . . ." I said somewhat more forcefully. What did she mean, "doing nothing but rescuing me"? Hadn't I rescued her in there somewhere?

"I should have known!" she went on. "My grandmother warned me about wizards! I should have realized her dire predictions would hold true for wizards' apprentices as well! You sit there and pledge eternal fealty, then the moment my back is turned, you gallivant off, looking for adventure and other women!"

"I do not run off all the time to see other women!" I shouted. Now she had gone too far!

"Well, perhaps I am being hasty," Norei replied, somewhat mollified.

I nodded. She was being much more reasonable now. I knew I should have spoken up sooner.

"So you're going to Vushta?" she asked more quietly.

I nodded. Perhaps she would understand after all.

"To the Vushta Art Theater?"

I nodded again. Somehow, Norei's voice seemed to be growing colder.

"To talk with whom, Wuntvor?"

"Why Hubert, of course, and uh . . ."

"See?" she cried triumphantly. "It's always dearest Norei this and sweetest Norei that, but the minute my back is turned, off to see another woman!" She shook both her fists at the heavens. "Off to Alea!"

"Um, er . . ." I responded. I had already explained to her a dozen times that Alea meant nothing to me.

"My grandmother was right all along!" she repeated. "I might as well go back to the Western Woods."

"But Norei," I managed at last, "my master—the meeting . . ."

"And you absolutely have to go see Alea personally and tell her about it? I understand! It is your duty as an apprentice! Men!"

"Norei?" I repeated. What else could I say?

"I will meet with the rest of you in an hour beneath the willow," she replied coolly. "As to what I will do after that, well, we will see."

She turned and walked quickly away.

I wanted to call to her again, but the words died in my throat. How could my beloved think such a thing of me? Would she really leave us and go back to her home in the Western Woods? I shook my head and headed back into Vushta. I didn't see how things could get any worse.

But, of course, that was before I turned the corner.

THREE

ON DEALING WITH WIZARDS
(a fable)

Once a wizard was on holiday, far from his native land. He had journeyed to a distant kingdom to see the wondrous sights, as well as witness local custom. And, on this particular day, he was on his way to see the most wondrous sight of all in this part of the world, the Grand Palace high atop Emperor's Crag. He walked down a broad highway, curiously devoid of traffic, with tall woods to either side, and as he turned a bend in the road, caught his first distant glimpse of the palace's golden towers.

"Go no farther!" a gruff voice cried.

The wizard, in a strange land full of strange customs, halted immediately. A tall man dressed in crimson walked briskly towards him from the woods.

"This is an official road, you know," the crimson-clothed man remarked as he approached. "And as you are walking upon it, you are subject to a toll. A piece of gold, please."

"A piece of gold?" the wizard repeated. It seemed to him a very hefty toll to pay when one was merely strolling toward a wondrous sight.

"Yes, yes," the other man responded impatiently. "I can see from your clothes you are a wizard, a man of learning. But I must have the toll. Unless, of course, you want to conjure up a broom and fly away from this road entirely." The toll collector allowed himself a little smile.

The wizard sighed. Still, he was in a strange land, full of strange customs, and one had to expect to put up with a little inconvenience now and then. He pulled his large and heavy money sack from his belt and handed a piece of gold to the other man.

"A wise man," the toll collector remarked, "for if you had not paid, I would have ordered the army to come out of the woods and kill you."

So that was the way of it, the wizard thought. Of course, he couldn't see an army. But the trees were so tall and close together that they could have hidden anything. The wizard loosened his belt so that he might once again tuck away the money pouch.

"Not so fast!" the other man demanded. "You have paid the toll, but you have completely forgotten the occupation tax!"

"Occupation tax?" the wizard replied.

"Another piece of gold," the toll collector said, smirking. "Unless, of course, you would like to call up a great storm to wash the road away."

"I see." The wizard recalled sadly how much he had wished to witness local custom. He reached back into his large and heavy purse.

"Ah, you have once again saved yourself from the army," the crimson-clad official drawled. "Oh, but I didn't mention, did I? That will be two pieces of gold. The occupation tax is double for wizards."

"The occupation tax is double for wizards?" the magician repeated in disbelief. He had to admit, by now he was getting a bit too much of a taste of local custom. Still, he did want to see the wondrous sight up ahead. He reached once again into his purse.

"What'll you do?" The other man sneered. "Turn me into a frog? But then there's the army, isn't there?" He jabbed the magician in the ribs. "Of course, that means you'll have to turn all of us into frogs, doesn't it? Oh, I forgot. While you have the purse open, there's one more tax you'll have to—"

There was a pause in the man's conversation.

"Ribbit, ribbit," the toll collector remarked at last.

And the wizard was on his way, and was soon marveling at great length at the wondrous sight, proud now of all he'd learned about local custom, and reveling in the newfound silence, which was only broken at nightfall from the direction of the lily pads.

—THE HOUSE AT WIZARD'S CORNER
(fourth edition)
by Ebenezum,
Greatest Wizard in the Western Kingdom

I turned the corner, onto the narrow street that led into the heart of Vushta.

But my way was blocked by three young men, all close to my own age and all dressed in brown. Two of them were very large, perhaps taller than even Hendrek or the Dealer of Death. One of the tall ones smiled in my direction, his grin missing a couple of teeth. The other big fellow seemed to hardly notice me at all. He appeared instead to focus all his attention on a long, slightly curved knife which he twirled absently between his palms.

The smallest of the three stepped forward. I was shocked to realize that he was only an inch or two shorter than I was. Exactly how tall were his companions?

"Excuse us, fella," the shorter one said. "You wouldn't know where we might be able to find some guy named Wuntvor, would you?"

"Yeah." One of the big ones laughed. "Wuntvor."

"Why, yes," I began somewhat hesitantly. My battle senses were instantly alert. My palm sweated where I gripped my stout oak staff. I searched hard to explain this sudden feeling. For some odd reason these three newcomers seemed slightly threatening. Still, it must be my imagination, the result of spending far too long fighting in the Netherhells, where you might find danger lurking behind every stalactite. I must remember, I told myself: In our recent battle to defeat demonkind, all of Vushta had banded together to fight creatures of every description. After that, what need did humans have to fight each other?

I looked into the newcomers' faces, one after another. After a moment's hesitation I answered, "I am Wuntvor."

"Really?" the shorter fellow said. Somehow, he didn't look at all surprised. "Not the same Wuntvor who is apprenticed to Ebenezum, a certain magician from the Western Kingdoms?"

"Ebenezum is the greatest mage in all the Western Kingdoms!" I replied far more quickly. I didn't like their tone. What were they implying about my master?

"Oh, no doubt, no doubt." The fellow doffed his cap. "I merely wanted to introduce myself and my companions here to the right person. You see, Wuntvor, we are apprentices, too. That's right. Just like you. Here, I want you to meet Slag . . ."

"Yeah." The big guy to his left laughed. "Slag."

". . . and over here is Vermin."

Vermin doffed his hat with his knife.

"They call me Grott," the shorter fellow continued as he placed his hat back on his head. "We're all very pleased to meet you."

"Yeah." Slag snickered. "Pleased."

Vermin played with his knife.

"Now," Grott said, "you may be wondering what three busy ap

prentices like us are doing, hanging around on street corners?" He smiled ingratiatingly. "Well, actually, we've been waiting here for you. You see, we have a little business."

"Yeah." Slag giggled. "Business."

Vermin used his knife to idly chip away large chunks of plaster from the building he leaned against.

"You see," Grott continued, "we represent a local organization, the Vushta Apprentice Guild."

"Really?" I replied. I had obviously misjudged these three completely. They were naught but a welcoming committee. How much luckier was I than Hendrek! I had a guild of my very own. I asked the three if they wanted me to join.

"Well," Grott went on, the smile still large on his face, "I don't think you quite understand. If you're an apprentice, you're in the guild. Here in Vushta, there's no way around it. And since you're a member, we've got a little proposition for you."

"Yeah." Slag guffawed. "Propo, uh . . . proposition."

Vermin moved casually to the corner of the building nearest to me. He began to pry bricks out of the wall.

"It seems your master and our masters have been doing a little business together, too," Grott said as Slag ambled across the road to a spot opposite Vermin. "And that business has led to an unfortunate situation. Now, because of your master, 'the greatest wizard in the Western Kingdoms,' all our masters are sneezing."

"Yeah." Slag smirked. "Sneezing."

Grott took a step in my direction. "You probably don't realize how upset this situation makes us. Let me therefore give you a couple of examples."

Slag and Vermin ambled toward me.

"Say you're a merchant in Vushta, used to paying a few pieces of gold each month as protection against evil sorcery. Now tell me, can a wizard who's allergic to magic protect anything?"

Grott didn't wait for my reply, but instead added: "Let me give you another example. Say you're an apprentice, used to an occasional forbidden delight. What do you say when that delight's manager refuses to let you get near it, just because your master's malady might be contagious?"

Vermin walked away from his wall, sidestepping the stack of bricks he'd piled on the pavement. He used his knife to pick his teeth as he sauntered in my direction.

"Only one more example, Wuntvor," Grott added ingratiatingly. "Say, once again, that you are a magician's apprentice. This could give you a special standing with certain young women. Your job prospects are good. Full-fledged magicians have lots of power. And the ones that don't sneeze can make lots of gold as well, especially in Vushta. Now, it seems to me that the wise apprentice would find time to spend with all these young women, and show each one of them personally the advantages of a sorcerous career. But an apprentice won't be able to do anything of the kind if he has to spend all his time taking care of a sneezing wizard!"

I suddenly found Vermin's knife at my throat.

"It's very simple," Grott continued, the smile gone from his face. "All this sneezing around here is making our lives a little difficult. But we have a simple solution. Your master got us into this. And you're going to get us out of it."

I opened my mouth to speak, but felt the knife point prick at my Adam's apple.

"We heard your master's hot stuff," Grott went on, "sneezing or no sneezing. We even heard you're pretty hot stuff, too, what with that jaunt down to the Netherhells and all. So we figure you can get everything back to normal by sometime in the very near future." He reached forward to gently stroke the knife blade at my throat. "Or else."

"Yeah." Slag towered over me. "Else."

"Are you threatening me?" I couldn't believe this. Fellow apprentices, resorting to violence! Is this what life in Vushta made of you? Perhaps I was happy I hadn't sampled any of the forbidden delights after all!

"Oh, no such thing." Grott pulled his hand away. His smile once again dominated his face. "We wouldn't think of causing you any harm. In fact, Vermin here is very good at improving the appearance of people he works on. He specializes in those little cosmetic extras, like cutting your ears back a trifle, or giving you an extra nose. But we wouldn't think of doing anything really violent." He winked at Vermin. "At least not yet."

"Yeah." Slag chortled. "Yet."

Vermin moved the knife point back a fraction of an inch, so that it but rested lightly against my throat.

"Well?" Grott prompted.

"Exactly what do you want me to do?" I asked. My hand still

gripped my stout oak staff. I wondered how many of them I might be able to disable before they overwhelmed me.

"Why, that's simplicity itself," Grott answered. "We just need results—say, a cure for all our sneezing masters, or, failing that, a large quantity of gold to be handed over to us to repay us for this inconvenience." The apprentice stroked his pointed chin. "I think one hundred pieces might suffice."

"One hundred pieces!" I exclaimed in disbelief.

"Oh, you are quite right." Grott smiled broadly at his two companions. "That was far too low an estimate. I am so sorry if I offended you. We'll have you bring us two hundred gold pieces instead."

This time I remained silent, glaring at my captors.

"There, there," Grott continued, "much more reasonable of you. And you will see we are reasonable as well. We do not expect a cure for our masters, or failing that, the gold, until moonrise tomorrow!"

"Moonrise!" I sputtered.

Grott shook his head. "Still talking back? Maybe we should leave you with something to remember us by. What do you think, Vermin?"

And Vermin finally said something: "Urracht!" he choked.

A hand, attached to an arm clothed in deepest black, lifted the large knife-wielder and tossed him a dozen yards down the road.

"I think this is possibly more fun than strangling wild pigs," a mild voice remarked. I twisted my head around. The Dealer of Death stood behind me.

I moved quickly, swinging my stout oak staff about so that its end caught Slag full in the stomach. He sat down abruptly with a groan. I retreated a step, wary of a further attack from Grott, before I realized he was already held in the Dealer's viselike grip.

"Should I strangle this one, too?" the Dealer asked eagerly.

"No, no," I replied quickly. "I think we need to talk with them."

"Oh," the Dealer answered in disappointment. With some reluctance, and without completely releasing his grip, he lowered Grott to a point where the apprentice's feet touched the ground.

"Much more reasonable," Grott whispered hoarsely once he had caught his breath. He nodded in my direction. "So I trust you will honor our request?"

"Request?" I could not believe my fellow apprentice's audacity. Slag was still groaning on the pavement, and Vermin, while he had picked himself up from his recent toss by the Dealer, had lost his knife and seemed to be wandering about in a bit of a daze.

"Perhaps," I added, "you don't quite understand the situation. You are facing more than one simple apprentice here. My companion is known only as the Dealer of Death, a member of a secret league of assassins. I can assure you that he knows a greater variety of ways to kill people than there are apprentices in Vushta."

The Dealer nodded eagerly. "I have been getting a bit rusty on the finer points, though. Can I try something really elaborate on one of them, say a little number called 'The Princess and the Spikes of Death'? That one always was a crowd pleaser!"

"No," I insisted, "I think it's better if we talk to them. They are, after all, in the same trade as myself, only slightly jaded, I am sure, by a lifetime spent in Vushta."

"Oh," the Dealer replied, trying hard not to show his disappointment. "Well, maybe I was being a bit too elaborate with the 'Spikes' idea. It's just so seldom one gets a chance to do anything really major in polite society. How about something a bit simpler, say 'The Shepherd Girl and the Hundred Screaming Points of Doom'? It doesn't have quite the showmanship of the other piece, but it is still quietly effective in its way."

"Please forgive the enthusiasm of my colleague," I told the other apprentices, looking specifically at Grott, who was slowly turning blue from the Dealer's somewhat looser hold on his neck. "If we can work together, none of this should be necessary. There is no need for threats, or for violence. I have fought demons and magical creatures from the Western Woods to Vushta, and then again down to the Netherhells and back, all for the sake of my master. I realize that you, too, fellow apprentices, are worried about the fates of your masters. But if we all work together, we shall persevere, and defeat whatever has overtaken the wizards, while we are ready for any other dastardly plan the Netherhells sends our way!" I threw my hands aloft, beckoning the others forward. "Join with me, fellow apprentices! Together, we can rescue Vushta! Together, we can save the world!"

"Does that mean I have to let this troublemaker go?" the Dealer asked with a frown. "I realize that even the 'Screaming Points of Doom' might be a bit much for the middle of the day. But I was still hoping to perform at least 'The Milkmaid and the Moment of Grinding Terror.' That's one of the most sedate deaths I know that retains any bit of style at all!"

"Let him go," I instructed the assassin.

Even though he didn't like it, the Dealer did what he was told.

"Much better," Grott said as he rubbed his neck. He stepped back three paces to join his fellows, who stood on either side of the street, each leaning against a building.

"So," Grott continued, "we expect either the cure or the money by moonrise tomorrow."

"What?" I replied in astonishment. "Haven't you listened to anything I said?"

"I would have preferred not to. As it was, I was too busy choking in a death grip to pay it much attention." The smile was back on Grott's face. "We have our orders, Wuntvor. Moonrise tomorrow, or else."

"Does this mean I get to perform the 'Moment of Grinding Terror' after all?" the Dealer cried joyously.

But the three apprentices were already some distance down the street, traveling at an amazing speed, considering their injuries.

"Remember!" Grott called before he disappeared around a distant corner. "There's more where we came from. We of the Vushta Apprentice Guild will not be stopped! Moonrise tomorrow!"

"Is it worth it to pursue them?" the Dealer inquired. " 'The Milkmaid and the Moment of Grinding Terror' is just as effective when performed in motion."

I told the assassin not to bother. We would deal with the Apprentice Guild later, if we had to. I must admit that at the time, I still held the vain hope that, in a cooler moment, the Guild might agree to work together with us after all. In the meantime, though, there was the meeting with my master to consider. I asked the Dealer of Death to join us beneath the willow.

"Ah," the Dealer replied with a smile, "time for action again. I shall meet you there." He flexed his large and powerful hands. "In the meantime, though, this recent encounter has left me vaguely dissatisfied. It is time I strangled a wild pig."

With that, the Dealer was gone as silently as he arrived. I turned and once again headed for the Vushta Art Theater.

A magnificently mellow voice spoke from the shadows before I had gone three paces.

"I would have saved you, you know, if the other fellow hadn't shown up," the voice crooned softly.

With that, the most wondrous beast I had ever seen stepped out into the light. Sparks flew where its shining hooves hit the cobblestones. It looked at me and tossed its head, the motion of its flowing mane taking my breath away.

It was the unicorn, a beast I had met once before in our journey across the Western Woods. Its incredibly white coat was doubly blinding here on the dark streets of Vushta, and I found it almost impossible to look at the sunlight reflecting off its golden horn.

"Forgive me," the exquisite creature murmured. "I just couldn't stay away."

"What do you mean?" I said, temporarily taken aback.

The unicorn looked at me with its soulful brown eyes. "I'm talking about you, you wonderful apprentice. It's not often that a beast of my sort finds someone really worthy, someone in whose lap I can lay my heavy head." The beautiful beast took a tentative step toward me. "It's worth taking a trip, even to a place like this, when you find a lap like that."

"All the way to Vushta?" I took a step away. I had forgotten how uncomfortable this beast made me. "Certainly there must be hundreds of laps in Vushta worthier than mine!"

"Vushta!" the beast snorted. It took another step in my direction. "They call it the City of Forbidden Delights, you know. Not much chance of finding virgins here." The unicorn sniffed haughtily. "Well, that is," the beast hastily added, "with certain exceptions." It nudged me gently with its golden horn.

"That's all very nice," I replied, trying to think of some way to escape this overamorous beast, "But I have errands—"

"Oh, yes, the meeting at the willow tree with the wizard. I overheard you from the alleyway." The magnificent beast sighed. "I've come this far, I can wait a little longer. I'll join you at the willow tree with the others. Then"—the beast paused significantly—"we'll talk again."

I hastily agreed, and ran down the street toward the Vushta Art Theater. Time was growing short, and I had to fetch two more of our company. I sped about the corner and caught my first glimpse of the towering edifice that housed the theater. The first time I had come here, I had been quite taken aback by the size of the place, until I thought for a moment and realized how large a stage they would need to have to accommodate a tap-dancing dragon.

I walked in through an entranceway marked Stage Door, waving my stout oak staff at the elderly man who shouted at me from the stool just inside. There was no time to tarry now, and no need to ask directions. I could hear the pair I sought rehearsing in the distance.

"Hit it, damsel!" the great, deep voice of Hubert the dragon exclaimed. He was answered in song by one of the sweetest sopranos I have ever heard.

> "Listen all you Vushtans, you'll be glad you came!
> We'll tell you of a young man, and his claim to fame!
> He might not be too bright.
> But still he did all right.
> We've got a hero, and Wuntvor is his name!"

The two then repeated the last line, singing together, followed by a spate of very loud tap dancing. I climbed a flight of stairs and crossed an area filled with large painted canvases depicting various scenes from both Vushta and the countryside. Some of them even seemed to suggest a forbidden delight or two.

The singing sounded much closer when they began again. Taking an extra moment to study a couple of the finer canvases, I neglected to watch where I was going and thus tripped over something that looked like rock but was nowhere near as heavy. The thing that wasn't a rock slipped away from me at alarming speed. I grabbed at a nearby canvas to steady myself. Unfortunately, the painted backdrop did not appear to be well secured either, and fell firmly over my head, covering my entire body and the floor on either side for some distance.

This was terrible! How could I fulfill my master's wishes if I was trapped in canvas? I could barely move beneath the weight. One misstep and I would stumble completely into the tangling cloth. Still, somehow I struggled toward the singers' voices:

> "Now Wuntvor is so clumsy, it's a wonder he's not lame!
> When he carries something, beware despite his fame,
> His marching down the street
> For he has two left feet.
> We've got a hero, and Wuntvor—"

The song was interrupted by a piercing scream. Alea's scream!

Something was wrong! Damsel and Dragon were in danger, and I was trapped in my painted prison, unable to come to their aid! I tried to call Alea's name, but my voice was muffled by the endless yards of canvas.

I stumbled against something hard.

"Have no fear, Alea!" Hubert's voice cried. "I've got this hideous creature now! Should I fry it where it stands?"

At that moment I finally discovered the end of the canvas, and rapidly pulled my head through the newly found opening. I looked straight up into a dragon snout.

"Then again," Hubert remarked, "perhaps I shouldn't."

"Wuntie!" Alea called, her voice tinged with delight.

I greeted both of them in turn. Hubert complimented me on my entrance and asked if I had ever seriously considered a career in show business. I told him I didn't have time to think of it now, and briefly informed the two of them of the situation at the Wizards College and the upcoming meeting with Ebenezum.

Hubert shook his head. "You shouldn't be too hasty in a decision of this sort. There's a place for you in our act! Besides, as you probably heard, we're working on a major new opus, 'The Ballad of Wuntvor,' for the big victory celebration this weekend. You could do a guest appearance! What a natural!" Hubert paused and snorted, producing two perfect smoke rings from his nostrils. "Of course," he added, "the way things are going, we may have to postpone the victory celebration . . ."

I agreed, and added that we should hurry, for the meeting was sure to begin shortly. All I had to do was get out of this restricting canvas.

"Oh, Wuntie!" Alea exclaimed. "Let me help you!" And with that, she rushed to my side.

What could I do? I knew that once Alea had her mind set on something, she had to have her way. She had called me Wuntie since we had known each other long ago in the Western Woods, and nothing I said to her now could stop it. We had meant something to each other in that long ago time, but it had been naught but a boyhood crush on my part, before I met Norei and discovered what true love really meant.

"Here." Alea giggled as she grabbed the pieces of canvas around my neck. "We haven't had a chance to be this close in weeks, Wuntie!" Her long blond hair fell in my face, tickling my nose. Her blue eyes were mere inches away from mine, as were her full, red lips.

It was getting awfully hot, trapped in this canvas. I began to sweat.

"I think I found where it starts," Alea cooed. "Wuntvor, I'm going to pull this way. If you pull opposite me, maybe we can unravel this." She giggled again. "I've always wanted to have a captive male."

"This is perfect!" Hubert exclaimed above us. "Are you sure you didn't want to go into show business? Talk about your escape acts! I tell you, it's a natural!"

Perhaps I overreacted then. Perhaps I was still far too worried about what Norei had said to me, and that if I didn't change my ways, she would leave me forever and return to the Western Woods. Perhaps I was worried what Norei might think if she found me in such close conversation with this other woman. Perhaps I thought about how far away the Western Woods really were.

Then again, perhaps I didn't want to be anybody's captive male.

Whatever made me do it, it happened thus: I pulled away from Alea, just as she had indicated. Unfortunately, I pulled away with far more force than she or even I was expecting. The canvas, amazingly resilient piece of fabric that it was, stayed firm, but the force of my movement instantly caused me to lose my balance. As I fell, I saw Alea swept off her feet, pulled by her own steel-fingered grip on the canvas. Once again she screamed.

"Then again," Hubert suggested, "you could perform a credible comedy act."

How could the dragon joke at a time like this? I was completely lost within the folds of the huge canvas. And what's more, Alea was lost with me!

This was not at all what I had planned to do.

I had meant to tell Alea, once and for all, about my feelings towards Norei. I had meant to tell her that for the time being it might be better if we did not spend any time in close contact. Now we were wrapped together, overwhelmed by a mass of scenery!

But I realized then that I was needlessly panicking; I, the apprentice who had rescued Vushta from the Netherhells. This was all an accident. Both Alea and myself were innocent, completely without ulterior motive. There was no need for my beloved to be informed of this little incident, ever. If I just stayed calm, I could extricate myself in no time, with no harm done.

"Pardon me," a woman's voice called outside my canvas prison, "but is Wuntvor here?"

I knew that voice. It was Norei!

"May I help you?" Hubert called in his most ingratiating tone.

"Well, mayhaps," Norei said hesitantly. I managed to peer again through a hole in the canvas. She looked up at the dragon, and did not see the point where Alea and I lay tangled upon the stage. "If you can aid me in finding Wuntvor." She blushed. How beautiful she was with those red cheeks! "You see, we had an argument. Oh, it was all my fault!"

She had come to apologize! I redoubled my efforts to free myself of the neverending canvas, doing my best to remain silent at the same time. If I could only get out of this one, Norei and I could live happily ever after!

"We had a fight over"—she paused—"well, over something stupid. I don't know what came over me. I think I wanted this whole trip to Vushta, with all the fighting, and all the nights not knowing whether I'd wake up in the morning or end up as some demon's dinner—I just wanted all that to be over. When I found that it wasn't, I took out my frustration on the person closest to me. And I'm afraid that person was Wuntvor.

"Oh, the argument was so foolish." She laughed as she looked about the room. "I have to tell him, to make him understand. Is Wuntvor here?"

At that moment I finally rolled free of the canvas.

"Wuntvor!" My beloved cried. "You heard me talking to the dragon, then? What can I say—" But her smile turned almost instantly to a frown.

"Norei—" I began.

Alea rolled out of the canvas and bumped into my posterior.

FOUR

"The truly professional wizard must consider the needs of not only humans, but every manner of creature he might come in contact with in the course of his sorcery. He is required to know, for example, precisely what sphinxes like to eat for a midnight snack; that trolls, as a rule, do not know the meaning of the word erudition, or that most fairies are violently allergic to horseradish. However, all these facts pale before the most important part of a wizard's knowledge, which is just exactly what each and every creature can afford to pay for your services."

—THE TEACHINGS OF EBENEZUM,
Volume XI

"What can I say?" my beloved repeated, although the tone of her voice had changed. "I know just what I can say, but I'm too civilized to repeat it in front of others!"

Norei turned and stomped from the stage, her footsteps somehow even louder than the noise the tap-dancing dragon had made earlier.

"I'm glad she's gone," Alea breathed on the back of my neck. "Now we'll have time to get reacquainted."

I didn't answer her. I was far too upset. Was Norei leaving me for the Western Woods? How would I ever see her again?

"Alea," Hubert reminded her softly, "we have to rehearse."

"Oh, Hubert! Honestly!" Alea pushed herself to her feet, somehow managing to lightly kiss my ear in the middle of the process. "Sometimes, working with a dragon . . ." She left the rest of the sentence unfinished as Hubert puffed impatiently.

"You'll forgive me, Wuntvor," she murmured, "but I have to get back to work. While you're very nice to dally with, the stage is my life."

I somehow managed to get to my feet as well. I might not be able to dally with Norei ever again. I felt as though my life were over.

But I had to get back to my master! While Norei was gone, I still had a purpose—to save Ebenezum, Vushta, and the Western Kingdoms from whatever machinations the Netherhells had devised this time. I would go boldly into battle, heedless of life or limb, with no one to mourn for me after I was gone.

I marched from the stage, heading resolutely for the street.

"Hit it, damsel!" the dragon yelled behind me.

Alea's voice followed me as I made my way back through the storeroom to the stage door:

> "Wuntvor's not that handsome, he's a hero all the same!
> It's not just that he's awkward, it's his face that
>   takes the blame!
> For you can't see his dimples,
> Beneath those mounds of pimples.
> We've got a hero, and Wuntvor—"

Their voices cut off abruptly as I walked from the theater into the street. It didn't matter. I wasn't really listening to the words. I was hoping to hear another sound, like the light, rapid footsteps of a young woman, returning to seek me out again, or mayhaps that same young woman's voice, saying she forgave me.

There was a noise ahead of me, a cart being pulled across the cobblestones, a man's voice crying cheerfully through the afternoon air. I looked ahead, full of the faint, foolish hope that where there was activity, there might also wait my beloved. Alas, it was naught but a costermonger going about his business. He tried to draw my attention to his wares, but I had no heart for it. He could go on mongering his costers around me for the rest of time, it made no difference. My thoughts would forever be elsewhere.

"Norei," I whispered to the empty street.

But enough was enough. I drew a ragged breath and reestablished a firm grip upon my stout oak staff. This mooning over lost love would do nothing to save us all from the clutches of the Netherhells. I had to return to the willow outside the Wizards College in time for the meeting. I had managed to gather all our allies—well, almost all.

I moved quickly to perform my final errand. It was on my way, at the corner of the field that the college used for their sorcerous athletic activities.

Dozens of furry faces seemed to light up as I approached their pen.

"Eep!"

"Eep eep!"

"Eep eep eep!"

I opened the door and was immediately surrounded by adoring ferrets. I worried sometimes, what with the way I had produced them —quite by accident, out of this old magic hat—that they all thought I was their mother. Their affection, especially right after I opened their pen, could sometimes be quite overwhelming. Still, I had grown rather attached to them on our travels to rescue Vushta from the Netherhells, and I admit that there had been one or two occasions when the hustle and bustle of Vushta had grown too much for me, and I had come to tend these cages, seeking solace.

"Come on now," I called softly, although I doubted that they really understood me. "It's time for us to go to a meeting."

"Eep!" they cried. "Eep eep! Eep eep eep!"

I laughed despite myself. They milled about me as I turned to lead them to the willow. What use had I for love? What need had I for human companionship? I had my ferrets to keep me warm!

Still, I didn't recall producing quite this many of them. They rubbed against my ankles and rose upon their hind legs to nuzzle my knees. A few of them, even merrier than their brothers and sisters, leapt joyfully for my head and shoulders so that they might rub their cold noses against my forehead and ears. There was a good score of them before me on the path, and two score of them to either side, while even more were emerging from their pen at a rapid rate.

Exactly how many were there? A momentary thought chilled me: Could magically produced ferrets reproduce magically as well?

"Come," I repeated, "there is no time to lose." I brushed the over-energetic creatures off my person and strode in the direction of the willows, being especially careful not to tread on any ferret parts as we made our way to the meeting. We skirted the large building that contained the Great Hall, and stepped into the college's main courtyard.

"Doom!" Hendrek hailed me, waving his warclub so that I might better see him beneath the willow. The ferrets all about me eeped merrily in reply.

A short, green blur paced rapidly back and forth behind the large warrior's bulk. It was Snarks, hopping, then walking, even running a pace or two, his fists occasionally darting out to hit something that wasn't there. Even allowing for his demonic demeanor, he seemed agitated.

"Oh," Snarks remarked distractedly as we approached. "I didn't know you'd be accompanied by a sea of rodents."

"Indeed?" I replied. "Rodents?" Just what did Snarks mean about my little charges? Perhaps I was being a tad oversensitive on the issue, but I thought the demon should show due respect for my ferrets. "Please, friend Snarks. These are anything but a sea of rodents!"

"What else could you call them, a living rug?" Snarks shrugged, as if it no longer mattered quite what they were. "Oh, well, I suppose they might make somebody a good coat someday."

"Coat?" I demanded. This was really too much. The ferrets nearest my feet, catching my mood, bared their teeth as they crept in Snarks' general direction.

The demon, seeing the change in my little charges, threw his hands up into the air. "Wait!" he called. "I am forced to agree with you. Ferrets are wonderful creatures, and a boon to our cause!"

I realized then that this was the second time today I had heard Snarks apologize. This went beyond mere agitation. Snarks was being pleasant and polite. There must be something seriously wrong.

I quieted my ferrets with a glance, and asked the demon what troubled him so.

" 'Tis a small matter," Snarks murmured, still intent, it seemed, on making light of the situation. But his anger broke through when he spoke again: "And it makes shoes!"

I had never seen the demon so undone before. "The Brownie?" I replied.

"The Brownie!" Snarks shrieked. "Always the Brownie!" He fell to his knees, his small, green fists flailing at the gnarled roots of the willow.

"Doom," Hendrek remarked.

I merely nodded, and gave myself a moment to collect my thoughts. For the first time since I had met him, Snarks seemed completely undone. What was even worse, his anguish concerned not an enemy, but another one of our allies, a magical creature who had helped us in the past and might be of use to us again.

I could see a potential for this situation to get out of hand. I wished then that I could have called my master over and allowed him to directly settle the dispute between demon and Brownie. But

Ebenezum's malady would not abide such close contact with these two magical creatures. Therefore, unless I wanted to see my master once again turned into a sneezing wreck, I would have to handle at least the up-close, personal end of this dispute. I looked at the demon and tried to think like a wizard. How would my master handle this?

"Indeed," I replied. "And yet you have dealt with the Brownie before for much of our adventures. Why, then, this sudden consternation?"

Snarks paused mid-tantrum. "Funny. I never thought of it that way. Yes, now that you mention it, I have stood up to the Brownie many times. I've even stood up to groups of Brownies!" I could hear the confidence creeping back into his voice. "After all, even in groups, they are still very short."

"Doom." Hendrek nodded encouragingly. "So you do not fear the Brownies?"

"No, not at all." Snarks allowed a demonic smile to settle upon his countenance. "Fear, no. Dislike, however, is another matter entirely. Yet that would not be enough to explain my actions." Snarks' smile faded as dark green furrows appeared on his forehead. "For I admit, I have been acting strangely. My behavior has been totally undemonic. What would my mother think?"

"Doom," Hendrek agreed. "Then you must fear something besides the Brownies."

Snarks stared at the large warrior. "You never cease to amaze me. First symbolism, and now this. And I used to believe your warclub did all your thinking for you!"

"Indeed," I interjected before Hendrek could become further embroiled in the discussion. "But has Hendrek hit upon the truth?"

"Is it fear?" The demon paused, and looked away from us to stare out into the middle distance. "In a way, yes. I fear it is this constant battle with my homeland. Even though I am a demon in exile, still I am a demon. When, at first, it seemed as though we had one great battle to win—to rescue Vushta from the Netherhells and defeat Guxx Unfufadoo, who I never much liked in the first place—well, that was a fight I could believe in. But now . . ." Snarks sighed.

"I was fine until I went back there," he continued. "I could have visited my mother, you know, when we returned to the Netherhells. But I chose to slink around like an outsider, as if my time with humans had tainted me." The demon looked from Hendrek to me and back again. "Which, of course, is a distinct possibility."

"Doom," Hendrek interjected, refusing to be lured away from the real topic. "Then you fear your mother?"

"Well, of course!" Snarks replied. "If your mother was a demon, you'd be scared of her, too! But that, I think, is beside the point. Returning to the Netherhells has dredged up old memories, and old emotions. Now, we find our battle might not be over. My real fear is that, the longer the battle lasts, the more these emotions will overwhelm me!"

"Doom!" Hendrek stated with grim finality.

"Indeed," I added, to show that I realized the weight of Snarks' problem as well. But I was afraid to share the rest of my thoughts.

I was chilled by how his complaints seemed so similar to those of my beloved. Both were tired of battle, and both seemed to be no longer quite themselves. I could think of no two creatures among my close acquaintance so dissimilar as Snarks and my young witch. Odd, then, that the demon's feelings should so echo those of Norei.

"Hello."

The mild voice was so close behind my shoulder that it made me jump. The black-garbed Dealer of Death strolled into our midst.

"I hear you are discussing problems. I, too, have a problem." The Dealer absently flexed his powerful hands. "One more profound than the recent shortage of wild pigs in the vicinity." He paused and looked at me, his usual smile gone from his face.

"You know, of course," he said slowly and precisely, being careful to flex his jaw and cheek muscles, "that I still hold a contract to assassinate at least three of you."

"Doom." Hendrek's hand moved quickly to the hilt of his warclub. Perhaps the warrior had hoped, as I had, that our time fighting side by side with the Dealer of Death had somehow negated the death contracts the assassin had on Hendrek, the wizard, and myself.

"There is no need to be hasty, good warrior," the Dealer remarked as he idly flexed his legs, "although the exercise certainly would be pleasant. Let me first tell you my thoughts on said problem."

Faster than the eye could see, the assassin snatched a buzzing gnat from the air and captured it within his closed fists. " 'Tis a funny thing about contracts. You might recall that there is no termination date on this particular piece of parchment. You might also recall that, through the wiles of the contractee, King Urfoo the Stingy, I end up paying to kill you rather than getting paid for my services."

The Dealer paused to clear his throat. Talking about this particular clause of the contract, especially since he was personally responsible for its negotiation, seemed to affect him emotionally. But at last the Dealer smiled, and as he began to speak again, he lifted aloft the hand that held the gnat.

"Because of these complications, I had thought about delaying said contract's completion. I was wondering if we might agree upon some future occasion, say perhaps when we meet in some future lifetime." The Dealer opened his fist, and the gnat flew away.

"Doom," Hendrek murmured, his voice tinged with relief.

"However," the Dealer continued, "life is seldom as simple as that. I also have my superiors in the Urracht sect to consider. It might be fine now to make a decision to delay your deaths, but what happens when my actions come up for their quarterly review?"

"Quarterly review?" Hendrek repeated, his hand once again reaching for the warclub. "Doom."

The Dealer nodded soberly. "The good assassin is accountable for every death. It's right there in our bylaws. The Urracht is a strict sect, but fair."

The Dealer stretched, languorously extending his huge shoulder muscles. "Before, as the battle was being joined, there was no time to think of contracts. Now, although I welcome the fact that the battle might soon be joined again, I worry more about just when such contracts should be fulfilled." He shook his head, a sad smile on his face. "I really should have killed some of you by now."

"Indeed," I interjected nervously, "but there have been extenuating circumstances. After all, the fate of the world may be at stake!"

"But will that be enough of a reason when my review comes up?" The black-clad assassin flexed his knees, obviously troubled. "Well, the fate of the world . . . It does have possibilities. I think my Urracht superiors may give me an extension." He hesitated again. "Still, a contract is a contract."

A deep voice shouted across the courtyard, causing even the brooding Dealer to take notice.

"Hey gang! It's showtime!"

Hubert the dragon circled overhead, angling to land in the grassy area at the courtyard's center. Alea waved to me from her perch at the base of the dragon's neck.

"Hit it, damsel!" Hubert cried as he executed a perfect four-point landing.

Alea began to sing:

"What's the show with so much class,
It stars a dragon and a pretty lass!
Yes we're the pair of Vushtan fame,
Who send the audience up in flame!
So if your theater's receipts are flaggin'
You know who to send for—Damsel and Dragon!"

"Just a little publicity," Hubert remarked as Alea handed him his top hat. "I thought it was time we classed up our act."

"I agree entirely," Snarks commented. "Let me know when you've come up with some way to do it."

"We've come for the meeting," Hubert continued, choosing to ignore the demon. "Are we on time?"

I told the dragon that they were perhaps a moment early and that we still awaited the arrival of my master.

"Early!" Hubert grinned. "What an opportunity! Damsel and I have been working up a new routine, including some brand-new snappy patter. We could not ask for a better audience than our friends here. Quick: Why did the dragon cross the road?"

"Wait a moment," Alea interrupted. "Shouldn't we be working on our song lyrics?"

Hubert harrumphed, sending a column of smoke into the air. "Alea, please." He turned to the rest of us. "It appears that the Damsel and I have some small artistic disagreement over song content."

Alea crossed her arms and glared at her partner. "We may have a disagreement, but I don't think there's anything artistic about it."

"Alea, please!" When the dragon snorted this time, flame shot from his nostrils. "Must we air our dirty laundry in front of our fans?"

"Exactly." Alea looked at the rest of us with a knowing smile. "And let me tell you, you've never dealt with dirty laundry until you've cleaned up after a dragon!"

She walked quickly over to where I stood. Somehow, I found her arm intertwined with mine. I remembered then that I had meant to tell this woman that our days of easy familiarity were over. But what with one thing and another, I hadn't quite gotten around to it.

"This all has to do with you, Wuntie." Her face was all too close to mine. Why did it always get warmer when Alea was around? "It's about your song: 'The Ballad of Wuntvor'."

"The Ballad of Wuntvor?" Snarks repeated.

"A deep and meaningful ballad!" Hubert boomed. "Perfect the way it is!"

"How could anything called 'The Ballad of Wuntvor' be perfect?" Snarks interjected.

"I feel we have gone slightly astray," Alea admitted. "We thought that by showing your fallibility, it would make your deeds that much grander. We wanted to show the human behind the hero. I'm afraid, Wuntie, that we made you a bit too human."

I realized then that I had heard bits of "The Ballad of Wuntvor" when I had come to fetch Damsel and Dragon earlier that day. I reconsidered the verses I had overheard in the theater. Now that I thought of it, that verse about my complexion had been a bit much. I told Alea I agreed with her, for that very reason.

"Complexion?" she replied a bit uncertainly. "Oh, yes, we *did* have a verse about that, didn't we? No, I'm afraid it was another verse entirely that made me realize we'd gone too far. The one about the stomach noises."

"Stomach noises!" Hubert retorted. "That verse? I'll have you know that I thought that particular verse was among the best . . ." The dragon hesitated. "Oh, dear. That was the one with the growl/howl rhyme scheme, wasn't it?" Gray wisps wafted upwards as Hubert cleared his throat. "Damsel, you may have a point."

"Complexion?" Snarks considered. "Stomach noises? Maybe 'The Ballad of Wuntvor' *is* perfect after all. Do you have a verse about posture?"

"No, we don't," Alea said thoughtfully. "Perhaps that would make a good substitution."

"Yes, of course!" the dragon replied. "We don't have to explore every nuance of Wuntvor's character. I think the twenty-eight verses we've already written cover most of his faults, anyway."

"Twenty-eight?" Alea asked, slightly surprised. "Oh, did you finally come up with a good rhyme for 'dandruff'?"

"No, I had forgotten all about that. I'm afraid I'd gotten caught up in that verse about nose hair. Thank you for reminding me, damsel. Perhaps we should have twenty-nine."

"Nose hair?" Alea clapped her hands in glee. "Oh, that's right! And then we contrast Wuntie's nasal curls with the nose hair of Guxx Unfufadoo? What pathos! A master's touch!"

"What can I say?" Hubert blew gently on his foreclaws. "I was born to write for the stage."

"Hello, Wuntvor," said a woman's voice so cold that I felt ice run up my spine. I knew, even before I turned to look, that it was Norei. "I don't know why I keep giving you another chance," she said in a voice barely above a whisper. "I thought, after walking out on you at the theater, that perhaps I had been hasty, that I should have listened to what you had to say. There might have been a reasonable explanation for why I found you wrapped up in a canvas with that woman." Her lower lip began to tremble. "Still, I came here thinking for some reason I'd give you one more opportunity to make a choice between us. Well, I see that the choice has already been made!"

What was my beloved talking about? Was she upset because I hadn't noticed her arrival? 'Twas true that I had become quite engrossed in the discussion of what should or shouldn't be in that song named after me, but that was understandable, wasn't it? Well, then there was the way Alea was holding onto my arm. That, perhaps, was a bit more difficult to explain, but I was sure if my beloved would but take a minute to hear me out—

"Norei—" I began.

"Don't even start!" she replied.

"But . . ." I added. What could I say? This was terrible. Now she would go to the Western Woods for sure! What could possibly be worse than this?

There was a small explosion by Snarks' foot. I used the momentary diversion to disengage myself from the clutching damsel.

"Surprise! Did you miss me?"

"You're right," Snarks replied. "Next time I'll have to take better aim."

It was Tap the Brownie.

"Good news!" he exclaimed in his tiny Brownie voice. "His Brownieship has given me another chance!"

"Good news?" Snarks repeated. "If that's good news, I'd hate to think what's bad news!"

"Oh, yes!" Tap added. "And in a few minutes we'll be visited by His Brownieship in person!"

"Yes, you're right," Snarks responded. "That's bad news." A shudder ran through the demon's sickly green frame. "His Brownieship?" Snarks wandered away to collect his thoughts.

Something poked me in the back. Could it be? Maybe she would give me a chance to talk to her in private! I turned quickly.

"Norei . . ." Her name died on my tongue. It was the unicorn.

"I said I'd come." The magnificent beast tossed back its flowing mane. "Unfortunately, it's much too crowded around here for us to *really* talk."

I told the unicorn that that was really too bad, but we had to wait for Ebenezum.

"I realized," the beast continued, its voice tinged with a magnificent melancholy, "when I followed you all the way from the Western Woods, that I would have to make sacrifices." The unicorn lifted its golden horn to the sky, its dark eyes staring into the distance. "If only my head were not so heavy. If only there were a lap somewhere where I might rest."

"Wuntie!" Alea called to me from a few feet away. "You weren't going to wander off and leave me all alone, were you?"

"Um, er . . ." I began. "I've been meaning to talk to you—"

"Wuntie!" Alea stopped and stared at the unicorn. "I remember this magnificent creature."

"Um, yes . . ." I began.

She walked rapidly toward us. "Well, don't you think it's time to introduce me?"

"Um . . ." I began. "Surely." Perhaps here was the chance I was looking for. While Alea and the unicorn were temporarily involved, I might at last seek out Norei and explain. I turned to the unicorn. "Do you recall this young lady—"

"I would rather not," the beast interjected. "Isn't there someplace we could go"—the creature allowed the slightest mournful sigh to escape from between its perfect teeth—"only the two of us?"

"My name is Alea." She smiled enough for her dimples to show. "I believe we met before. In the Western Woods."

The creature shrugged its silken shoulders and pointed its golden horn in my direction. "I was speaking with Wuntvor. Isn't there someplace quiet we can go? This sort of thing always happens when unicorns get stuck in crowds." The beast snorted its magnificent defiance of the ways of the world. "If only I hadn't wanted to see you so badly! If only I could find a place to lay my weary head!"

"I have a very nice lap," Alea suggested.

"This is what happens when unicorns get stuck in crowds in Vushta!" The beast nudged my shoulder gently with its horn. "It seems I am offered a never-ending succession of laps! But never"—it paused to nudge me again—"the right one."

"Wuntvor!"

"Norei!" I replied, for it was she, the woman with a voice only slightly more frigid than the coldest of winter days.

"We have been waiting here for quite some time. Isn't Ebenezum ever coming?"

Now my beloved was becoming impatient. It seemed very unlike her, as if, when she lost her faith in me, she had lost her faith in my master and all of Vushta as well.

I swallowed hard, knowing that whatever had happened to her, it was all my fault.

"Norei," I began. "We have to talk. No matter what you may think of me—"

"Weren't we talking?" the unicorn reminded me.

"Later," I said, ignoring the beast's insistent golden horn. "Norei, we've been through a great deal together—"

"Oh, for a lap to rest my weary head!" the magnificent beast interrupted.

"But I've already offered you mine!" Alea interjected. She glanced at me as she sidled toward the unicorn. "If Wuntie wants to waste his time elsewhere, let him. After all, I'm available!"

Alea ran around the beast so that she might sit directly in front of it. The unicorn's well-polished hooves took a pair of steps in the opposite direction.

"Oh!" the beautiful beast moaned. "To be in want of a lap in Vushta!"

I looked up to see Norei standing directly before me. Her lips trembled as she tried to speak. Finally she managed: "Wuntvor? You started to tell me something. What—"

"It's after me again!" Snarks ran between us, his lips curled back in a grimace of fear that showed his every fang. "The Brownie is after me!"

But I turned my attention back to my beloved. I could not let the crisis of the moment dissuade me from my task. What Norei and I meant to each other was too important for that.

Snarks ran on. The Brownie followed.

"Norei," I tried again. "In our brief time together, we have become very—"

"I just want to help you with some Brownie etiquette!" Tap yelled at the retreating demon. "Like those times when you should refer to

His Brownieship as the Master of Buckles, or mayhaps the King of Sole—"

"Wuntvor," Norei said, taking my head in her hands. "Are you trying to say—"

The unicorn's majestic horn came between us, pulling us apart.

"Why not rest awhile?" Alea insisted as she pursued the grandly trotting beast.

"Ahem. There are laps, and then there are laps," the unicorn replied haughtily.

"Norei—" I began, as Snarks ran screaming between us once again.

"And you need instruction in some of our sacred ceremonies!" insisted the Brownie, close upon the demon's heels. "You know, like the ritual tying of laces—"

"Wuntvor!" Norei complained. "It's impossible to talk to you!"

"Yes, it is, isn't it?" the unicorn agreed sadly. "Oh, what a heavy head!"

"Wuntvor!" another voice called out from across the clearing. It was the voice of my master, Ebenezum.

"Norei—" I turned to excuse myself, but my beloved was already marching away to the opposite side of the willow, with no sign that she had even heard me call her name.

But I had no time to worry about what would happen now. Ebenezum needed me. I jogged across the grass to my master.

"Wuntvor," the wizard addressed me as he pulled upon his long, white beard. "I am sorry to have kept you, but it has taken me somewhat longer to confer with my colleagues than I had at first anticipated." He nodded to both sides. I followed his gaze, and saw a pair of wizards, one left, one right, each a good twenty paces distant, and twenty paces beyond each of them, another pair of magicians, and so on. I realized then that wizards circled the entire courtyard.

"Indeed," Ebenezum replied to my questioning glance. " 'Tis but a precaution against further mischief on the part of the Netherhells. We wizards are close enough to form an effective magical unit, but not so close as to affect our immediate maladies."

My master scratched at the shock of white hair that protruded from beneath his handsome wizard's cap. "But we must discuss our plan, for even with precautions such as these, who knows when another . . ."

Ebenezum paused as we both heard a low rumble which seemed to come from deep beneath the earth. The ground where we stood began to shake.

I knew this kind of quake. This was no little Brownie explosion. This was an attack, by the demons of the Netherhells!

"And so it begins," my master remarked grimly.

FIVE

"The successful wizard must plan to spend a fair amount of time away from home, whether in the company of other mages or working for the common man.

"I have known the occasional wizard who had attempted to buck this trend and work completely and forever alone, but there is danger here as well. A close personal acquaintance of mine locked himself inside his lair for sixteen years, until at last he discovered a spell for turning dirt into gold, and spent the last few months of his exile amassing a great pile of his magical wealth.

"What could be wrong? you might ask. Ah, but sixteen years away from human contact had taken its emotional toll. This wizard had become afraid to even walk outside his home, and confessed to me, through his closed and bolted door, that he was even more afraid to leave his horde of gold, and cursed his riches for a burden!

"The solution, of course, was simple. Whenever such a tragedy occurs to a fellow sorcerer, the wise wizard should always be prepared to take the burden from their hands."

—WHEN BAD SPELLS HAPPEN TO GOOD WIZARDS
(fourth edition), by Ebenezum,
greatest wizard in the Western Kingdoms

Ebenezum nodded to the wizard on either side of him, and they, in turn, nodded to the wizards on either side of them. Everyone seemed to be nodding, although it might have been the earth shaking at our feet that caused heads to bob up and down so. My master raised both his arms, and the other wizards in the circle mimicked his action, so that all arms pointed to the sky. Then the whole circle of magicians called out a string of syllables as one, their voices close to drowned out by the crashing rumble of the ground, and slowly lowered their arms so they pointed at right angles to their wizardly frames.

"Now!" Ebenezum shouted above the earthquake.

The circle of mages all turned their outstretched palms to the ground and pushed.

The quake noise seemed not quite so loud as before.

The wizards pushed downward, seemingly against the air, although their arms shook as if they were struggling with a great weight.

The ground beneath my feet was not lurching about so violently as it had before.

The wizards' palms were now parallel with their waists as they continued to struggle against the invisible force. I looked back to my master. Sweat matted his white hair to his forehead.

But the noise of the quake was quieting. It was now no louder than distant thunder. And the earth beneath my feet was hardly moving at all.

The magicians pushed their hands as far as they could reach down their sides.

The earthquake stopped. For an instant the world around us was completely silent. And then the birds began to sing.

"Master!" I called, almost overcome with joy. "You have defeated the attack of the Netherhells! How . . ."

I paused in my exclamation when I realized that Ebenezum, along with every other mage in the circle, was now lost in a sneezing fit.

My master was the first to recover. He blew his nose quickly on a silver threaded sleeve, then beckoned me to come closer.

"Indeed," he began, "we have won. But you have seen the cost." He swept out his arm to include the circle of wizards, all the rest of whom were sneezing still. "And what has worked once may not work again. The Netherhells will be more prepared next time. We will have to develop new counterstrategies."

My master stood and regarded me for a silent instant as he tugged absently at his beard. "Wuntvor, it is time we had another talk. What we wizards of Vushta can do against the Netherhells will result in nothing more than a stalemate. I'm afraid we have need once again for someone not afflicted by my malady to make another quest."

I swallowed hard. Whatever my master wished of me, I knew I would obey.

"Must I go to the Netherhells again?" I asked, and this time my voice barely qualified as a whisper.

My master shook his head. "Indeed, no. Our salvation, if we are to find it, lies elsewhere, although I fear your new destination is not much preferable to traveling in the land of demons. Wuntvor, little as I like to do it, I must send you to the Eastern Kingdoms to enlist the aid of their leader."

"Eastern Kingdoms?" It was the first I had ever heard of them.

"Indeed," my master agreed with my confusion. "We in the magical trade do not discuss the Eastern Kingdoms overmuch. I suppose we are embarrassed by any associations with them. You see, Wunt, things are"—Ebenezum cleared his throat—"different there."

"Different?" I inquired.

My master nodded his head. "They have strange customs thereabouts." He paused, considering his words. "They have a different way of looking at the world." He paused again, and when he spoke for a third time, it was in a whisper. "But mostly, they have Mother Duck."

"Mother Duck!" I exclaimed.

"Indeed," Ebenezum continued in a whisper. He stroked his mustache agitatedly. "No so loud, Wuntvor, if you please."

He stared at the ground and surreptitiously motioned me to walk with him a little farther from the crowded clearing. Rarely had I seen my master so uneasy. I glanced briefly around the courtyard in which we stood. Those wizards who had recovered from their sneezing fits all seemed to be glaring in our direction.

"Mother Duck?" I repeated, this time matching my master's quieter tone. "Who is Mother Duck?"

"Who indeed?" my master replied. "She is the ruler of the Eastern Kingdoms. She is also the reason that none of the wizards here want to visit her domain."

"Doom!"

I had become so engrossed in my master's conversation that I hadn't heard the approach of Hendrek and Snarks.

"Forgive us for eavesdropping," the large warrior began, "but you wizards have only narrowly averted a skirmish with the Netherhells. We were wondering if we might be able to offer you any aid."

"It also gave us an opportunity to get rid of the Brownie." Snarks, who stood somewhat farther away to avoid affecting my master's malady, nodded his head happily.

My master pondered briefly. "Perhaps you heard that Wuntvor will have to go on another quest? He will once again need companions to aid him and protect him against dangers along the way. Still, I do not think we can utilize all the magical and heroic allies who have gathered here. I believe a small fast-moving group would be best for our purposes. Once all the wizards have recovered, we will discuss strategy and determine the party that will best serve our needs."

"Doom." Hendrek nodded his head, acknowledging the wisdom of my master's counsel.

"So we have a chance to leave Vushta?" Snarks added. "Not that Vushta isn't a wonderful place"—he glanced nervously at the area around his shoes—"but some of the creatures that tend to congregate in the area . . ."

"Doom," Hendrek agreed. "It will do my warclub good to once again taste battle."

"What's this about tasting battle?" I started at the nearness of this new voice. The Dealer of Death had once again snuck into our midst.

"My master has suggested another quest," I explained.

"Yeah!" Snarks rejoined. "One without any Brownies!"

There was a miniature explosion at the demon's feet.

"Did somebody call?" a small voice demanded. "Come on now, I'm sure I heard my name."

"Why would anyone mention you?" Snarks asked defensively. "You've heard of the phrase 'beneath notice'? I think that that perfectly fits anyone who doesn't come up even to my knees!"

The Brownie shook his head sadly. "It's tragic to meet a being who can't see the beauty of Brownie Power. I'm afraid I tried to show our friend here the glories of Browniedom too quickly. Listen to me, friend Snarks!"

"Sorry," the demon murmured, trying hard to maintain his composure. "Not interested."

Tap tugged at the demon's robes. "I will start where I should have all along: In the beginning, long ago, before there were Brownies . . ."

"Maybe I'm interested after all!" Snarks brightened momentarily.

". . . or before there were demons," the Brownie continued, refusing to be sidetracked. The little fellow looked at the rest of us. "Or before there were wizards, or warriors, or apprentices, or trained assassins. Before all these things, there was the Great Shoe!"

"Now I'm really not interested!" Snarks exclaimed as he began to sidle away from the little person.

"I'm not very interested, either," another voice said behind me. "At least, I'm only interested in certain very special individuals."

It was the unicorn.

"But what I wouldn't do for those individuals!" the magnificent beast continued. "Oh, if only I could find a place to lay—"

"If you'll excuse me." My beloved stepped between me and the unicorn's horn. "I thought that I might like to be included in the discussion. Who knows? Perhaps I can be of some help"—she looked pointedly in my direction—"at least for that short time that I am still available."

"Hey, what's going on here!" A deep voice cut off the unicorn's complaint. "It looks like a victory celebration, damsel! But what sort of celebration would it be without entertainment!"

The Brownie continued his speech, eyes closed, in a clear, high voice, as if everyone else was not shouting simultaneously. ". . . and the Great One looked out upon the void, and saw nothingness. So the Great One reached out its laces to the Void, and said 'Let there be shoes!' "

"What we need here," the dragon continued, "is a funny story from our new act. How about this one? Seems there was this thirsty dragon decided he needed to have a drink. So he goes into this local tavern, see—"

"Ahem," my master intoned, holding his nose against the ever-increasing scents of magical creatures in the immediate vicinity. "I think, Wuntvor, that the time has come for us to consult briefly in the college library. Alone." He turned and called to the others. "Wuntvor and I will return anon. Please wait for us. We beg your—"

My master sneezed once. He turned upon his heel and rapidly strode across the courtyard. I did my best to keep up.

"And there were shoes!" the Brownie continued behind us, his voice filled with wonder. "And boots, and sandals, and slippers with pointy toes—"

"So, anyway"—Hubert's booming voice drowned out the little person's—"the tavern keeper brings the dragon a tankard of mead and says, 'That will be five hundred golden crowns.' Then the barkeep adds, 'You know, we don't get many dragons—' "

Ebenezum slammed the door of the library after I had followed him inside.

"I fear," my master remarked, "That this situation may be getting out of hand."

I agreed with the mage.

Ebenezum pulled absently at his beard. " 'Tis always the way when great magic is involved. One way or another, magic creatures appear in great numbers and stand around being magical. Unfortunately, it can be very disruptive"—he paused to blow his nose—"especially considering our present circumstance. Like all things sorcerous, magical creatures must be kept under strict control. They need a firm hand. They need a leader."

"Master?" I asked, not quite seeing his point.

"Indeed." The wizard fixed me with his steely gaze. "They need you, Wuntvor."

"Master?" I repeated, a bit of panic in my voice.

"Yes," Ebenezum continued. "There's no use denying it, Wuntvor. This situation needs a leader, a focus to direct all those magical actions we will require to defeat the Netherhells. Unfortunately, my malady prevents me from being that focus. And now all the wizards in Vushta seem to have caught that same malady. It is therefore up to you, Wuntvor, to become the magician who will lead our forces to success."

I did not know what to say. Me, Wuntvor, a mere unschooled apprentice, the leader of all our forces? I was quite overwhelmed by the amount of faith my master held in me. I looked at the wizard, resplendent in his new robes of deepest blue, and he nodded solemnly.

I swallowed and took a deep breath, careful to stand at my full height. Perhaps my master was right after all. I had shown that I could perform magic in a pinch, both in our trip to Vushta and in my quest to the Netherhells. Now that I thought of it, I *had* conjured dead fish and turned myself into a grackle.

Very well. I folded my arms and nodded, ready to fulfill my destiny.

"Indeed," my master continued when it became apparent that I had no objections. "Now we must prepare for your quest. And Wuntvor, the best preparation a wizard can have is that of a ready mind and positive attitude towards what is to come."

"Indeed," I replied, ready to shoulder a wizard's responsibility.

"Therefore," Ebenezum resumed, "you must keep a cool head, no matter what should occur or what people should tell you. There are many rumors about the Eastern Kingdoms, and while most of them are completely unfounded, there are many in Vushta who enjoy spreading these rumors about." He paused to stroke his mustache thoughtfully. "You should know, then, to pay no heed to the stories of

Mother Duck's kingdom, especially those about her cooking magicians and heroes in those ovens she keeps for her giants. And, of course, give not a thought to those unfounded tales about how she can twist the very fabric of reality and turn men into beasts and shrubs." Ebenezum's great white eyebrows rose as he made his final point. "Remember, no matter what happens, your magic will be able to save you!"

Beasts and shrubs? Then again, it occurred to me that there might be some situations that required spells other than grackles and dead fish. I cleared my throat. Perhaps I had objections after all. But how would I best be able to express them to the mage?

"But master," I began hesitantly, "will I be able to learn the spells required? I mean, my magical background—"

" 'Tis true, Wuntvor." Ebenezum nodded sagely. "I have been slightly remiss in your education. During your first two years of apprenticeship I had meant to begin your course of magical lessons. Still, you know how things go—one thing leads to another, and the time is gone before you know it. Well, it is no use crying over broken spells. We will have to remedy your lack of education, beginning now."

Ebenezum turned to the rows of books that stood behind us. "Indeed, Wuntvor. I brought you to the library for more reasons than to free ourselves of the crowd. There is a certain tome here that I feel might be of assistance to you." Holding his nose, he scanned the shelves.

"There!" he said at last, pointing to an aged volume on the uppermost shelf. "Could you reach it for me?"

I pulled down the book, which was bound in dark blue velum. At first glance it was a quite impressive-looking tome, although the parchment within appeared a touch dog-eared, as if it had seen frequent use. The cover bore a title, in highly illuminated script of pure gold leaf: *Magic for the Millions—A Home Study Course.*

"A home study course?" I replied.

"Even more than this," my master intoned. "It is the finest home study course ever invented."

"Pardon, master," I asked with some trepidation, "but what is a home study course?"

"Indeed." The mage pulled at his beard. " 'Tis a series of lessons that are self-contained, so that you might gain the advantages of a schooling in magic without actually attending the school. There are a great many advantages to learning magic in this method. Think,

Wuntvor. For one thing, you don't have to sit through the study halls, and you'll never catch yourself glancing at the classroom hourglass while your teacher goes on and on about something you could care less about." The wizard sighed. "Of course, you also aren't able to try out for the sports teams, sorcerous soccer, and the like, and I would imagine that the senior play might have to be a monologue—but I digress." Ebenezum paused to clear his throat and straighten his robes.

Study halls? Sorcerous soccer? I had no idea what my master was talking about. I hoped there was enough in this book so that I might make some sense out of it. I hastily opened the cover and read aloud the words imprinted on the first page:

"Compiled by Ebenezum, Greatest Wizard in the Western Kingdoms. Fourth Printing."

"Indeed," my master remarked. " 'Twas part of my association with the Famous Wizards School. Made me quite a bit of—but that is beside the point. We must address our present task!" He waved with a flourish at the book I held in my hands. "You have before you everything you need to become a full-fledged wizard, competent in all the basic sorcerous arts—alchemy, healing with herbs, love potions, how to predict the arrival of tax collectors. And that is but the mere beginning!"

Love potions? All thoughts of quests and battles with the Netherhells fell away from that one glowing thought. My master had said love potions, hadn't he? I tried to contain my excitement. Perhaps there was some way Norei and I could be reunited after all! I could barely wait to begin this "home study course." Love potions, indeed!

"No matter what danger you might face," the wizard resumed, "within this book there is a magical solution. If you would turn to the back, you'll find an index."

I struggled to put thoughts of a happy reunion out of my mind, and did as Ebenezum bade, opening to a page titled "Easy Wizard's Index." I scanned quickly down the righthand column:

Demons, who are about to eat you, 206, 211
Demons, who are about to tear you limb from limb, 207
Demons, who are about to thrash you soundly, 206–7
Demons, who have already begun to eat you, 208 . . .

"As you can see," my master continued, "quick reference to this index can prepare you for virtually any eventuality. In all, I think this home study course will go some distance toward remedying your lack of education. Of course, while you are on the quest you might have difficulty in mailing your lessons, but we'll devise some method to overcome that."

I closed the tome and looked to my master. The index certainly did seem thorough. I was happy that he was so sure of my success. There was a damp spot on the velum where my sweaty palm grasped the book. Suddenly my brain was no longer filled with thoughts of my beloved. Instead, the words I had read in the index were sinking into my overworked consciousness: "Demons, who have already begun to eat you . . ."

I had been thinking too much of Norei and not enough about the quest. I would have to study this book in some detail before I began my journey. Then, when there was time, I would study the love potions.

"Indeed," my master remarked. "I have also spoken with Snorphosio, and he shall supply you with a map of the region." He pulled at his beard. "Or at least what we know of that region. But what say, Wunt, that we go over the introductory lesson together? I may have to hold my nose a bit, but I think I can make it through. If we work on it now, in the library, we should be able to speed through it without interruption."

I had barely reopened the book when the earth began to shake again.

"Then again," the wizard muttered, "we may never again be able to do anything without interruption."

I hurriedly followed my master back into the courtyard, ready for our next confrontation with the Netherhells.

Or so I thought.

SIX

"Demons do not generally make the best of friends, unless, of course, you like to center all your social activities around eating, and furthermore, enjoy serving yourself as the main course."

—THE TEACHINGS OF EBENEZUM, Volume XLI

"To the circle!" my master cried as he ran from the library. The other wizards, alerted by Ebenezum's warning, hastily moved to their preassigned positions.

The circle of wizards raised their arms as one. Then in unison each magician began to sneeze.

The quake intensified. The ground heaved, shaking me from my feet. By the time I regained my balance, I saw that a great rift had appeared in the earth at the center of the courtyard. I watched, horrified, as a demonic apparition rose from the bowels of the Netherhells to fill that rift.

The quake ceased as suddenly as it had begun. I gripped my stout oak staff as the dust settled, and I could clearly see what the foul fiends of the Netherhells had brought into our midst.

It appeared to be a stout oak table, behind which sat five of the largest and ugliest demons I had ever seen. The one in the center pounded on the table with a huge gavel.

"I now bring this attack to order!" the thing announced in a voice far too coarse to be called gravelly.

What sinister trick of the Netherhells was this? I turned to my master, but he was lost, sneezing deep within his robes. It was up to the warriors, then. I nodded to my fellows still standing amidst the sneezing mages.

"Doom," Hendrek agreed.

We all took a cautious step forward.

"Wait a moment!" the slightly smaller, purplish demon cried from the end of the table. "Who gives you the authority to begin the attack? We have to have a consensus here!"

"My dear Blecch," the demon with the gavel calmly replied. "I beg to differ. We don't need a consensus. In cases like this, a simple majority is fine."

"Majority?" Blecch laughed derisively. "My fellow demon is completely out of order!" It pounded its demonic fist on a large and ugly tome that it had just opened. "It states clearly here, in the *New Netherhells Bylaws*—"

The demonic group seemed a bit disorganized. If we were going to win, we should attack now.

I lifted my stout oak staff above my head, and with the mightiest cry I could muster, ran towards the demons. Luckily, my fellows followed my lead. As I ran to face our enemy, I glimpsed Hubert galloping, Hendrek trundling, and the unicorn prancing magnificently forward to attack.

The Dealer of Death got there before all of us.

"Point of order!" one of the demons cried. "We seem to be under attack!"

"I vote for retaliatory action!" Blecch added. "All in favor say"—he paused as the Dealer grasped him by the throat—"Urracht!"

"No, no," the gavel demon insisted. "A show of hands is more appropriate. All in favor?"

The four demons not currently being strangled raised their hands. Blecch, with some considerable effort, managed to follow suit.

"It's unanimous, then!" the gavel demon announced. "Time for the boiling blood!"

All five demons turned to regard the Dealer.

The man in black gasped. His face turned bright red and steam shot from his ears. Blecch gave him a gentle push. The Dealer collapsed on the ground.

"Now we can get on with our own attack," the gavel demon remarked.

"I think not!" Blecch countered as it massaged its throat. "We still have not resolved this important procedural issue. To recklessly continue without putting this matter to rest would be a breach of authority one might expect of Guxx Unfufadoo!"

"What?" the gavel demon blustered. "You dare compare me with the ex-Grand Hoohah? Just for that, Blecch, I'll—"

We never found out what the demon would do, for that was the moment my fellows and I attacked.

"Point of urk!" Blecch yelled as the dread warclub Headbasher came squarely down upon his purple head.

I swung my stout oak staff at the demon on the table's far end. "Point of order!" it cried as it deftly ducked the blow. The staff bounced harmlessly off the table, forcing me to stagger back a pace.

"I think we should vote on retreat!" the ducking demon continued.

The demon at table's center lifted its gavel to pound for order, but found the wooden mallet burnt from its fingers by Hubert's dragon fire. "Show of hands!" the demon yelped. It didn't wait for any response from its fellows, who were busy fending off Snarks, myself, and the unicorn. "Majority rules!" the ex-gavel demon shrieked.

The table and its occupants disappeared in a puff of smoke.

"Doom," Hendrek muttered as his enchanted club swept the air where a demon had sat scant seconds before.

"What an exit!" Snarks whistled in admiration. "Unfortunate, wasn't it, that it was the only successful part of their attack?"

I turned to Norei, who knelt over the prostrate Dealer of Death. He lay so still. A chill slithered down my spine.

"Is he—" I began in trepidation.

"I feared the same," Norei replied quickly. "But there is still a spark left deep within him. The demons' attack appears to have put him in a deathlike trance. And who knows how long that life spark will last?"

"Doom," Hendrek intoned, echoing the sympathies of all those assembled.

The chill I had felt when I had seen the stillness of the Dealer had stayed with me. We seemed to be facing a new and very different strategy from the Netherhells. As ineffectual as their first attack had been, the threat somehow seemed much more sinister.

I heard a nose blow behind my right shoulder. My master stepped forward.

"Indeed." He spoke as if he had read my thoughts. "An attack of this nature can be truly serious. I have never before seen this particular Netherhells strategy, but I have read about its devastating effect in my ancient wizardly lore." He paused to blow his nose a final time. He wiped his mustache clean and redeposited the kerchief in one of his voluminous sleeves.

"From observation," the wizard resumed, "it appears that this particular plan of attack has fallen out of use among the demons as well, for the proficiency of the strikes against us has so far been somewhat lacking. However, we should not let this temporary incompetence lull us into complacency." He extended his foot to gently nudge the still form of the black-clad assassin. "We have seen from the current condition of the Dealer of Death that this new strategy can be devastating. The forces of the Netherhells are stubborn. They will come against us again and again, until they get their attack right. When that happens, I fear we are all doomed, for there is no Netherhells strategy deadlier than the one we saw today: Conquest by Committee!"

"Doom!" Snarks exclaimed in agreement. " 'Tis the only thing worse than the Grand Hoohah."

"What—" I began.

"You don't want to know!" Snarks interjected rapidly.

"Indeed," my master continued. "This situation makes it that much more imperative that we begin the quest for aid at once." He motioned to the other mages, most of whom seemed to have recovered from their sneezing bouts. "We must confer for but a minute, and then the selection shall be made." He turned to Norei. "I am sorry, young witch, that we will have to exclude you, but I feel such a move is for the best. You see, I have discovered that when magic arises, my malady becomes contagious."

My master turned and walked back in the direction of the library, the other wizards at his heels. I paced in the opposite direction, eager to pick up the Home Study Course where I had dropped it in the heat of battle. On my way there, I chanced to pass close to my beloved, who shook her head in disbelief.

"Can you believe it?" she asked.

Well, I could believe anything that came from those beautiful lips. Still, of late, whenever I had tried to express my devotion to Norei, it seemed to come out incorrectly. I decided, therefore, to take the safer path.

"Believe what?" I asked.

"Your master kept me from casting a spell in the recent battle. I did not know that was his intention at the time, of course. He kept leaping in front of me, his head covered by his great robes, so that all I could hear were his muffled sneezes. Norei chuckled. "I thought the great wizard had taken leave of his senses."

I nodded solemnly at Norei's explanation. With hardly any thought of his own malady, Ebenezum had prevented this young witch from suffering a similar fate. He was, truly, a great wizard. How many times had he saved me from similar misadventures? But with that thought came another: How would I survive my coming quest without him by my side?

I turned to Norei, intent on confiding my doubts. But my beloved was nowhere to be seen in the milling aftermath of battle. Was this what it had come to, then? Had I lost Norei's confidence completely? Would I be forever alone, without another soul to speak with?

There was a small explosion by my feet.

"A happy Brownie hello!" an equally small voice exhorted. "You haven't perchance seen my student hereabouts?"

"Your student?" It only occurred to me once I had spoken that he must mean Snarks.

"Yes, the green fellow," the Brownie replied, confirming my suspicions. "That rapscallion led me to the official college bootery. Well, let me tell you, time can really fly when you get a chance to examine quality footwear. And how much more fascinating is it when that footwear is magical!" The Brownie whistled softly. "There was one pair of ruby slippers that really caught my . . ."

Something pricked at my throat. I found it was a knife. It was attached to an arm, which was attached in turn to Vermin, that large, unspeaking member of the Vushta Apprentice Guild.

"What a surprise!" said Grott, whom I was sure could do enough talking for the both of them. He doffed his cap and bowed in what I thought was a rather exaggerated manner. "To find you here at the Wizards College just after a battle. But how fortuitous. It seems we have a little unfinished discourse."

A huge shadow blocked the sun. I looked up to see Slag grinning at me.

"Yeah," the huge man said. "Disco— uh, disc—." He swallowed. "Yeah," he began again. "Seems."

"It also seems," Grott continued all too jovially, "that a certain party of our mutual acquaintance has just had his blood boiled and can no longer come to your rescue!"

"Yeah," Slag smirked. "Seems."

"So we simply waited until the courtyard here was a little less populated," Grott continued. I glanced about me as much as the knife at my throat allowed. It was true. My surroundings were quite deserted. "When that happened, we knew it was time to become reacquainted and remind you of our simple demands: A total cure for our masters, or four hundred pieces of gold for—"

"Hey!" a small voice piped from near my foot. "Are these fellows bothering you?"

"Eh?" Grott said. "What's this?" Obviously, in their haste to threaten me again, my three fellow apprentices had completely missed my tiny companion. Grott glared down at the Brownie. "Oh, an insect of some kind."

"Only if insects are equipped with Brownie Power!" Tap exclaimed.

Grott laughed at that. "No matter what defenses an insect has, it can easily be squashed."

"Yeah." Slag chuckled as he raised his foot. "Squashed!"

The Brownie danced, a frown of concentration on his tiny face. The laces on Slag's rapidly descending shoe suddenly snaked out and tied themselves around the man's arms, causing the large apprentice to totally lose his balance. Slag fell beyond the Brownie with a considerable crash.

"What happened?" Grott demanded.

"Yeah." Slag struggled to put words in a sentence. "What . . . uh, shoe . . . uh, tie. No. Untie!" The large fellow pointed gleefully to his unlaced boot, happy that he had found the right word.

"What?" Grott repeated incredulously. "Oh, never mind. We'll figure it out later, after Vermin takes a little prize from our apprentice friend here. Something to remember you by, Wuntvor, a little keepsake—say, a piece of your ear."

Vermin's knife pressed even harder against my throat.

"Don't worry," Grott added. "We'll give it back to you when you deliver the four hundred pieces of gold." He cleared his throat and smiled. "Did I say four? So sorry. A slip of the tongue. I meant, of course, five hundred pieces. Vermin, if you would?"

"Not while there's Brownie Power around!" Tap cried triumphantly.

"What?" Grott's voice held a note of panic. "What's happening to my shoes?"

"Yeah!" Slag replied hoarsely. "Untie!"

And that was what Grott's soft leather boots were doing: the laces seemingly untying of their own accord. The knife was no longer at my throat, so I was free to turn my head and see the same thing happening to the footwear of both Vermin and Slag. Six sets of laces untied, then stretched to perhaps three times their natural length, swatting away the apprentices' hands when the guild members tried to control them. Then just as rapidly the individual laces found each other and tied new knots, so that Grott, Slag, and Vermin were joined together by their footwear.

"I'm warning you!" Grott screamed as his feet were pulled from under him. "A cure for our masters or six hundred pieces of gold!"

The six shoes, with the apprentices' feet still inside, began to bounce up and down.

"Did I say six hundred? I meant seven hundred!"

The bouncing grew more pronounced.

"Eight hundred!" Grott, Slag, and Vermin caught each other's arms to keep from falling. The shoes bounced away from me and the Brownie. "No! A thousand!" Their bouncing took on height and speed as the three took great six-foot leaps across the courtyard. "And by moonrise tomorrow, or you'll really sorry!"

Their leaps grew higher still, so that by the time they reached the far end of the courtyard, their final jump sent them clear over the Great Hall.

"A thousand?" Grott shrieked with all his might. "That is not enough! Twelve hun—"

His voice was cut off by the intervening building.

"What will happen to them?" I asked the Brownie.

"Eventually they will reach the Great Vushta Canal," Tap replied. "There, they will sink." He grinned broadly. "Is that Brownie Power or what?"

I had to agree with the little fellow. He certainly did have a way with shoes.

"Wuntvor!"

My master's voice called to me from directly outside the library. He approached, trailed by his fellow wizards. The crowd of heroes and magical creatures was also filtering back into the courtyard, although Snarks, on spotting the Brownie, seemed content to lurk about in the extreme edges of the greenery, generally behind some concealing bush or boulder.

My master stopped a few paces before me. "It is time for our decision," he intoned.

"Indeed?" I replied.

"Indeed," my master rejoined. "Heed well, 'prentice, what transpires in these next few moments. Your life, very probably, will depend upon it."

SEVEN

"The working magician will sometimes find himself in less than ideal circumstances. For example, say you are employed to fight some dire enemy, and having begun the fight, find the enemy has hired a wizard as well. The professional magician, ready for any eventually, will thereupon redouble his efforts while constructing mystical barriers against the other mage.

"But the enemy has also hired assassins, equipped with enchanted weapons, to kill our hypothetical magician. In such cases the fully prepared wizard will reach deep inside himself for those special inner resources, gained through years practicing the magical arts, that will help him to survive.

"But then it grows even worse, as our mage discovers the enemy has enlisted the services of a demon horde who are headed straight for our magician's redoubt to tear him into little pieces and then serve those pieces, impaled with toothpicks, as a part of their victory celebration. What, then, is the working wizard to do?

"The first thing to tell yourself is not to panic. Remember, rather, to keep a calm head, and to heed these words that have helped other wizards, in similar situations to your own, throughout the ages:

"When in doubt, run."

—THE TEACHINGS OF EBENEZUM,
Volume LXXXII
(annual supplement)

So the moment of decision had come at last. I was relieved, in a way. Now, at last, I could put all the petty little things that had been happening of late behind me and concentrate on the quest.

"Get away from me!" Snarks shrieked.

"You are only delaying the inevitable," the Brownie replied calmly as he chased the frightened demon across the courtyard. "We must prepare you for the arrival of his Brownieship. Soon you will know the truth about shoes."

"Indeed," my master interrupted, primarily, I suspect, to regain my attention. "As the rest of our group assembles, let me give you a final reassurance. As you know, my malady prevents me from joining you personally on your quest into the realm of Mother Duck. However, you will not be without my guidance. I have made arrangements so that we will stay in constant contact—"

My master sneezed.

"Must you?" the unicorn chided as it stepped between us. "You'll tarnish my wondrous golden horn." The beast shook said horn dry, the golden sheen flashing magnificently with reflected sunlight. It turned its amazingly soulful eyes in my direction. "I only wanted a few"—it paused—"private words with our"—it paused again, blinking at me—"young hero."

My master sneezed in disbelief.

"Indeed," I said quickly, doing my best to substitute for the temporarily ailing wizard. "Do you think it might be possible to give the two of us a moment's privacy?"

The unicorn looked at me in shock, as if I had wounded it by the very suggestion we might not want it around. "So that's the way it is, then," it murmured, its voice soft and mournful. "I, the most magnificent of beasts, am to be turned away. Who would have thought it would come to this?" The creature glanced at me a final time, its eyes filled with wondrous despair. "If only my head were not so heavy!"

"There, there," I said, momentarily taken aback by the unicorn's show of anguish. "Nobody's disputing your magnificence." The unicorn stopped moaning softly to itself and looked at me. "In fact, it is that very magnificence that would stop us from fully concentrating on an important decision. That is why you must leave. After all, how can we defend ourselves when we are blinded by your beauty?"

"Yes, being as wonderful as me can be a tremendous burden," the beast agreed as it tossed its shaggy mane from its eyes, a gesture that took my breath away. "It's good to know that others can realize that." The creature once again looked deep into my eyes. "And it's also nice to know"—the unicorn paused meaningfully,—"that you care."

"Indeed," I replied after a moment's pause.

The unicorn nodded a final time and strutted away, the royalty of magic creatures.

My master blew his nose. "Indeed," he remarked once he had regained his breath. "With such diplomacy, Wunt, you may become a first-class wizard after all. I had feared that my malady might stunt your growth in the wizardly arts. But now I see that you have used the adversity of the past few weeks to your advantage." The wizard beamed at me. "After dealing with Brownies and unicorns, Wuntvor, you should be able to handle regular clients with both hands tied behind your back while you are concurrently balancing a ball upon your nose and midway through a short, refreshing afternoon nap."

I was quite taken aback. Rarely had my master heaped any praise at all upon me, and never, I thought, had he complimented me quite so directly. For the first time I began to feel just a bit like a hero.

"But there are things we must discuss," the wizard added quickly. He pulled for a moment at his long white beard. "Now, let us see. You have been given the home study course, and I mentioned that we would stay in contact, although I have not yet explained the means—"

The earth shook, ever so briefly. I feared another Netherhells attack until I saw that Hubert had landed in front of us, accompanied by his beautiful partner, Alea, who sat upon the dragon's back.

The two began to sing:

"The young man, he came from the West,
Bound on a Mother Duck quest!
From his grim task he would not sway,
Though certain death stood in his way!
But Wuntvor was bound to endure,
Though he would get eaten for sure
By dire creatures out for his blood,
Who would then stomp his bones in the mud,
And break them in two for a wish!
They'd hollow his skull for a dish,
And make a soup using his eyes.
From the rest, they'd make Wuntvor Surprise!
Although they might spit out an ear,
While they noisily chomped on his—"

"Indeed!" my master interjected very loudly, at the same time holding his nose so that the dragon's scent would not bring about another sneezing fit. "I am sure this is all very musical, but what does it have to do with our present situation?"

"Good wizard," the dragon replied, bowing so low that his snout touched the ground. " 'Tis but a small token of our appreciation for being included in this adventure. You know that we feel it is our duty to lighten the grim load of responsibility with an occasional entertainment. And what better time than right now, with a new quest about to begin!" The dragon tossed his head aloft, shooting forth a banner of flame.

"Yes," my master began. "But—"

"So glad you agree," Hubert replied quickly. "Let me tell you, it was a dilemma. This is such an important moment, we wanted to choose something appropriate. After much discussion, we decided that a touching farewell song would be best, and so put together a haunting melody tinged with sadness as we send our hero off to certain doom. You know, the sort of thing that tugs at the strings of your heart. We humbly think that if you are here to provide the wisdom, we are here to provide the art."

Tug at the strings of my heart? I had felt more of a reaction to the song in my stomach.

"Indeed," I attempted to interject. "But—"

"Thus," Hubert continued, "we thought it appropriate to give you a small sample of our strengths now, when you are about to choose those who are to go on this most important mission. Yes, that is correct: Damsel and Dragon would like to volunteer! The expedition surely needs a couple of cheerful minstrels to keep spirits high in times of trial! We laugh at demons! We sneer at sorcery! We scoff at danger!"

The dragon chortled, producing a pair of smoke rings from his nostrils. "Plus, should we succeed, think of the publicity! 'Damsel and Dragon Help Save the World from Demonkind!' " Hubert sighed happily. "We will be booked forever!"

Hubert's dragon jaws closed with a snap. Apparently his oration was over.

"Indeed," my master replied after a moment's hesitation. "Thank you for your offer. I assure you it will receive careful consideration."

Alea blew me a kiss as the two of them left to join the crowd. Ebenezum took a second to tend to his nose.

"Sometimes," he remarked as he once again tucked his dark blue handkerchief, tastefully embroidered with silver moons and stars, within his voluminous sleeve, "I long for the days when it was just the two of us, Wunt, struggling across the Western Kingdoms toward Vushta, with only nature and the forces of the Netherhells to contend with." He shook his head. "But this is no time for nostalgia. It is time for action. Now where were we? We have covered the home study course, and delved, however briefly, into the fact that I shall still be able to advise you. Now, I think it is time for a bit of wizardly advice. Heed my words carefully Wuntvor, for they may mean the difference between success and failure, life and death, a carefree existence for us all or an eternity of pain and torture at the hands of—"

"Doom." Hendrek's voice resounded over my left shoulder. "Forgive me for interrupting, but they have brought the weapons."

"Indeed," my master replied as he glanced over his shoulder. "So they have. Now, if you would excuse us for but a moment—"

"Doom," Hendrek interjected. "You must forgive one further interruption, but as we speak of weapons, I feel I should remind you of my prowess with Headbasher. If you are about to go on a quest, how much better if you are to include a man inured to battle like myself, a warrior, steeped in blood. A berserker, ready to kill at the slightest provocation."

"Indeed," Ebenezum concurred. "Still—"

"A lit fuse," Hendrek glowered. "A powder keg ready to explode. It is best that a trained mercenary like myself does not remain idle." He fingered the sack that held Headbasher. "Please consider me when you choose companions for the quest. Doom!"

And with that, the large warrior left us.

"Well," Ebenezum remarked. "And now quickly back to our discussion, before we can be interrupted—"

Someone cleared her throat behind me. It was the most musical throat-clearing I had ever heard. It had to be Norei.

"Excuse me," she said, looking straight at my master. "I know it's rude to interrupt, but I was wondering if you might be able to give Wuntvor a message from me."

"Norei!" I began. Why wasn't she speaking to me? "But—"

"I am well aware that you are about to choose those among us who are to accompany Wuntvor on a quest of some importance. I wanted to inform you now, so that there would be no misunderstanding, that I do not wish to be among those included."

"Norei?" I gasped, astonished. What did this mean? "But—"

"I want to be very firm about this," my beloved continued. "You see, Wuntvor and I once meant something to each other." She sighed wistfully, as if recalling some far distant memory.

"Indeed?" my master remarked as he stroked his beard in thought. He glanced in my direction.

"Norei?" I asked forcefully. Whatever her problem with me, I would do my best to solve it now. "But—"

"It is for this very reason," my beloved continued as if she had not even heard me, "that I do not wish to be included in any other adventures. The very nearness of that apprentice would remind me of better times, happier moments that Wuntvor apparently never wishes to repeat. Therefore, you should not even consider me for the quest. That is"—she paused, her eyes fluttering ever so slightly (dare I hope?) in my direction—"unless you really need me."

Ebenezum cleared his throat rather noisily. "Well, I will be certain to tell Wuntvor of your wishes. And we will assuredly take your feelings into account when choosing our party."

"Norei?" I called a final time. She seemed to hesitate as she turned away. My heart quickened. Perhaps she would give me one last chance.

"Oh, Wuntie!" Alea called to me as she skipped across the courtyard. Her ash-blond curls shone blindingly as they bounced in the sunlight. "Hubert wanted me to talk to you about that act we were going to do together!"

To my dread I saw my beloved Norei mouth Alea's last few words: "Act we were going to do together?"

Norei looked at me for the first time. From the intensity of the emotions in her eyes, I wish she hadn't.

Alea interposed herself between Norei and me. "You'll excuse us, won't you dear?" Alea called over her shoulder to my beloved. "Wuntie and I have things to discuss."

It was too much for the young witch. "Act?" she yelled. "Things to discuss? I'll give you—"

She stopped abruptly, caught short by the sudden appearance of a golden horn so wonderful it put even Alea's hair to shame. The unicorn pushed between me and the two others.

"Pardon me, but are these women bothering you?" the incredible beast inquired.

"Um . . ." I replied.

"Bothering you!" Both women cried in unison.

"Um . . ." I repeated. This was all going too fast for me. What should I say?

"I never bother Wuntie!" Alea insisted vociferously. "Wuntie and I were having another of our sensitive conversations about—"

"You wouldn't know a sensitive conversation if one bit you in the—" Norei interrupted just as loudly.

"Obviously, then, my first reaction was quite correct," the unicorn sniffed. "A sensitive lad like you needs protection"—it paused meaningfully—"and perhaps a little guidance." The beast looked soulfully into my eyes. "I thought if I took a more active interest, you might see the light. Who, after all, can resist a unicorn? Especially when the alternatives are such as these."

All three of them turned to look at me. I swallowed loudly and turned to look at my master.

"Indeed," the wizard said as he stroked his mustache. "Wuntvor and I must confer privately about the choice of weapons."

My master hastily pulled me aside.

"What do you mean," I heard Alea shout behind me, "I wouldn't understand a sensitive conversation?"

My master spoke to me quickly, in hushed tones. "We have a situation here that would best be left alone for a time."

"So you want sensitive?" Norei retorted. "I'll make you sensitive!"

"Say the time it takes to complete a quest," my master added.

"Of course," a third voice remarked calmly, "no one is as sensitive as a unicorn."

"Oh, shut up!" Norei retorted. "You're nothing but an overstuffed horse!"

"Or perhaps two quests," the wizard amended. I could see the wisdom in my master's words. "But we must confer quickly now, before we suffer further—"

"I never want to hear about shoes again!"

My master almost tripped over the rapidly traveling Snarks. I suppose it was only natural, then, that I should trip over the Brownie.

"You must face the inevitable—yelp!" Tap shrieked as he collided solidly with my left foot.

As I picked myself up, I was startled to see Snarks on his knees, clutching frantically at my master's robes.

"Oh, great wizard," the demon pleaded. "I have heard there's another quest in the offing, and I was wondering if I might be considered —" The demon drew back as he saw Tap stand and happily brush himself off. "No, I'm not wondering at all!" Snarks added quickly.

"Take me on the quest! I don't care where it is! As long as there aren't any Brownies!"

I turned and began to apologize to the little fellow, but Tap waved me to silence.

"No harm done," he remarked cheerfully. "Brownies don't bruise easily. It's one of the advantages of being built short. You're much closer to the ground when you fall. Besides, I should have been looking where I was going. Once I get talking about shoes, though . . ."

The Brownie sauntered casually in the demon's direction. Snarks shrieked and ran. I looked after him with astonishment. Before today the demon had always had a ready answer for everything. Could one Brownie make that much of a change?

Ebenezum blew his nose and tapped me on the shoulder.

"Indeed," my master whispered hoarsely. "Quick—"

"Eep! Eep! Eep!" My ferrets, dispersed by the recent battle, seemed to be regathering around us. As happy as I was to see them, I had to admit that their joyful cries made it difficult to listen to anything else in the immediate area.

"Oh, never mind," the wizard muttered. "Let's look at the weapons."

The aged wizard Snorphosio nodded as we approached. He was tastefully tucking his own recently used handkerchief within a bright red sleeve.

"We have here what weapons we could find in the college storeroom." The scholarly mage sniffed. "I am afraid there have been some problems."

"Problems?" Ebenezum asked.

"Yes." Snorphosio nodded his head sadly. "Although who among us does not have problems? It is in the nature of existence, is it not, for wizards must exist like any others. And what is the true nature of a wizard's existence except—"

"Exactly what problems are there?" my master interrupted.

"Oh, certainly," Snorphosio murmured. "Forgive my digression. But is not digression itself a problem that wizards must—" He stopped and cleared his throat self-consciously. "Yes. Pardon. The problems. First, it appears that during Vushta's recent trip to and from the Netherhells, the weapons storeroom got jumbled about a bit. We opened the door to find everything in incredible disarray. On first sight it reminded me of the chaos that is the core of all our existences and the problems I had mentioned before that dog a wizard's every waking—"

"Indeed," my master interposed. "So something is wrong with the weapons?"

"With the weapons themselves, no." The scholar shook his head. "As far as we know, they are in prime working order. Of course, we cannot tell for certain if they are working properly—"

"And why is that?" Ebenezum jumped in before his fellow could begin another digression.

"All the weapons seem to have lost their labels," Snorphosio replied a bit sheepishly. "We can't quite tell what does what anymore."

"Doom." I noticed then that Hendrek had silently lumbered up behind us.

"Indeed?" Ebenezum frowned and pulled on his beard. "Does anyone have a knowledge of the storeroom?"

"Not a very complete one, I'm afraid." Snorphosio shrugged. "I'm sure you know how it is. Things pile up, you get way behind in cataloging. Again we return to the nature of life, don't we, and man's feeble attempts to extract order out of chaos? But what, exactly, is the true nature of order? What right have we, as magicians, to impose—"

"What can we do to find magic weapons for the quest?" my master retorted.

"Well," Snorphosio admitted, "that's another problem. None of the wizards have been able to reach very far into the storeroom. The sneezing problem, you see. We did manage to drag out one chest full of smaller weapons, however." The scholar patted a huge strongbox whose top reached up to his waist. "There may very well be something of value herein."

"May very well?" Ebenezum exploded. "Can't you tell?"

"Well . . ." Snorphosio hesitated. "No. The label problem, you know. One has to be careful around unlabeled enchanted weapons. Besides the sneezing problem, some of these things are quite powerful, capable of warping the fabric of the universe and ending life as we know it." The mage cleared his throat once again. "However, we don't think any devices with that kind of power are that small." He tried to smile and failed. "At least," he added, "we hope not."

"Hope?" My master seemed to be trembling with anger by now. I had hardly ever seen him so upset. He wasn't using any "indeeds" at all.

"Oh, we have not been sitting idly with this problem on our hands,"

Snorphosio assured him. "In fact, one of the younger magicians among our number boldly volunteered to test the weapons enclosed to see what might be useful."

"A bold mage indeed," Ebenezum remarked, his anger momentarily subdued. "And what were the results?"

"Well . . ." The scholar tapped the box. "Our suspicion is that the young fellow's still in there somewhere." He sighed, but then smiled. "However, before he disappeared he did manage to give us this!"

His smile broadened as he held aloft a thin sliver of wood. "This, gentlebeings, is Gllzbchh's Toothpick."

"Doom," Hendrek remarked in awe. "I have never seen a weapon so small. How deadly is it?"

"Deadly?" Snorphosio frowned. "Well, it is not exactly deadly?"

"Doom," Hendrek replied. "Then the weapon is truly dangerous?"

"Well," the scholar allowed, "in point of fact, you couldn't even call it exactly dangerous. You can take my word for it, though, that it is very, very annoying."

"And that is all you have found?" my master demanded.

"No, no, of course not!" Snorphosio insisted. "Well, actually, in point of fact, yes, it's as far as we got when our poor compatriot disappeared. However, we do have a few more weapons we can offer. Such as this!" He decisively pointed at a nearby oak.

"And what, precisely, is 'this'?" Ebenezum asked with some disdain.

"Why, it's a magic tree of course." The scholar sounded somewhat hurt that my master had not instantly recognized the enchanted vegetation. "And let me tell you, I got an extremely good price on it, too. Bought it from a renegade demon, actually, fellow in a bright checked suit who sold weapons slightly used."

"Indeed," my master responded, making a visible effort to calm himself. "And how would my apprentice be expected to carry a tree?"

"Carry it?" Snorphosio mused. "Why would he need to—oh, dear, he is leaving the vicinity, isn't he? What to do?" His tentative fingers prodded the oak's unyielding trunk. "Maybe we could break off a magic branch?

"Wait, wait!" the scholar continued when he saw the look and the color of my master's face. "All is still not lost. We have not considered the weapons left over from the last quest!"

"Doom," Hendrek remarked for us all.

"Now, now," Snorphosio insisted, "they are perfectly serviceable.

Well, more or less. We have been having some trouble with Cuthbert. The sword claims to have been traumatized by all that battle. Refuses to come out of its sheath. I'm sure all it needs is a good talking to."

No one commented. Snorphosio quickly continued: "Then, of course, there is Wonk, the Horn of Persuasion."

"No, no!" everyone cried in unison. "Anything but Wonk!" I still remembered the effect the horn had when it was blown, and would do anything to see that it was *never* blown again. I had to face it. There were some weapons just too horrible to use.

"So there are no weapons my apprentice can take with him?" my master demanded.

"Well, no, not exactly." Snorphosio handed me the enchanted toothpick. "Well, actually, that is more or less correct."

"And so Wuntvor must go off to face the unknown with nothing but his wits and my assistance?" My master sighed. "Oh, well. He has done it before. Come, we had best pick companions before something else happens."

That's when the earth began to shake again.

"Doom!" Hendrek intoned. "I shall show you my prowess against the Netherhells. You are bound to take me on the quest!"

"I will surely be among those chosen," a magnificently modulated voice remarked. The glorious beast pranced forward in the afternoon sun. "Who can say no to a unicorn?"

"Quick, damsel!" Hubert rejoined. "We will confuse the enemy with our dancing and snappy patter! Then we shall be the quest's Official Entertainers!"

"I will show my fellow demons exactly how unwelcome they are!" Snarks added. "And I'd be glad to do it anywhere, especially anyplace without Brownies!"

"More demons?" Tap laughed delightedly. "Bring them on! I will tell them all the truth about shoes!"

"Even I will not desert you!" my beloved Norei added. "And you can tell that to Wuntvor when you get the chance!"

"Eep! Eep! Eep!" my legion of ferrets added, eager for the coming fight.

My master nodded to the other wizards, who formed a circle around the center of the quake.

The table with the five demons erupted again from the earth. Everyone paused for a long moment. I noticed the magicians close by me were holding their breath, perhaps to give them a few minutes longer in the face of this demonic enchantment.

"Quick, my fellows!" I shouted as I gripped my stout oak staff. "Forward to the attack, before they have a chance to vote!"

The gavel demon at table's center smiled evilly. "You are too late! We voted this time before we came to the surface so there would be no dissent. Prepare, pitiful mortals, to have your blood boiled!"

"Now!" Ebenezum shouted as he removed his fingers from his nose. And all the wizards sneezed as one.

"Point of—glub!" a demon shrieked as he was swamped by nasal effluvium. The entire table seemed totally undone by the sudden shower.

Without another word the dampened demons disappeared beneath the earth.

"Master!" I cried. "You have beaten them again!"

"Only by surprise," Ebenezum replied when he was done blowing his nose. "I fear it was our last guaranteed strategy. Next time the demons shall win."

I looked about me. All was confusion. Hendrek pounded Headbasher against the spot where the demons had sat but a moment before, while Damsel and Dragon tap danced close behind. Snarks beat a hasty retreat, pursued by the Brownie. The other wizards had fallen to the ground, all lost to their sneezing. The unicorn seemed somehow above it all, looking down at the proceedings from behind the length of its golden horn. The ferrets were everywhere, eeping merrily. And Norei, my beloved Norei, was nowhere to be seen.

"It will take far too long to choose companions," I remarked grimly.

"Indeed," my master replied. "It seems to take far too long to do anything." With that, Ebenezum once again succumbed to a bout of sneezing.

"Then I shall go alone," I stated, though no one was particularly listening. "I shall bring help from the Eastern Kingdoms. Do not worry, master. I shall not fail."

Having said what was necessary, I grabbed my stout oak staff and my pack, which contained both Snorphosio's map and the home study course. No one seemed to have heard my speech, and no one seemed to notice my leaving. Still, I was glad I had spoken.

I would have been happier still if I truly believed what I had said.

EIGHT

Nothing would stop me now. There was no reason to look back. My beloved Norei apparently no longer needed me. Besides which, I had a world to save.

I left Vushta the way I had entered, through the adjacent town of East Vushta, where I had first fought side by side with the members of the Wizards College Extension Program to save their neighbor city from the clutches of the Netherhells. From there, though, my path was different, leading me away from the shores of the Inland Sea into parts of the world entirely new to me.

I refolded Snorphosio's map and tucked it back into my pack. I had passed the East Vushta Extension College some moments before, and here the road split, one fork leading into the hills, the other down to the seashore. I once again shouldered my belongings and headed inland, toward my destiny.

I was amazed at how fast I left the city behind me. While the buildings and shops of East Vushta were quite a bit smaller than those of the City of a Thousand Forbidden Delights, they were still built close together, the streets surrounding them thronged with people. Once into the hills, however, what cottages I saw grew quickly smaller and farther apart, each one in worse repair than the one before. The last couple of shacks I passed were obviously deserted, at least of human occupants, although great, dark birds made their nests here and there amidst the collapsed walls.

As the homes grew sparser the trees grew thicker and the road, paved with brick where it left East Vushta, soon became naught but packed earth. A scant few minutes walk beyond that, it had deteriorated to two wagon ruts between tufts of sickly yellow grass. I paused to again look at Snorphosio's map, but according to the scholar's drawing, there was no way I could have made a wrong turn. There was but one road to the Eastern Kingdoms, and I was on it.

Still, I was happy to be on my way. My life had a definite goal once again. I had not realized how much I wanted this kind of purpose until it had been offered to me. I wondered, absently, if questing was habit forming. My pack again on my back, a firm grip on my stout oak staff, I found myself taking broad strides down the rut that passed for a road. I began to whistle one of the little ditties I had learned from Damsel and Dragon.

Something whistled back.

At least that was what I thought at first. But what initially had sounded like a whistle soon became a low moan, then rose in volume, transformed to a howling gale. The wind was upon me all at once, as freezing as it was sudden, as though it had appeared from the worst day of winter, rather than the late summer day around me. The gale hit with such force that I could no longer move forward, but had to struggle merely to remain standing.

Then the wind was gone, as quickly as it came, and the forest grew still once again. I thought for a second that I heard faint laughter in the far distance, but decided after a moment that the sound was more likely the aftereffects of the winter wind upon my ears.

I brushed the ice crystals from my shirt and continued on my way. I wondered if this sort of thing happened all the time in this particular forest. With such weather conditions, I could understand the lack of local habitation.

I walked on for some moments without further incident. Perhaps, I thought, I had just been the victim of some freak late-summer squall, the kind that brings hailstones to shine brightly for a moment before they melt under the summer sun. The trees, rather than blocking my view of the sky, seemed to be thinning hereabouts, and I thought I saw a clearing just ahead.

I began to whistle once again.

Once more my whistle was answered. This time the spot where I stood seemed somehow protected from the main force of the gale, but the wind whipped savagely overhead, almost bending the trees in two. I was inundated by torn leaves and small branches and, as the great oaks and maples groaned above me, I feared that the larger boughs might break off and rain down on me as well.

The second wind vanished as quickly as the first. The trees seemed to shake a final time, then resumed their still and silent vigil.

Did I hear laughter again?

It had to be my imagination.

For the first time since I had begun my journey, I considered that perhaps I should have waited for companions after all. I had gripped my stout oak staff so firmly during the second windstorm that my fist ached. But my staff seemed scant protection against a phantom wind with the full force of winter behind it. What else could I do?

It was then that I remembered the Home Study Course in my pack.

I could not restrain the slightest of smiles. So I was not defenseless after all! I had merely to look up, say, "Winds from Nowhere" in the index, and all would be explained, including, I imagined, a magical remedy or two. Perhaps they would even have a listing for "Winds from Nowhere, Caused by Whistling"!

I whipped the pack quickly from my back, almost losing my balance in my enthusiasm. I would prove more than a match for whatever force or being was creating these bizarre weather patterns. Still, I hesitated as I glanced briefly overhead. Perhaps it would be best if I moved out from beneath these trees.

Once in the clearing, a beautiful little meadow dotted with wildflowers, I again set about my task. I placed my pack on the long grass and knelt down beside it, quickly thrusting a hand inside to locate the home study tome.

I drew my hand out just as quickly. My fingers had found something else in the pack, something unexpected, something that didn't feel like a book, or a map, or an enchanted toothpick. Not only that, when I touched it, it moved.

Had whatever caused the wind placed another surprise in my pack? Visions of miniature demons equipped with two or more sets of teeth flitted through my frightened brain. Cautiously, I threw back the flap that had sealed the bag so that I might see the contents in bright daylight. I was no longer on my knees, but balanced on the balls of my feet so that I might make a quick retreat if whatever I found inside proved to be particularly nasty.

I slowly leaned forward, peering into the pack's dark recesses.

There! Something moved again, a dark body darting behind the massive Home Study Course. Did it gibber at me as it fled my grasp? I took a ragged breath. There was nothing I could do but reach in to move the book.

I did just that, cautiously, with exceeding patience, ready at any second to feel tiny, dire fangs piercing the skin of my knuckles. But the stowaway remained hidden. I swallowed. I had faced worse threats than this from the Netherhells. And should I rescue the Home Study Course, I would have a means to banish this problem as well.

It was The Moment of Truth.

I grabbed the book and whipped it from the pack. Now!

Two small brown eyes met my astonished gaze.

"Eep!" the ferret cried.

I laughed. So I had not managed to leave Vushta unaccompanied after all. My new companion was small, even for a ferret, probably not yet fully grown.

"Hello, there," I remarked to the newcomer. "Decided to come for a ride, did you?"

"Eep!" the ferret replied joyfully. I stroked its tiny head with my thumb. I realized I was smiling. For some reason, having this small furry fellow around made me feel that half of my troubles had vanished into the air.

Still, if half my troubles were gone, that meant that the other half remained to be dealt with. That's why I held the Home Study Course in my hand. It was time to look up "Winds from Nowhere" and face my problem directly.

I opened the tome to the index at the rear, flipping rapidly to the W's, eager to find an answer. The last page began "Wombats, use in potions." Too far. I would have to backtrack. I turned back a page. Here it was:

"Winds (see also breezes, gales, hurricanes, storms, tornadoes—"

I never realized the entry could be so long! I whistled softly to myself.

And my whistling was answered.

This time the gale came low. My head and arms were still warmed by sunshine, but my legs and feet were frozen where they stood. The wind roared over the meadow. Wildflowers froze and crumbled, while the grass turned from brilliant green to a dead, lifeless gray. And the wind was followed by laughter, much louder this time, and even colder than the gale that preceded it.

I glanced quickly back at the book, doing my best to ignore my frostbitten lower extremities. My eyes rapidly scanned the entries:

> Wind charms, simple and complex
> Wind chills, their cause and prevention
> Wind chimes, their use in spells—

The entries were even longer than I first imagined. My gaze darted more rapidly still, past entries on wind choirs and wind chores, and on to how to make winds churn. The entries seemed to go on forever! My palms sweated where I held the book, despite the freezing gale. What could I do?

"You won't find anything in there," whispered a voice twice as chilling as the wind.

I looked up into a face I knew, if you could call it a face. I would know those dark robes and that grinning skull anywhere. I was looking at Death.

"So pleased to see you again." Death's voice was the sound of brittle leaves blowing in the wind. "Did you like our little game?"

"G-game?" I whispered back.

Death softly whistled, and the winds howled all around. He laughed, and the air was still again, but it no longer seemed to be the air of summer. It was replaced by the winter chill which nipped at my fingers and set my teeth to chattering.

"You do remember," Death replied, "how fond I am of games?"

I did indeed. My master and I had first met Death in the cursed Valley of Vrunge, where we had been surrounded by ghosts not only dragging chains and moaning, but doing all the things they had done in life, from fighting wars to making love. All of that cursed night we spent in the valley, in fact all of life itself and death beyond, was a game. Or so said the creature Death.

"So glad you remembered." Death spoke as if he could read my mind. "It makes what I have to say next so much easier." He pointed a bony finger at my chest. "For you see, apprentice, I have wished to speak to you for ever so long." The creature laughed again, a dry chuckle like the sound of crumbling stone.

"Everyone dies," Death continued, his skull-grin somehow even wider than before. "And everyone should come to me. That is the

natural order of things, after all. But . . ." He paused, and I thought
I saw a flash of red deep within his night-black eye sockets. ". . .
there are some meddlers who like to change what is natural, who like
to create heroes who are eternal and forever beyond my grasp!" Death
paused again, smoothing his robes with bony fingers. "This, however,
I have accepted with time. Perhaps people need their eternal heroes. It
makes everyone else's deaths so much more poignant, and so much
more hopeless. But there is one other I shall never accept, one the
gods have created to mock me for all eternity!"

Death swept his arms wide toward the meadow. A few flowers and
blades of grass had survived the winds. They all perished in that instant, rotting and falling into dust as I watched.

Death turned back to gaze at me. I looked away, afraid that I might
be drawn within those dark sockets and find myself falling for all
eternity. The creature spoke again, his voice louder and tinged with
anguish.

"Why could I have not seen that time before who you truly were? It
would have been so easy to dispense with you in the Valley of Vrunge
had I but known your true identity"—Death's voice had become as
shrill as the howling wind—"THE ETERNAL APPRENTICE!"

I turned back to the apparition. What had he called me?

"The eternal apprentice," Death repeated—more, it seemed, to
himself than to me. "Forever aiding heroes in his bumbling, well-
meaning way, and forever accompanied by any number of magical
companions. As long as he is with these companions, he is beyond my
grasp. I cannot even have him when he dies, for he is immediately
reincarnated into another bumbling form!"

The apparition's bony hand grabbed my tunic. "How unfair it all is!
But one day as I was reaping souls, I had an idea. The eternal appren-
tice is always snatched from my grasp the moment he dies. But what if
I could somehow get him alone when he was still alive?"

Death's hand pulled me closer. His breath smelled of decay. I
turned my head away, trying to draw untainted air into my lungs.

But Death would not be deterred. "So I made a point to join your
little group, very discreetly, of course. Don't look so surprised! I am
always with you. After all, people die a little every day, sometimes in
body, sometimes in mind. I only needed to speed the process a bit, to
wither a little here, rot a bit there. I will admit, there was dissension
among your fellows before I came. Ah, but how a little Death can
improve the quality of that dissension."

The apparition grasped my chin with his other bony hand. He drew my face to his again.

"No one has escaped my effect."

So that was Death's game! He had worked his discontent among my fellows, as when he sent the Brownie against Snarks, ten times worse than they had been before, somehow undermining the demon's confidence in the process. In smaller ways he had set Snarks against Hendrek, the Dealer of Death against Ebenezum, even, I remembered now, Damsel against Dragon. Then there was the spread of the malady among the wizards! Was the creature before me responsible for that as well?

And what of Norei's reaction to me? I was chilled by the thought. How insidious was Death!

"And so all in Vushta became Chaos." The apparition chuckled, his spirits renewed. "What could a poor apprentice do if he wanted to save his master, but leave the chaos behind and strike out alone for the cure!"

Death threw his head back and laughed so hard that his bones rattled.

"And now, at last, I have you alone." He dragged me forward, until my chin was almost touching his chest. "At last, accursed apprentice, you are mine, for all eternity!"

I felt the pack shift on my back.

"Eep!"

Death recoiled in horror. "What is that?"

The apparition had loosed its grip on me! I staggered back, gasping the chill but untainted air. And with that breath came a rush of emotions that had been somehow suppressed. Death had mesmerized me. I had listened to his explanation as if I were in a trance, beyond fear, even beyond reason. Now, though, my tiny friend had startled him. Now I had a chance.

"I am never without companions!" I said boldly. "You are wrong, Death. I am not alone. I have brought a ferret!"

"Eep!" my companion added.

Death screamed. His voice echoed the final agonies of countless souls, a sound so horrible that it almost caused me to lose my new-found resolve.

"Will you never be alone? I had some doubts before. I feared you were perhaps a bit too bumbling for the one I seek. But now I know."

His skeletal hand shook as he pointed at me. "You are truly the Eternal Apprentice!"

"Eep!" the ferret retorted.

"But wait . . ." Death paused, instantly composed. "Who stands in the way of my goal? Only a dumb animal. And a ferret at that! After all, who can say if a ferret could even properly be called a companion?" Death's skull leered at me. "I think I shall take you after all. People are said to cheat death all the time. Who will know if Death cheats just this once?"

Death made a fist, and I felt icy fingers around my heart. I couldn't catch my breath. Was this the end? I thought, one final time, of Norei.

"Eternal Apprentice!" Death crowed. "You are mine at la—"

There was a small explosion by my feet.

"Hey, guys!" an equally small voice piped. "It's Brownie time!"

And I heard a scream so intense that Death's earlier cry seemed but a whisper.

NINE

"Even wizards must deal with unwelcome visitors. They eat your food, interrupt your spells, perhaps even criticize your conjuring. What's a poor wizard to do? A mage can, of course, use his other magic to banish these guests, or perhaps even better, turn them into some less offensive form of animal or vegetation. In fact, many beautiful tower gardens have been begun by such a happy accident.

"Unfortunately, by the very nature of his or her occupation, the average wizard will sometimes attract company that is just as magical as the mage, say a rival sorcerer or some form of enchanted creature. These unwelcome guests are somewhat more problematic. They tend to frown on being changed into a harmless herbivore, and become absolutely livid at the suggestion that they might look good as a hanging vine on the veranda. Besides this, they might have the additional audacity to actually change the spells their host wizard conjures, as well as calling up any number of other troublesome residual magicks as they settle in for what seems to be the remainder of the host wizard's lifetime.

"But even though one may not at first be able to rid oneself of such unwanted companions, the resourceful wizard should not despair. In fact, should the wizard simply be prepared to instantly change name, occupation, and country of residence, that wizard should probably have no further trouble whatsoever."

—THE ONE MINUTE MAGICIAN—A
WIZARD'S GUIDE TO BETTER
MAGIC MANAGEMENT
(fourth edition) by Ebenezum,
Greatest Wizard in the
Western Kingdoms

"Did I interrupt something?" Tap inquired.

I stared at the Brownie. Hadn't he heard Death's ear-piercing scream? And the words that followed still rung in my ears with a chilling clarity:

"I will get you yet, apprentice. The next moment you are truly alone, you are mine!"

Tap frowned up at me. "You seem distracted. If I'm in the way, just let me know. Brownies never stay where they're not wanted."

I hastily assured him that he had done no harm. I glanced around quickly, concerned lest Death have one more game to play. But the spectre seemed to have vanished. Only the ravaged hillside, devoid now of all the colorful plantlife that had graced it but a moment before, attested to the fact that he had been there at all.

The Brownie followed my gaze. "Do you like to stare moodily at piles of dirt? While it is generally not in a Brownie's cheerful nature to criticize his companions, I must say that I could think of better places to stop by the side of the road than this creepy corner.

"But enough of this gloom and doom!" The little fellow jumped happily around so that he stood between me and the barren hill. "That's one of the reasons I'm here, you know—to help you on your quest with one of those things we wee folk are best at: Good, down-to-earth Brownie advice!"

Down-to-earth Brownie advice? The joy I had felt when the Brownie first arrived seemed to be draining rapidly from me. It didn't help that Tap had begun to hop about again, giggling merrily as he bounced. Perhaps, I thought, there might be some way to reason with the small fellow, if only he would stand still long enough.

"Um . . ." I began. I waved my hands at him, hoping the gesture would quiet him down.

"And a happy Brownie hello to you, too!" Tap waved back. His moving hands seemed to make his jumps even higher. "That's more like it! I knew a little hopping about would cheer you up immediately. That's Brownie Power!" After a few more ecstatic leaps, the little fellow paused to add: "I am here, of course, for other reasons as well."

There was a distant crash in the forest. I turned, full of trepidation. Was Death coming back? I put a finger to my lips in an attempt to caution the Brownie to silence.

"And what are those other reasons?" Tap continued as if he hadn't heard anything but the sound of his own voice. "First, of course, is the might of Brownie know-how! We little folks have hundreds of years of shoemaking experience. And let me tell you, that really counts for something in the know-how department!"

There was another crash in the forest, both louder and, I imagined, closer. I failed at that immediate moment to comprehend exactly what connection shoemaking had to our present situation. I cleared my throat in an attempt to interrupt the small fellow.

"Nasty cough you have there," Tap remarked. "But speaking of counting for something, Brownies do count, you know. We may be small, but we think big! That's another thing you have in your favor—the joy of Brownie enthusiasm!"

The smashing and crashing was definitely closer now, and accompanied by guttural screams. Another thought chilled me to the bone: Maybe it wasn't Death at all. Maybe it was demons, come to stop me from getting help for Vushta!

"But basic-Brownie protection doesn't stop there," Tap continued merrily. "For at its center is the greatest gift of all, the thrill of Brownie magic; a wizardry that shines like bright leather, full of spells laced with the best intentions!"

The commotion in the forest was becoming louder still. Besides the crashing, I could now hear the sounds of rending and tearing, as if some force was demolishing the very trees and bushes that made up the woods. The guttural screams continued as well, although now I could also hear the somewhat lesser cries of terrified forest creatures as they rapidly fled the scene. And the noise was close enough now so that I could clearly tell where it came from—directly in front of me, behind the barren hill.

"And then, of course, there is one more reason for believing in Brownie Power . . ." Tap continued, but paused when he saw the look of extreme consternation upon my countenance. The rending and screaming continued unabated, loud enough so that the Brownie had to shout in order to be heard.

"Um," I said, glancing above the Brownie to the far side of the hill. "Don't you think we should do something?"

"Well, if you think it's time." Tap did a small dance, limbering himself up for the magic to come. "But why so upset? Is it that little noise in the woods? Brownies are ready for everything! You never have to worry when there's Brownie Power around!" The little fellow sighed. "We'll pause then, and deal with the commotion. I guess I'll just have to wait to tell you about how I'm supposed to transmit messages between you and Ebenezum."

"What?" I shouted at the small fellow. Then the wizard had sent the Brownie! Perhaps I was glad to see Tap after all.

"Well, tell me—" I began.

My question was interrupted by the loudest shriek I had heard so far.

"Oops," the Brownie remarked as he stared at the top of the hill. "Then again, maybe Brownies aren't ready for *absolutely* everything."

I followed the Brownie's gaze to the summit of the barren rise before us. There stood two demonic figures. Much worse, they were demons I had met before.

"There they are!" The creature on the left pointed and waved. He was wearing a checkered suit. "I told you our magical weapons wouldn't let us down!"

Brax the salesdemon turned to his companion. The other demon grunted, a guttural sound not unlike the screams we had heard but moments before.

It was this second fiend whose appearance caused my blood to freeze, whose immense size, immense claws, and immense teeth, led one's gaze away even from the other creature's extremely loud attire.

The second demon was Guxx Unfufadoo. Guxx, the fiend who had given my master Ebenezum his sneezing malady, and who had, until recently, been involved in a plot for the Netherhells to subjugate the surface world to his demonic administration! He had almost won, too, for the demon had only been stopped when I managed to capture a strand of his nosehair and return it to Ebenezum and his fellow wizards for them to effect a counterspell.

So, if you looked at the course of events in a certain way, I was the only reason Guxx was not now ruler of both the world above and below. I was the only reason he had not retained the exalted title of Grand Hoohah (whatever that was; I had been told not to ask) and was instead wandering upon the surface world with but a single companion instead of his usual retinue. I was the only reason that he did not have fantastic amounts of gold and jewels at his disposal as well as all of humanity as his slaves, but instead seemed to be a penniless outcast far from home.

I took a moment to swallow, although my throat was far too dry, and wondered if Guxx Unfufadoo might be the slightest bit annoyed. I wondered if the demon had indeed sought me out for a purpose, perhaps as a practice ground for his amazingly sharp claws and incredibly sharp teeth, so that they might not fall into disuse. Or perhaps Brax, who made his demonic living selling slightly used enchanted weapons, had come along with the express purpose of providing Guxx with the nastiest of his wares for my disposal.

Both demons smiled at us and waved. They began to descend the hill.

Whatever the two had in store, I had no doubt it would be fiendishly hideous. Not to mention very, very bloody.

I drew myself up to my full height, my stout oak staff firmly in my hands. It was not much protection against rending claws and teeth, but it was the best I had, and I would use it to my fullest. I had often feared the worst in my encounters with the Netherhells. Now that the worst was here, I was ready for it.

"Yes!" Brax called down to us. "You are the very creatures we were seeking. No, no, don't run away! Demons are very fast, it would be completely useless. In fact, we want to be your friends!"

Friends? I lowered my staff to stare at the two demons. Maybe there was something worse than the worst.

Guxx grumbled darkly as they approached. His voice sounded like gravel being ground to dust. He flexed his claws and gnashed his teeth. I could see the dark glow of the fires of the Netherhells in his eyes. I attempted to swallow again, and wondered exactly what kind of friendship they were looking for.

The two demons paused as they reached the bottom of the hill a scant few feet away. They were so close that I could smell the brimstone on Guxx Unfufadoo's breath.

"Now!" Guxx intoned.

Brax quickly reached into a large, leather bag he carried and drew out a tiny drum. He began to beat upon it with a regular rhythm. With that, Guxx stepped forward and began to intone:

> "Guxx Unfufadoo, noble demon,
> Wrongly shunned by Netherhells traitors,
> Forced to walk the surface pathways
> Until he can regain his kingdom!"

The large blue demon nodded at his smaller companion.

"That is why we are here," Brax added. "Banished from the Netherhells because of Guxx's failure."

The larger demon's claws snaked out to snag the fabric of Brax's suit.

"Again!" Guxx ordered.

Brax hastily returned to beating on the drum. The larger demon began anew:

> "Guxx Unfufadoo, never failing,
> Greatest of demonic heroes,
> Those that scoff at his great prowess,
> Will find they will soon be eaten!"

Brax paused in his drum beating to add. "Well, failure wasn't the exact word I meant. The real word I meant to use was, um—"

"Continue!" Guxx commanded. Brax went back to his drum.

> "Guxx Unfufadoo, hungry demon
> Has a plan for those who mock him,
> Has these claws, so good for rending,
> And these teeth so good for chewing."

"I meant setback!" Brax hurriedly amended. "That was it. Not failure! No, no. Never failure! Nothing but a setback!"

This time Guxx's clawed hand lifted Brax completely from the ground.

"Again!"

Still aloft, Brax beat on the drum as Guxx intoned:

> "Guxx Unfufadoo denies setbacks,
> He will destroy those that bring them.
> Guxx the mighty he will beat them,
> Tear off all their limbs and eat the—"

A look of horror spread across the large demon's countenance. He tried to stop himself, but it was already too late. He began to sneeze.

He dropped Brax in the process. The smaller demon sighed and readjusted the jacket of his checkered suit. "You now know of Guxx's fate. At the end of the battle he caught your master's malady. Once, his fearsome rhymes gave him ever greater power. Now, whenever he rhymes, even if it should be by accident, he sneezes."

"Buckles and laces!" exclaimed the Brownie, whom in the excitement I had almost forgotten. "So his magic has been turned against him!"

" 'Tis true," Brax concurred. "This misfortune has forced Guxx Unfufadoo into talking nothing but blank verse."

So that was what you called what the large demon had been spouting. I agreed that it certainly was a tragedy. Guxx sneezed again, a truly horrible sound from such a demonic nose.

"Well," Brax said, "at least now he'll stay quiet for a while." He took a further moment to straighten his checkered creases. With Guxx temporarily indisposed, he seemed much more his old salesdemon self.

"I suppose you want an explanation," Brax ventured with a laugh. "I understand that humans are like that."

"Brownies are like that, too," Tap added from where he now stood by my side.

"I'm sure you are!" Brax replied jovially, quick to include another potential customer. "I suppose it is only fair. And while I explain, you'll have the opportunity to learn about some prime, previously-owned weapons that I luckily thought to bring along. And all I need is your signature in blood. Only a formality, really. You'll heal in no time, and a magic weapon will be yours! Just think: no money down, a lifetime to pay!"

So Brax had weapons? Well, we could certainly use them, what with the unknown Eastern Kingdoms before us and a committee of demons likely to show up at any moment to vote on the best manner for our demise. And then there was Death, who wanted me for his very own. But what weapon could one possibly use against the creature that embodied the end of life itself?

"No rush," Brax added cheerfully. "Guxx Unfufadoo and I plan to be with you for quite a while, and you may purchase a weapon at any time during that period! You see, that's why we came here—to be your companions on your forthcoming quest!"

"Buckles and laces!" the Brownie exclaimed.

I was somewhat taken aback by this information as well. Until his defeat, Guxx Unfufadoo had been our direst enemy, ready to destroy us by any means possible. Our first encounter with the fiend had caused my master's malady, and further altercations had led to no end of bloodshed and destruction of property. Now this foul creature, risen from nocturnal slime pits hidden deep beneath the earth, wanted to be my ally?

"Um . . ." I ventured.

I remembered then what Death had said about companions. If I was who the spectre said I was, I always had to have them. Maybe Guxx and Brax couldn't help themselves. Because of my nature, they had to become my companions. They had no other choice. I marveled at my newfound power. To attract such otherworldly creatures as these, I must be irresistible.

"It is no wonder that you are at a loss for words," Brax added quickly. "What a surprise to be joined in your quest by the greatest of all demons. And what an honor!" He shook the bag by his side. "Now, admit it! How much better you would feel with a new weapon the equal of your newfound companions!"

It was true. A formidable weapon might make me feel better. Especially a weapon that would protect me against demonic teeth and claws.

"Interested, hey?" The salesdemon tugged at my sleeve. "Well, wait just a second while I fetch a contract. . . ."

Tap the Brownie tugged at my other sleeve. "Think carefully about this. What need have you of weapons from the Netherhells when you have Brownie magic!"

I remembered Brownie magic from some of our prior battles. The weapons began to sound better all the time. But Tap's interruption reminded me that the Brownie had said he was in contact with my master. Perhaps it would be prudent to contact and speak with Ebenezum before I entered into any sort of a bargain with demons.

"I've got the contract right here." Brax had reached into his bag and pulled forth a sheaf of parchment almost as large as my Home Study Course. "Yes, it does look a little imposing, doesn't it? Just a lot of Netherhells legalisms, I assure you. Nothing to worry about at all, at least not in this lifetime. And you only have to sign it once, for a weapon that might even protect you against whatever you're looking for on this quest!" The demon smiled as he flipped to contract's end.

"Um . . ." I replied. This was all going too fast for me. There seemed to be no time to contact my master, even if I knew how to use the Brownie to do so. Still smiling, Brax waved a sharp-edged pen in the direction of my index finger. What should I do?

There was a great sneeze, and the contract went flying from Brax's hands. Guxx Unfufadoo had regained his feet.

"But—" Brax cried, but his protestations died with a single glance from the larger demon.

"Begin!" Guxx Unfufadoo demanded.

Brax shuffled through the bag quickly to find his drum. As soon as it was in his hands, Guxx chanted:

> "Guxx Unfufadoo, great companion,
> Joins the noble surface heroes,
> He will make their quest successful
> For the glory of demonkind!"

Brax shrugged his checked shoulders. "I guess we'll have to talk about the weapons later." He glanced up at the larger demon, who glared back at him.

"Oh, that's right!" Brax said nervously. He drew a piece of parchment from his sack and read it without inflection: "Excuse me, but since we are going to be your companions on this venture, I hope it isn't too impudent to ask exactly where we are going?"

"Why," Tap chirped, "to the Eastern Kingdoms, of course!"

"The Eastern Kingdoms?" Brax hesitated, the parchment falling from between his fingers, and turned pale (in actuality, he turned a much lighter shade of green). "Isn't that where they take heroes and bake them into loaves of bread?"

I assured the demon that I had discussed the matter with my master, and Ebenezum had said the tales were greatly exaggerated.

"Exaggerated?" Brax retorted. "What does that mean? That they only bake heroes into rolls and muffins? I had no idea that when you set out on a quest you were going to—"

Guxx raised one of his clawed hands above his head, instantly silencing his lackey.

"Again!" Guxx stated. Brax picked up the drum and began to beat.

> "Guxx Unfufadoo, fearless demon,
> Accompanies them to the East.
> Enemies shall know no quarter!
> He shall rend them, man or beas—"

The large demon started to sneeze before he had finished the last syllable, falling instantly to the ground.

"Alas." Brax shook his head sadly. "The big fellow has rhyming in his blood. Now where did that contract go?"

"Hold!" I demanded. I had had enough for the moment of epic verse and Netherhells contracts. Of course, the fact that Guxx Unfufadoo was temporarily indisposed didn't hurt, either. I would get some answers!

I asked why the two demons were really here.

"Well . . ." Brax looked over his shoulder at the indisposed Guxx. "He can't hear a thing while he's sneezing. Very well. We are genuinely here to help you on your quest, for that is the best way for Guxx to gain revenge on those who banished him."

Really? The demon's honesty took me by surprise.

"Um . . ." I began. But no, if I were to be master of this situation, I would have to think clearly. How would my master handle a situation like this?

"Indeed," I began again. "And then, I imagine, Guxx will eat me."

"Oh, on the contrary," Brax replied, somewhat taken aback. "I don't think Guxx plans to eat you at all. That is," he amended, "at least not in the near future."

"Indeed?" I asked. "But isn't he mad at me?"

"He's probably furious, but that's beside the point. It's all a matter of priorities, you see. First he must destroy his opposition in the Netherhells, then return there to reestablish his rule." Brax smiled his best salesdemon's grin. "You will be happy to know that then and only then will he come back and eat you."

Somehow, I did not find this particularly reassuring.

"So we will come with you on your quest," Brax continued. "Or you can refuse our help, and Guxx could simply eat you now. That's one thing about having a demon of his magnitude as an ally. You always know exactly where he stands!"

I also knew exactly what he ate. It didn't help.

Brax frowned. "Now where is that contract?" He peered around in the gathering gloom. Our encounter with the demons had taken the final hour of daylight, and night was rapidly coming upon us.

"Indeed," I said a final time. "So you think it is convenient to join me in order to serve your own ends?"

"Yes, more or less," Brax reiterated, somewhat distracted. "That, and the rumor that you're the Eternal Apprentice." He glanced back in my direction. "You, I know it's silly—well, let's face it, it's ridiculous—actually, it's more ludicrous than anything. Anyway, Guxx is not one to discount rumors. Any rumor!" Brax smiled at me and shook his head. "You?" He snickered softly.

The salesdemon turned to regard the barren hill, now a black shape against the starlit sky.

"How am I supposed to find my contract in the dark?"

I wished him luck, and told him that I would be retiring for the night. I walked away, motioning Tap to follow. The Brownie and I would need to have a discussion.

And there was one more thing I had to do before I went to sleep: consult my Home Study Course. There might be nothing in there to prevent one's meeting Death, but there surely must be a spell or two for exorcising demons.

TEN

"One should never attempt a spell without sufficient practice. Then again, one should never get eaten by demons, either, or have to go without a date on Saturday night."

—SOME THOUGHTS ON APPRENTICESHIP
by Wuntvor, apprentice to Ebenezum,
greatest mage in the Western Kingdoms
(a work in progress)

"We have to talk." I whispered urgently to the Brownie. "How do we get in touch with my master?"

"Have no fear!" Tap reassured me heartily. " 'Tis as easy as making shoes."

"Say!" Brax called cheerfully across the field. "I think I've finally found the contrac—" The salesdemon's voice was abruptly cut off as he found a set of long, nasty-looking purple claws resting on his shoulder. The claws belonged to Guxx, who seemed to have stopped sneezing for the time being.

"Begin!" Guxx bellowed in the other demon's ear. Brax hastily dropped the contract and picked up his drum.

Guxx took a deep breath and recited:

> "Mighty Guxx, the best of demons
> Has no fear of this Duck's ovens!
> We shall join you, boldly, bravely;
> All will flee in fear before us!"

The demon raked his claws through the air for emphasis.

"Indeed," I replied when I realized that the former Grand Hoohah was waiting for a reaction. "Nice to have you along. Now if you'll excuse me—"

"Continue!" Guxx roared. Brax beat his drum.

> "Mighty Guxx says we should hurry!
> There are many who would stop us;
> Traitor demons, down below here,
> Who want this world for their foul reason!"

"Indeed," I answered again. "Um . . . indeed."

Apparently it was going to be more difficult to quiet Guxx down than I had first imagined. Still, there must be some way I could get a moment free to talk to the Brownie. I decided to try another strategy.

"Good advice, I am sure," I called to Guxx as I continued to walk away. "And we will hurry, I assure you, as soon as we get a good night's sleep." I paused to yawn and stretch. "Now, if you'll excuse—"

"Persevere!" Guxx screamed. Brax continued to beat.

> "Guxx Unfufadoo, never tiring,
> Guides our heroes into battle!
> Who needs sleeping? Who needs eating?
> When this great demon leads us onwards!"

I cleared my throat. "Indeed," I murmured. Guxx seemed to be a demon used to getting his own way. What could I do?

Tap looked up at me with some consternation. "Is it time for Brownie Power?"

I glanced at the little fellow. What did I have to lose?

"Indeed," I asked. "What kind of Brownie Power did you have in mind?"

"It's a challenge, all right," Tap agreed, glancing at the heavily clawed and muscled Guxx. "But Brownies are always ready for a challenge. How do you think we came up with high-buttoned shoes?"

"What if—" The Brownie shook his head. "No. The demon would slice through any shoe I could conjure. Even a really big shoe." He paused a moment in thought. "How about . . ." The little fellow's frown deepened. "No, that thing wouldn't even notice a rain of buckles and laces."

"Does all your magic have to center on shoes?" I asked with a hint of hysteria.

"I beg your pardon!" Tap replied, a hurt edge in his voice. "Brownie magic may be specialized, but what we do, we do with style."

I quickly apologized, explaining that there was a certain set of sharp, purple claws too much on my mind. The Brownie said he quite understood.

"I know!" Tap clicked his heels together and began to dance. "You have given me the answer, apprentice. Style is the key. Brownie style! All our problems are solved. I will show them the wisdom of the Brownie Way!"

"In—deed," I replied slowly. Brownie style? Still, after my initial shock, I realized the little fellow's idea had a certain merit. After all, I knew from my own encounters with the wee folks' ideas that getting a lecture on Brownie philosophy would probably slow the demons down far longer than any physical force we could possibly imagine.

I told Tap to go ahead. He skipped merrily over to the demons whilst whistling a happy tune.

Now was the time for me to get to work. While the others were occupied, I would at last have a minute to look through the Home Study Course. My first priority was to find a spell to banish demons. Once I had accomplished that, I could contact Ebenezum and get on with my quest.

I hunched down, careful that my back was facing the others, and rummaged quickly through my pack. After taking a brief moment to pet my ferret, I pulled forth the Course and turned rapidly to the index, anxious that I should find the spell before the rapidly fading daylight vanished entirely.

I found "demons" in the index almost immediately. It wasn't at all difficult; the entries went on for pages. I quickly looked down the left-hand column.

Demons, summoning for special occasions, page 612
Demons, summoning on short notice, page 623
Demons, summoning multiples thereof: odd numbers,
    pages 634–6; even numbers, pages 637–9
Demons, summoning specific colors, page 944

I turned back a page, searching the "Demon, B"s for "banishment." My gaze jumped at random among the entries:

This was taking forever. I flipped the page again, and there it was, at
the top of the right-hand column.

I stopped reading, and rapidly turned to page 487. There was the
heading, in bold letters:

BANISHMENT
THE ALL-PURPOSE REMEDY

"This spell," the book went on, "is particularly effective in dealing
with demons, and so simple and direct that even beginning wizards
can accomplish it with ease."

I couldn't help but grin. Effective? Simple? Direct? This was the
very thing I had been looking for.

"Shoes?" I heard Guxx bellow behind me.

"Yes!" Tap yelled back with almost equal force. "Shoes are the
answer; the only answer! Let me explain . . ."

The Brownie's voice thankfully lowered to a more conversational
level which I could no longer understand. I returned to the Home
Study Course and the spell that I would accomplish with ease.

Spell Variation No. 1: Banishing Demons.
Just follow the few simple directions below, and any demon in your
vicinity will instantaneously be banished from the surface of the
world.

Oddly enough, the next paragraph was printed in bright red:

WARNING: FOLLOW THESE DIRECTIONS EXACTLY. SUBSTITUTIONS
CAN LEAD TO DISASTER!

Why did they print a warning if the spell was so easy? Perhaps it was explained in the introductory portions of the book, somewhere in the four hundred eighty-six pages preceding this one. Maybe I should try to read a little bit more.

"More shoes?" Guxx screamed from halfway across the field. I turned to listen. "Brax!"

Brax pounded on his drum as Guxx intoned emphatically:

> "Guxx Unfufadoo, peerless demon
> Has heard enough of Brownie prattle,
> Has waited long enough for humans,
> And will lead us into batt—"

Great clouds of dust rose about him as Guxx succumbed to a sneezing fit.

Brax sighed. "It's a shame when a natural rhyming talent like that has to go to waste." He paused a moment to straighten the lapels on his checkered suit. "Now, if you'll permit me to change the subject—"

Tap tried to continue his lecture, but Brax was too fast for him.

"No, no, my good Brownie!" Before the Brownie could protest, the demon quickly retrieved the sheaf of parchment from where it had fallen in the grass. "I'm sure 'Stitching techniques for proper heel placement' is a fascinating subject. But we do have this contract here, and we all know from experience that Guxx will only sneeze for so long."

I looked back at the salesdemon, waving his contract above the faltering Brownie. It appeared, at least this time, that Brownie Power had failed.

"Wait!" Tap interjected hastily. "It's, uh—time for a demonstration!" He jumped into a speedy dance.

The demon's feet were suddenly covered by shiny brown shoes.

"Not bad," Brax murmured, temporarily distracted from his salesmanship. "Do they do anything?"

"Do they *do* anything?" Tap replied with the slightest of hurt tones. "These are shoes!"

Brax stared at his newly covered feet. He did not seem that impressed. "So?"

"Don't you know about the joy of shoes?" Tap asked in astonishment. "They are an art form, and one of the great inventions of the modern world!"

"Really?" Brax nodded solemnly. "But they don't do anything?"

"Of course they do things!" Tap seemed to be getting a tad over-excited. He paused to catch his breath. "I mean, they keep cold air away from your feet, for one thing. And you know those little sharp rocks that hurt the soft undersides of your feet? Well, now that you have these . . ."

I turned back to my book. It didn't look like Tap could keep Brax distracted much longer, and Guxx was likely to stop sneezing at any moment. I had to banish this pair before they interfered any further with my quest. Warning or no warning, this spell would have to do. I had no time to worry.

I quickly read the spell.

Make sure you have sufficient quantities of all the following before you begin:

½ batwing, crumbled

One left eye of newt

¼ cup dried duckwort blossom

One medium toad gizzard

One pinch salt (to taste)

Mix the above ingredients in a large cauldron . . .

I stopped reading. Cauldron? Toad gizzard? Left eye of newt? Follow these directions exactly?

How could I? I didn't have any of those things!

"And look at those laces!" Tap continued quickly, his voice rising again. "Why, the practice you can get tying knots . . ."

The demon casually kicked the shiny brown shoes off his feet, sending them sailing high above the cloud of dust that encased the sneezing Guxx.

Tap was horrified.

"I'm through fooling around," Brax said with a smile. "Let's talk contracts. I already know about shoes. In fact, I have a pair just for you. A pair that does more than keep your feet warm. That's right, Brownie, I'm talking about a pair of—magic shoes."

"But you threw away—I mean, those were perfectly good . . ." Tap's voice faltered. "M-magic shoes?"

"Absolutely correct." Brax patted the little fellow's pointed cap. "I could tell from the first time I met you that you were the kind of

Brownie who likes to step ahead of the pack. And how better to do that stepping than in a stunning set of enchanted footwear?"

Tap, eyes and mouth both opened wide, took a step toward the demon. "En-enchanted footwear?"

Oh, no! Brax had found the Brownie's weakness. Soon Tap would be laboring under a Netherhells contract probably even worse than the one that doomed Hendrek.

I had to banish the demons now! The general spell I had found would do me no good. But the index had been full of others.

I looked up "Demons, banishing on short notice":

There will often be times when demons will not have the courtesy of allowing you the time to perform one of the more intricate and civilized banishment spells found elsewhere in this tome. At this point, you have two options: to run, screaming, from the demons until you find some spot where you might perform those civilized spells, or use the short, dirty little magick that follows.

PLEASE NOTE: BE SURE TO FOLLOW THE DIAGRAMS EXACTLY!

The warning at the end was, again, printed in red. Still, there didn't seem to be any arcane ingredients necessary to the spell that followed, only a series of hand and foot gestures. I should be able to handle this one easily.

"What—what kind of enchanted footwear?" Tap asked dreamily.

"Only the very best, I assure you," Brax replied heartily, "with firm leather soles and bright blue tassels!"

"Blue tassels?" Tap responded, a beatific smile spreading across his face. "Bright blue tassels."

There was no time to waste. I began to follow the instructions in the Home Study Course—exactly.

"First," I said aloud, "perform the rite of the Mystic Rooster, to notify the spirits that you command their attention."

I placed my right hand above my head as the book indicated and crowed.

"What's that?" Tap yelped, his trance temporarily broken.

"Only the young human, clearing his throat," Brax assured the Brownie. "That's not important now. We were talking shoes."

Tap nodded. "Shoes."

I crowed again, but neither Brownie nor demon took further notice.

"They'll make you a Brownie among Brownies, and all you have to do is sign on this dotted line." Brax riffled the contract before him. "Don't worry about all the fine print. Merely Netherhells' legalities, of interest only to the demons who enforce these things. One small signature and the shoes are yours."

"Small?" Tap blinked. "Are you saying that Brownies are small?"

"Why not at all!" Brax assured him. "Once you have these shoes, you'll be a big man in the Brownie set. Here, let me show them to you."

The demon opened his sack and looked inside.

"I think they're right over here, below these magic false teeth and this magic imitation housefly." He rummaged deeper still. "Oh, yes! And this magic antelope's horn. Unfortunately, it only works on other antelopes. Ah, I think I see them towards the bottom."

It was time to proceed with my spell. I quickly read the second set of directions: "Next, perform the Rite of the Mystic Sparrow, to instruct the spirits to fly to your aid."

I spread my arms to my sides, as instructed, and waved them up and down, while at the same time bending my knees and emitting a high, chirping sound from between my teeth.

"No, I'm sorry," Tap said, looking back at me. "That doesn't sound at all like clearing a throat."

"But who knows what he got in there?" Brax murmured. "Besides, we have a contract to sign."

I chirped again. I didn't see any sign of spirits. Was this thing working?

"Might be the hiccups," Tap ventured.

"Yes, it might!" Brax replied with the slightest bit of irritation. "But what does that matter when we're talking about *magic shoes?*"

I chirped again for good measure, hoping the spirits could hear me.

"Whooping cough?" Tap mused. He glanced back into the demon's gaze, and the questioning look dulled in his eyes. Brax stared at the Brownie. The smile reappeared on Tap's tiny face.

"Yes," he whispered happily. "Magic shoes."

"That's a bit more like it," Brax replied merrily. "Once we get the contract signed, we can ask the young human what he's doing. Maybe it's a hobby of some sort." Brax went back to searching in his bag.

Perhaps it was time to go on to the third part of the spell, I decided. The demon dropped his sack as purple claws surrounded his neck. "Begin!"

Even in Guxx's stranglehold, Brax managed to pick up his drum.
The blue and purple demon chanted:

"Guxx Unfufadoo, Mystic Demon,
Knows when he sees magic brewing,
Sees when humans give him trouble,
Says that wizards soon get eaten!"

The Brownie shook his head as if to clear it.

"Him?" Tap pointed at me. "A wizard? If he was a wizard, why
would he need Brownie magic?"

Guxx glowered at me, flexing his claws.

"Yeah," Brax added. "The little fellow's right. I mean, what kind of
magic can you make by clearing your throat? It's easier to believe this
guy's the Eternal Apprentice than"—he snorted—"a wizard!"

Both Brax and the Brownie had a good laugh.

Guxx still glowered, but the other's arguments seemed to have kept
him, at least for the moment, from attacking and eating me.

If I was going to banish them, there would never be a better time.
There was nothing to do but finish the spell.

I glanced quickly to my Home Study Course: "Now it is time for
the Mystic Warthog, to instruct the spirits to banish the demons from
the surface world."

I quickly curved my hands to either side of my nose, like tusks, and
began to snort, stamping my feet in the described rhythm.

"Magic!" Guxx screamed, and leapt for me, claws extended.

Somehow, I managed to stand my ground and finish the spell, although the sight of an onrushing demon somewhat unnerved me.

And then I thought: I had stomped my foot seven times. Hadn't I?
Guxx was still rushing forward to rend and tear. I had lost count.

I stomped once more to be sure.

And Guxx froze in mid-stride.

The spell was working! Brax seemed frozen as well, drum in one
hand, contract in the other. The spirits must be at hand. I snorted a
couple more times for good measure. Soon the banishment would
begin.

The ground began to shake. What was going on? The Home Study
Course had said nothing about this.

The quake beneath my feet intensified. It took me a moment to
realize that I hadn't banished anyone.

Instead, I had summoned the Netherhells!

ELEVEN

"The professional magician must always be ready for the unexpected, for who knows what magic might bring? Thus, one should always be prepared when performing sorcery, and have on hand a full knowledge of all the latest banishment spells, a good half-dozen well planned escape routes, and perhaps most important, a constant supply of clean linen in the guest room."

—THE TEACHINGS OF EBENEZUM, Volume IX

Oh, no. What had I done?

The shaking earth before me tore asunder, and from that rift in the ground rose a great oaken table, complete with five demons. This was far worse than I had thought. I had somehow summoned the entire dread legion of the Netherhells' Conquest by Committee!

"Point of order!" the small, somewhat sickly looking demon at the end cried.

The much larger demon at table's center pounded its gavel. "Yes, yes. What is it this time?"

"Beg pardon," the small, sickly demon remarked in a voice so brash that no one, anywhere, at any time, would ever pardon anything it said. "Look around us. We don't appear to be where we should be. I really thought someone should mention that."

"What do you mean?" the gavel demon demanded. "We followed the most recent burst of wizardly energy, and here we are."

The gavel demon was so busy glaring down at its shorter committee member that it had not bothered to study the surroundings. This, I thought, might be my chance. If the demonic committee was going to pause for a discussion, maybe there was time for a counterattack after all!

"Beg pardon," the small sickly demon continued, "but there don't appear to be any wizards." The demon smiled, totally self-satisfied. "I thought someone should mention that, too."

The gavel demon looked about in astonishment. "By the Netherhells! For once our small, sickly member is correct. There don't appear to be any wizards! Is this not then Vushta after all?" The demon paused to look about suspiciously. "Careful now! This could be some sort of surface world trick."

Oh, would that I did have a trick! Maybe, I thought, if I looked quickly, I might find something in my Home Study Course. But what?

"Point of order!" the small, sickly demon screamed.

The gavel demon looked at the other fiend with half-closed eyes. "You've already had your point of—"

Small and sickly shook its head emphatically. "This is an entirely different one." It pointed its diminutive and pale hand across the field. "Isn't that the former Grand Hoohah standing yonder?"

They had spotted Guxx! I would have to act quickly. I opened the Course to the index. But what to look under? Mayhaps "Demons, immobilized by magic"? I flipped to the back of the book.

"Oh, my," the gavel demon murmured, nodding at the silent Guxx. It coughed politely, a truly unpleasant sound. "Excuse us, your immenseship." The gavel demon tried to smile. "Didn't mean to bother you. Just passing through, don't you know."

Guxx, frozen immobile by magic, did not reply. I scanned the pages quickly, searching for "Demons, immobilized . . ."

"Your magnificenceship?" the gavel demon ventured. "Surely you understand."

Guxx stood there like a statue. The gavel demon began to sweat. I looked down at my book again. I spied an entry for "Demons, immersed in syrup." I was getting close.

"Your superiorship?" The fiend fell to its knees. "Please give us a chance to explain!"

I quickly scanned the next entry. "Demons, immodesty at parties." But "immodest" came after "immobile"! That meant the entry I was looking for did not exist!

I stared blankly at the book. The answer had to be in there somewhere. Didn't it?

"Point of order!" the small demon yelled. "The Grand Hoohah hasn't moved—"

"So what if the Grand Hoohah hasn't moved?" the gavel demon screamed hysterically. "If the Grand Hoohah doesn't want to—"

"Beg pardon," the small fiend continued. "I believe he hasn't moved because he cannot move. See how the birds flutter about him, as if he were a tree or standing stone. He appears to be frozen, perhaps by some diabolical surface spell."

"What are you . . ." The gavel demon paused to peer at the immobile Guxx. At that very instant a sparrow alighted on the former Grand Hoohah's nose.

"Frozen?" the gavel demon whispered.

Frozen! I thought. Of course! I quickly thumbed through the index to F.

"I just thought someone should mention that," the sickly demon added with a grin.

"Frozen. You don't say. Frozen." The gavel demon wiped its brow and pounded its gavel. "Who cares about the old Grand Hoohah anyway? It is time for the committee to rule!"

Here it was! "Frozen demon, on a stick, page 212." On a stick? Somehow, that didn't sound right. Still, it was my only hope.

The large demon pounded the gavel again. "All in favor of attack?"

Four of the five demons raised their sharp and ugly claws. I would have to hurry before my blood was boiled!

"Very well," the gavel demon rapped. "Majority—"

"Point of order!" the small, sickly, dissenting demon shrieked.

It appeared that I might still have a moment. I quickly turned to page 212.

"I am sorry," the gavel demon said in a very loud voice that didn't sound sorry at all, "but the vote does not have to be unanimous in a case like this."

The sickly demon pulled a huge tome from beneath the table. "But it says right here in the Netherhells bylaws . . ."

I had a tome of my own to look through. I found page 212 and quickly read through the text. Here it was!

"FROZEN DEMON ON A STICK: For the wizard that enjoys entertaining, here's the perfect end to a delightful meal—"

I stopped reading. This wouldn't do at all.

"But there aren't any wizards!" the gavel demon screamed. "You said so yourself! Surely the rules are different when there aren't any wizards!"

"Point of—" the other demon began.

"Oh, no, you don't!" the gavel fiend exclaimed. "The rest of us are going to attack without you!"

So this was it. There'd be no more time for the Home Study Course. I dropped my book and picked up my stout oak staff. I knew it wasn't much protection against the might of the committee, but it was all I had. I hoped that with the help of the Brownie, who now stood on one side of me, and my ferret, who had emerged from the pack to stand on the other side, that we, together, might make an accounting.

"Come, fellow demons," the gavel demon extolled. "It is time to boil blood!"

"Oh, no, it isn't!" another voice boomed, high above me.

Who could it be? Demonic reinforcements, wishing to boil our blood even more efficiently than before? With some trepidation, I looked aloft.

"Look out!" cried the voice, both loud and deep. "Make way! Clear a path! Watch your heads!"

The voice belonged to Hubert the dragon, who carried the damsel Alea upon his back. The two of them appeared to be landing in our midst.

The demons scattered. Three of them took their table with them.

"Thank you," Hubert said, once he had settled his huge dragon bulk on the ground. "We always do like to make an entrance."

"Point of order!" the sickly demon interjected.

The gavel demon ignored the other's cries, turning instead to the newcomers, its gavel raised above its head like a weapon. "How dare you tell the Committee of Conquest it isn't time to boil blood!"

"Simplicity itself," Hubert replied. "No matter what the occasion, without Damsel and Dragon it simply doesn't happen!"

"Doesn't . . . happen?" If the gavel demon had seemed upset before, now it was absolutely livid, the once rich blue of its scales turned a shiny purple. I had to admit that even I was taken aback by Hubert's remarks, perhaps because I had never thought of boiling blood as an "occasion." Still, the arrival of Damsel and Dragon had, at the least, temporarily stopped the demonic attack. Perhaps I should give the Home Study Course another try.

"I'll show you what doesn't happen!" the gavel demon shrieked after it had managed to control its breathing.

"Of course. Certainly," Hubert replied affably. "But first allow us to introduce ourselves. Damsel, if you would get me my hat?"

Alea reached into the satchel strapped to Hubert's back and extracted a cylindrical purple hat with a snappy brim. She placed it firmly on Hubert's head.

"But—" the gavel demon began.

"No buts about it," Hubert replied. "We have to get to know each other. And what better way to get acquainted than with a little song and dance?"

"What?" the gavel demon bellowed. "Don't—"

Damsel hopped down off the dragon's back and Hubert began to sing:

> "The trouble with demons, as everybody knows,
> Is when you stomp them, they squish between your toes."

"Between your toes!" Damsel chorused.
Hubert continued:

> "The trouble with demons, as everybody sees,
> Is when you kick them, they splatter on your knees."

"Right on your knees!" Damsel echoed.

The demons stared at them, open-mouthed, their yellowed teeth glinting in the sun. I would never have thought to neutralize a Netherhells attack with song and dance, especially a song and dance about squishing demons. Still, Hubert had told me many times: "There is no such thing as a hostile audience, only inadequate performers." Now, it seemed, he was out to prove his point.

The strange thing was, the song and dance worked. Maybe it was the newness of their performance, the incongruity of song and dance just before battle, the true horribleness of the dragon's singing voice, or perhaps simple shock. Whatever combination of factors neutralized the demons, they only sat and stared, stupefied.

Let's face it. Even I was dazzled by Damsel and Dragon's fancy footwork. Mesmerized like the others, I completely forgot about my Home Study Course.

Damsel and dragon sang together:

> "They're not much of a treat
> Because they're no good to eat.
> Too spicy! And their claws,
> Will give your stomach pause.
> But the trouble demons do
> Is when a demon troubles you!"

"Yeah!" Damsel and Dragon shouted. "So let's give a little advice."

Hubert waved his tail in Alea's direction. "Take it, damsel!"

Alea launched into a series of complicated dance steps, much like I had seen the Brownie use when he was performing his magic.

"Say, big fellow," she called out to Hubert. "Do you know why demons don't accept jobs from dragons?"

"Why, yes, Damsel!" Hubert blew a smoke ring. "They're always afraid of getting fired!"

They danced together for a moment, the dragon's footsteps shaking the earth.

"But tell me, Damsel," Hubert said at last. "I understand you'll never date anyone from the fiery pits of the Netherhells."

"Yes, it's true," Alea sighed. "It's just that they keep reminding me of old flames."

The two danced some more.

"Say, Damsel," Hubert began.

"Yes, Dragon—" Alea replied.

"Do you know demons don't like the surface world?"

"No, but if you hum a few bars, I'll fake it!"

When I look back on it now, I realize that line was where Damsel and Dragon went wrong. That final joke was far too old and far too horrible. It snapped the spell their impromptu show had cast. The demons simply couldn't take it anymore.

"Boil the dragon's blood!" they chorused as one.

"I'm pretty hot-blooded already," Hubert quipped. "Comes from having a forest fire in your lungs." But the demons had all gathered behind their table and were staring intently at their adversary.

Hubert stumbled and almost fell on top of Alea. The Committee's concentration was too much for him. His top hat fell from his head. He gamely tried to finish his routine, but his movements seemed to have more stagger and less dance in them with every passing moment.

I had to do something. But what? I had learned from bitter experience that the Home Study Course might not be the best resource when one was hurried. And I could think of no better reason to hurry than what was transpiring between Hubert and the demons.

"Is it time for Brownie Power?" Tap asked.

"It's time for anything!" I cried. "Anything you can think of."

Tap nodded grimly. "You want the works, you got it!" He began to dance with purpose.

A dark brown cloud rolled in to fill the sky. The smallest demon shouted "Point of order!" but the others were too busy boiling blood to listen.

Then it started to rain slippers, directly over the demonic committee.

"Not enough!" Tap grimaced. "Brownies do it better!"

He danced faster. The rain turned first to sandals, then to shiny shoes with buckles. A couple of the blood-boiling demons glanced up.

"You're getting to them!" I shouted encouragingly.

Tap shook his tiny head. "Still not enough. Brownies do it best!" He danced so fast that I could no longer see his feet.

The rain turned to thick, heavy boots.

The committee cried out in alarm, shielding their heads and staring up at the boot-laden sky. Hubert stood up and shook his large body. The spell had been broken!

"All right, Damsel," he began. "Time for another chorus. A-one and a—" The dragon gasped.

I glanced back at the committee. They were once again concentrating their collective will on the dragon, the boots bouncing harmlessly from their brightly scaled bodies. Their demonic hides were too thick. Once the initial surprise was gone, they had returned immediately to boiling blood, knowing the shoes would do them no harm.

With a final groan, Hubert sank to his reptilian knees. Alea ran quickly out of the way as the dragon's great bulk crashed to the ground.

"Not enough," Tap gasped. "Brownie Power not . . ." And he, too, fell to the ground, beyond dancing another step. The boots stopped falling. The demonic committee stood behind their table, directing their unanimous blood-boiling stare at the quickly fading dragon.

The Brownie had failed. It was up to me. If Hubert was to live, I would have to distract them. Somehow. I ran towards the table, the loudest scream I could muster upon my lips.

"Die, fiend!" I shouted as I swung my stout oak staff.

"Beg pardon," the small, sickly demon replied as it deftly ducked beneath my blow, "but I think not." And it picked up the huge volume of Netherhells bylaws to defend itself.

I backed away from the massive weight swinging in the demon's hands. Would that I had brought my own Home Study Course and we could have fought book to book. As it was, my stout oak staff was no match for the heavy tome. One swing of the bylaws and my weapon snapped in two!

"Point of order!" the sickly demon screamed as it leapt atop me to press the amazingly heavy tome against my chest. I was pinned instantly against the ground, as if I had the bulk of the mighty Hendrek pushed into me. I couldn't breathe! I would be crushed to death by the Netherhells bylaws!

The demon on my chest cackled. "The vote is unanimous, and the final results are dea—" The demon's sentence ended in a surprised screech.

"Eep! Eep!" came the answering screech of my ferret, who leapt straight for the fiend's astonished countenance. The demon fell backwards in shock, and the bylaws slid from my chest.

I did not move for a moment, attempting to regain my breath. I turned my head and saw that Alea kneeled by the fallen Hubert.

"Oh," Alea sobbed. "What can we do?"

"I will die . . . performing!" Hubert replied with a groan. "It is the way . . . it should be! Hit it, Damsel!"

Alea began to dance before Hubert's prostrate body as the dragon sang as best he could:

"The trouble with . . . demons," Hubert gasped, "as . . . everyone believes, is that . . . they don't go well . . . with crackers . . . and they don't . . . go well . . . with . . . cheese."

"Not good with cheese!" Alea chorused with tears in her eyes. Hubert would go to his death a showdragon!

The demons chortled behind their table. They knew when they were winning. And Hubert was by far the strongest among us. Only his dragon fire had any hope against the combined demonic might of the Netherhells committee. With Hubert defeated, they would destroy the rest of us in less time than it took to say "Point of order!" Nothing could save us now!

Then Guxx Unfufadoo began to sneeze.

TWELVE

"Demons are sadly lacking in the social graces. They are just as likely to eat you with the salad fork as with the proper utensil, and after they've gobbled up two or three humans, they seldom even cover their mouths when they belch. Still, if you insist on inviting a demon to your next gathering, it will make for a fascinatingly different party, especially if you seat some of your least favorite guests on the demon's side of the table."

—Ask Ebenezum: The Wizard's Guide
to Perfect Etiquette, fourth edition

It took me a moment to comprehend what had happened. Guxx had suddenly, miraculously, recovered from his frozen state. At first I had no idea why. Then I realized that the former Grand Hoohah only sneezed when exposed to poetry. And that, after a fashion, is just what Damsel and Dragon had given him in their "Trouble with Demons" song.

Damsel and Dragon had assaulted Guxx's frozen ears with rhyme after rhyme, so that at last his sorcerous malady had overwhelmed whatever spell I had laid upon him, the stronger magick winning out in the end. I was sure, though, that the crucial moment came during the dragon's last verse, the one that paired "believes" with "cheese." Almost a good rhyme, but not quite; the sort of poetry Guxx used to thrive on!

"Point of order!" the small demon screamed as it pointed at the sneezing Guxx.

"I see it!" the gavel demon replied. "I think this situation calls for a brief conference." The five demons huddled together.

Slowly Guxx was recovering. The sneezes were becoming fewer and further between. The former dictator of all the Netherhells staggered over to the still-frozen Brax.

"Begin!" Guxx rumbled in the other's ear.

Brax blinked, and began to beat his drum.

> "Guxx Unfufadoo, noblest demon,
> Greets this group of demon traitors,
> Has one question for these demons:
> How would they like to be murdered?"

"Murdered?" the small, sickly demon ventured. "How about 'Not very much'?"

Guxx pointed a quivering claw at the small demon and yelled again in Brax's ear: "Continue!"

Brax beat and Guxx intoned:

> "Guxx informs you: He can eat you;
> He can rend you; he can tear you;
> He can squash you; he can stomp you.
> 'Not very much' is not an option!"

"All in favor of retreat!" the gavel demon exclaimed.

The Committee disappeared before they could even take a vote.

Quiet descended over the field, the only sound the muted beating of Brax's drum.

"They're gone?" Hubert sniffed. "Oh, well. They weren't much of an audience." The dragon tipped his hat in my direction. "Still, you can't say we didn't give them their money's worth."

"Oh, Wuntie!" Alea ran towards me across the field, her long blond hair streaming behind her in the wind. "You were so brave, facing those demons all by yourself!"

"Hey!" a weak voice said by my feet. "What about me?" The Brownie seemed to be recovering, too. "Don't I count for something? Well"—the small fellow paused, then added in a whisper—"maybe I don't."

"Eep eep!" my ferret commented.

But Alea only had eyes for me. She was approaching rapidly, her arms outstretched to embrace me. My throat suddenly felt very dry.

"It certainly was dramatic there for a few minutes," Hubert mused. "What do you call that staring routine of theirs?"

I told the dragon they referred to it as boiling blood.

"Boiling blood?" Hubert nodded his approval. "It has a ring to it. I wonder if we could incorporate 'the dying dragon' into our act. What pathos!"

And in that instant Alea was upon me.

"Oh, Wuntie!" she whispered as her form pushed against mine.

"Um," I replied. Before I could say more, her lips were covering my own.

"You were so brave back there," Alea gushed between kisses. "So bold, so . . . so foolhardy!" Her lips swept in for another attack, but I managed to dodge them long enough to wriggle from her grasp.

"Alea!" I gasped. "Please!" I did my best to catch my breath. "We are on a quest!"

"But that's just it!" She smiled fiercely. "There's something about a man who . . . who . . . *throws* himself at danger!"

I saw fire in the damsel's eyes. I took a step away. Alea managed to reach out and catch my wrist anyway. This was too much. Didn't she realize the importance of our mission?

"I'm sorry, Alea," I insisted, disentangling myself again from her embrace. "Whatever you have in mind, the quest must come first."

"Is that so?" She smiled meaningfully at me as she stepped even closer than she had been before. "Well, my bold"—she paused to ruffle my hair—"quester. Perhaps while we are"—she paused to rub her shoulder against mine—"questing, we will at last get a little time to spend"—her hand drifted down from my head, grazing my neck and spine—"together."

"Um," I remarked. "Uh . . . indeed." I had the feeling that her definition of questing might be somewhat different from my own.

"Now that I'm with you," she added, "I'm not even afraid of being baked into bread."

"Baked into bread?" a small voice piped from near my feet.

Alea nodded. "That's what they do to you in the Eastern Kingdoms."

"Why would they do that?" Tap inquired.

"So that the giants can eat you," Alea answered.

"Oh," Tap replied. Somehow, he didn't seem to be his old self. The smile was gone from his voice, the bounce from his step. And perhaps most shocking of all: since his shoe defeat, he hadn't even referred to Brownie Power.

"Recommence!" Guxx shouted from the spot where he stood, half-way across the field. Brax rebeat his drum.

> "Guxx Unfufadoo, noble leader,
> Tells you 'Have no fear of giants!'
> Follow me to Eastern Kingdoms,
> And my claws will shred their ovens!"

Guxx roared as he finished the verse, sweeping his extremely long, extremely sharp claws through the air for effect. I knew what this meant. He wanted to take over the quest!

Guxx glowered meaningfully in my direction. What could I do? I no longer had even my stout oak staff for protection.

"Uh," I remarked. I wondered if there might be a way I could quickly glance through the Home Study Course without raising the demon's suspicions.

A great shadow fell over me. I looked up to see Hubert, who casually blew a smoke ring in Guxx's general direction.

"I think not," the dragon replied softly. "Wuntvor is the leader of our quest. We follow him."

"Reassert!" Guxx screamed. Brax continued his rhythmic accompaniment.

> "Guxx Unfufadoo, natural leader,
> Does not follow any human,
> Leads the bravest into battle,
> Eats any who disobey him!"

The demon paused to show his teeth.

"I trust that is your final word." Hubert coughed gently, then inhaled and removed his top hat.

"Proceed!" Guxx added. Brax took his drum and proceeded.

> "Guxx Unfufadoo, never beaten,
> Leads no matter what the dragon—"

Two great gouts of flame burst from Hubert's nostrils, searing a patch of ground mere inches from Guxx's toes. Brax lost the beat, jumping away from the fire with a yelp. Guxx stared down at the charred earth for a moment before concluding his verse.

". . . Then again, there is no reason,
Not to hear some more discussion."

"Bravo," the dragon replied. "And our reasoned discussion should
begin with our leader, Wuntvor." He glanced down at me. "Well,
Wuntvor? Anything you want."

Guxx grumbled darkly, but made no further move. Hubert had
given the quest back to me, and I knew exactly what I wanted. No, as
much as I yearned to rest and put a good meal in my belly, there was
something we all needed more:

I had to contact Ebenezum!

"I must be alone for a moment," I said, much more solemnly than I
felt.

Guxx glared again at the scorched grass, then paced away from the
others. Brax followed at a distance, obviously fearful of his master's
mood. I turned to Hubert and thanked him for his efforts.

"Think nothing of it," the dragon said with a toss of his head. "We
know where our interest lies. After all, when was the last time you saw
a demon applaud?" He chuckled derisively. "They have no appreciation at all of the vaudevillian arts."

The vaudevillian arts? I wasn't too sure if I had any appreciation of
those myself, but I thought it rude to mention that thought to a
dragon who had so recently saved me. Instead I asked Hubert and
Alea to leave me with the Brownie.

Damsel and Dragon readily agreed.

"Come on, Tap," I said to the small fellow by my foot. "It's time for
Brownie Power."

Tap frowned up at me. "Are you sure?"

This was far worse than I thought. I had to be careful not to frown
back at the Brownie. How would my master handle something like
this?

"Certainly," I replied with a cheerful smile. "Don't you remember,
Brownies do it better?"

Tap turned to stare at the ground. "Do they?"

This was not going to be as easy as I had hoped.

"Of course they do!" I knelt down and patted the Brownie's back
with my index finger. "Didn't you tell me that Brownies have it all?"

"All of what?" Tap looked up at me and sighed. "Somehow, none of
it seems to matter anymore. I failed. I . . . I couldn't save you with
my shoes."

"Indeed?" I replied. "But we are still here and safe, aren't we?"
Tap nodded mutely.

"And we're here in part because of your brave efforts. Your shoe attack gave Hubert enough time to sing his final verse, the verse that reawoke Guxx and, ultimately, saved us all."

The Brownie paused in thought. "Then Brownie Power didn't fail you?"

"No, it just worked in a way we didn't expect." Like everything else that has happened to me since leaving the Western Woods, I added to myself. I remembered what Ebenezum had said about my leading a charmed life. I thought again about what Death had told me about the Eternal Apprentice.

"So you see," I added aloud, "now you have saved my life more than once."

"I . . . I have, haven't I?" Tap's voice was filled with wonder.

"Indeed," I added. "Never fear. Brownies have their proper place in the scheme of things."

"And an important place it is, too!" Tap added, the old verve back in his voice. "That's Brownie Power!"

"Indeed it is," I coaxed. "The same Brownie Power with which we're going to contact Ebenezum!"—

"You need to contact Ebenezum?" Tap laughed. "Well why didn't you say so? 'Tis time for Brownie magic!"

"Indeed," I replied.

Tap began a dance even more complicated than the one he used for the rain of shoes. A breeze sprang up from nowhere, lifting the dirt and dead leaves into a tall, brown cloud that circled around us like a wall so that we were hidden from the eyes of others. But the cloud kept its distance, so that I had no trouble breathing and Tap could continue his dance.

Tap winked up at me. "Are you ready?"

Somewhere in the far, far distance, I heard a sneeze. A wizardly sneeze.

"Indeed!" my master's voice called, faint but clear. "Be with you in a second!"

The wall about us intensified, turning from the color of yellow mud to that of dark, rich earth. Then suddenly, directly in front of the spot where Tap was dancing, there appeared a point of light upon the wall. The Brownie whistled and cheered as his feet flew from step to step.

The light grew, filling fully half the circle in which we were enclosed, and I realized I was looking at the courtyard of the Wizards College at Vushta, just as I had left it, except for one thing.

In the center of the yard was a giant shoe.

"Now that's Brownie Power!" Tap exclaimed.

"Indeed?" the shoe replied. "You wished to speak with me, Wuntvor?"

It was my master, the great wizard Ebenezum!

THIRTEEN

"What happens when you encounter a gigantic and hideous creature who sports huge fangs and claws and breathes great streams of flame? May I suggest that you make friends as quickly as possible."

—THE TEACHINGS OF EBENEZUM, Volume XXIV

It took me a moment to collect my thoughts.

"I'd appreciate it," Tap mentioned as he madly moved his feet, "if the two of you would communicate. I've already learned once today" —the Brownie gasped in air—"that I cannot dance forever."

"Certainly," I replied, a bit abashed. I realized I was having some trouble addressing the wizard in his shoe disguise. I shouldn't have been surprised, really. Ebenezum and the Brownie had used the protective abilities of the giant shoe once before, when the wizard and I found ourselves in the midst of a union meeting of mythical monsters, a magical situation my master could only survive from within the protective shoe leather. Now Ebenezum was called on to confront magic from a great distance. Under the circumstances, the enclosing shoe made perfect sense.

Still, I had looked forward to seeing my master's long white beard and stately robes, tastefully embroidered with silver moons and stars. Somehow, talking to a shoe was nowhere near as reassuring.

"Um . . ." I began.

"Yes, Wunt?" my master-inside-the-shoe prompted.

Where should I start? So much had happened since I had left Vushta. Perhaps I should begin with the attack by the Netherhells. Or mayhaps it was more important to reveal Guxx's startling turnabout when he joined the quest.

Instead I decided to tell him about my meeting with Death.

"Indeed?" my master remarked when I was finished. "That could explain a great many things. When you left Vushta so suddenly, I felt there must be some deeper reason. That was why I sent the Brownie after you. But Death called you the Eternal Apprentice?"

The shoe paused and rocked back on its heel. "Death is an enigma, Wunt. His power is one of the most natural things in the world, the ending of life. Still, few wizards of repute have endeavored to study Death's power, for fear of what that knowledge might bring. Thus, while Death is with us every day, we know little of his true nature. However, the very concept of an Eternal Apprentice is a fascinating conjecture." The shoe's laces wriggled as if the wizard was moving about inside. "Indeed. I will have to think on it. In the meantime, Wuntvor, you seem to be following the best path. Do you wish any further advice?"

I wished any and all advice the wizard could give me, so I told him about Guxx, and our recent altercation with the Netherhells.

"I see." The whole shoe appeared to nod solemnly. "It sounds like an uneasy alliance at best. And yet if Death is correct in his accusations, Guxx has joined you as another companion, a situation that could work to your advantage."

The shoe creaked as Ebenezum no doubt leaned forward against the leather. Did I see his steel-gray eyes studying me through the eyelets?

The Brownie waved his tiny hands in my direction. "I hate to bring . . . this up, fellows," he managed, breathing heavily, "but this Brownie's power has . . . almost worn . . . through."

Now that he mentioned it, I noticed that Tap's once fancy footwork was becoming more of a shuffle than a dance. The magic image of Ebenezum's shoe flickered and began to grow indistinct around the heel.

"Very well," my master continued. "We shall hurry. Wuntvor, one part of Death's story seems to be correct, and that is his information about companions. According to what you have told me, you left Vushta hurriedly because it seemed that the entire town wanted to accompany you. That was apparently the case, for moments after we realized you had disappeared, everyone who desired to join your quest had disappeared as well. I fear, Wuntvor, that half of Vushta is following you upon the road, wishing to be your companion."

I was quite taken aback. It appeared that this quest might get somewhat larger than I had at first anticipated.

And then the true meaning of the wizard's statement sank in.

"Everyone?" I breathed, almost fearful of considering the possibility. Could my master mean that Norei was rushing to join me as well? I had almost given up hope, but now—

Tap stumbled and almost fell. He slowly dragged his feet back and forth, as if they were made of lead. The shoe was fading.

"Whoever plans to meet you, I am sure you will see them soon enough," Ebenezum continued quickly. "We need to discuss strategy, and I fear that the Brownie cannot dance forever. I believe that my fellow wizards have recovered sufficiently to best that demonic committee one more time. We shall try to draw the next Netherhells attack here, a ploy that, if nothing else, will serve to further confuse them and give you time to finish your quest. That's the advantage to fighting committees, you know; the chance of confusion increases in direct relation to the number of committee members. But make haste, Wuntvor. Enlist Mother Duck to our cause and we will be able to defeat the Netherhells forever!"

"That's it!" the Brownie gasped, falling on his face. Ebenezum disappeared, and the brown dirt wall settled to the ground. That meant it was time for action.

I cheered heartily. My companions all looked at me with some surprise.

"No time for sleeping!" I scooped the Brownie up in my palm and beckoned with my free hand to Guxx and Brax, Damsel and Dragon. "Onwards, fellow beings. We seek the Eastern Kingdoms!"

I quickly gathered up my pack, once again containing both ferret and Home Study Course. I left the remains of my stout oak staff behind; I would find a replacement along the way. I began to whistle one of Damsel and Dragon's ditties. All was right with the world. Norei was following me!

I heard a rustling in the bushes behind me. Could it be? Would my prayers be answered so soon?

I turned and walked quickly toward the dense underbrush. "Is it you?" I whispered.

I got no reply, save the sound of heavy breathing. It did not sound like Norei. And yet, what if she had run all the way from Vushta to be with me? Would not her breath be labored as she tried to draw air into her sweet lungs? Perhaps she was afraid to step out and meet me when she was not yet at her best. But now that she was so close, I could not bear to wait another moment without her! I would have to coax her out of hiding.

"Are you in there?" I murmured softly.

Was it my imagination, or did the breathing get louder?

"If you've come all this way, why not come out and see me?" The bushes rustled again. Was she coming out at last?

"Come on, now," I prompted. "You know how much I've missed you."

And with that, a head forced its way through the undergrowth; a head topped by a golden horn.

"How long I have waited for you to say that!" The unicorn stared at me with its large, limpid eyes. "Others of my kind might have scoffed at me, for galloping after you all the way from Vushta. But you should know by now that you are one of the few mortals for which I would" —the unicorn paused, tossing its splendid head so that its horn shone in the sun—"work up a sweat."

"Well," I replied, a bit taken aback. This had not quite worked out as I had planned. "But you don't understand. You see, I thought—"

The unicorn glanced past my shoulder at my other companions, who had turned to watch us.

"I see now," the magnificent beast whispered conspiratorially. "You're shy about sharing your feelings in front of all your friends. I understand perfectly. Unicorns know all about shyness." It nudged me gently with its golden horn. "We'll talk about this later"—the beast snorted briefly in the direction of the others—"when we're alone."

"Indeed." I cleared my throat and turned to face the others. "The unicorn has volunteered to join our quest!"

No one seemed particularly excited by the prospect of the unicorn ally, but then no one objected, either. I turned east and waved for the others to follow.

"What we need," Hubert called from where he lumbered along behind me, "is a good marching song. The sort of thing to lift the spirits and make the miles fly by!"

Alea looked up at him: "Were you thinking of singing number 126?"

"A perfect choice!" the dragon agreed. "Shall we? Once you learn the chorus, everyone, feel free to join in."

Damsel and Dragon began to sing:

> "If we are bold, if we are brave,
> If we believe in true romance,
> If we are questing, with a world to save,

We'll save it all with song and dance!
If we are mighty, if we are true,
If we are to win the battle long,
How can we conquer? What can we do,
Unless we do it first with dance and—"

Guxx ran in front of the singing, dancing couple, dragging Brax behind him. "Now!" he screamed above the din of the song.

Brax regained his feet and started to beat.

"Guxx Unfufadoo, reasoned demon,
Asks that you would cease your singing,
Asks if you could stop your rhyming,
Asks if we might walk in silence."

The demon blew his nose for emphasis.

"What?" the dragon cried happily. "But you just haven't gotten into the spirit of the thing. It gets better as it goes along. Listen to this."

Damsel and Dragon sang together:

"If we are brave, if we are bold,
If we believe that truth just grows,
Then come on and do what you're told.
Bring a song to battle and tap those toes!"

"Continue!" Guxx screamed in response. Brax pounded on his drum.

"Guxx Unfufadoo, annoyed demon,
Demands you stop this caterwauling,
Demands you spend this trip in silence,
Or there will be some retribution!"

"Did someone say something, Damsel?" Hubert inquired.

"Not that I heard, Dragon," Alea replied as she pirouetted.

"Oh, well." Hubert blew a smoke ring in the shape of a fly. "Must have been an insect somewhere. But we have another verse!"

"We have hundreds of verses!" Damsel added. And they sang again:

"If we are true, if we are mighty,
You'll hear us singing down the street,
Come on now and don't be flighty,
Just come with us and slap those fee—"

"Overwhelm!" Guxx shrieked in a voice so loud that it shook the trees.

Brax pounded on the drum with renewed force.

"Guxx Unfufadoo, enraged demon,
Informs those who still are singing,
Soon enough they'll find those voices,
Stomped to bits by feet of demons!"

"Damsel?" Hubert remarked. "I feel another verse coming on."

"Indeed!" I yelled over everyone. "I've had enough . . ." I paused and coughed to get my voice back down to a reasonable level. "I've had enough of your petty arguing. This is a quest, and we're all on it together. Therefore, for that period of time remaining before we reach the Eastern Kingdoms, I demand that there be no more vaudevillian singing or Netherhells declaiming! Anyone who doesn't agree is free to leave the quest. Is that understood?"

Guxx and Hubert glowered at each other, but both continued to walk with the rest of our party.

The unicorn trotted up to my side and tossed its magnificent mane.

"I've never seen this side of you before," the golden horned beast murmured close to my ear. "It's quite a revelation." Its dark, soulful eyes looked deep into my own. "Oh, I love it when you talk tough!"

I noticed that all the others in our band were watching me again.

"Maybe," Alea nodded to Hubert, "he's going to be a wizard after all."

I walked on ahead. The others followed. They were beginning to truly accept my leadership. Alea said I would be a wizard after all. And for a minute I believed her, at least until we came to that next clearing; the one with the big painted sign:

You are in the vicinity of
THE EASTERN KINGDOMS
Are you sure you want to be?

The Brownie climbed onto my shoulder to get a better look. "What does that mean?"

"I think," Alea answered, "It has something to do with giants baking bread."

"Nonsense," I replied. I didn't want their spirits to plummet now, when we were so close. "There could be any number of meanings to that sign."

"Like what?" the Brownie asked.

I couldn't think of an answer.

From deep within the trees behind the sign, another voice spoke. "Doom," it said.

FOURTEEN

"Why are wizards your friends? Surely it is because they are reputed to be able to create vast sums of gold from the empty air. You do not agree? Then it must be because they can predict with astonishing accuracy the next visit of the royal tax collector or the royal mother-in-law. Still no? Then you must certainly agree that it must be that they have been rumored to take those people with whom they are not friendly, and turn those individuals into mice and swine? Surely you see my point of view by now. Let me put it to you this way: Would you rather oink for a living?"

—excerpted from the lecture series "Why Wizards Are Your Friends," given in part by Ebenezum, greatest wizard in the Western Kingdoms (See footnote)

"Doom."

I would know that deep, resonant voice anywhere.

"Are we just going to stand around in the bushes all day?" another, infinitely more grating voice added. "I didn't come on this quest to spend my days standing in shrubbery!"

I knew the second voice as well.

There was a great crashing and banging in the bushes. I saw the doomed warclub Headbasher flash through the green.

The warrior Hendrek emerged a moment later. "Doom," he remarked. "I cleared a path."

The truth-telling demon Snarks followed him out. "I don't see why

Footnote: The above lecture was, unfortunately, never completed, due to an altercation in the audience, some of whom had been turned into swine.

you bother using that club of yours. Why don't you just push your way through? Any bush would have to yield to your greater size."

"Doom," Hendrek replied.

"Indeed," I interjected. "I am glad to see you as well. You have come to join our quest?"

"Well, it was better than spending all our time around a bunch of sneezing wizards," Snarks answered. "Plus, this questing thing tends to get in your blood. Hendrek and I both felt it was time to go out and rescue something. It's much better than sitting on your hands in Vushta, especially considering the unwelcome small fry that have been showing up lately. Any chance to get away from—" Snarks stopped and stared. "What's that on your shoulder?"

"Brownie Power!" Tap called out.

The demon turned a slightly lighter shade of green. "Maybe I enjoyed standing in the bushes after all."

Tap, seeing the demon's distress, hopped off my shoulder and skipped toward Snarks. "I haven't been feeling quite myself lately, either," the Brownie admitted. "Now that you're here, though, everything's going to be as happy as a Brownie jamboree!"

"I was afraid of that," Snarks moaned.

For once I sympathized with the demon. As much as it pleased me to see Tap's spirits returning, I feared that even I would not be capable of surviving a Brownie jamboree.

"Doom." Hendrek lifted his dread warclub Headbasher. He had seen Guxx.

Guxx had seen Hendrek and Snarks as well. He poked at Brax with a pointy claw.

"Begin!"

"Indeed," I remarked as Brax picked up his drum. "You remember what I said about anybody who sang or declaimed on the quest?"

Brax stopped beating. Guxx glared at me for an instant, then whispered in the other demon's ear.

Brax cleared his throat when the former Grand Hoohah was done. "My ruler would like to tell you the following." Brax smiled uneasily. "Let's see. Guxx Unfufadoo, noble demon . . . um, that he certainly is . . . um, sought to greet our new companions, sought to tell them he was friendly . . . and, uh . . . oh, he sought to welcome them to questing."

Hubert snorted derisively. "That sounds an awful lot like declaiming to me."

"Indeed!" I exclaimed, before this could go any further. "This arguing is going to get in the way of our quest. Perhaps I have been too harsh. A little modest declaiming might be in order after all."

"Agreement!" Guxx shouted. Brax began to beat his drum.

Hubert snorted a short burst of flame. Brax stopped beating, glancing apprehensively at the vaudevillian lizard above him.

"No," the dragon insisted. "If he gets to declaim, we get to sing and dance."

Alea looked up at her partner. "What did you have in mind?"

Hubert paused a minute to consider. "How about number 216?"

" 'The Demon Slaughter Polka'?" Damsel nodded approvingly. "Well, it's certainly bouncy enough."

"Indeed!" I interrupted quickly. Somehow, this was getting out of hand all over again. "No singing, no declaiming. The edict stands."

Snarks and Hendrek both looked at me.

"Doom," the large warrior whispered. " 'The Demon Slaughter Polka'? I thought we were all supposed to be friends on this quest."

"How can you possibly make friends with a dragon who sings?" Snarks asked. He glanced at the former Grand Hoohah. "For that matter, who could possibly trust a demon politician?"

I told Snarks and Hendrek how Guxx had come to join us. I also mentioned that Guxx and the dragon had had a small difference of opinion. But I also thought again about what Death had told me when we met. He had sent friend against friend back in Vushta to get me to meet him alone. Now I heard dissension all around me once more. Could Death be intensifying our quarrels to ruin our quest? If so, he must still be following our progress, something that I should never forget, even when we were being attacked by demons.

I shuddered to think what would happen if Death did get me alone.

"Wait a moment," Snarks queried. "Guxx joined you because he thought you were the Eternal Apprentice?"

"Doom," Hendrek remarked.

"It is a frightening thought," Snarks echoed. "Eternal Apprentice, huh? Does that mean you'll have those same pimples throughout the rest of time?"

"Indeed," I remarked, somewhat distracted. "I think not." I was their leader now. I would have to act like one. How would Ebenezum handle this? I stroked my chin in thought.

"Indeed," I said again. "What we really need here is some strategy. The Brownie and I recently contacted Ebenezum—"

"That's Brownie Power!" Tap exclaimed from where he ran by our sides. I looked down at the little fellow. He seemed to be his old dancing, smiling self at last. Both my talk with the Brownie and his summoning of Ebenezum seemed to help him, although for a while he looked as if he might still slide back into despair. Now, though, the arrival of Snarks seemed to have revived his spirits completely.

The demon Snarks shivered visibly as the Brownie approached. I ignored both of them and continued. ". . . and when I spoke with Ebenezum, the wizard told me that many of our allies in Vushta are coming on their own to join this quest." I nodded first towards the unicorn—keeping its distance from the others, but still a member of our party—then at Hubert, Alea, and the Brownie. "Of course, we have also been joined by two denizens of the Netherhells, but it is almost impossible to even approach Guxx and Brax without being assaulted by unrhyming verse. Talking strategy is completely out of the question. Damsel and Dragon, I am afraid, are almost as hopeless—"

"Theater people," Snarks agreed.

"Doom," Hendrek added.

"But now that I have been joined by those who were my companions on our successful campaign to rescue Vushta, I feel strategy is a priority. Especially because we are already on the edge of the Eastern Kingdoms." I nodded at the large warning sign.

Hendrek read it. "Doom," he concurred.

"But come, we must resume our march. It grows dark. We should get as close to our goal as possible!" I waved for the others to follow us, and they did so. There were enough of them by now to form a substantial line. I led them down the trail into the next wooded area, with Snarks and Hendrek still by my side.

I realized, then, that they had accepted me as their leader. But why wasn't I happier about this turn of events? As soon as I asked myself the question, I knew the answer. I would not be happy with anything until I knew the whereabouts of one more traveler from Vushta—one who was dearer to me than all the others I had left behind. Still, how could I broach the subject without letting my emotions interfere with my leadership? But I must know!

I would ask, I decided, but I would do so casually.

"Now, as to strategy," I continued, the soul of casualness. "Our first priority, I would think, would be to assess our strengths. We have gathered quite a compliment together on this march, and we may even be joined by more. Tell me"—my voice caught in my throat for a second as I asked the next question—"is anyone else coming from Vushta to join us?"

Snarks and Hendrek both shook their heads.

"No one?" I prompted easily. How could they have forgotten Norei?

"Doom," Hendrek replied. "We are the slowest of those to follow you. We are the last."

"It wouldn't have happened if this large fellow had followed my diet and exercise guides," Snarks added. "But he won't listen to me. Nobody listens to me. And we could only lumber so fast after you."

It occurred to me, then, that perhaps Norei hadn't followed after all. But that couldn't possibly be!

"Are you sure there was nobody else?" I insisted.

"Planning to join you here?" Hendrek shook his massive head with finality. "None that we passed."

This was terrible! After what Ebenezum had said, I had simply assumed that Norei would join us, and looked forward to at last explaining those few small misunderstandings that had happened between us recently. But what if she truly did not want to see me again? Would I never get the chance to tell her that I might be the Eternal Apprentice?

But I had to get hold of myself. This wasn't the way for a leader to act. I had no time to pine for lost love. I had to stride boldly forward, vanquishing foes and righting wrongs, making the world safe for Vushta and magicians everywhere. So what if Norei was gone from my life forever?

"Indeed," I said one final time. "Are you sure there was *absolutely* nobody else?"

"I think it's time for a new question," Snarks retorted. "Something that relates more to the quest, like, 'What's your favorite color?' "

"Doom." Hendrek looked back at me and frowned. "Why do you keep asking?"

"Indeed," I replied to give myself a chance to think. Despite my best efforts, my feelings about Norei were taking their toll on my supervision of the quest. Would it weaken my leadership even further if I were to admit how much I missed her? Perhaps I was becoming too strident in my questioning. I recalled that when I first decided to broach this subject, I had resolved to be as easygoing as possible.

So far I had failed miserably.

I took a deep breath. I would simply have to appear even more casual, and everything would be fine.

I looked casually at Snarks and Hendrek. "I don't know," I began, scratching casually behind my ear. "I was just . . . curious." I yawned even more casually. "There were some others we might be able to use. For example, how about"—I paused, casually picking a name out of the air—"Norei."

"Oh!" Snarks exclaimed. "That's right! Your heartthrob. How could we forget—"

"Doom," Hendrek interrupted the demon. "Norei will definitely not be joining us."

What? Norei not joining us as at all? All casualness left me as I demanded how Hendrek could be so sure.

Snarks spoke up first. "I'm afraid this is one time the immense one here is right. We passed her on the way here."

So they had seen her. That meant she was on the road to the Eastern Kingdoms! But what they said made no sense. Why had they told me—

"Doom." Hendrek spoke before I had a chance to frame a question. "She has too much pride to join you. Not after, as she told us, what happened in Vushta. She will, however, follow at a respectful distance in case you get into trouble."

"Indeed?" I said. I did not know what to feel. One part of me was overjoyed that she cared enough about me to hover near, ready to protect us should disaster strike. But another part of me despaired of ever speaking to her again. And if I never spoke to her again, how could I possibly explain what had really happened?

"Doom," I whispered.

"Hey!" a gruff voice retorted. "Watch where you're going!"

"What?" I said. It was hard to make out shapes in the gathering gloom. But it was true that in my grief over losing Norei, I had not watched my feet, and thus had walked into and toppled what appeared to be a pile of short pieces of wood.

"Who's there?" I called.

There was no further response. The woods around us were deadly still.

"Doom," Hendrek explained. "It appears to be another sign."

I realized the large warrior was not speaking metaphorically when I looked where he pointed with his club. While I wasn't paying attention, we had walked into another small clearing. In the center of that clearing, just beyond the lumber I had disturbed, was another large expanse of white wood. The light was fading around us more rapidly than I had realized, but I could still barely make out the words:

It's not all that far to
THE EASTERN KINGDOMS
Sure you don't want to turn back
now?

"Friendly sort," Snarks remarked.

"Doom," Hendrek added again.

"But we're not turning back. We are almost to our goal." I glanced at the woods around us, completely black in the descending darkness. "I think it is time at last to make camp. It is too dark to go farther."

"Doom," Hendrek repeated, glowering out at those same woods. "There is something out there."

He was right. We had all heard the gruff voice in the dark. I kicked at the wood by my feet. "Use this to build a fire. We will take turns at sentry."

I scanned our surroundings once again, but could see nothing but the forest, close to us on every side and far too quiet.

"Gentle beings!" I turned to the rest of our party. "We camp here tonight, sleeping close together. We move again at first light. We are at the edge of the Eastern Kingdoms."

I paused. Did I hear something move out in the woods? It was my imagination, wasn't it?

I cleared my throat and added: "I fear that tomorrow the quest begins in earnest!"

FIFTEEN

"The sages say that under certain circumstances, extensive traveling in strange lands can be both entertaining and educational. This is true, for there are few things more educational than putting one's hand or foot too close to a ravenous demon or mythological beast met in these same travels. And what of using what limbs you still possess to escape from said hungry creature? Well, let me assure you that that escape will be far more entertaining than the alternative."

—THE TEACHINGS OF EBENEZUM, Volume XXXV

So we would camp at last. Unlike the last time I had made this suggestion, when Guxx had first decided that he was going to lead our party, there were no protests from any of our group. Besides having to inform Alea that when I spoke about sleeping close, I did not necessarily mean her and me, we settled down without further incident.

I realized that I had brought no food in my haste to leave Vushta earlier, but everyone else, apparently, had not been so shortsighted. Hubert had brought an immense amount of supplies (it is amazing how much a dragon can carry on his back), and Hendrek had brought a sizable sack as well, although the large warrior seemed intent on consuming as much as he had contributed. Guxx and Brax elected not to eat with us, something that, quite frankly, I was perfectly happy with, being a bit afraid of finding out exactly what the demons *did* eat. But the rest of us sat down to a filling meal around the camp fire we'd built from the pieces of the warning sign.

Our bellies full, the rest of our party settled down to sleep. I had elected to take the first watch. There was some thinking I had to do, some things I had to work out if I were going to successfully lead these others to brave the perils before us. I threw another bit of wood into the fire and stared at the flames. Somehow, I could not keep the quest foremost in my mind. Another thought kept driving all others away:

How could I get Norei to speak with me again?

I turned from the flames. The fire didn't hold any answers. The ferret nuzzled my knee as it finished off the scraps I had saved for it. At least this little animal still had some affection for me. But it wasn't the same. The night was growing cold. Soon the ferret would retreat to the warmth of my pack, and I would be left here, all alone.

Of course! I was astonished how simple the answer was when it came to me. The pack! The Home Study Course was in my pack! That was the answer to my problems with Norei. For had not even my master, the great wizard Ebenezum, mentioned that the book contained love potions?

That was it! How simple! How perfect! I would use my magic to bring her back!

I quickly pulled the tome from my pack and turned so that I could read it by the light of the fire. I turned to the index, under L. Here it was!

"Love potions, all purpose, page 33."

All purpose? What need had I to go any further? I flipped rapidly to the proper page.

"What kind of idiot did this?"

I looked up from my reading. It was the gruff voice, calling from the woods.

Somebody coughed. I looked around the fire. It didn't seem to be one of my compatriots; they all were sound asleep. I heard the cough again. It came from the forest as well, on the opposite side of the clearing from the gruff voice.

Whoever was out there, I was surrounded.

I closed the book. Love potions would have to wait. There was something out there, something from the Eastern Kingdoms; maybe even something that wanted to bake me into a loaf of bread. Oh, how I wished I still had my stout oak staff!

"You'd better watch out."

That voice was right behind me! I spun quickly, clutching the Home Study Course as a shield.

It was Brax.

"I couldn't sleep," the demon said. "I heard voices. I came over to warn you. The situation looks pretty tense." He paused a moment to straighten his checkered lapels. "A weapons salesdemon *lives* for times like these. In fact, I just might have a little something here . . ." He let the rest of the sentence hang in the air.

So Brax wanted to sell me weapons? "Sorry," I replied. "Not interested."

"That's all you have to say?" The demon looked grieved. "Not interested? I tell you, I'm losing my touch." He dropped the heavy sack he was carrying. It fell to the ground with a clank. "Oh, how being Guxx's rhythm section cramps a salesdemon's style!"

I told the salesdemon to be quiet. There was something out there.

"There certainly is!" Brax whispered. "And how much better you'd feel facing it with one of my previously owned weapons!"

"No, I wouldn't," I replied.

The demon sighed. "My timing is gone completely!"

"You're in a lot of trouble!"

Brax and I looked at each other. It was the gruff voice from the woods!

"Mayhaps I should answer it," I ventured.

"Mayhaps," Brax agreed. "And don't forget, I have a sack full of weapons. No down payment, easy terms, at least one lifetime to pay."

I decided to ignore the demon and respond to the voice instead.

"Hello!" I called to the night. "And a good evening to you!"

"What's it to you?" the voice yelled back.

Well, whatever the thing was, it was talking to me, even though it didn't sound very friendly. I decided to try again.

"I merely thought that, if you had a problem—"

"Who asked you anyway?" the voice interrupted.

"Well," I continued, trying to keep a cheerful tone, "it's just that you shouted at us, and I thought you wanted to communicate, like any civilized being—"

"So's your old man!" the voice rejoined.

My mouth snapped shut. I was at a loss for words.

"I think you'd get much better results with a previously owned weapon," Brax whispered.

I was beginning to agree with the salesdemon. But obnoxious as the voice was, how could I slay what I could not see?

"Doom," a voice rumbled at my side. "You have no need of previously owned weapons." I looked over and saw that Hendrek watched us from a sitting position.

"Indeed," I said to the large warrior. " 'Tis true that I have you and the others in our party to protect me from harm. Still, there may come times when I must fight on my own and need a weapon to help me survive."

"Doom." Hendrek nodded his head. "We have brought your weapon." He reached over to shake Snarks.

"I'm awake!" the truth-telling demon grumbled. "How could anybody sleep with all this shouting going on!"

"Doom," Hendrek replied. "Give Wuntvor his weapon."

"All right! All right!" The demon sat up with a groan. "That's the problem with questing; it doesn't give you any leisure time. It's just quest, quest, all the time quest." He rummaged through his own sack. "Here it is!" He pulled something long and shining from the sack and threw it in my general direction. "Now can I go back to sleep?"

I recognized the weapon in its dark blue scabbard before I had even caught it. It was Cuthbert.

I looked to Hendrek. "But I thought the sword refused to come out of its sheath?"

"Doom," the warrior answered. "We persuaded it."

Snarks laughed. "If it didn't come out, we were going to melt it down into ornamental paperweights."

The sword almost sprang from its sheath as I pulled it free.

"Can you imagine?" Cuthbert cried. "Ornamental paperweights? The very idea. A sword has some pride, you know!"

"Indeed," I remarked, wondering how much I should agree with the weapon. Even with my substantial magical background, I always found it a little difficult to converse with a sword. Especially a sword like Cuthbert, who was a bit of a coward, particularly when it came to anything even potentially violent.

"So," I added after a second's pause, "you are prepared to do your duty?"

"Well . . ." Cuthbert paused in thought. "You can use me to threaten. Any blood, though, and we will have words!"

"I am certain we will," I agreed. "But you shine in the dark as well." In fact, Cuthbert had done that very thing in our quest through the Netherhells, lighting our way through countless caverns.

"Oh, certainly," Cuthbert responded jovially, quite pleased that I had asked. "And I shine very nicely, too."

"Quite true. And that is the very thing we need now!"

"Why didn't you say so? Having me go on and on about bloodletting! I should have known you wanted much more civilized magic. Give me but a second while I brighten up!"

The sword glowed, first a dull red, then orange, then yellow, then blinding white.

"How's that?" Cuthbert asked.

"Perfect!" I answered. I held the sword before me and marched toward the spot where I had last heard the gruff voice.

"No fair!" the voice yelled. A short figure, perhaps half my size, leapt from the shadows and ran back into the trees. I heard other running feet as well. And one of the runners was coughing.

I stood at the edge of the clearing, listening to the fading sound of feet scrambling over broken branches and dead leaves. It was far too dark to follow them, even with a magic sword. Besides, I had a feeling we'd meet again, soon enough.

"Indeed," I said to the sword.

"That's it?" Cuthbert said in relief. "I feared, when we went running toward the woods—well, never mind. That's fine. Any time!"

I sheathed the sword and returned to the camp fire.

"Doom." Hendrek nodded. "I will take the next watch."

I didn't argue, but settled down with the Home Study Course to read myself to sleep.

The morning was magnificent. The sun was golden as it peeked through the trees, turning the leaves a bright, translucent green. Even the moss-covered rocks seemed to glow in the gentle morning light.

Alea rushed around the dying campfire to my side, her pale blond hair attractively mussed from sleeping.

"Oh, Wuntie!" she thrilled. "Isn't it wonderful?" She waved at the scenery around her. "It's like we woke up in some fairy land!"

"Hey!" a high voice yelled by my feet. "Watch your language!"

We both looked down at Tap the Brownie. The little fellow shrugged defensively.

"Well, no one ever calls it Brownieland, do they?"

"It doesn't matter what you call it," a beautifully modulated voice said from just past my shoulder. "This is a magic place. We have entered the Eastern Kingdoms."

I turned to look at the unicorn, and it was as if I had never seen that wondrous beast before. Its white coat and mane were blinding in the morning light, the color of newfallen snow in the high mountains. And its golden horn shone as if that gold were molten and the horn itself held the light of the sun. It pranced upon the bright green sward, beneath a sky the color of a brilliant robin's egg.

When I had first seen the unicorn, it had taken my breath away to see such magnificence in our everyday world. Now, though, the unicorn was even more incredible, surrounded by a world as beautiful as the beast. It was enough to stop your heart and be overjoyed that this might be the last thing your eyes beheld before you went to the grave.

This was where the unicorn belonged. I had no need to ask why the creature knew this place was magic. These Eastern Kingdoms, this "fairy land," as Alea had called it, was where the unicorn must have been born.

"Come," the unicorn said. "I will lead you."

I quickly instructed the others to gather up their belongings and follow us.

"Do you know the way to Mother Duck's?" I asked the unicorn as I shouldered my pack and the Brownie once again climbed onto my other shoulder.

"I know much about this place," the splendid beast answered. "For many years it was my home, until I found a reason"—the beast glanced significantly in my direction—"to seek other things outside. There are all sorts of sights I might show you." It lowered its wondrous eyelids, halfway closing its soulful eyes. "I know . . . private places as well."

"Indeed," I replied. "I am afraid that our need to meet with Mother Duck precludes any extensive side trips."

"As you wish." The unicorn sighed. "I only pray that when our business is done, you spare some small thought for those of us with . . . other needs." With that, the wondrous creature turned and walked down a trail into the woods. I beckoned for the rest of our group to follow.

Our first hour or two was uneventful. We traveled slowly but steadily through the Eastern Woods until we heard the hammering.

"Doom," Hendrek commented behind me.

I cautioned the others to be quiet. Perhaps we might be able to sneak up on the noisemakers. Normally, the tremendous racket my own group caused would have made this quite impossible. However, the hammerers were so incredibly loud that I felt we might still have a slight chance.

Cautiously, the unicorn led the rest of us down the trail.

Hendrek walked up to my side.

"Doom," he whispered. "Who could they be?"

"Well they certainly aren't Brownies!" Tap retorted. "Listen to that noise. No technique at all!"

I motioned both of them to be silent. I thought I heard voices. And sure enough, as we walked I could hear the rudiments of a distant conversation.

"What do you think you're doing?" The voice was the same gruff one I had heard the night before.

"Why are you picking on me?" a somewhat more highstrung voice replied. "Why does everybody always pick on me?"

Someone else yelled something incoherent. Then somebody coughed. I would recognize that cough anywhere. We were approaching whatever had surrounded us the night before!

I walked into the rear end of the unicorn. It had stopped to listen to the voices. I apologized to the magnificent beast, and it said it understood perfectly, especially since we were in public.

"Why did you stop?" I asked the beast.

The unicorn tossed its mane distractedly. "I know those . . . individuals up ahead. I was thinking about taking another route. One that would avoid them."

"Doom," Hendrek remarked. "Are they dangerous?"

"Well"—the unicorn considered—"no, not really. But they're very, very unpleasant. Why don't we take another trail? It will only add on half a day's march."

I told the unicorn we couldn't afford the time. We would have to march toward the hammering.

The unicorn sighed. "If they won't listen to me, what can I do?" Reluctantly, it led us down the road once again.

We turned a bend in the path and there they were, hammering together another sign:

> You are now entering
> THE EASTERN KINGDOMS!
> Don't say we didn't warn you

But who were they?

Or, more specifically, *what* were they?

SIXTEEN

"When meeting happy woodland creatures
Be careful what you do,
For many woodland creatures
Are only happy eating you!"

—"Woodland Wonderland" (verse six), excerpted from
THE DAMSEL AND DRAGON SONGBOOK
(still awaiting publication)

"Oh, no! Not you again!"

One of the hammerers scowled in our direction. The other half dozen or so turned to look at us as well.

"See?" another of their number shrieked. "I told you they were picking on us!"

"Oh . . . wow," a third added. Still another one coughed.

I wondered again exactly who, or what, these fellows were. They were short, about the size of Snarks, although their features were not demonic in the least. They had large, round heads, and bushy brows that seemed to accentuate their emotions, so that the fellow who scowled at us seemed the very picture of disgust.

There was an uncomfortable silence, broken only by one of the fellows' continued coughing. Very well. This situation called for leadership. More than ever before, it was time for me to live up to my position on this quest.

"Indeed?" I queried. "I am afraid we cannot 'pick on you,' as you put it, until we know who you are."

One of the small fellows jumped down from where he had been working on the top of the sign, wringing his hands as he approached us.

"Oh, certainly, certainly, most honored sirs," he began. "Please take no offense from the manner of my fellows."

"They cannot be Brownies," Tap asserted. "No manners at all."

"Oh, might I please beg your pardon?" the hand-wringing hammerer pleaded. "Oh, noble sirs, who are obviously far more knowledgeable than myself and my poor companions—"

"Speak for yourself!" the scowling fellow interjected.

The hand-wringer smiled apologetically and continued. "But as I was saying, although I am sure that we are as mud beneath your feet—"

"Oh, yeah?" the scowler retorted.

The fellow of the wringing hands smiled even more apologetically. ". . . indeed, some of us are more like the worms in the mud beneath your feet . . . but as unworthy and pitiably valueless as we are, I believe you should know the smallest bit about us before you pass judgment."

"Indeed?" I prompted.

"Certainly! Oh, incredibly so, most valued sirs. And so, as inconsequential as we may be"—he glanced at his fellows. "Please! No further comments!" He cleared his throat—"I thought that I might introduce us. Of course, as you worldly-wise travelers have no doubt already surmised from our compact stature and industrious work habits, we are dwarves."

"Industrious work habits?" Tap began. "They couldn't buckle a shoe, much less hammer—"

I instructed the Brownie to quiet down.

"Dwarves?" I asked instead. This was interesting. I had heard of a group much like this one in an old tale, back when I was a boy. Could such stories be true in the Eastern Kingdoms? I decided it would do no harm to inquire.

"Could you be—"

"No, no, most esteemed sir!" the hand-wringer interjected before I could finish my sentence. "Although that would be an excellent guess, I fear it is incorrect. You see, we are the other ones."

"Indeed?" I replied. "The other ones?"

The fellow nodded rapidly, overjoyed that I understood. "Yes, we are the Seven *Other* Dwarves!"

Snarks stepped to my side. "Other dwarves? You mean there's more of these things around here?"

"What's it to you?" the scowling fellow inquired.

"Doom," Hendrek replied, the enchanted warclub Headbasher swinging free in his enormous hand.

"Now, now," the hand-wringer hastily interposed, "most incredibly intelligent and well-mannered visitors—to whom we are but the blemishes upon the worms crawling in the mud beneath your feet—I beg of you to but allow me to introduce my poor and most certainly overrated companions, and I shall be eternally grateful."

"Indeed?" I said again. I had my doubts if I wanted this fawning fellow to be eternally grateful (or eternally anything else) on my behalf. However, I had the feeling that if we did not suffer through his introductions, we might never find Mother Duck.

I asked the dwarf to proceed.

"Oh, bless you!" the hand-wringer cried. "I grovel at your feet in thankfulness. Even though I am no more than the dirt on the blemishes on the worms in the mud—but no, let my pitifully inadequate words introduce my fellows—"

"You can say that again!" the scowler barked.

The hand-wringing dwarf pointed to the fellow who had just spoken. "This is Nasty. As you remarkably fine gentlemen can certainly ascertain, he lives up to his name."

"I suppose it has to be me next!"

The hand-wringer nodded to a dwarf to the left of Nasty. "Touchy," was all he said.

"Do you have to be so abrupt?" Touchy wailed.

"I'd ignore them, if I were you," said the dwarf to Touchy's left. "I don't intend to have anything to do with them!" The speaker turned away, his nose in the air.

"And Snooty," the first dwarf added.

Another dwarf wandered into Snooty's backside.

"Why don't you look where you're going?" Snooty yelled. "Oh, why do I have to put up with such a lowlife?" The dwarf lifted his nose even farther aloft, imploring the heavens.

The fellow who was performing the introductions placed a hand on the bumper's shoulder. The other dwarf blinked repeatedly, as if he couldn't quite focus his eyes.

"And this," the first dwarf continued, "is Spacey."

"Oh," Spacey remarked, somewhat distracted. A moment later he added: "Wow."

The first dwarf waved his hand to include those fellows in the background. "And here, of course, we have Dumpy, Noisy and Sickly."

Dumpy moaned, Sickly coughed, and Noisy dropped something.

"Oh!" the first dwarf exclaimed, as if the thought had just occurred to him. "But most esteemed sirs, I have neglected to introduce my own ridiculously deficient self." He bowed low, kissing the dirt before my feet. "Most wonderful, most magnanimous, most enlightened gentlemen, who are so high above me that I am but a pinprick on the ground beneath your eyes; nay, even more, a pinprick upon a pinprick—"

"Get on with it!" Nasty yelled.

"Oh." The dwarf stood again, still all smiles, but also still not quite looking me in the eye. "Certainly. I, honored sirs, am Smarmy."

"There's no doubt about that," Snarks remarked.

"Indeed," I replied. "Very nice to meet you. Now, if you will excuse us, we must be on our way."

"Oh, no!" Smarmy cried. "A hundred thousand pardons, most incredibly wondrous sirs, but that would never ever do. Now that you are in our less than worthless company, I am piteously afraid that this is where you must stay."

"Doom." Hendrek raised his club above his head. "Are you trying to take us prisoner?"

"Oh, most certainly not!" Smarmy pleaded. "We would never use force against such honored gentlebeings as yourselves. However, as lowly and degenerate a speaker as I am, might I ever so gently *suggest* that you become our prisoners?"

"Indeed?" I replied, restraining Hendrek from using his club. "And why would you make that suggestion?"

"A million pardons that I should be so presumptive, oh astonishingly insightful travelers, but my humble suggestion, though probably barely worth your consideration, is in every likelihood a thousand times better than the alternative."

"Indeed?" I queried. "And just what is the alternative?"

Smarmy smiled even more apologetically than before, but his reply was only two words:

"Mother Duck."

"Where?" Touchy screamed.

"Oh, that I would have to deal with such people!" Snooty added haughtily.

"Oh . . . wow," Spacey remarked.

Sickly coughed. Dumpy moaned. Noisy dropped something.

"Doom," Hendrek murmured.

"Very probably," Smarmy agreed. "Especially if Mother Duck catches you wandering around alone in the Eastern Kingdoms with-

out her authorization. I sincerely believe that your chances are far
better if Mother Duck catches you wandering around the Eastern
Kingdoms with us."

I felt two small but strong hands grip my shoulders. An incredibly
worried face framed by blond hair thrust against my nose.

"Oh, Wuntie, I told you!" Alea whispered. "We'll be baked in the
giant's ovens!"

I gently moved Alea to one side, whispering back that we would
talk once I had learned all our options.

I nodded again to Smarmy. "Indeed. In both your scenarios,
Mother Duck catches us. Is there no other alternative?"

Alea clung tight to my arm. "We'll be mixed with flour and yeast,"
she murmured half to me, half to herself, "and baked into bread!"

Smarmy shook his head grimly, as if he were telling me the saddest
thing in the world. "Alas, not in the Eastern Kingdoms. Mother Duck
catches everybody."

"It's not fair," Alea continued. "My mother didn't raise me to die
being mixed with yeast."

Guxx Unfufadoo stepped forward, dragging Brax by his side.

"Commence!" he shrieked. Brax positioned his drum and com-
menced.

> "Guxx Unfufadoo, demon leader,
> Does not care who this Duck catches,
> Has no fear who this Duck threatens,
> Rather fancies Duck for dinner!"

"Is that so?" Hubert retorted. "To my side, Damsel! Number 341!"
Alea left my side at last to rejoin the dragon.
They sang:

> "We've got a toast of just one kind,
> For those we know with a ruling desire.
> You might possibly change your mind,
> When you've been toasted by Dragon Fire!"

"Indeed!" I shouted at the top of my voice. "You've both had your
say! You are now even. There will be no further singing or declaiming.
The truce goes back in effect *now.*"

Hubert and Guxx glared at each other, but neither spoke further.

I spoke again to Smarmy, "Still, the two of them do have a point. I doubt Mother Duck has ever encountered anything like us before. After all, we have demons and a dragon on our side."

"Not that it's going to do you any good!" Nasty sneered.

"Why do I have to always be around when these unpleasant things happen?" Touchy demanded of no one in particular.

"Oh . . . wow," Spacey added.

"I know that if I had my way, I wouldn't be with any of you!" Snooty exclaimed distantly.

Noisy dropped something. Sickly coughed. Dumpy moaned.

"Oh, most nobly deluded sire," Smarmy replied when his fellows were finally done, "the remarkable show of force that you mention might work elsewhere, but not with Mother Duck."

"Indeed," I answered. Somehow, this was going all wrong. We were on a mission to save the surface world, not start a war. I would simply have to explain myself better. "But you realize that a show of force is the last thing on our minds. We come in peace, to tell Mother Duck of a great threat that affects the Eastern Kingdoms as well as our homeland."

Smarmy wrung his hands in agreement. "All the more reason to join with us. When Mother Duck finds you, which she will whether you are with us or not, she will assume you are with our unworthy band for a purpose. She will then at least wait a few seconds for an explanation before deciding your fate."

"Doom," Hendrek interjected. "Deciding our fate?"

"Yeah, bumpkin!" Nasty added. "Or you could say 'choosing your death' instead!"

"Who are you calling a bumpkin?" Snarks demanded.

Nasty pointed at the warrior. "This blimp over here!"

"That's going too far!" Snarks rejoined. "Wuntvor, lend me your sword. Only I can call Hendrek a blimp!"

"Doom," Hendrek agreed. He swirled Headbasher through the air above Nasty's head.

"Indeed!" I called again. "Put down your weapons and lower your voices. There is no need for battle. In fact, a fight might keep us from our goal of meeting Mother Duck."

"How right you are, learned young master!" Smarmy chimed in. "That is why you must stay." The dwarf stopped wringing his hands, and wiped them nervously on his worn, brown leggings. "But to be totally frank, honest, and candid with you, there is a further reason as well. You see, if we do not capture you, Mother Duck will 'decide our fate' as well."

"She's like that!" Touchy agreed. "Oh, why do I always have to get into the middle of these things!"

"Indeed?" I replied. "Then perhaps we should travel with you. And as we travel, perhaps you can tell us something about this Mother Duck."

"Then you will be our prisoners?" Smarmy shouted gleefully. "Oh, a thousand thousand thanks. You have no idea what this means to my humble band, especially in terms of continued longevity."

"Fine," I said. "Now that we are under your care, what do you wish us to do?"

Smarmy frowned. "Oh, dear. We're supposed to do something? Yes, that would be a very good idea, wouldn't it? Mother Duck is very big on that, calls it 'advancing the plot,' she does. Oh, deary dear. Most of the time we simply hammer, you know, and put up these warning signs. Oh, my." The dwarf paused, frowning, then smiled for an instant before shaking his head and frowning again.

"I'm afraid I haven't the faintest idea," he said at last.

I told the dwarf it might be something to think about. He agreed wholeheartedly, said that he would consult with the other dwarves and definitely have a plan by morning.

I turned to my companions and instructed them to make an early camp. Mother Duck sounded like a very difficult character indeed. I had to do some thinking as well, or we might all wind up as some giant's dinner.

"Oh, Wuntie!" Alea trailed after me. "Something is wrong," she called. "You are so preoccupied these days. Have your feelings changed for me? Has the magic gone from our relationship?"

I turned back to stare at the damsel as she rushed forward to fling her arms around me.

Of course! That was the answer!

SEVENTEEN

" ' 'Tis as plain as the nose on your face' is another annoying remark that sages make. Think on it. When was the last time you went walking down the street, looking at your nose?"

—THE TEACHINGS OF EBENEZUM, Volume I

Magic!

It was so obvious, I didn't know why I hadn't thought of it before. I felt like kissing Alea, but stopped myself for fear it might lead to other things.

The only way we were going to survive the Eastern Kingdoms was through magic. But exactly what magic?

I thought at first of contacting Ebenezum. Yet what could he do at this great a distance? Besides, with what the Brownie had already been through, I doubted he had the energy for anything pertaining to Brownie Power. And even if the Brownie could manage to contact my master, it was the kind of magic, what with a dancing Brownie and a great cloud of dust, that rather called attention to itself.

But perhaps most important of all, I did not yet know the Seven Other Dwarves' true intentions. Even without talking to Ebenezum, I realized it was important to keep our various magical abilities to ourselves until I knew a little better what they had planned for us.

That was the real problem—just when should we use our magic? Perhaps it would be best to wait until we confronted Mother Duck. Then, if need be, I could resort to the Home Study Course. True, many of the recent spells I had attempted from that tome had not worked out quite as I had planned. Still, the law of averages demanded that I would eventually get a spell correct. Didn't it?

But no. I realized that the less time I had to master a spell, the more chance I had of it going awry. Handling emergencies with the Home

Study Course would have to remain a last resort. I needed someone here with a real mastery of magic.

It was then I knew. My heart quickened with the realization. We truly needed Norei.

"Wuntie?" Alea whispered huskily in my ear. "When you squeeze me like that, all my doubts are forgotten."

"Um?" I said. "Oh." In my enthusiasm for my new plan, I had forgotten that I had a young, attractive blond woman in my arms—a young, attractive blond woman who was looking very fixedly into my eyes. What could I say? "Indeed. Well, I'm afraid we don't have time for any of that right now, Alea. I must make plans."

"Oh, I'll forgive you this time," Alea said throatily as she stroked my arm. "When you hug that *recklessly,* I can wait."

"Yes . . . well," I replied. "Indeed." I shook the young woman from my arm and shrugged the pack off my back.

"Why don't you watch where you're throwing things?" Touchy demanded from somewhere behind me. The pack seemed to have landed in the vicinity of his head.

"Um . . . indeed," I began, somewhat distressed by this turn of events. "I beg your pardon—"

"You should beg our pardon for ever crossing our paths!" Snooty demanded.

"Oh, why bother with them!" Nasty remarked to his fellows. "They're all going to be eaten by giants anyway!"

Sickly coughed in our direction, and Dumpy's moan had a sinister undertone. Nasty told Noisy to walk over to me and drop something on my foot.

This seemed to be getting out of hand. Without Smarmy here to act as spokesbeing, the other dwarves were becoming definitely hostile. And where was Smarmy? Before he disappeared, didn't he say something about deciding our fate?

Maybe I should talk to Ebenezum after all. But where had Tap gotten to?

Noisy stumbled toward my pack. Was the dwarf going to attempt to drop it on my foot in retaliation?

"Watch out, Noisy!" Touchy screamed. "He's got a weapon!"

Who had a weapon? Were they talking about me?

Then I remembered I was wearing Cuthbert. Perhaps I should draw the sword and confront the dwarves with naked steel. That would certainly end all this confusion for good. Still, I wanted to avoid violence if I possibly could. Oh, why did everything always have to get so complicated?

I really wished I could talk again with Ebenezum. If only there were some way . . . .

Noisy once again trundled in the direction of my pack. I placed my hand on Cuthbert's hilt as a warning.

It was then I remembered.

Of course! Cuthbert was more than your everyday sword. Not only could it talk, but the sword had other magical properties as well. I had used it repeatedly to contact Ebenezum when I was in the Netherhells.

Then that was the answer! I had no need to wait for the Brownie; I would use Cuthbert instead. I looked around me at the glowering dwarves. Perhaps it would be best to talk to my master now, before the situation got any worse.

"Stand back, varlets!" I called as I attempted to pull the sword from its sheath.

The sword didn't budge. I tugged at the hilt with both hands, but it made no difference. It appeared to be stuck.

"Cuthbert?" I inquired with the slightest edge of desperation.

"I'm not coming out," the sword replied, its voice muffled but distinct. "I can hear raised voices. I know when there's going to be bloodshed."

"The only blood shed around here," Snooty remarked disdainfully, "will be yours."

"Eaten, eaten, eaten!" Nasty added.

"See?" Cuthbert retorted. "It's quite cozy in my sheath, thank you very much."

Snarks rushed to my side. "Ornamental paperweights," he whispered to the sword.

"Is—is that so?" Cuthbert replied, obviously wavering. "Well, maybe holding down paper wouldn't be such a bad job after all."

Noisy leaned down to pick up my pack, then stomped towards me with a smile. Hendrek stepped to my other side, Headbasher in his hand.

"Doom," the large warrior remarked.

Snarks leaned even closer to the sword. "Ornamental paperweights sculpted to look like me."

"A sword has some pride!" Cuthbert sprang from its sheath. "Stay away, now! Don't force me to do anything rash or"—I felt the sword shudder in my hands—"messy."

Noisy paused, looking doubtfully down at the pack in his hands. And then the pack moved.

Dumpy moaned uneasily. Sickly coughed a warning.

"Watch out!" Touchy shrieked. "It's one of those Western Kingdom tricks!"

"Eep!" the ferret screamed in Noisy's face. The dwarf dropped the pack and ran.

"Indeed!" I called, wishing to stop this nonsense as soon as possible. "We come in peace. We wish you no harm!" Mayhaps, I thought, I should resheathe the sword I now waved in my hand as a sign of my good intentions. And yet if I restored Cuthbert to its sheath, I somewhat doubted my chances of getting it to come back out again.

The dwarves continued to scowl at me, believing my brandished sword rather than my words.

"You just wait for the giants!" Nasty exclaimed.

I replied that it might be far better if both our parties waited for a while and settled down for the late afternoon and evening as we had first intended. The dwarves grumbled and walked off to eat on the far side of their newly erected sign. I told my companions that we should settle down as well, and added that I would take the first watch. I needed time for quiet contemplation.

Our current situation was becoming more unpleasant with every passing moment, and it promised to get much worse. The dwarves were not quite openly violent, but I had met friendlier demons in the Netherhells. I knew I had to take some action, but I thought it best if I tried something quiet. I feared that even contacting Ebenezum with the sword might draw too much attention. It would do me no good to speak to my master if, as a by-product, I managed to start a riot.

"Doom." Hendrek approached me. " 'Tis not a good situation for a trained warrior."

"Hey, Hendy," another voice said behind me, "this is not a good situation for anybody. Especially those among us not now equipped with high-quality, previously-owned magical weapons."

I did not have to turn around to identify the speaker.

Brax, straightening the lapels of his checked suit, strolled around in front of us. Hendrek lifted his enchanted club Headbasher as I hefted Cuthbert, showing Brax that we, at least, both had our magical weapons.

"No bloodshed!" Cuthbert squeaked.

"Now, now," Brax quickly added. "There is no need for a show of force. Our current situation constrains all of us. Yonder dragon cannot sing, my master Guxx cannot declaim, and I can find little time to ply my sincerely honest and valuable trade. We must do what we can to keep our spirits up."

"Doom," Hendrek agreed, eyeing Brax meaningfully. "How much better I would feel if I could bash something."

"Come now, Hendy, I haven't demanded payment on your high quality warclub since—"

"Something in checks," Hendrek interrupted.

"Now, just hear me out," Brax replied. "You may not like your payment schedule, but you have to admit that your dread Headbasher has given you first-rate magical service."

"Doom," was Hendrek's only reply.

Brax nodded briskly. "And that's exactly what you'll have if you can't properly defend yourself against whatever's going to happen here in the Eastern Kingdoms."

He lifted the bag he carried with him and shook it. The bag clanked significantly.

"Do you know what this bag is filled with? That's right—magical weapons; practically every weapon you'll ever need. We have broadswords, rapiers, daggers, penknives, letter openers, and corkscrews. And that's not all! Also in this pack you'll find powders, poisons, philters, and potions, and a surprise or two besides! And I'm willing to give it all to you for a special group rate! That's right, all the weapons in this sack can be yours for one low price, payable with the simplest Netherhells contract imaginable!" He hefted the clanking sack again. "How much would *you* pay . . ."

He paused, smiling up at me as if expecting an answer. He wanted to sell me all those weapons? I swallowed hard. What should I do? If he were to offer me only one or two, I definitely would have refused, fearing the Netherhells contracts. But all of them? What power they would give us! Maybe they were the magic we needed.

"Uh . . ." I began.

"Don't answer yet," Brax interrupted, whipping still another weapon from behind his back, "because you also get this enchanted battle ax at no additional charge! That's right, this cleaver goes through your enemies like a knife through butter. And it also slices vegetables!" He removed a carrot from his coat pocket and tossed it in the air. The battle ax neatly cut it in two. "It's great for making tasty snacks!"

"Quiet down over there!" Nasty yelled from the other side of the sign.

"Dwarves would probably make tasty snacks," Brax added, tucking the ax once again behind his coat. "Well, what do you say?"

"No bloodshed!" Cuthbert warned.

I looked at Hendrek.

"Doom," the warrior remarked.

Hendrek and Cuthbert were right. Upon sober reflection, I realized that stockpiling weapons was not the answer. From all I had heard of Mother Duck, I felt we had more of a chance convincing her through reasoned discussion than with a show of force.

"Sorry," I told Brax, "but your weapons do not fit in with our plans."

"Plans?" Brax asked. "We have plans?"

"Well, we will have plans," I assured him. "They will definitely be completed by tomorrow."

"Oh, but do we have plans for you!" Snooty called from beyond the sign.

"Should we"—Sickly coughed—"let the giants"—he coughed again—"get them?"

"Nah," Nasty replied. "I think we should save them for Mother Duck!"

They all laughed and coughed together.

I told Brax and Hendrek to ignore the derisive dwarves and get some rest. I tried to remain as calm as possible, casually flexing my sword arm as my companions turned back to our half of the campsite. I decided that at least for now, it wouldn't do any of them any good to see how truly concerned I was. For I felt this was one of the most serious situations I had faced since I had begun to quest. Whether we were going to encounter giants or Mother Duck, we needed all the magic we could muster. And not the blunt, brute-force magic of Brax's slightly-used weapons. We needed thinking magic.

I had to get Norei to join us.

But how could I contact her? And even if she knew of my problem, how could I be sure she would respond to my request? Once, not so long ago, we had been as close as two could be. Now I feared she would never talk to me again. Oh, if only we could start anew, like the two lovers we were meant to be!

I stared at my pack. But there was a way to start anew!

I reached inside and, briefly petting the ferret, lifted out the Home

Study Course. I would have to consult it one more time after all. But I would do it slowly, carefully, not allowing any mistakes. I had to succeed, if I were to gain Norei once again by my side.

My heart pounded in my ears as I turned to the index. My decision was made.

I would have to use the love potion.

EIGHTEEN

"What, exactly, is love? Why it's the most wonderful, even greater than the most wonderful—no, it's the greatest, even greater than . . . no, that still doesn't quite explain it. Rather, it's like the dawn light shining over a field of the most beautiful wild—but perhaps that is too metaphorical. But you know the feeling? Yes! Is there anything better? There's no need to answer. I'm glad I was able to explain."

—SOME THOUGHTS ON APPRENTICESHIP
by Wuntvor, apprentice to Ebenezum,
greatest mage in the Western Kingdoms
(a work in progress)

Here it was, on page 44: "The Universal Love Potion Spell." To my surprise, it was the least complicated spell I had found in the entire Home Study Course, full of simple ingredients and simple gestures. In a way, though, that made sense, for what could be more pure than love? I quickly set about locating the ingredients: fresh spring water, green leaves and wildflowers, as well as a few dried twigs for a fire. I then moved to the farthest edge of the clearing so I could pursue my magic without interruption.

I checked the incantation a final time. There was still one ingredient missing! I quickly ran and fetched Cuthbert.

"What are we doing?" the sword demanded as I picked it up. I assured it that I would do nothing violent in nature. I simply needed its sharp edge to cut off a lock of my hair.

"So I've been reduced to barbering?" Cuthbert replied, obviously not happy with the situation. "Don't you think a pair of magic scissors would be better for that kind of work?"

I asked him if he'd rather help out on a spell that required blood.

"Now that you mention it, you are getting a little shaggy around the ears," the sword allowed. "Would you like me to take a little off the top, too?"

I laid the suddenly subdued sword to one side and began preparations for the spell. First the making of the fire, then the burning of a leaf and a flower, then a spray of water into the flames; all performed, of course, with the proper incantations. Now it was time for the fresh-cut hair. I waited for some new remark from Cuthbert, say how my hair oil would dull its blade, but the sword only whimpered as I sawed.

I tossed the hank of hair into the flames. The fire burned bright blue. Now I would only have to say the final words and the spell would be complete.

But my concentration was broken by a noise, a rustling in the bushes just opposite where I stood. What could it be? Perhaps another visitor from Vushta? I realized I wasn't breathing. Could the spell have worked before I had even completed it?

"Why, look who we have here!" a distinctly male voice called.

"Yeah," another voice mocked. "Here."

I knew who it was even before I felt the knife at my throat. Grott, Slag, and Vermin, the three representatives of the Vushta Apprentice Guild, had found me.

"Thought you could get away from us by simply going on a quest to the Eastern Kingdoms?" Grott drawled as he emerged from the bushes. "How foolish that was, especially since your solution to our little problem is long overdue!"

"Yeah," Slag added as he, too, stepped into view. "Long."

Vermin's blade pressed against my throat.

"Um," I said. I had completely forgotten about these three and their demand for a cure for their masters by moonlight tomorrow. Except by now their deadline had come and gone; it would have been moonlight yesterday. I thought my forgetfulness was understandable, considering what had happened since my last meeting with the apprentices. But I wondered if there was any way I could get them to agree with me.

Still, I could not help but be impressed with their dedication in their search for me. If only they would use that fortitude in our cause! Unlike myself, who had spent most of the last months caring for a sneezing wizard, they had probably been learning magic from their mentors! If they could but put aside their quarrel with me for a time, what allies they would make!

"Indeed," I replied. "So you have followed me all the way into the Eastern Kingdoms. But things are different here from the safe streets of Vushta. In these strange lands we are all in peril for our lives. Under these circumstances, don't you think we could forget our little differences and all work together, for the good of Vushta and the surface world?"

"You have no cure, then?" Grott growled. "Well, perhaps we will forget after all, once Vermin has carved himself a small memento from somewhere on your chest. But remember, there is still a better way." Grott's smile turned positively jovial as he added: "Our forgetfulness can be bought, for a mere thirteen hundred pieces of gold."

"Thirteen hundred?" I blurted. Their price had gone up yet again.

"Uh—" Slag interjected.

"Oh, did I say thirteen hundred?" Grott waved his hand apologetically. "So sorry, a slip of the tongue. I meant to say fourteen hundred."

"Fourteen?" I exploded. "Where—"

"Uh, Grott," Slag interrupted, pointing past the other apprentice's shoulder.

"Not now," Grott replied curtly. "We are doing business." He nodded pleasantly in my direction. "Where will you find those fourteen hundred and fifty pieces of gold? Why, you're a magician's apprentice, after all. We thought you could come up with something."

"Indeed," I answered. This particular conversation was getting me nowhere. While I admired my fellow apprentices' single-mindedness in pursuing their goal, I felt their talents could be put to much better use in our present situation. But how could I convince these three to join us?

"I do not have the gold," I told the grinning Grott. "Nor do I have a cure for the malady that afflicts all our masters. However, if you were to stay and work with me in the Eastern Kingdoms, we will certainly encounter many wonders. Who is to say if, among those wonders, we might not find a cure? And who can say how much gold we might find besides?"

"Stay?" Grott replied. "Well, we will not go very far. After all, we have an investment here."

"Yeah," Slag hastily added. "Here. Uh. Listen, Grott—"

"Not now, Slag. You're ruining my timing!" Grott turned back to me and nodded sadly. "Poor Wuntvor. We do think it is a shame that you have neither the cure nor the gold. And just so you remember how important our business dealings are, I think it's time that Vermin took his little souvenir. That way, you'll be even more eager to have the fifteen hundred pieces—"

Grott broke off abruptly. A strained look came over his face. "Vermin, is that you?"

But, of course, Grott's knife-wielding companion still had his blade at my throat. Grott's back was pressed against the bushes. He reached a hand around to feel behind him.

"Slag?" Grott inquired.

"Yeah," Slag replied. "Unicorn."

"I certainly am," a magnificently modulated voice spoke from the bushes. "And a more wondrous and deadly beast you will never meet. Now, if you would please move yourselves into the middle of the clearing, where we can see what everybody is doing . . . ?"

Grott and Slag both obliged. The unicorn followed, his horn pressed into Grott's spine. Vermin pulled the knife away from my throat to warily study the mythical creature.

"Don't even think about it," the unicorn stated, "unless you want to become part of a picturesque tableau." The splendid beast snorted, the sound like the ringing of deep and sonorous bells. "You know, the kind of tableau that features great gouts of blood flying everywhere and poor humans writhing in their death agonies as the unicorn rears triumphantly, dark bloodstains tastefully mottled on its shining golden horn? Surely you've seen the scene. It's on thousands of tapestries."

"But you mistake our intentions!" Grott exclaimed hurriedly. "After all, we are but poor apprentices, just like Wuntvor here. We only wanted to have a little talk."

"And I imagine you like to talk with knives?" The mythical beast pawed the ground meaningfully. "Well, I like to talk with my incredibly sharp, glowing golden horn."

Grott's smile seemed a bit forced, "Vermin," he remarked between clenched teeth. "Why don't you put away your knife?"

The other apprentice sheathed his blade.

"Now, we were discussing the best way for Wuntvor here to furnish us with fifteen hundred and fifty pieces of gold."

"I think it might be time," the unicorn replied, "to discuss instead where you would like the holes gored in your body."

"Yeah," Slag said. "Good-bye." Both he and Vermin ran for the underbrush.

"Wait for me!" Grott bolted away from the unicorn with a speed I had never seen in him before. "Remember!" he called to me over his shoulder. "Sixteen hundred pieces—" And then he, too, was lost in the bushes.

I told the unicorn that I didn't know how I could express my thanks.

"I have an idea or two," the incredible beast replied. "My head's gotten awfully heavy after all that threatening."

"Indeed," I responded, "Perhaps later. Unfortunately, at this moment I am in the middle of a spell."

"Sorcery?" The unicorn sniffed. "But aren't *I* magic enough?"

I apologized again. The unicorn walked slowly back toward camp, a broken mythical beast.

But what had happened to my spell? I turned to my fire, but the flames had gone out. There was nought left but a few glowing embers. And I was so close to success! I had completed all but the very last portion of the spell. What should I do?

Someone stirred among the sleepers. I thought I heard a muffled "doom." My altercation with the apprentice guild must have roused some of my fellows. I had no doubt that one or more of them would be joining me momentarily. That made my decision easier. I did not have time to entirely begin the spell again. I would have to complete it as quickly and best as I could.

I piled what twigs and leaves I still had atop the fire's remains and blew on the embers until flame started to lap around the dry wood. I would have to finish my incantation speedily and hope for the best. I looked at the flames. The fire was the wrong color, bright yellow flames where they should be blue.

Well, that was easily solved. I reached for Cuthbert.

"Now what?" the sword demanded. "You can't fool me! I heard the threats!"

"Indeed," I answered. "I assure you that we are now quite alone. I only need you to cut a bit more hair."

"Barbering again?" was Cuthbert's response. "Is this going to be a regular activity? I mean, things like this get out, they could ruin a sword's reputation. I can hear the other magic swords now. 'So how you doing, Cuthbert? Shave any faces lately?' Oh, the shame!"

I ignored the sword and used its edge to chop off another chunk of hair.

"It's not that I don't have dreams," Cuthbert continued as I worked. "It's all this traveling around. It gets so wearing, especially when your owner won't put you back in your scabbard. Oh, would that I could settle down, away from all this bloodshed and strife. Perhaps a nice wall somewhere, hanging half drawn from my sheath so that I might watch the hustle and bustle around me. But no. I am forced to lead the life of a vagabond sword, traveling through whatever bloodstained region my master—"

I put the sword back in its scabbard. I had to concentrate. I looked a final time at the spell in the Home Study Course.

"Having done all these things"—the book said—"the final step is most important. Taking a hank of fresh-cut hair from your head, plunge it into the fire and recite the words below. Remember, as you recite these words, place in your mind the image of the loved one you wish this spell to affect. The fumes of this potion will then reach out to your beloved, wherever he or she may be. Again we emphasize, concentrate on your beloved, for the strength of this spell will vary with the purity of your thought."

I threw my hair into the fire and the flames again burned blue.

"Norei," I whispered, then began the incantation.

"Doom!" boomed from the campsite.

"Now that's Brownie Power!" Tap answered.

"Let me go," Snarks retorted, "or we'll have Brownie Power for breakfast!"

"In my humble and most likely worthless opinion," Smarmy added, "the little fellow is completely correct."

Then everybody started to talk at once. I glanced back at the fire, but the blue flames were gone. And what of the love spell? I would have to hope that my incantation had worked before I was interrupted.

The voices back at the camp were growing louder by the moment. My companions and all the Seven Other Dwarves seemed to be shouting at once. I supposed I would have to go back and quiet things down.

"Indeed!" I called out as I walked towards them.

"Wuntvor?" they cried in unison. A sudden silence fell among them. That was odd. Maybe they were accepting my leadership at last.

But why were they all looking at me so strangely?

NINETEEN

"There are many definitions of love. The starving man, about to chew greedily on a roast chicken leg, is sure to give you one predictable view. The recently cooked chicken, however, may be of a different opinion."

—THE TEACHINGS OF EBENEZUM, Volume LVIII

"Oh, Wuntie!" Alea screamed. "At last we can be together!" She ran towards me, smiling as though she hadn't seen me in weeks.

"Oh, no, you don't," the unicorn thundered magnificently. "I saw him first!" And with that, the mythical beast also galloped in my direction.

I stopped, open-mouthed. What was happening here?

Guxx stepped forward, dragging Brax after him.

"Elucidate!" the chief demon cried. Brax winked at me and began to beat on his drum. Guxx bellowed in my direction:

> "Guxx Unfufadoo, heartfelt demon,
> Wants to speak of admiration,
> Wants to pledge his faith undying,
> Wants to get to know you better!"

"Oh, yeah?" the dragon bellowed. "Well, you ain't heard nothin' yet!" He began to sing:

> "Here's an apprentice that's just the nicest,
> You want him there in any crisis,
> Even though he's kind of awkward and shy.
> His adolescent charm is so revealing
> How could clumsiness be so appealing?
> You could say that Wuntvor's my kind of guy!"

This was getting stranger by the moment. And Guxx and the dragon were once again ignoring my edict about declaiming and singing. Perhaps an "indeed" would be in order here.

But before I had a chance to utter a single word, Alea was upon me. Literally. She threw herself against me, and I could not keep my balance. Then, once I was down, she covered me with a barrage of kisses.

"Uh," I began. "Al—" I found that I didn't have enough time between kisses to speak her full name, ". . . eee . . ." Instead I was reduced to uttering but one syllable at a time. ". . . a!"

"That's my name," she purred, "and from your lips it becomes music!"

"Alea!" I repeated, trying to take advantage of this few second's reprieve. "Would you please"—she started in again—"let"—I tried to struggle, but it was no use—"me"—her grip was like iron—"breathe!"

She lifted her lips from my own, a look of concern on her countenance. "Oh, forgive my ardour, most dear Wuntvor. It's just that I have missed you so."

She missed me? But I had only been standing on the other side of the clearing! What madness was this?

"Stand away from that innocent lad, you hussy!" a magnificently dynamic voice demanded. "You are not worthy to kiss his toes!"

"What?" Alea stood up and glared at the unicorn.

"Yes," the unicorn sighed, "and what wonderful toes they are! Not to mention his legs, his arms, his shoulders, his ill-cut hair! And"—the splendid beast paused, somewhat overwrought—"what of his lap?" A small groan, half despair, half desire, escaped from between the unicorn's pearly teeth. "I dare not speak of it, lest the thought drive me wild!"

But Alea was ready to speak and more. "What do you mean, I'm not worthy of Wuntvor's toes? I'll have you know that I'm one of the most sought-after performers in all of Vushta."

"My point exactly," the unicorn replied dryly.

"Hah!" Alea retorted. "Look at this hair"—she grabbed two great handfuls of glistening blond strands—"these lips" her exquisite mouth pouted tantalizingly—"this exquisite womanly form!" She proceeded to pat other parts of her anatomy. "This is what Wuntvor desires! Not some overstuffed horse with a bump on his nose!"

"Overstuffed!" the unicorn responded, pawing the ground. "Bump on my nose? I would be offended, if those words had not come from an *actress!*"

"How dare you!" Alea demanded. "I'll act all over *you*, you big, stupid—" She sputtered, waving her fists at the magnificent beast.

I stood up as the two of them argued. They seemed to have forgotten about me completely. I walked past them towards the others.

"Doom," Hendrek greeted me as I approached. "But perhaps not, now that you are here." To my horror, the large warrior smiled.

"Good old Wuntvor!" Snarks shook my hand. "Why, you're the best clumsy, pimply-faced apprentice with bad posture I've ever had the pleasure to know!"

Snarks had complimented me. I stared stupidly down at the hand he had so heartily shaken. Something was definitely amiss.

"Oh, Wuntie!" Alea called from where I had left her. "Don't run from me, lover! I cannot exist without you!"

"How can someone like you know what love is?" The unicorn snorted proudly. "A mythical beast like me *is* love."

It couldn't be. I felt a cold spot, deep in my innards, as if I had a snowball in my stomach. They were all talking about—but, no. I shuddered to even think of it.

Could something have gone wrong with the love spell?

"Wuntvor!" Alea commanded. "We must be together always. I must feel you in my arms!" She ran towards me again.

"You cannot fight it!" the unicorn cried as it also galloped in my direction. "Your lap and my head were destined to be as one!"

"Indeed," I remarked hastily, glancing at my nearby companions. "Uh, fellows? Could you keep those two away from me for a little while? I need to think."

"Doom," Hendrek grinned. "Anything for you."

"Of course!" Snarks skipped after the warrior. "I tell you," he said musingly, "I just want to pinch his pimply-faced cheek."

Hendrek and Snarks were joined by Guxx, Brax, and Hubert. That was good. The five of them would save me, at least temporarily, from the overaffectionate advances of Damsel and unicorn. I could not doubt that it was the love conjuration. But what had gone amiss?

I had followed the spell exactly as instructed by the Home Study Course; except, of course, that I had let my hair burn before I had completed the magic, and so had added some more. Perhaps I had made the spell too powerful. But I had thought of Norei when I finally completed the spell! At least, I had thought of her for an instant. Then there had been that commotion between my companions and the dwarves, and my attention had been temporarily distracted.

Could it be?

The ball of ice in my belly turned to a boulder. I had turned to look at everybody in mid-spell. Did that mean I had worked my love spell on the entire camp?

The Seven Other Dwarves smiled at me.

"Why, Wuntvor's not such a bad fellow, compared to some I could name," Snooty remarked.

"Yeah," Nasty added. "Actually, he's kind of cute."

"Why didn't you ask me?" Touchy interjected. "Anything you want, Wuntvor, we're at your service!"

"Indeed," I replied. What else could I say? The spell was insidious. Everyone in camp seemed to be affected. Those who hadn't liked me before had become my friends, and those who had previously been attracted to me, I would have to fight off with Cuthbert.

But what of Norei? My magic had originally been meant for her. This, then, was the final irony. In dissipating the spell, had I lost her forever? The ice seemed to overtake my whole form.

"A happy Brownie hello!" Tap called from somewhere near my ankle. "And may I say it's a pleasure to work for you! It fills my heart with Brownie admiration!"

"That's true," Smarmy added, stepping up next to the little fellow. "That's what we call Brownie Power!"

"Indeed?" I said, although my heart wasn't in it. My heart was far away, with a woman I would never see again!

"Yes!" Tap agreed with the dwarf. "And all that great Brownie Power is here for you, the most worthy of worthies!"

"Oh, dear," Smarmy interrupted. "But may this humble and obviously pitiable fellow beg to differ? While this young human is certainly worthy, not to mention lovable as lovable can be, he is most unfortunately completely lacking in Brownie magic!"

"Too true," Tap agreed sadly. "But can we fault him for being far too tall and far too human? Remember, we Brownies must be generous with our gifts."

Smarmy nodded happily. "That's Brownie Power!"

Snarks returned then. "We've got the girl and the horse under control, at least for the moment. I just thought you'd like to know. I am at your service." He eyed the Brownie suspiciously. "Do you need me to take care of anything else?"

"Oh, most humbly no," Smarmy answered. "We Brownies will take care of everything!"

Snarks turned a deeper shade of green. The dwarf's remark seemed to render him temporarily speechless.

"Indeed?" I asked, curious despite my misery. *"We* Brownies?"

"Well, perhaps this worthless individual is counting his dragons before they are hatched," Smarmy admitted. "Or at least, I was worthless! But I was fortunate, for Tap took me aside and showed me the way." Smarmy smiled down at the Brownie. "I have seen the truth in Brownie Power, and Tap has accepted me as one of their own!"

"I've already made him an honorary Brownie," Tap added. "All he needs is ratification from the Brownie Council!"

"I am a little large," Smarmy explained, "but Tap says they will in all probability make an exception."

"Soon," Tap piped merrily, "there will be Brownies everywhere!"

"Doom," Snarks whispered.

"It has been a dream I've had," the Brownie continued, "to show others the wisdom of the Brownie Way, ever since I came here to prepare the way for his Brownieship . . ."

The Brownie paused, turning a shade of green almost as colorful as Snarks.

"His Brownieship!" Tap whispered, true horror distorting his countenance. "I forgot. All this talk of quests, and I so wanted to teach Snarks—his Brownieship would go to Vushta, expecting me—" The little fellow hit his forehead with the palm of his hand. "Oh, dear, is my buckle bent! My lace is frayed for good!"

"Indeed," I commented. I felt sympathy for the small fellow. As surely as I had forgotten about the Vushta Apprentice Guild and their demands, Tap had not remembered that his Brownieship was still to arrive in Vushta with an important message. And when the Brownie's ruler finally came, Tap would be far away in the Eastern Kingdoms!

"You could always go back to Vushta," Snarks suggested, "and stay there."

"No, my place is here with Wuntvor. A Brownie never backs out on a quest." Tap paused, his face a mask of anguish. "Oh, I will never make shoes again!"

"Alea!" the dragon roared behind me. "Forgive me Wuntvor! I could not fry a dancing partner!"

I turned to see the damsel almost upon me. She grabbed me by the shoulders and wrenched me to the ground.

"They tried to keep me away from you," she whispered hoarsely. "Rather they should try to keep the sun out of the sky!"

"Um," I replied.

"Or grass from growing in the ground!" the damsel continued, hugging me close. "Or water from filling the ocean! How can I say it?" She smiled with sudden inspiration. "I know! I will sing it instead!"

"Must you?" Snarks asked.

Alea ignored him and burst into song:

> "He's my apprentice!
> He's the only one for me,
> And Heaven sent us
> To live forever happily!"

"Apparently she must," Snarks remarked. Across the clearing, I heard Guxx begin to sneeze.

"Oh, Wuntie!" Alea squealed, and launched into the second verse:

> "He's my apprentice!
> And what am I to do?
> The perfect world is lent us,
> In love with my little Wuntie-poo!"

"Could this get any worse?" Snarks wailed.

And then the unicorn was in our midst, snorting wonderfully at Alea.

"You think to win this lad's favor with your song?" The beast tossed its splendid head, its mane flowing magnificently in the wind. "Well, we mythical creatures know poetry as well. Remember, a unicorn *is* art!"

The beast turned to look at me with its large, soulful eyes.

> "Oh Wuntvor, do not be forlorn,
> For you can stroke my golden horn."

It tossed its head, its forelocks blowing wonderfully in the evening breeze.

> "There's no need to suffer pain,
> When you might ruffle my wild mane."

The unicorn paused, lowering its head so that its wondrous horn almost touched my lower ribs.

> "And you needn't wander 'round the map,
> For I'll lay my head upon your lap."

"I was wrong," Snarks whispered. "It got worse."

Alea stood, ready to confront the mythical creature. "What do you mean," she demanded, "reciting poetry for my Wuntie? Don't you know I'm the one that can give him what he needs?"

The unicorn shook its perfect mane. "All 'your Wuntie,' as you call him, needs, is a magnificent horned head upon his lap!"

"Is that so?" Alea screamed, rushing the unicorn. "I'll give you a magnificent horn . . ."

They were at it again. I crept away from them as quietly as I could. Still, escape was only a temporary solution. I knew they would be on me again in a matter of moments. I had to get out of this somehow, and I feared I needed more magic than was at my command.

It was time to call on Ebenezum.

"Tap!" I beckoned to the Brownie. "I need your help!"

Tap and Smarmy rushed to either side of me.

"At your service, oh glorious leader!" the Brownie chirped.

"I need to contact my master, now," I informed him urgently. "Are you up to it?"

Tap hesitated. "That means talking to Vushta? But what if his Brownieship . . ." He sighed, then grimly straightened his jerkin. "No, you are right. This is a job for Brownie Power!"

Smarmy applauded. Snarks asked to be excused.

"Yes, we are ready," Tap answered at last, his tiny voice filled with determination. "For Smarmy here will help me dance. It will be his first lesson in Brownie magic!"

"Indeed?" I said, wondering if the dwarf were up to it. But I had no time to argue. If I didn't get my master's assistance, I didn't know how I was going to get out of this.

"Very good." Tap nodded to Smarmy. "Now follow me. First you move your right foot, cool and tight, then you wriggle to the left and you . . ."

I glanced nervously about as Tap finished giving the honorary Brownie his instructions. Alea was tugging on the unicorn's mane while the beast used its horn to muss the damsel's hair. This was getting ugly. I urged the Brownie to redouble speed.

"For you, anything!" Tap cheerfully agreed.

"That's Brownie Power!" Smarmy added.

All four of their feet began to move so fast that I could no longer follow them. We were surrounded by dust. The world around the three of us disappeared in an instant, replaced by the brown wall on which images of Vushta already flickered.

"Master!" I called.

"Wuntvor?" my master asked just before he sneezed. "I will be ready for you in but a moment!" I knew that meant he had to reach the protective enclosure of his gigantic Brownie shoe.

The picture on the dust wall began to gain definition and color. It was the courtyard of the Wizards College, with Ebenezum's shoe at the very center. I caught a glimpse of one sleeve of my master's robes, the dark blue tastefully embroidered with silver moons and stars, as Ebenezum lowered himself within his protective barrier. The sight of the robe was oddly reassuring, as though I were looking at a little bit of home. I was doubly glad, then, that I decided to contact my master; I felt calmer already. For the first time in quite a while I felt that perhaps everything would truly work out for the best.

The earth shook.

Oh, no, I thought. Not now! The Netherhells couldn't be attacking again!

But the quake was not repeated, at least not for a moment. And when it came a second time, it was again a single tremor, as if someone had made a mallet from a thousand trees and was pounding it slowly against the earth. It had to be something other than the Netherhells. Didn't it? I could not see or hear outside of the dust cocoon. I hoped that whatever it was, it would allow me enough time to speak with Ebenezum.

The ground shook again, with such force that it knocked all three of us from our feet. Without Tap and Smarmy's constant dancing, the dust cloud began to settle and our surroundings became dimly visible.

I did not at all like what I saw outside.

"Buckles and laces!"

Tap and Smarmy saw it as well, and could do nothing more than stare, open-mouthed. The dust around us was almost gone.

"Indeed!" my master called. "Wuntvor—"

But the spell was broken. And in its place stood the largest shoe I had ever seen, perhaps five times the size of the one that contained Ebenezum.

"Is this Brownie Power?" Smarmy said in awe.

Tap shook his head. "I believe this is even beyond us."

I decided I should breathe again. But if this wasn't Brownie Power, what was it? Then I noticed that the shoe was connected to a pants leg that rose into the sky.

There was another noise. It was either a mountain falling or the loudest voice I had ever heard, saying "Oops!"

"What do you mean, oops?" Touchy demanded.

I looked up, and I do mean up, at a figure whose hair brushed against the clouds. The tallest creature I had ever seen smiled apologetically and waved to his left.

"I seem to have crushed this half of the forest," the giant replied, somewhat abashed.

"Well, if you'd only stop dragging your feet!" Nasty replied. "Can't Mother Duck find any better help?"

"Come on, fellows," the giant chided. "Is it my fault if they don't build trees any bigger?"

"The trees are perfectly fine for me," Snooty insisted.

"Well, you still have all the rest of them. As you see I carefully placed my right foot in this clearing." The giant glanced back at his other foot, which was resting in the distance on a recently deforested hilltop. "Oops. Well, I'm afraid you've lost a few more. If only forests didn't have trees so close together."

"So that's why you've come here?" Nasty demanded. "To destroy our homeland?"

"On the contrary!" the giant insisted. "Destruction is the farthest thing from my mind."

"Pity it isn't the farthest thing from your feet," Nasty snapped.

"Never mind," the giant rumbled. "I am here on official business. You see, Mother Duck has heard that strangers have entered her domain. Strangers whom I must carry away!"

"Strangers?" Sickly coughed.

"Not here!" Noisy bellowed.

"Begging your extremely enormous pardon," Smarmy added, "but we have seen no strangers. Rather, we have only been visited by our extremely close friend and his companions."

"Is that so?" the giant mused. "No strangers? Then I suppose I must carry off an extremely close friend and his companions."

"No!" all Seven Other Dwarves wailed together as they clustered around me. "You can't take him!"

"Ah." The giant smiled. "So this is their leader. That makes things simpler. He will be taken and questioned first."

"Oh, no, you don't!" Hubert the dragon shouted defiantly. "I'll make Wuntvor glad that he included us on his quest. Take that, giant!"

The dragon reared to his full height and shot a lance of flame at the giant's knee.

"Oh. That feels good," the giant remarked as he gently picked up Hubert and placed him to one side. "Mayhaps when we have a little more time, I will have you play some fire over my sore shoulder."

The giant reached for me. Each finger was the size of one of the trees he had just crushed. What should I do? I thought of drawing Cuthbert, but even if I could persuade the sword to emerge from its sheath, I doubted that the giant would feel much more than a pinprick no matter how I sliced and cut. He was huge! I had met giants before, but this fellow from the Eastern Kingdoms was three times the size of those we had in the west. Besides that, he was apparently in no mood to talk the situation over.

What could I do? I panicked and ran.

The giant's hand cupped down before me, splintering the outer edge of the woods.

"Excuse me," the giant apologized as he lifted me aloft, "but that's what is going to happen if you try to get away."

It was hopeless, then. I could only wait, a firm grip on my sword and pack so I would not lose them as the giant lifted me aloft between one huge thumb and forefinger. He placed me in the palm of his other hand.

"Comfy?" he asked.

"But you can't take him—" Smarmy began.

"Sorry, but it's been ordered by Mother Duck." The giant paused, surveying all those who stood in the clearing. "Would anyone care to question her?"

The dwarves all stared up at me, grim and silent.

"Good. We are off, then."

In a single stride we were out of sight of the others.

So I had been captured by a giant from the Eastern Kingdoms, to go to who knew what fate? For all I knew, this huge fellow was taking me to Mother Duck, which was where I wanted to go in the first place.

Of course, there were those stories about the giant's ovens that everyone kept going on about. Still, Ebenezum had told me to beware of rumors. Perhaps this situation was not as bad as it appeared.

"Please answer one question," I ventured. "Does Mother Duck really take intruders and bake them into bread?"

"Oh, that." The giant coughed gently into his free hand. "Let me put it to you this way. Which do you prefer, whole wheat or pumpernickel?"

TWENTY

"Before I came to be in the service of the wizard Ebenezum, greatest mage in the Western Kingdoms, I sometimes thought of life as nothing but confusion, with the world a whirling ball of chaos in which anything could happen to you and, given sufficient time, probably would. Since I have become an apprentice, however, I have revised my views, and now consider my earlier worries and fears nothing more than a glimpse at everyday reality."

—SOME THOUGHTS ON APPRENTICESHIP,
by Wuntvor, apprentice to Ebenezum,
greatest mage in the Western Kingdoms
(a work in progress)

Whole wheat or pumpernickel?

No! It would not be! I rebelled at going to my death, completely powerless.

But I wasn't completely powerless! My sword might not do any good against one so large, but I still had my pack, and within that pack was my Home Study Course! I soon had the pack off my back and the book in my hands. Now all I had to do was look up G in the index.

"Eep!" the ferret cried, jumping out of the pack and onto the giant's hand.

"Eh?" the giant said. "What's that? Oops!"

The hand fell away beneath me, and I fell with it. The ground rushed toward me with alarming speed. Both book and ferret went flying away.

I landed with a slap in the once again steady palm.

"Sorry, there," the giant remarked. "Hope I didn't shake you up too much. Didn't see that cottage. Well, at least it used to be a cottage. But what were you doing? You weren't trying to get away, were you?"

I glanced up at the giant. What could I do now?

I heard a tiny, tiny "eep" from far below.

I wished there was something else, anything, that would save me from my doom. But the Home Study Course was gone, and my ferret, too. I shook the pack a final time in frustration, as if I might get some magical solution to mysteriously appear.

Into my hand fell a small sliver of wood. A sliver of wood that had been given to me in Vushta!

What could I do? I was desperate. Perhaps I could distract the giant long enough to attempt an escape. I held the toothpick out to him.

"How about this?" I challenged.

The giant laughed. "How about what? You are actually holding something? I cannot see your threat."

I placed the toothpick in the palm of his free hand.

"What is this? A tiny sliver of wood? Odds bodkins!"

The wood grew in the giant's hand. It was then I remembered that this was no ordinary toothpick, but a weapon given to me by the wizards of Vushta!

The giant grasped the thing, which had grown to the size of a substantial tree trunk, between two great fingers.

" 'Tis a magical tooth pick!" the giant cried in surprise. "Mayhaps I shall use this. I can feel some bread stuck between my molars."

Smiling, the huge fellow brought the mystic wood to his enormous mouth. But he cried in surprise as the pick leapt from his hand, straight into his mouth!

"What?" the giant mumbled. "Methinks this wood has a mind of its own." He wrinkled his brow. "Oh, that feels good. No, not there! My gums are much too sensitive." He frowned. "I'll put a stop to this!"

He reached around his teeth with the fingers of his free hand. "Where are you?" He grunted. "Almost! The thing is bewitched. I will have it in a minute."

He ceased to speak then, for a time, cocking his head this way and that and prodding about his jaws with various combinations of fingers. His movements became more frantic as the minutes passed.

"It is only a toothpick," he said at last, pausing to calm himself. "I *will* get it free. If I could just rzzssmm."

"I beg your pardon?" I asked politely.

The giant pulled his hands from his mouth. "Reach it. That's what I said. If I could just reach it. But I am afraid I will need bff hrrzmms!"

"I'm sorry?" I asked.

The giant frowned down at me. I could tell he was getting annoyed.

"*Both hands!*" he repeated as he once again extricated his fingers from his mouth. "I will need both hands. Excuse me, I will have to put you down. There! A finger back here will do it. Almost. It's stuck just behind this tooth. I'll just dislodge it here and everything will be frsgglggsm."

So it was that I found myself back on the ground again as the giant staggered away, both hands stuffed in his mouth. I was free! The weapons of Vushta had once again done their work. And speaking of weapons, I realized that I still carried Cuthbert, thrust through my belt. The sword, which seemed so ineffectual when I was in the grip of the giant, somehow appeared much more useful now that I was back on solid ground.

Now all I had to do was find my way back to my companions and the dwarves. I had no idea how far the giant had carried me, although I imagined he took half a mile in a step. How many steps had we gone? Ten? Twenty? Certainly not more than thirty.

I swallowed grimly. I could be quite some distance from my companions; half a day's march or more. At least I knew the direction the giant had come from. Well, at least I thought I did. He had staggered around a bit as he tried to dislodge the enchanted toothpick. I would just have to make my best guess and hope I came across copses of ruined trees about the size of a giant's footprint. Who knew? If I could retrace the giant's footsteps, perhaps I might be able to regain the Home Study Course, and my ferret, too!

Clutching Cuthbert's handle for reassurance, I set out into the forest in what I hoped was the correct direction.

The woods were thicker here than they had been where we met the dwarves. The trees overhead blocked out what little evening light remained, save for a faint, rosy glow to the west, and I had to be careful not to run into tree trunks or what scraggly underbrush grew in the darkness. I could recognize no landmarks, for the giant had carried me here far above the trees. At last, despairing of having to walk through inky blackness, I drew forth Cuthbert. I would need his light to proceed farther, and with the sun gone, we would have to guess at the direction of our companions.

"Where are we?" the sword whispered once I had drawn him forth.

I told Cuthbert that I did not know exactly. We had to find our companions, and I would need his light.

"A civilized response," the sword replied as it glowed obligingly. "There has been so much shouting and movement of late, that it is nice to have a few moments of quiet. It seems as though, lately, every time I've been drawn, it's to fight some sort of monster or hideous demon. I tell you, it's enough to make a poor sword paranoid."

"Well," I replied, "all you have to do for now is light my way. I assure you that we are quite alone."

But as soon as I finished speaking, a wind sprang up, a chill night wind that turned my clothes to ice against my chest and legs.

"What's that?" Cuthbert cried.

The sword was answered by a chuckle so dry it would drain the water from a stone.

"Yes, Wuntvor," the same dry voice rasped, "you are alone, for the first time in ever so long."

I knew who it was even before I spun Cuthbert about to illuminate his skull-like visage.

"Is that who I think it is?" the sword whimpered.

Death sighed, the sound of winter's coldest gale.

"Ah," he said, "alone at last with the Eternal Apprentice."

What was he talking about? Even now I was not without companions. I held one in my hand.

"No, I am not alone!" I shook Cuthbert at Death. "I have my sword!"

"Leave me out of this!" Cuthbert wailed.

Death chuckled again. "Is this what you call a companion? A magic sword? No, I am sorry, apprentice, to escape my touch you will need more than an inanimate object." Death shrugged back the sleeves of his robes to reveal his white-bone arms. "But there is nothing I can say today that you have not heard before. You are mine now. Don't you think it's time we went to my domain?"

Death stepped towards me. He reached out a skeleton hand. I took a hasty step away, waving Cuthbert wildly before me.

"There are other uses for a sword!" I cried, desperate for some defense.

Death laughed. "Poor child. Neither can you hope to kill me. Death, my dear apprentice, holds a monopoly on killing."

Cuthbert whimpered again, and shook in my hand. "No, you don't!" I exclaimed, saying anything that came into my mind that might give me another few seconds of life. "You've called me the Eternal Apprentice! And you know I have companions! And uh . . . I'm sure they'll come and join me any second now!"

"That means we'll have to hurry, doesn't it?" Death grinned. "Come to me now, and the Eternal Apprentice shall be mine at last."

But a streak of reddish-brown leapt between Death's bony legs!

"Eep! Eep!" the streak exclaimed. My heart leapt within my chest. My ferret had found me!

"Oh, come now, Wuntvor," Death remarked, the slightest trace of irritation entering his sepulchral tones. "You know a ferret is not much of a companion either. If I am already taking the Eternal Apprentice, I do not think it would bother the cosmic forces overmuch if I were to take one tiny ferret as well."

I took a deep breath, knowing that Death's words should lead me to despair. But my hope had sprung anew. My ferret had found me much faster than I had thought possible. Perhaps I was not as far away from my other companions as I had imagined.

"But quickly, now," Death intoned. "I have other deaths to attend to."

His bony fingers leapt at me with astonishing speed. I reacted with a yell, lost my balance, and fell to the forest floor. Death's fingers closed above me.

"Come!" Death commanded. "This is childish! You are delaying the—"

For one brief instant the night around me was turned to day.

"There you are!" sang a voice from above.

I would recognize that raspy baritone anywhere. The light in the sky was Hubert's dragon fire! I saw the great wings spread wide as Hubert circled for a landing.

Death screamed the agonies of a thousand souls. "I will not be thwarted again! I will have you *now!* Though it may threaten the cosmic balance, I shall take ferret, and dragon, and apprentice, too!" One hand still reached for me. With the other, he pointed to Hubert. "Come now. In an instant it shall be done."

"What's going on here?" the dragon asked as he landed. "It certainly looks dramatic."

"Dragon! Ferret! Apprentice!" Death opened his jaw to shout: "I TAKE YOU N—"

"There you are!" half a dozen voices shouted at once. And all about me, stepping out of the woods, were my companions, with Norei at their center!

Something that felt like the north wind but sounded like a scream of rage stopped everyone where they stood. Then the gale was over as suddenly as it had begun. I turned around and Death was gone.

Hubert was the first to break the silence.

"Yes," the dragon whispered. "That certainly *was* dramatic."

"Indeed," I replied, somewhat shaken by the incident myself. I looked to the others, half expecting Alea and the unicorn to rush me at any moment with new protestations of affection. And what of Norei?

"Hello, Wuntvor," Norei said as she walked towards me. All the others, Alea and the unicorn included, kept their distance. "We were rather worried about you."

"Indeed?" I replied "Um . . ."

"It all started," Norei continued when it became evident that I could not finish my thought, "when I detected some errant magic in the area. I'm still not sure exactly what it was—well, it might have been an airborne love potion; either that or something to do with animal husbandry. At least that's what I think the spell was. Frankly, it was so awkward and diffuse that it was hard to tell. Somehow, though, the spell reminded me of you." She laid a reassuring hand upon my shoulder. "Not that I think of you as awkward"—she paused, then smiled—"except perhaps in an endearing sort of way."

I did not know what to say. Norei was speaking to me again!

"Indeed," I whispered hoarsely.

"And it's lucky I came along when I did," Norei added. "Can you imagine, not only had you been spirited away by a giant, but it did turn out to be a love potion after all, and all these around us had been affected! Well, the spell was so clumsy that it was simplicity itself to remove it, but then we had to rescue you as well."

"Doom," Hendrek interjected. "Luckily, something seemed to happen to the giant's sense of direction. We spotted him soon after we set about our search, stumbling about, back towards our camp. But you no longer seemed to be with him. Hubert went on ahead, to see if he could spot you."

"Which I did within a matter of moments," Hubert remarked proudly. "It's my theater-trained senses, you know. I can always smell out an audience."

"Indeed," I said at last. "I thank you all."

"I should say you should thank us!" Nasty sneered.

"Why do we always have to be the ones to go and rescue people?" Touchy demanded.

Sickly coughed. Noisy dropped something. So Norei really had counteracted my spell. Things, apparently, were back to normal.

"But how have you fared in finding Mother Duck?" Norei asked.

"Indeed," I replied, grinning at Norei. I could not take my eyes off her! "We are very close." How welcome a sight was her fire-tinged hair, her eyes of deepest green. "The dwarves assure me of that." How many times had I longed for this vision! "Um, could we talk alone for a minute?"

"Well, I suppose so, if you insist." Norei's smile broadened as she spoke.

I insisted, and told the others Norei and I needed a few minutes for a conference. The two of us walked through the trees until we were out of sight of our numerous companions.

"Norei," I whispered. I took her hand and drew her to me. It had been ever so long!

"Is this, perhaps, a new definition of the word conference?" she began sternly. But then she laughed. "I have missed you, too, Wunt—"

The quake came before she had time to finish her sentence.

"Oh, no!" I cried. " 'Tis the Netherhells!"

But it was much more than that, for at that moment there came a great crashing from the bushes. Were my companions rushing to join me?

And then there was a knife at my throat.

Grott and Slag stepped out from behind the knife-wielding Vermin.

"Ah," Grott sneered. "We are so happy that you have found a quiet spot at last. We hope the young lady doesn't mind if we have a little talk?"

"Indeed," I replied. "This young lady is a witch."

Grott and Slag got a good laugh out of that one.

"Yeah," Grott added. "And I'm the great wizard Ebenezum!"

"Yeah," Slag remarked. "Great."

There was another quake beneath our feet, much worse than the last.

"Indeed," I said when the quake had run its course. "And do you realize that we are about to be attacked by the Netherhells?"

Slag and Grott thought that that particular comment was even more hilarious.

"Look," Grott said, wiping the tears from his eyes. "Your pitiful attempts at distracting us are too funny for words. What are you going to tell us next, that our shoes are untied?"

"Yeah." Slag glanced hastily at his feet. "Shoes."

Grott frowned. "Well, perhaps that was a bad example. Anyway, all this talk is distracting us from our real purpose. We've come to collect the seventeen hundred pieces of gold you owe us."

"Seventeen hundred?" I exclaimed.

"And twenty-five," Grott added. "That's right. Seventeen hundred and twenty-five pieces of gold. Unless, of course, you've come up with a cure for our masters?"

"Wuntvor?" Norei turned to me. "Who *are* these people?"

That's when the earth tremors *really* started. Vermin fell to the ground, almost losing his knife. The rest of us soon followed.

When the dust cleared, we saw a table, behind which sat five demons.

"Oh, my," Grott commented. "You weren't kidding about a Netherhells attack, were you?"

"Point of order!" The small, somewhat undernourished demon at the far end of the table turned to regard the larger fellow who held the gavel. "Exactly where *are* we?"

The larger demon pounded his gavel. "We are in the presence of magic!"

"Where?" his undernourished comrade barked. "All this time you've been saying 'I know where Vushta is!' But have you been able to get us there?"

Grott stepped rapidly to my side. "Uh, about those seventeen hundred and fifty pieces of gold—I suppose we could negotiate."

The other three demons behind the table were becoming restive as well, grumbling as their two fellows continued their argument.

"I tell you," the gavel demon insisted, "I came here because I was following a spell."

"Of course!" the undernourished fiend shouted, shaking a finger at the other's gavel. "You don't mention it was the only spell you managed to find since we started looking. You also didn't mention that, of all things, it was a love-potion spell!"

"Not necessarily," the gavel demon said defensively. "The spell could have had something to do with animal husbandry."

Grott tore his gaze away from the fighting demons long enough to glance at Norei. His pale complexion became paler still. "Uh . . ." he began hesitantly, "Wuntvor, old comrade, you were joking when you mentioned Norei was a witch?"

"Indeed," I answered, "no."

"Indeed?" Grott replied. "Well, about those eighteen hundred and fifty pieces of gold . . . Perhaps we can agree on some sort of time-payment scheme."

"Wuntvor?" Norei asked. "What do you want me to do with these, uh . . . people?"

Before I was able to reply, I was interrupted by a particularly loud quarrel among two of the demons. After a moment the three other fiends managed to pull them apart.

"Hey," one of the noncombatants asked, "why are we fighting each other? There are humans over there!"

"That's right!" another demon wearing a flowered hat added. "And some of them probably know the way to Vushta!"

"Does that mean we can't eat them?" asked the only demon who hadn't spoken.

"Of course not," the flower-hatted fiend replied. "We have to find out where Vushta is. Then we can eat them."

"Let's just say you owe us nineteen hundred pieces of gold," Grott said hastily. "We'll discuss the exact terms when we're back in Vushta. Slag? Vermin?"

Unfortunately, Vermin took the mention of his name as a signal that it was once again time to take a memento from somewhere in the vicinity of my nose. He leapt for me with his knife as Norei barked a short, guttural spell. A tiny whirlwind sprang up around the three apprentices, spinning them away.

"Wuntvor!" Grott screamed above the wind. "That's nineteen hundred and twenty-five you owe—"

They spun into the arms of the committee.

"Do you think these three will do?" the flower-hatted demon asked as they grabbed the Vushtans.

The undernourished demon chewed and swallowed Vermin's knife. "Umm. Tasty."

"Fine," the gavel demon ordered. "Toss them into the hole."

Grott wrenched his head around to give me a final glance as he was pushed into the pit.

"Remember, Wuntvor, two thousand and fifty—" Then his voice was lost in the distance. Slag and Vermin quickly followed.

"Now," the gavel demon continued, "I think it's time we got down to some serious blood boiling."

"What's going on here?" a voice called out of the woods behind us. It was a woman's voice, as full of authority as that of my master. I knew who that voice belonged to even before I saw the bonnet and the high-buttoned shoes.

It was Mother Duck. She was a woman of middle age, rather tall, almost my size, and imposingly built as well. Everything about her, from the way she surveyed the crowd before her to the bold way she marched among us, said that she was a woman used to command.

The rest of my companions and the Seven Other Dwarves all rushed to join us.

"Doom," Hendrek remarked. " ' 'Tis the Netherhells."

"Yeah," Snarks added. "Don't you guys know when to quit?"

"I think we should boil that demon's blood first." The undernourished fiend pointed at Snarks.

Snarks started to shake as the Netherhells committee concentrated.

"Buckles and laces!" Tap exclaimed. "Could this get any worse?"

There was an explosion in our midst. Tap moaned.

"It's . . ." he managed weakly after a moment, "it's his Brownieship!"

"No thanks to you," his Brownieship stated darkly.

"Excuse me," Norei mentioned, "but certainly we should consider helping Snarks before the demons boil his blood?"

Norei had a point. Things had been happening so fast in the past few moments that I hadn't had time to react the way a leader should.

"Companions!" I called to those around me. "Forward! We must save Snarks from the committee!"

Hubert asked if I was absolutely sure about that, but even he joined the fray. The demons were badly outnumbered, what with Hendrek and his club, Guxx and his claws, Hubert and his dragon fire, not to mention Brax and any number of previously owned weapons. Then Norei joined in with her magic while Alea and the dwarves threw rocks to distract the fiends. It was time for me to talk quickly with Mother Duck.

"Indeed!" I called to the gray-haired lady. "I have traveled from far Vushta to seek your help."

"But wait!" his Brownieship interrupted. "You have not heard my urgent message!"

"I am sorry," I replied, "but there is no time just now. Mother Duck—"

I was interrupted by the descent of a giant shoe, crushing at least a dozen trees.

"Oops," the giant remarked.

"Richard!" Mother Duck looked up at the large fellow. "I'm glad you finally found us. Is this the one?"

Richard the giant peered down at me. "The one with the toothpick? Yes." He kicked his foot petulantly. Another two dozen trees met their untimely end. "Pumpernickel and whole wheat are too good for him. I think we should make him raisin toast!"

"Now, now, Richard," Mother Duck chided. "I have other plans."

"Are you sure you don't want to hear my pronouncement?" his Brownieship inquired.

"Oh, listen to him!" Tap entreated. "Please listen to him!"

His Brownieship glared at Tap. "I used to know a Brownie once who looked a lot like you. Of course, he would have waited in Vushta for me."

Tap moaned something about his eyelets being lost forever. I couldn't stand to see the little fellow in such pain. I would let his Brownieship make his pronouncement as soon as I introduced myself to Mother Duck.

"I will be with you in one second," I assured the Brownies.

"Indeed," I continued. "Mother Duck, as I was saying, I have come here from far-distant Vushta to seek your aid on behalf of my master, Ebenezum, and all the other magicians at the great Wizards College."

"Aid?" Mother Duck asked. "What sort of aid?"

I explained to her about the Netherhells plans to take over the surface world, culminating with the attack going on behind us even as we spoke.

"That?" Mother Duck shook her head curtly. "I can take care of that." She marched smartly off in the direction of the fighting.

I looked back to his Brownieship. "Now," I said, "I can hear your pronouncement."

"Wha—" His Brownieship tore his gaze away from the giant's enormous shoe. "Sorry. What wonders one finds in the outside world. Nice stitching, too." He reached inside his jerkin to retrieve a small roll of parchment, then glanced up at me and cleared his throat.

"A Brownie Pronouncement."

His Brownieship unrolled the scroll and read:

"To Whom It May Concern: Be it known that through certain arcane and difficult procedures known only to the ancient and revered society of Brownies, we have determined a fact of utmost importance that we believe has great impact on whatever quests are currently in progress. To be more specific, we have uncovered certain facts regarding Mother Duck. To be even more specific, these facts concern Mother Duck and the recent treaty she has signed with the forces of the Netherhells, dividing the soon-to-be conquered surface world into two kingdoms, one ruled by demons, the other by Mother Duck. For this reason, your proposed overtures to Mother Duck would seem . . ."

The Brownie's voice died as Mother Duck returned.

"It's been taken care of," she remarked dryly. "Even demons know that if anything happens in the Eastern Kingdoms, it is done by me."

"Oh, most certainly, Mother Duck," Smarmy agreed as he ran after her. "Anything you want us to do, Mother Duck?"

"I was going to ask her that!" Touchy blurted.

"If anyone should be asking things of Mother Duck—" Snooty began.

"Of course!" Mother Duck interrupted her dwarves with a smile. "Mother Duck has things for everyone to do. Now, why don't you be good little dwarves and gather together all the other intruders. They are now our prisoners!"

"Certainly, Mother Duck!" the dwarves shouted more or less together before they ran off to capture my companions. But then we would be prisoners of allies of the Netherhells! What could I do?

"Indeed," I began, "perhaps you did not—"

The woman turned to regard me with her penetrating blue eyes, as clear as a bright winter sky. "Mother Duck has things for everyone to do," she repeated.

"Indeed," I tried again, "but if you would only listen—"

"Mother Duck wants you to be quiet," she interrupted again. "Richard, if you would?"

The giant's hand scooped me up from behind, knocking my legs out from under me. I found myself once again in the giant's palm, a hundred feet above the earth.

"Where do I take him?" Richard rumbled. "To the bakery?"

"Oh, no, no," Mother Duck chortled happily. "You'll have to do without your bread, at least for a little while. Once I found out that this fellow was the Eternal Apprentice, why, my plans for him changed ever so much." She clapped her hands gleefully. "Oh, my. Mother Duck is going to have such fun!"

"To the Storybook, then?" Richard asked.

"Oh, yes, the Storybook!" She laughed brightly. "Take him there at once, my lovely giant and my energetic dwarves!"

"To the Storybook," Richard repeated, stepping carefully away from Mother Duck, heading, I assumed, deeper into the Eastern Kingdoms. We were soon out of sight of all the others.

"Indeed!" I called up to the giant. "What is this Storybook?"

The giant shrugged his massive shoulders. "You probably would have preferred the bakery," is all he would say. And he continued to carry me off into the night.

I sat back down in the giant's palm, helpless, at least for the moment, to alter my fate. There were so many questions: Would I see my companions again? Would I get a chance to talk to Mother Duck and somehow show her the error of her ways? Would I even live long enough to see tomorrow's sunrise?

"And what," I whispered aloud, "about Norei?"

Yet as dramatic as all these queries were, they paled before the one question that would not leave my head:

This time, had I failed my master forever?

AN
EXCESS
OF ENCHANTMENTS

To Heather,
who likes this sort of thing . . .

ONE

"Things are not always what they seem."

—Words (which some expected to be his
last) spoken by Ebenezum, greatest
wizard of the Western Kingdoms, when he
was discovered in close and personal
consultation with Queen Vivazia of
Humboldt by the queen's husband, King
Snerdlot the Vengeful. Unfortunately,
the following statements made by the
king to his elite assassin guards, as
well as the reply uttered by the wizard
as he climbed down the battlements of
Humboldt castle in his nightshirt,
have been lost to posterity.

Once upon a time, in a land very, very far away, there traveled a young lad who wanted to see the world. Now this lad's name was Wuntvor, and he wished to be an adventurer and visit that distant place from which every morning came the sun. As he grew toward manhood, he would look out his bedroom window each dawn as he awoke, and watch the sun rise. He began to think of it as his friend, and he imagined the blazing orb beckoned to him, calling Wuntvor to come and see its home.

So it was that Wuntvor left his native land and journeyed east. He walked for many days, until the days turned into weeks, but Wuntvor did not despair, for he was young and his heart was pure. The weeks became months, and still Wuntvor traveled on, for, although the sun seemed no closer than when he started, he knew that if he but tried hard enough and long enough, he would reach his goal.

Still, the way was long and tiring, with hills and mountains to climb and rivers and oceans to cross. Even one as young and pure of heart as Wuntvor found himself doubting the wisdom of his journey from time to time. So it was on a particular evening, when the sun had journeyed all the way from its home in the east to its resting place in the west. Wuntvor was weary from his day's march, and decided to camp in a secluded glen by the side of a babbling brook. He spread out his bedroll and ate a meagre meal of bread and cheese, listening to the nightbirds overhead.

"Alas," he said at last, more to himself than to the birds. "Will I never find the home of the sun?"

And a voice answered him:

"Why ever would you want to do that?"

Wuntvor started, realizing that the voice came from a small man who stood by his knee. After he caught his breath, Wuntvor answered:

"It is what I have always dreamed of. It is my heart's desire."

"Really?" said the small man, who was dressed all in brown and sported a pair of translucent brown wings. "Well then, you have come to the right place."

"And just what place have I come to?" Wuntvor inquired.

"Why," the little fellow said with a big smile, "you have come to f-f-fairyland—" He had quite some difficulty pronouncing the word. "—of course."

"Of course," Wuntvor agreed. "And if this is fairyland, who are you?"

"Why, I am—" The little fellow paused and frowned. "If this is f-f-f-fair-fairyland—" The fellow paused again. His face had turned a bright blue. He took a breath and resumed his speech. "If this is—uh —that place, then I must be a f-f—" His two tiny fists shot into the air. "I am no such thing. I am a Brownie! And proud of it! More than proud! In smallness there is greatness! Brownies forever!"

Wuntvor blinked. Something was wrong here. An old lady stormed down the hill. She did not look happy.

It was then that I remembered where I was.

"No! No! No!" the old lady screamed.

I was in the Eastern Kingdoms, but I had not come here to follow the sun. Rather, I was on a mission of some sort, sent here by my master, the great wizard Ebenezum. Unfortunately, several things had gone wrong. I remembered that, also.

"Can't you even get a simple fairy tale straight?" the old lady demanded. I recognized her now! Her name was Mother Duck. And she was the reason I had been sent to the Eastern Kingdoms!

"I beg your pardon," the small fellow in brown said drily. I knew this person too! His name was Tap! It was all coming back to me at once, as if I had just awoken from a dream.

The little fellow added:

"I do not do fairy tales."

"Is that so?" the old woman queried, her index finger stabbing at the wee man. "No one talks that way to Mother Duck!"

The little fellow took a step back as he hesitantly replied, "I—I would do a Brownie tale!"

"Would you now?" Mother Duck replied. "Well, this is my kingdom and these are my stories. And what we do in this kingdom is make up fairy tales—whether you like it or not. You'll become a part of my stories, and you will like it!" Her mouth twisted into a cruel grin. "We'll just have to make the spell a little stronger."

"Never!" the Brownie bravely retorted. "No spell is as strong as Brownie pride!"

"We'll see." Mother Duck stared intently at the little fellow.

"I am sorry," Tap insisted, doing his best to ignore the old lady's stare, "But I am a Brownie, and will be until my—uh, that is—I am— uh, aren't I—um—welcome to fairyland, home of the happy-go-lucky fairies! Like me!"

Tap tried to perform a happy-go-lucky skip, with little success. He didn't look happy at all.

"Very well," Mother Duck remarked with a heavy sigh. "That's one problem taken care of." She regarded me critically. "I trust you are going to be cooperative?" She turned her gaze from me to look to the heavens. "Why must I suffer so for my art? Why can't they understand what I'm trying to create?"

I didn't know what to do. I remembered now that I had been sent here by my master to try to win Mother Duck over to our side in the war with the demons of the Netherhells, who were using their fearsome Conquest by Committee in an attempt to take over the surface world. However, once we had arrived in the Eastern Kingdoms, we learned from one of our allies, His Brownieship, King of all the Brownies, that Mother Duck had already signed a pact with our enemies.

Unfortunately, it had been too late to escape. We were captured, and I was carried away by a clumsy giant named Richard to take part in something Mother Duck called her "Storybook." Was that where I was now? I had seen Tap the Brownie, but what had happened to my other companions? This Storybook didn't seem so bad. There must be some way to escape, some way to . . .

I looked up to see Mother Duck staring at me. My mouth opened of its own volition, and I began to speak words over which I had no control.

"Once upon a time," my mouth said, and again: "Once upon a time."

"Excuse me," a deep voice sounded from behind me.

I blinked. My mouth snapped shut. The spell was broken.

"What is it?" Mother Duck demanded. "Can't you see I'm creating?"

"Sorry," the voice said. "I was looking for Mother Duck."

"Well, you've found her!" The woman's tone was filled with rage.

"Oh," the voice replied. "So pleased to meet you."

I tore my eyes away from Mother Duck and turned to regard the newcomer. He was not at all what I expected. For one thing, he was totally covered with thick brown hair. For another, he appeared to be built like an animal, although he was standing on his hind legs. He wore no clothes, save for a green cap inscribed with the words: "Do it again, Celtics!" If I didn't know better, I would have sworn this creature was more animal than human. In fact, I would have sworn he was—

"My name is Wolf," the hairy newcomer said.

Exactly.

"I can see that," Mother Duck replied. Her anger seemed to have abated somewhat. Even she was taken aback by the animal's manner.

"Jeffrey Wolf, to be precise," the newcomer continued rapidly. "And I think *you'll* be glad you met me."

"I certainly hope so," Mother Duck said, "for your sake."

"For *both* our sakes," Jeffrey replied smoothly. "I trust I've come to the right place. You *are* the Mother Duck who does fairy tales?"

The old woman laughed through her nose. "No one else would dare to call themselves Mother Duck."

"Quite assuredly." Jeffrey smiled, showing two rows of very sharp teeth. "I like a woman who knows who she is and what she wants. And what you need in your fairy tales is a talking wolf! Just think of it! What an opportunity!"

"Possibly," Mother Duck agreed, slowly. "I won't kill you just yet, then. A talking wolf? Not as good as an Eternal Apprentice, but I suppose it does have possibilities."

The Eternal Apprentice! The words came rushing at me with the force of a winter wind in July. So there were still other things I had yet to remember. Like the fact that I had met Death on my way to the Eastern Kingdoms, and he had called me the Eternal Apprentice, a person destined to always aid heroes, a person who furthermore was clumsy but lovable, and who was always accompanied by any number of companions. And the dread apparition also told me that this apprentice was someone who could not truly die, but instead, as soon as his earthly body expired, would be reborn into another body, so that his soul would always be free from Death. Unless, of course, Death caught that person alone and snatched that person in that instant to his grave.

I remembered now how barely I had escaped the foul fiend. What else had I forgotten from my past? And if this Eternal Apprentice thing was true, how did I know that Death would not come and snatch me while I was under one of Mother Duck's spells?

I could not let this woman control me again. I would have to escape, and somehow reunite with my other companions. But how could I get away? We seemed to be surrounded by forest. I realized I had no idea quite where I was. I would have to wait, and hope that something Mother Duck said would give me a clue.

"I'm glad you see how valuable a talking wolf could be!" Jeffrey said when Mother Duck stopped scowling. "When do I start work?"

"What?" Mother Duck demanded. "When do you start work? As soon as I decide that I shouldn't have the giants carry you away to bake you in their bread!"

"But, madam!" Jeffrey waved both his forepaws, entreating the old woman to listen to reason. "I'm the opportunity of a lifetime! Think of it! A talking wolf! What symbolism! What possibility for metaphor!"

"What an ingredient for the giants' bakery," Mother Duck replied summarily. "Richard!" she shouted. "Oh, Richard!"

I heard a rumbling in the distance. I had hoped to somehow escape while Mother Duck and the wolf argued. But Richard had captured me before. I knew there was nowhere I could run where the giant would not find me again.

The rumbling grew closer and louder, so that I discerned that it was really two noises, one a repeated pounding, as if someone was dropping Bog Womblers from a great height to fall upon the earth below. The second noise was a repeated crashing, as Richard accidentally crushed everything in the vicinity of his path.

The wolf did not look at all happy about this turn of events. "Who," he inquired, somewhat hysterically, "is Richard?"

"Oops!" a great voice declared from high overhead. Richard had arrived.

"Richard?" Mother Duck inquired of her very large lackey.

"I'm sorry I asked," the wolf moaned. "I'll just be going—"

"I hope you didn't need that cottage back there," Richard pleaded. "It was right next to that muddy river bank, and my foot slipped ever so slightly—"

"Don't worry about it, Richard," interrupted Mother Duck, her voice tinged with fatigue. "I can have the dwarves build another. In the meantime, I have a job for you."

"Let's not be hasty, now," Jeffrey interjected. "I have too great a talent to be baked away!"

"You also have too big a mouth." Mother Duck pointed at Jeffrey. "Richard, make sure the wolf stays quiet while I work. If not—"

The giant grinned. "Whole wolf bread."

"Exactly," the old lady agreed. "Understand. I must have silence when I create! Now—" She paused to look at me.

What could I say? There must be some way to keep from coming under her spell again. What would my master have done? Argued with her, probably. Attempted to get her to see reason. Very well, that was what I would have to do as well. I opened my mouth. "Indeed—," I began.

But the next words that came out were, "Once upon a time."

Once upon a time. Once upon a time.

TWO

"There are two sides to every issue."

—Words (which some were surprised he
was still alive to speak) uttered by
Ebenezum the Wizard to the elite
assassin guards of King Snerdlot the
Vengeful, after the king decided to
question the parentage of some of his
offspring by Queen Vivazia, who did have
a habit of long and personal
consultations with gentlemen wearing
wizard's robes. Few realize, however,
that the fleeing Ebenezum was at the
time disguised as a costermonger
(although on closer inspection his garb
might have passed for a wizard's
nightshirt), and furthermore, that he
managed to cast Gleebzum's Spell of
Universal Guilt among the assassins,
which caused them to spend the rest of that afternoon
repeatedly arresting each other.

Once upon a time, a young lad named Wuntvor traveled far from his
native land, seeing the sights and having many adventures. So it was
that he came over a hill and saw a bright and verdant valley spread
before him. Brilliant sunlight shone down on green trees and golden
crops, and Wuntvor thought that he had never seen a place as beautiful as this in all his travels.

He left the hilltop and began his descent into the valley. But he had
not gone a dozen paces before he saw a handpainted sign hanging

from one of the beautiful, green trees. And on that sign, in large red letters, someone had painted a single word:

DANGER.

Wuntvor paused for a moment, and stared at the sign. Was someone trying to warn him? But danger of what? And where could any danger be on such a fine day as this?

So Wuntvor continued upon his way, whistling merrily as he studied the wildflowers that bordered the path on either side. He came to a broad field of wild grass and clover, and saw that on the far side of that field wound a lazy blue river.

Wuntvor looked along the trail he followed, and noted that in the distance it led to a narrow bridge that crossed the wide expanse of water. Well then, he thought to himself, that is the way that I must go. But he had not walked a dozen paces before he found that a giant boulder blocked his way. And on that boulder was painted a single word, in red letters three feet high:

BEWARE.

Wuntvor paused for a long moment to regard the message on the boulder. This was the second warning he had received since he had entered the valley. But what were these messages trying to tell him? What, or whom, should he beware of?

At length, Wuntvor decided that it was much too fine a day to beware of anything. Let the fates do what they must, he thought. On a sunny afternoon like this, he could best whatever was thrown in his path!

And with that, Wuntvor skirted the boulder and continued down the trail to the bridge. He had not gone a dozen paces, however, before a large man stepped out from behind a concealing hedge. Wuntvor studied the newcomer with some surprise, since he was the largest man the young lad had ever seen, being massive in girth as well as height. The large fellow was dressed in a bronze breastplate, which was somewhat dented and tarnished, and wore an elaborate winged helmet on top of his massive head. He raised a giant club above his head, and uttered but a single word:

"DOOM."

Wuntvor took a step away, being somewhat taken aback by this new turn of events. Was this the danger that the first sign spoke of? Was this what he had to beware of, as the boulder had cautioned? Yet the large man did not attack. Instead, he simply stood there, the giant club still raised above his massive head.

"Pardon?" Wuntvor said after a moment.

"What?" the large man asked.

"I beg your pardon?" Wuntvor expanded.

"Oh," the large man answered. "Doom."

"Yes," Wuntvor prompted. "But what kind of doom?"

"Oh," the large man answered again. "Down at the bridge."

Wuntvor smiled. Now he was getting somewhere! "What about the bridge?"

"Doom," the large man replied.

But Wuntvor wasn't about to give up. "At the bridge?" he prompted again.

The large man nodded his head and lowered his club.

"That's where the danger is?" Wuntvor added. "That's where I have to beware?"

The large man continued to nod.

"But what is the danger?" Wuntvor insisted. "What do I have to beware of?"

"Doom," the large man insisted.

Wuntvor began to despair of ever getting any real answers out of the large fellow. He gazed down the path at the distant bridge. It certainly looked peaceful enough. Just what was this big fellow trying to warn him about? Wuntvor decided he would try to gain a definite answer one more time.

"Indeed," he began, for there was something reassuring to Wuntvor about beginning sentences in this way, "you tell me that my doom waits on yon bridge?"

The large fellow nodded again, smiling that Wuntvor had understood his plea.

"And yet," Wuntvor continued, "there is no way that you might explain to me what that doom is?"

The large fellow shook his head sadly.

"Doom," he agreed.

"Why not?" Wuntvor demanded, upset with this turn of events.

The large fellow looked all around. When he was convinced they were all alone he spoke to Wuntvor in a voice barely above a whisper.

"I am here as a warning," was all he said.

Wuntvor bit his lip so that he would not scream. After he had regained his composure, he asked:

"But can't you at least inform me what you are warning me about?"

"Doom," the large fellow replied sadly.

"Why?" Wuntvor demanded.

"Because that is the way fairy tales work," the large fellow answered.

Wuntvor blinked. Fairy tales? What was this about fairy tales? The lad felt some faint memory stirring at the back of his brain. A word floated toward his consciousness. Mother. Mother what? Of course, now he remem—

"Once upon a time." Wuntvor's lips moved, saying words he could have sworn he never thought. "Once upon a time."

He shook his head violently and stared at the large man again. "Can you tell me nothing about the bridge?"

"Doom," the immense fellow pondered. "Perhaps I can ask you a question or two. Would you by any chance have a good deal of gold?"

At last! Wuntvor thought, I shall get some information.

"No," he answered. "I am but a penniless traveler, out to seek my fortune in the world."

"Doom," the other responded. "Still, all is not yet lost. Are you good at riddles?"

What was this large fellow talking about? "Riddles?" Wuntvor demanded. "What do riddles have to do with anything?"

"Doom," the immense one replied, nodding to himself as if he had confirmed something he'd known all along. "I suggest you turn around and go the other way, unless you fancy yourself as troll fodder."

And with that, the large fellow turned and disappeared behind a sizable hedge.

"Indeed," Wuntvor mumbled to no one in particular. Somehow, he did not feel he had gained much information at all.

But after a moment's thought, Wuntvor decided to go to the bridge anyway. After all, hadn't he left his native land to seek adventure? He had the feeling that this bridge he was approaching, as small and innocent looking as it was, might contain so much adventure that he could return home immediately after crossing it.

He was not a dozen paces from the bridge when he heard a voice.

> "Ho, young traveler!
> We have advice:
> If you want to cross,
> You will pay a price."

And with that, a horrible creature leapt from beneath the bridge and landed less than a dozen paces away from the startled Wuntvor. The creature's skin was a bright shade of yellowish-green, but that was nowhere near as startling as the horrible fact that it wore clothing filled with purple and green checks, not to mention that it held a brown, smoking thing between its teeth.

The creature removed the brown, smoking thing (which was quite foul smelling besides) from between its jaws, and spoke again.

> "Now that you're here
> You won't get old,
> Unless you give
> This troll some gold."

"Indeed," Wuntvor replied. So this, at last, was what he was being warned about. Wuntvor thought, somehow, that he should feel more cheered by finally learning the truth. The truth, though, left something to be desired.

The hideously garbed creature smiled with even more teeth than a creature like that should have, and sauntered toward the lad. Wuntvor decided that what he mostly wished at this precise moment was that the large fellow he had so recently spoken with had been more specific in his details of the danger's exact nature, so that Wuntvor might be currently pursuing his adventures in an entirely different location from where he was at present.

The creature pointed at Wuntvor. More specifically, its sharp yellow claws pointed at Wuntvor's belt as it spoke again.

> "Gold need not be
> My only reward,
> I'll take instead
> Your meagre sword!"

Wuntvor looked down at his belt. He had a sword? It came as a total surprise to him. Shouldn't a person remember if he was wearing a sword?

Well, he reasoned, as long as he had a sword, he might as well defend himself.

"What are you doing?" the sword screamed as Wuntvor yanked it from the scabbard.

The sword spoke! Wuntvor almost dropped the weapon. He definitely should have remembered a sword that could talk. The lad frowned. Something, he thought, is not as it seems.

"I would like an answer," the sword insisted. "As your personal weapon, I think it's the least I deserve."

"Indeed," Wuntvor responded, wishing to grant the magic sword's wishes. "I was merely drawing you forth to slay yon horrible creature."

"Merely?" the sword began, but whatever it had to say next was lost beneath the creature's new rhyme.

> "Ho, young traveler,
> Your valour growing.
> Sad to say,
> I must be going."

And with that, the garishly garbed creature dove under the bridge.

"Merely?" the enchanted blade repeated.

Wuntvor glared at the sword. "Who are you, anyway?"

"Is that a trick question?" the sword responded, a suspicious edge to its voice.

"Nay," Wuntvor insisted, although he doubted, under the circumstances, that he would know a trick question even if he spoke it. "I fear I am under a spell of forgetfulness, and hoped that a magic sword might know the truth."

"Why didn't you say so?" The sword brightened perceptibly. Wuntvor had to shield his eyes not to be blinded by the glow.

"That's exactly what we magic swords are for," the blade continued. "My name is Cuthbert, and I'm a first-class example of sorcerous weaponry. What else do you need to know? Your name is Wuntvor. You do remember that? Good. Do you recall that you are on a quest for your master—Hey!"

The sword screamed as it fell from Wuntvor's hand, which had gone suddenly numb. But the lad had no more thought for his discarded weapon. All he could think of were the words upon his lips.

"Once upon a time," he said. "Once upon a time."

And, as if in answer, he heard a second voice come from beneath the bridge.

"Ho, young traveler,
No need to fiddle!
You'll simply die
If you miss this riddle."

And with that a second creature leapt onto the path, less than a dozen paces from Wuntvor, who was nowhere near as startled this time, having come somewhat to expect such occurrences. The second monster was a bit different from the first, a tad shorter and more of a putrid gray-green in color. Its clothing was more conservative as well, as it wore dark, almost monastic-looking robes that ballooned around its short body in great folds.

"Riddle?" Wuntvor inquired. This must be the second thing the large fellow warned him about. A riddle that, according to this creature, he could simply die from. Wuntvor suspected the creature was not speaking metaphorically.

The sickly green thing smiled broadly and pulled a piece of parchment from beneath its robes. It read in a clear, high, annoying voice:

"With this riddle,
The seeds are sowed:
Why did the chicken
Cross the road?"

The monster licked its chops, obviously intending a quick and tasty meal. The lad had a difficult time even thinking about the riddle.

Wait a second. Wuntvor stared hard at the riddling horror. A chicken crossing the road? That wasn't difficult at all. His aged grandmother had told him the answer to that one a thousand times.

"To get to the other side!" Wuntvor shouted triumphantly.

"Get to the other side?" the green thing mused. "Well, I suppose that's possible. Just a moment." The creature reached within its voluminous robes and pulled forth a sheaf of parchment.

"No, no, I'm afraid the answer is as follows—" It cleared its throat and announced portentously:

"A newspaper."

What? Wuntvor thought. What was a newspaper?

"It is not!" the lad insisted angrily. "Everyone knows that chickens cross the road to get to the other side!"

The creature shook its head sadly, reaching within its robes with its free hand to draw out a knife and fork. "Perhaps that sort of thing happens wherever you come from," it answered as it scanned the sheaf of parchments. "I do remember seeing that answer somewhere. Ah, here it is: 'To get to the other side.' I'm afraid though, that it's the answer to another riddle entirely. Uh—here it is—'What's black and white and read all over?' "

"What's black and white and red all over?" Wuntvor repeated.

The creature nodded triumphantly. "To get to the other side!" It paused, waiting for some sign of recognition from the traveler. "You see now, don't you?" it prompted at last. "You see, because it's black and white and read, it has to cross—" The thing paused and stared for a moment at the parchment. "Well, perhaps it is a little difficult to explain. It has to be correct, though. I assure you, Mother Duck uses nothing but the very latest equipment. So there's no chance for a mistake." The thing blinked, as if it couldn't quite believe what it was saying. "Well, not that much of a chance."

Mother Duck? The lad frowned. Where had he heard that name before? And why did he have an almost uncontrollable urge to say "Once upon a time"?

"Other side?" the thing said, more to itself than to Wuntvor. "What kind of stupid—" The creature stopped itself and, after a moment, coughed discreetly. "Well, perhaps, in the very slight chance there was an error, we should give you another opportunity. It's your life at stake, after all." The green thing riffled through the pile of parchment. "Oh, here's the old chestnut about four legs, two legs, three legs. She's got to be kidding. There must be something with a little more verve than that." The creature turned the page. "Let's try this one."

The monster cleared its throat and spoke in a loud, even more annoying voice: "How many elephants can you get into a Volkswagen?"

It paused, staring at the parchment in disbelief. "Where did she get these questions, anyway?" The creature flipped another page, frowning as it quickly read the text. "Let's see. I don't suppose you have any idea what a—'lightbulb' is? I thought as much."

The thing crumpled the parchment in its green claws. "I'm sorry, this is ridiculous. What am I doing in a stupid fairy tale, anyway?"

Fairy tale? Wuntvor remembered the Brownie. And that woman the thing had mentioned. What was her name? Mother something. It was on the tip of his tongue. Mother—

He had it!

"Once upon a time!" Wuntvor cried in triumph. Wait a second. That wasn't the point he was going to make. Was it?

"Once upon a time," he said again for good measure.

And again, as if in answer, a third voice, far gruffer than either of those that spoke before, came from beneath the bridge.

"Ho, young traveler,
Not yet beaten;
Prepare yourself now
To be ea—"

But instead of completing the rhyme, the third creature began to sneeze.

"Are you just going to leave me here?" the sword demanded.

The sword? The sword! He looked down to where he had dropped it. Somehow, Wuntvor had forgotten all about the magic weapon again.

"Yeah!" the green thing shouted at Wuntvor. "And just what are we doing in this stupid fairy tale when we're supposed to be on a quest?"

A small brown fellow appeared by the lad's foot. "I couldn't agree more! Fairy tales! Just think how much better it would be if it were a Brownie tale!"

The green thing had recoiled at the very sight of the little fellow. "Don't ever agree with me!" he shouted, then looked back to Wuntvor. "There are simply certain things I cannot cope with."

"I suppose I'm just going to lay in the dust forever," the sword moaned, "left here to rust, forgotten by my owner—"

The checkered monster was suddenly in their midst. "Are you tired of your lot in life, enchanted sword? Well, come with me, and I'll offer you foreign sights, adventure—"

"It's ruined! It's ruined!" a woman's voice called from somewhere far up the hill.

Wait a second, Wuntvor thought.

There was something about all this chaos that was disturbingly familiar. He looked around and remembered that the robed creature was Snarks, a demon who was forced to speak nothing but the truth, no matter how unpleasant that truth might be. And there, in his checkered suit, was Brax the traveling Salesdemon, purveyor of previously owned enchanted weapons, "Every one a Creampuff!" And the sword was Cuthbert, a weapon that was unfortunately a bit of a coward. And he had seen Tap the Brownie during his last fairy tale.

His last fairy tale?

That's right! He was a prisoner of Mother Duck, who was currently storming down the hill toward them, pursued by a hairy fellow who looked rather like a wolf standing on his hind legs, sporting a green cap. Hadn't he seen this fellow before somewhere, too? Wuntvor shook his head.

I wondered what else I didn't remember.

Somebody was sneezing, but it didn't sound like my master. A large, blueish-purple, and quite horrible creature crawled from a ravine beneath the nearby bridge. It grabbed a corner of Brax's sportcoat and blew its nose.

> "Guxx Unfufadoo, noble demon,
> Wants no more of fairy stories!
> Will no longer obey Mother;
> Will turn Mother into ducklings!"

"Is that so?" Mother Duck replied drily. "And what seems to have upset my little demon so?"

Guxx advanced on the old lady, his talons spread wide, ready to rip and shred. As he lifted his claws above the woman to prepare for the kill, he uttered three final words:

"No more poetry."

THREE

The wise wizard should, if at all possible, avoid making plans during a crisis. The only problem with this advice is that the mage often discovers that the crisis has already made plans for the wise wizard.

—*The Teachings of Ebenezum,*
VOLUME VII

Guxx advanced on Mother Duck.

The old woman stood her ground. "Don't you think for a minute that you can defeat me. Once upon—"

"Did I hear someone mention poetry?" a booming voice called from the direction of the bridge. I turned away from Guxx to see Hubert the dragon landing in the river, the beautiful Alea astride his broad blue back. But wasn't there something different about the damsel? Perhaps it was that she was wearing a new gown of royal blue. Then again, I did not remember her blond tresses as being so long that they covered most of the dragon's back.

Still, all this fairy tale business seemed to be jumbling my memory. At that moment, I could not swear to anything.

"We'll give you something better than poetry!" the dragon called. "Hit it, Damsel!"

The beautiful Alea sang in a clear, high voice:

> "All your troubles don't mean a thing,
> Whether you're rich, whether you're poor;
> Forget your troubles and dance and sing,
> For Damsel and Dragon are the cure!"

With that, she did an impromptu dance across Hubert's scales as the dragon beat time with his wings.

"If they're the cure," Snarks mumbled, "give me the disease."

"What are you two doing here?" Mother Duck demanded, forgetting Guxx to concentrate on the new arrivals. "You were supposed to wait on the other side of the bridge!"

"We were?" the dragon asked. "Well, why didn't someone tell us about this? We *can* take direction when required. We're theater people, you know."

"Well, I was going to give you the role of your careers!" Mother Duck seemed to be getting upset. "You were going to be the climax of the fairy tale!"

"Oh, is that what we were doing?" Hubert laughed apologetically. "I was wondering about that. I mean, for some reason, there we were, humming this idiotic ditty about 'Once upon a time, once upon a time.' Then—zap!—we suddenly remembered who we were and what we were doing here, and next thing we knew, there was this tremendous commotion outside. What could we do but investigate?"

"That's right!" Alea chorused. "Damsel and Dragon are always where the action is!"

"Well, this time you'll wish you were where the action wasn't!" Mother Duck raised her hands above her head. Was she going to conjure?

Guxx leapt for her with a roar.

It all happened so quickly, I wasn't quite sure what had transpired. One minute, the heavily muscled demon was flying through the air, straight toward the old lady. Just as his sharp and deadly claws were about to reach Mother Duck, however, the demon somehow managed to perform a complete somersault in midair and land on his back in the mud at the river's edge.

"Must we be tiresome?" Mother Duck murmured. "I could eat demons like you for lunch. Why do you think the Netherhells were forced to sign a pact with me?"

A chill ran through my frame as I remembered the true severity of our situation. Not only were we prisoners of this woman, but Mother Duck had already allied herself with the evil forces of the Netherhells, a demonic horde who wished to control the surface world for their own foul purposes. My fellow questers and I had been sent to try to enlist Mother Duck in our cause by my master and his fellow wizards of Vushta, now all afflicted with a dread malady that caused them to sneeze whenever confronted by sorcery. This malady made them easy prey for the magical might of the Netherhells, and it appeared that all might be lost for the surface world unless we might gain the aid of the mysterious woman who controlled the Eastern Kingdoms. Once we had met this woman, though, we discovered that Mother Duck had already allied herself with the forces of darkness.

Was there no hope, then, of saving Vushta and the rest of the surface world from an eternity of Netherhells domination? I choked back a cry of anguish. If I foundered in despair, all would be lost.

Indeed, I thought to myself, trying to calm my fears enough to rationally deal with the problem. How would my master, the great wizard Ebenezum, handle a situation like this?

That was easy. I knew he would have continued with his noble purpose, no matter what the odds. There was only one answer, then. As difficult as it appeared, I had to somehow find a way to get Mother Duck to change her mind.

"Indeed!" I called out to Mother Duck, who was still glowering at the mud-covered Guxx. "I was wondering if we might talk about this pact of yours."

"Eh?" The woman glanced at me as one might regard a passing insect. "Ah. The Eternal Apprentice. Now, now, don't worry your mythic little head about those things. Mother Duck knows what's best for you."

"Indeed?" I replied, rather taken aback. Mythic little head? This was going to be more difficult than I thought.

Guxx pointed a claw at Brax the Salesdemon, who had managed to help his fellow creature rise from the mud.

"Begin!" Guxx exclaimed. Brax began to beat on a drum that he fished out of a sack he had been carrying over his shoulder.

> "Guxx Unfufadoo, muddy demon,
> Follows Wuntvor, noble quester,
> You will listen to the 'prentice,
> Or you will feel Guxx's fury!"

The large demon cracked his massive knuckles for emphasis.

Mother Duck yawned. "Must we continue to be so tiresome? No one needs to feel anybody else's fury. We're here to make fairy tales."

The hairy fellow with the green cap trotted over to the old woman. "And speaking of fairy tales, may I say that I can see any number of ways to improve your presentation?"

Mother Duck stared glumly at the hairy fellow. She seemed a bit out of sorts.

"Ahem," the hairy fellow replied, glancing at me and doffing his cap. "Pardon me, but I don't think we've been introduced. Wolf's the name. Jeffrey Wolf."

I began to introduce myself in turn when I was interrupted by the very loud noise of Hubert emerging from the lake.

"But you haven't had a chance to see our act!" the dragon called to Mother Duck. "Now, however, that you have dealt with that untimely interruption, it's time to begin!" The trees shook as Hubert tap-danced his way into our midst.

Mother Duck stared at no one in particular. "What have I done to deserve this?"

"I've asked myself the same question a thousand times," Snarks confided in the old woman.

"Shall we tell them about our new dance craze?" Alea piped up.

"That'll wow them!" the dragon agreed. "Ah-one and ah-two—"

Alea jumped from the dragon's back, careful to sweep her incredibly long hair aside so that it wouldn't get in her way. The two began to sing:

> "Don't you act so nonchalant,
> Let's both go where the dancing's hot!
> Cause you can go wherever you want
> When you're doing the Dragon Trot!"

Mother Duck regarded the performers, all the color drained from her face. "All I want to do is create," she moaned. "And now this."

Damsel and Dragon continued:

> "First you fling your right foot, fast and free;
> You might crush a bush, you might crush a tree.
> Then you kick your left foot, what a romp;
> And if they don't like it—Stomp! Stomp! Stomp!"

Damsel and Dragon crushed a large amount of underbrush under foot for emphasis before they launched once again into the chorus:

"Don't you act so nonchalant,
Let's both go where the dancing's hot!
Cause you can go—"

"Twenty-three years," Mother Duck went on. "I've been doing this
for twenty-three years, and never, ever . . ." Her voice died before
she could finish the sentence. Alea began to dance between the dragon's toes, as, high above her, Hubert performed selected birdsong imi-
tations.

Mother Duck shook her head. "My dear mother always told me I
should go into another line of work. You'll never go hungry if you
become a General Witch Practitioner, she'd always say. And love
potions! You can get rich with love potions! But no. I had to follow my
own muse and get involved with characters like this."

Damsel and Dragon launched into yet another verse:

"Next you take your tail and swish it around;
Be sure to flatten everything down to the ground;
What you can't stomp down you can certainly push.
Say, hey, you're a dragon so crush! Crush! Crush!"

Guxx Unfufadoo began to sneeze.

Mother Duck looked about her entreatingly, as if, somewhere in her
Eastern Kingdoms, there might be something that would enable everything to make sense. It was an amazing transformation. This once
strong woman, the mistress of all she surveyed, suddenly looked like a
tourist lost without her guidebook. A moment ago, she had flicked
Guxx Unfufadoo away as if the demon lord were some insignificant
gnat. Now, Damsel and Dragon seemed to have totally undone her.

Not that I hadn't seen it happen before. As the demon Snarks might
say, when you watched Damsel and Dragon perform, it was like giving a whole new definition to the word "entertainment." Faced with
an act of Damsel and Dragon's character, Mother Duck didn't have a
chance.

Still, it was an amazing transformation. Perhaps this would be a
good time to make my proposal.

"Indeed," I began as the duo launched into another chorus. "I was
wondering—"

"Where have I gone wrong?" Mother Duck asked, turning to face
me. "I'll be honest with you, I've never felt quite comfortable with the

whole thing from the very beginning. Even my name—Mother Duck. Oh, it's not a bad name, mind you, but it doesn't have quite the snap I was looking for. If your fairy tales are going to be remembered throughout history, your name should have some snap. Don't you agree?"

"Uh,—" I answered. "I suppose so. But I wanted to talk about Vushta—"

"What about something more regal," the old woman suggested, "like Mother Swan?"

"Very nice," I replied rapidly, "but about your pact with the Nether—"

Mother Duck wrinkled her nose and shook her head. "No, a swan's much too fussy. I think it should be a common everyday bird, one that people could relate to. Like Mother Sparrow? No, that's a bit plain. Mother Grackle, maybe?" The old woman made a face, shaking her head as soon as the words had left her mouth.

Damsel and Dragon continued. Did the song have no end?

"Now you know how to do the Dragon Trot,
It's the best dance craze we ever got!
You know being a dragon is such a joy,
And if they don't like it: Destroy! Destroy!"

Damsel and Dragon ended with a flourish, bowing to everyone gathered in the clearing.

"Over?" Mother Duck whispered. "It's over?"

"Did we hear a disappointed cry in the audience?" Hubert queried. "Is it time for an encore?"

"No! No!" their audience replied en masse.

"Indeed," I added hastily, eager to have them out of the way so that I could get back to my discussion with Mother Duck. "Why ruin a perfect performance by dragging it on needlessly? Rather, let us remember your song for its brilliance and brevity."

Hubert nodded solemnly. "The apprentice has a point."

Mother Duck nodded in turn. "Furthermore," she stated, the power once again in her voice, "if you attempt to sing a song like that again, I will be forced to cast a spell of eternal silence over you." She pointed both her aged but still nimble hands at Hubert. "Think carefully, or you could spend the rest of your life as a silent dragon."

"A spell of silence?" Hubert replied, aghast. "A silent dragon?"

But Alea nodded her head knowingly. "Don't you see?" she told the dragon. "She's never seen actors from the theaters of Vushta before. She's obviously afraid of being upstaged."

"Oh, dear." The dragon sighed in agreement. "It's the price you have to pay when you play the provinces."

"Good," Mother Duck stated. "I'm glad that's settled. I'm afraid I was a bit startled by your first song and dance. I assure you that next time I will be prepared for anything you have to offer." She flexed her conjuring fingers absently. "Remember, the next time I hear the Dragon Trot, you lose your vocal chords."

A solitary smoke ring rose from the stunned dragon's nose. She had done what I thought impossible—rendered Hubert speechless.

Mother Duck allowed herself a smile. She was in a good mood at last. It was time to make my plea!

"Indeed," I began. "Now that you have dealt with that small problem, perhaps we may talk in earnest."

"Hmm?" Mother Duck replied, as if she had forgotten all about me. "Oh, the Eternal Apprentice? Yes, I did rattle on there a bit, didn't I? Well, you shouldn't worry about it. I have quite recovered. In fact, I think it's almost time for our next fairy tale."

"Indeed?" She couldn't leave now! I had been so close. She had to hear me out! "But—"

"Now, now, don't keep interrupting Mother Duck. That's a good myth figure. There's no need to get upset." She smiled condescendingly. "In fact, with what I have planned for you, I think you'll need to conserve your strength."

She stood, hands on hips, and surveyed all who stood around her. "The first two fairy tales didn't work, but I've learned from my mistakes. I was thinking too small. You and your companions keep breaking out of the narrow confines of the tiny stories I have been giving to you. But no more. I am going to concoct a fairy story the equal of all of you." She sighed happily. "With luck, it will be my masterpiece!"

"A worthy goal," Jeffrey the wolf agreed. "But just think how much more resonance your stories would have, not to mention symbolism that might speak to a dozen unborn generations, if your tales featured clever talking wolves?"

Mother Duck sighed. "I've had just about enough outside interference. Maybe I should have Richard take you away after all. I mean, what kind of fairy tale would use a talking wolf?"

"What kind of fairy tale?" Jeffrey emitted a barking laugh. "Listen, lady, I've got some great ones. How about this little kid who has to take this basket of goodies through the woods to her grandmother's house. But the wolf, you see, eats the grandmother and takes her place."

Mother Duck looked at the wolf with new respect. "Really? Well, it does have some interesting elements. I like the kid and the grandmother. A nice family angle. The woods and the goodies aren't bad either. They lend necessary color, I think. And the wolf eating the grandmother gives us that good old fairy tale violence that children love so much. What happens next?"

Jeffrey smiled, pleased with the approval. "Why, I eat the kid, too! Is that great or what?"

"You eat the kid, too?" Mother Duck made a face. "Who would want to hear a fairy tale like that?"

"What do you mean?" Jeffrey replied, somewhat miffed. "It's really popular in the Wolf family."

"It only proves, if you want a good fairy tale, you've got to tell it yourself." And with that, Mother Duck climbed back up the hill. Jeffrey the wolf trotted right behind her.

My hope faded as Mother Duck walked away. I had completely failed in my plea for her to change allegiance. How could I get her to see our side of the issue if she wouldn't even talk to me?

But again, I would not let myself crumble into despair. For my memory was still returning, and, as Mother Duck had surveyed those gathered in the clearing, I had looked around as well. And, as I looked around, I remembered. Here were my companions, Tap the Brownie, Hubert and Alea, and the three demons: Snarks, Guxx and Brax.

And I remembered that I had more companions . . .

First, where had Hendrek gone? The large warrior had appeared in the second fairy tale, warning me of "Doom" if I crossed the bridge. Yet, I had not seen him at all since I had regained my senses. True, Mother Duck might simply have placed him elsewhere, to prepare for the next part of her fairy story. Somehow, though, I wondered, for there were others that I had not seen at all.

One was the vain unicorn, who had followed me all this distance wishing to put its head in my lap. The unicorn, though, had been born in these Eastern Kingdoms. It had known of Mother Duck from before our present quest. Perhaps it also knew a way to avoid her powers. Of course, it could be waiting for me in the next fairy tale as well. So could the Seven Other Dwarves, who could not really be called companions, as we had met them so recently upon our travels, except for the fact that they had tried, unsuccessfully, to protect me from Mother Duck.

I had to face it: it all could be random chance, all controlled in some arcane fashion by the mistress of fairy tales, Mother Duck. Yet, somehow, I sensed a plan behind all these defections, because one more person was absent from this clearing, and had somehow absented herself completely from Mother Duck's spells. This last person gave me hope, for the final fugitive was my beloved, the young witch Norei.

Norei! When I thought of her, everything fell into place. I knew the real reason I had come on this quest. Oh, certainly, I came to save my master, the great wizard Ebenezum, not to mention rescuing the wondrous metropolis of Vushta, city of a thousand forbidden delights, and the entirety of the surface world from the devastating evil of total defeat at the hands of the Netherhells. But I had personal reasons for my quest as well, reasons in their own way as important if not more so than the grand goals we had set out with on the quest to the Eastern Kingdoms. And those reasons could be summarized in one word:

Norei!

She was my *real* reason for being on this quest. But then, she was my real reason for everything. I had met other women before my young witch, had even fancied myself for a brief moment in love with one or two of them. Ah, they had been naught but schoolboy crushes, every one, even my liaison with the lovely Alea before she left the Western Woods to join the theater; but it took meeting a woman like Norei to show me the error of my ways.

So it was that I risked my life in the Eastern Kingdoms. I needed to make the world a safe place for Norei and me to be together, a place where we might, if things were to work out as I hoped, grow old together. True, Norei and I had had a few small misunderstandings when we had been together in Vushta. Oh, nothing insurmountable, I was sure, just a tiny confusion about a meeting or two I had had with Alea, and what small problem I had getting the actress to see that whatever had once been between us was now gone. In fact, I had almost succeeded in this goal, and would have gladly explained the few difficulties that still remained to my beloved Norei, if the young witch had still been talking to me. But, of course, she wasn't, because of an incident with Alea and some canvas, not to mention—but, perhaps it was all a bit too complicated to dwell on at present. I would better spend my time devising some way to contact Norei, for I felt it was only with the aid of the young witch that we would escape Mother Duck's clutches.

But Mother Duck had walked away. My companions and I were alone; beyond her control for the first moment since we had met. Why was I sitting here thinking when I could be acting? I did not know when an opportunity like this would come again. We would have to talk quickly and make plans before the old woman on the hill wove her spells about us once more.

"Indeed!" I called to my fellows. "Gather 'round. We must talk!"

The Brownie, Damsel and Dragon and the three demons all came forward, forming a rough half-circle around me.

"It appears that Mother Duck has left us alone for a moment. We must foment some sort of plan. There is no way we may complete our quest while we are trapped by this woman's power. In addition, we all know the situation in Vushta, with every wizard there sneezing at the mention of sorcery. Each moment we are imprisoned, the forces of the Netherhells are that much closer to victory. What can we do?"

"Perhaps a cheerful song might help," Hubert suggested.

"Then again," Snarks interrupted, "perhaps it might not."

"Begin!" Guxx instructed Brax, who was still holding the drum. Brax beat as Guxx declaimed:

> "Guxx Unfufadoo, noble demon,
> Will put an end to Netherhells traitors;
> Will help the 'prentice defeat Mother—"

He glanced at the dragon before continuing:

> "Will put a stop to poetry forever!"

The demon smiled, satisfied he had made his case.

"And I have exactly the right used weapons to do the job!" Brax added.

"Is it time for Brownie Power?" Tap asked.

"Indeed," I replied. "It is time for Brownie Power, and Demon Power, and Damsel and Dragon Power as well. Our strength is in our diversity. We all saw how Mother Duck became a bit undone by the surprise of Hubert and Alea's song. Imagine how shocked she would be if we all used our abilities at the same time?"

"Oh, Wuntie!" Alea exclaimed, rushing over to give me a powerful hug. Her silken blue dress rubbed against my rough shirt, her long blond tresses fell in my face. "How brilliant!" She stepped away to look at me candidly. "I've always wanted to date a genius."

I cleared my throat and looked at the others. Why did the temperature always rise whenever Alea was near?

"Um—er—very well," I continued. "While we still have time, I will quickly outline the plan." I glanced about to make sure I had everyone's attention.

"Now we begin with—uh—we begin—" I was having trouble forming the words. Sweat trickled down my brow. "We—" I tried again. "—Once upon a time."

Alea frowned. "What was that, Wuntie?"

"Oh, no!" Hubert shouted. "I think he's been—he's been—once upon a time."

"You people are making less sense than usual!" Snarks complained. "What's all this—once upon a time?"

"No! It's time for Brownie—" Tap faltered. Both he and Alea said the four words together.

"Once upon a time," Guxx Unfufadoo chimed in. "Once upon a time."

And Brax beat along on his drum.

FOUR

"Here we go again."

—Words (which many were surprised were
not posthumous) spoken by Ebenezum after
he had managed to elude both King Snerdlot
the Vengeful and the monarch's elite
assassin guard by cleverly using the maze
of secret passageways in Snerdlot's
castle, only to open a door to discover
he was once again in the bedchamber of
Queen Vivazia. The queen was, of course,
overjoyed to see him still alive, not to
mention quite hot and sweaty from his
recent pursuit, and therefore
crossed the room in record time to give
the wizard a comradely embrace. Ebenezum
ceased his struggle a moment later, for,
upon reflection, the wizard realized
there were certain things from which
there was truly no escape.

Once upon a time there was a traveler named Wuntvor, who happened
upon a little man in the woods.

"Are you a fairy?" Wuntvor asked the little man.

But the little fellow made a face. "Not this time, thank my lucky
shoes. No, good sir, I am genuine Brownie, and furthermore, sir, it is
your lucky day."

"My lucky day?" Wuntvor said, taken quite by surprise.

"Yes, you're the only other person in this fairy—uh—" The little fellow stopped himself. "—*Brownie* tale, so I guess it has to be you. It *is* your lucky day."

The Brownie stood there, waiting expectantly.

"Thank you," Wuntvor said at last, not knowing what was expected of him.

"Aren't you going to ask why?" the Brownie demanded, tapping his tiny foot.

"Why?" Wuntvor obliged.

"Yes," the Brownie agreed. "*Why* is it your lucky day! Oh, I guess you did ask. Pardon me. My mistake. Performance nerves, I guess. Well, it is your lucky day because you are to be granted seven wishes."

"Seven wishes?" Wuntvor asked.

The Brownie nodded.

"I thought the usual was three," the lad stated.

The Brownie nodded.

"Then why seven?" Wuntvor inquired.

"We're running a special!" the Brownie exclaimed.

"Oh," Wuntvor replied.

"Well, aren't you surprised? Aren't you excited?"

"I guess so," Wuntvor responded, not really sure of anything. He had the nagging feeling that he had been here, or a place very much like here, sometime before.

What was that? Somewhere, in the distance, Wuntvor heard voices arguing. An elderly woman was complaining about how no one understood artists.

"Once upon a time," Wuntvor said. He blinked. "Seven wishes? You're really going to give me seven wishes?" He looked down at the little man in wonder.

"That's more like it," the Brownie replied. "I mean we wee folk expect some enthusiasm for our efforts, you know? That's right, seven wishes for anything you want!"

Anything he wanted? The lad was quite impressed with this opportunity, although he was the slightest bit scared as well. Seven wishes were a mighty responsibility, and Wuntvor knew all the old stories about farmers and fishermen receiving wishes and squandering them on puddings and the like. He would have to think about this, for he was a young man, abroad to seek his fortune, and this seven wishes thing might be just the chance he was looking for. But, even though he had more than the usual three, Wuntvor knew he would have to use every wish wisely.

"Well," the Brownie said, foot once again tapping. "I'm waiting."

"Uh—" Wuntvor replied in surprise. "I have to start wishing now?"

"Hey, give me a break. You've got seven wishes, here. We Brownies have things to do. Time is shoes, you know!"

Oh, well, Wuntvor thought. Why not? He had to start this wish business some time. He'd have to make the first one a good one.

"Indeed," he began, for that word seemed to help him to think. "I —um—wish I had a stout weapon to protect me from danger."

"Granted!" the Brownie exclaimed.

There was a muffled sound from the direction of his belt, like someone hollering behind a closed door.

"Eh?" Wuntvor said, or a sound very much like that. He looked down, and noticed that there was a sword and scabbard hanging from his belt. The lad grabbed the hilt of the weapon and pulled it free.

"It's about time you let me back out!" the sword exclaimed. "Do you know how boring it can get in there?"

"Pardon?" Wuntvor asked, confused by the weapon's complaint. "About time for what? Have we met before? You are the sword I wished for as the first of my seven wishes. I don't understand what you are talking about."

"First of seven wishes?" the talking sword mused. "Oh, that means we're not still—we're in an entirely different—I see. Excuse me. When you're stuck in a scabbard day in and day out, you lose track of time. I didn't realize we had started another fairy tale."

"It's a Brownie tale!" the little fellow contradicted.

"Wait a minute," Wuntvor interjected. He had been confused from the beginning of this whole thing, and somehow, anything that anybody said to him only seemed to make it worse. He stared at the sword. "You mean you were around here all along?"

"Hey," the Brownie said defensively, "I didn't say you had to wish for something you didn't already have!"

The lad looked open-mouthed at the Brownie. Had the little fellow tricked him?

"You should be more careful with your wishes, you know." The sword chuckled softly to itself. "Before long, I'll bet you'll be wishing for puddings!"

Then he had been tricked, and had had the sword at his belt all along. But why hadn't he remembered the sword? He *had* felt awkward from the first about being in this fairy tale, or Brownie tale, as if he had done something like this before that he could not quite recall.

And he hadn't been all that surprised to see the sword at his belt. So maybe he had remembered after all. Or maybe he was remembering that he had remembered it all before.

Wuntvor shook his head. It was very confusing. He simply couldn't remember.

"Well," the Brownie prompted, "we're waiting."

The lad decided he would not let the little fellow fluster him. He didn't know quite how he had gotten the sword, but he had it. This Brownie would cause him to squander his wishes if he wasn't careful.

Wuntvor decided to study his surroundings before he made another wish so as to avoid any more obvious mistakes. He stood at the edge of a bridge over a wide but slow-moving stream. The path wound away from him, up a grassy but steep hill. And on the summit of that hill stood a tower, with but a single window at the very top, a window from which, at this moment, poured thick, gray smoke.

What did this mean? Would his adventures lead him to the smoking tower, or should his fate lead him to the other side of the river? There was something about the bridge, too, that made him the slightest bit uncomfortable, although of course he could not remember exactly what it was, except he could swear it had something to do with poetry.

"Well," the Brownie prompted, "what's it going to be?"

Yes, Wuntvor thought, what was it going to be, the other side of the river or the tower on the hill? He looked again at the sinister gray turbulence roiling from the window above. Actually, if he were to have his preference, he would as soon have all his adventures in places other than smoking towers, thank you.

Well, he'd cross that bridge when he came to it. Or had he crossed it already? The lad glanced back at the river with a frown. If only he could remem—

Wuntvor shook his head sharply, as if he might dislodge any cobwebs that were growing between his ears. Whatever had happened before, it was time to make another wish.

This time he would wish for something a bit more difficult. And something perhaps that was not as dangerous as adventuring to the tower at the top of the hill. And—dare he hope?—something of more lasting importance than any single adventure.

"I wish—" Wuntvor hesitated, wanting to get the words just right. "I wish I could meet a fair damsel to be my own true love."

"Granted!" the Brownie responded cheerfully. "If you'll simply follow me?"

With that, the little fellow started up the hill, toward the smoking tower. The lad glanced up again. Did he see flame shoot through the gray clouds?

"Wait a moment!" Wuntvor exclaimed. "Where are we going?"

"Exactly what I would like to know!" his sword chimed in.

"To meet a fair damsel, just like you wanted. Come on. When you wish for something, you've got to follow through. That's part of the Brownie Code."

"Indeed?" Wuntvor asked, trotting tentatively after the Brownie, who moved very quickly for one so small. "But what if I don't wish to go to the tower?"

The little fellow shook his head. "Sorry, Brownies don't do non-wishes. You'll have to talk to some other magical subspecies about that. Besides, what are you worried about? You still have enough Brownie wishes left to waste one or two." And with that, the Brownie turned away again and resumed his rapid climb.

Left to waste? Wuntvor wasn't sure he hadn't wasted the two he had already wished. Still, he supposed he'd never know unless he followed the Brownie to the tower. The lad decided to climb the hill.

Smoke still poured from the window. And as he climbed the steep slope, Wuntvor detected a deep rumbling, something he half heard and half felt shaking the ground beneath his feet. What precisely was going on up there?

Wuntvor decided to ask the Brownie.

"Excuse me," he said, increasing his stride to catch up to the little man. "Could you tell me exactly why we're going to this tower?"

"That depends," the Brownie said cagily. "Could you put your question in the form of a wish?"

"What?" Wuntvor exploded. "Must I use my wishes for everything?" His hand tightened around the hilt of his weapon. "If I weren't a hero and role model to unborn generations—"

"Careful now!" the sword cautioned him. "You know I don't like to be used for threats. It upsets my delicate balance."

The Brownie covered his head with his tiny hands, as if to ward off the lad's blows. "Hey!" he shouted as he continued up the hill backwards. "Don't blame me. You should see the wish quota I have to fill. Why do you think we're giving away seven wishes at a pop? For our health, maybe? It's tough being in the fairy tale—uh—*Brownie* tale business. If you're not on top of it all the time, your limelight gets stolen by a golden goose or something!"

"Indeed," Wuntvor replied, feeling his grasp of the situation once again slipping away, "perhaps we should continue to the tower."

"That's more like it!" the Brownie cheered enthusiastically. "I don't suppose you'd want to rephrase that as a wish, either? Just asking! Let's get to that tower."

The Brownie turned and ran up the last third of the hill. Wuntvor was hard put to keep up with him.

"One maiden coming up!" the Brownie announced.

Wuntvor was too busy catching his breath to think of an appropriate answer. The rumbling was much louder up here. He could definitely feel it through the soles of his boots. The lad wondered if he wanted to meet a maiden who caused rumbling like that. Still, he had left his native land in search of adventure, and he supposed this qualified as that sort of thing.

"Ready?" the Brownie prompted.

Wuntvor took a deep breath and nodded.

"You got it," the wee fellow replied. "Now all you have to say is 'Fair maiden, fair maiden, let down your hair!' "

"Fair maiden?" Wuntvor said tentatively.

"It's part of the second wish!" the Brownie insisted. "Say it!"

"Very well." Wuntvor looked up at the tower and did just that.

"Fair maiden, fair maiden, let down your hair!"

He heard a woman's voice call down above the rumbling:

"So you may climb my golden stair!"

Golden stair? Wuntvor frowned. What did that mean?

Something plummeted from the window above. Something golden and shining. It was heading right for him!

Then everything went black.

FIVE

A wizard needs to be many things beyond a mere magician. Among the skills a student mage must cultivate is play-acting, a talent which may be more important than it might seem at first glance. "Why acting?" the novice wizard might ask, but the benefits will soon become apparent when that same mage must "act up a storm" for a spell that is not quite going as planned. And as to "playing," well, it is only after such a spell has gone horribly wrong, bringing destruction and great financial reversals upon your clients, that you realize how useful "playing dead" can be.

—*The Teachings of Ebenezum,*
VOLUME XXII

"There you are."

Wuntvor groaned, blinking in the bright light.

The Brownie smiled apologetically. "I suppose I should have warned you about the hair. When it grows as long as all that, it gets pretty hefty. Here. I've swept enough of it aside so that you can crawl free." He waved for Wuntvor to follow him.

The lad crawled through the opening, then stood and turned to see what had befallen him. He whistled softly. The Brownie was correct. There was more hair here than he had ever seen in one place before. The entire side of the tower was covered with it; cascading golden blond strands that reached all the way to the window high above. And the hair was so long that it gathered in great masses upon the ground, forming valleys and tiny hillocks all its own, so that it looked like some miniature and yet strangely hirsute landscape spread out before him.

"Well," the woman's voice called to him. "Are you going to climb up or not?"

"Oh, most assuredly he shall!" the Brownie shouted. The little fellow nudged Wuntvor's ankle. "Well, you want your damsel, don't you?"

Wuntvor nodded, a touch troubled by these proceedings. Shouldn't there be some way to meet a fair maiden without having to climb up her hair? Still, in a way he supposed it was his fault. He knew from his childhood reading that whenever you got involved in wish stories you had to be incredibly specific, or this sort of thing always happened.

He stepped forward and gathered enough hair in his hands to make a thick rope. He gripped the strands as best he could and hoisted himself aloft.

"Ouch!" came a cry from far overhead.

Wuntvor looked down doubtfully at the Brownie.

"Hey," the little fellow shrugged. "You want your maiden, you've got to do what she asks. That's the way this wish stuff works. No pain, no gain."

Wuntvor grabbed a hank of hair above him and pulled himself up again.

"Ooooh!" This time, the noise from the window was more of a moan than a sharp cry.

Wuntvor looked up to the window far overhead. "Are you sure you want me to do this?"

And the melodious voice called down:

"Would you just hurry and get up here before you pull out *all* my hair?"

Well, Wuntvor thought, one should never argue with a fair maiden. If climbing was what she desired, Wuntvor would ascend.

"Yow!" the cry came from the tower, and "Oof! Eeee! Erk! Yorp!" and other exclamations of a similar stripe, every time Wuntvor pulled himself farther up the rope of hair. The lad redoubled his efforts, for he wished to put an end to the maiden's suffering as soon as possible.

At last his hand grasped the stone window sill. He grabbed the sill with his other hand as well, and hoisted himself up so that he could throw his leg across the ledge.

"Well," the maiden remarked upon seeing him. " 'Tis about time." She wrinkled her brow and rubbed her head. "Next time, I may choose to be rescued by a lighter hero."

Wuntvor began to stammer an apology.

"Oh, nevermind," the damsel replied. " 'Twas not your fault, after all. I was the one who asked you here. Now, if you would give me a hand, we need to haul up my hair."

So Wuntvor helped the maiden to gather her hair from the tower wall and return it to her sitting room. As they were involved in this procedure, which was quite time consuming, the lad thought to make polite conversation. Thus he commented upon the length and lustre of her hair, and wondered how she kept it so.

"You don't know the half of it!" The damsel, who was quite attractive when she had her hair pushed away from her face, rolled her eyes heavenward. "Nobody ever told me having long hair would be like this. Brushing it a hundred strokes takes all day! And when it gets snarled"—she laughed ruefully—"it's murder!"

Suddenly, the rumbling began again, deep within the tower, so loud that Wuntvor had to cover his ears for a moment until it passed.

"What was that?" he asked with some trepidation.

"Oh, nothing." The fair damsel shrugged. "Only the dragon."

A dragon? The Brownie had never said there was going to be a dragon!

Wuntvor walked back to the window and scowled down at the little fellow.

"You'd better get up here!" the lad warned.

"Is that a wish?" the Brownie hollered.

Wuntvor wanted to scream. He could see it happening; one way or another, the Brownie would make him squander all his wishes. But perhaps there was another way. Maybe Wuntvor could help the maiden escape without ever having to confront the dragon.

"Wait there!" he called to the Brownie, then turned about and walked back to the sitting room, where the fair damsel was trying to find enough nooks and crannies in which to stuff her tremendous locks so that she might have room to breathe. Before he did any rescuing, the lad decided, he should ask the maiden's opinion on the matter. He briefly outlined what he considered the options to be, then asked what she desired most.

"What do I want most?" the damsel replied, fluttering her long and copious lashes. "I want to sing!"

"Sing?" the lad repeated, somewhat surprised.

The damsel nodded, cheerful at last. "When you've been trapped in a tower as long as I have, you can't imagine how much you long to do a musical number for an audience. Even an audience of one." She flashed her lovely smile. "It was so nice of you to ask me. I'll do a little ditty that's always been one of my favorites."

She cleared her throat, and, to the lad's astonishment, began to belt out a song:

> "Am I afraid of dungeon towers?
> Oh no, not little me.
> My locks can unlock any door;
> My curls will set me free."

She grabbed a mass of hair and stared at it, enraptured, as she sang again:

> "Men can come and go;
> I really couldn't care.
> But I'm in love,
> I'm so fond of,
> My glorious, glorious hair."

The damsel curtsied, apparently finished with her performance. The rumbling returned, somehow more rhythmic than before.

"Oh, thank you, Hubert!" the maiden called. "Thank you *all* so very much." She smiled at Wuntvor again. "It's gratifying to work with a dragon that appreciates my talents."

Wuntvor realized then what the heavy pounding that filled the tower really was. It was applause—dragon applause. The lad had some trouble comprehending exactly what this meant. He decided to take a direct approach.

"But you are held a captive in this tower!" he said to the maiden. "Don't you want to escape?"

The maiden bit her lovely lip. "Oh, I suppose so," she said after a moment's pause. "But the dragon would have to come along as well."

If the lad had been puzzled before, now he was totally confused. This made no sense whatsoever. Dragons were meant to rumble, and threaten, and possibly devour, but never ever to applaud. And as to escaping and taking the dragon along—what had the Brownie gotten him into? Next time he saw the little fellow, they would have words.

In the meantime, though, he would have to hurry to stay with the maiden, who was leaving the sitting room by the second door, which

led into the tower's interior. Wuntvor sprinted just behind, careful to
stay ahead of the massive curls that swirled along the floor beside him.
"We go down these stairs," the maiden said. They were in the end of
a short corridor. "Hubert waits below." She began her descent.

The lad followed once again, realizing that he would have to completely rethink his opinions on the relationship between damsels and
dragons. Unless, perhaps, there was some more sinister motivation
behind the damsel's actions; that, perhaps, she was adept at luring her
young suitors to their doom, say, as a dragon's lunch? But no,
Wuntvor dismissed that idea almost as soon as it occurred to him. No
one as sweet and lovely as the maiden before him could be involved in
such treachery. But then another, even less pleasant thought struck
him with the force of a winter storm.

"Does the dragon do musical numbers as well?" he asked, trepidation once again in his voice.

"Well," the maiden admitted, "he used to, but there are a few difficulties with his present contract." She shook her head sadly. "If he
uses his voice in an improper fashion, there could be dire consequences. But you didn't come here to hear our problems. It's time to
talk to Hubert."

She continued down the stairs. The lad could think of nothing to do
but follow. The worn stone steps seemed to wind about the inside of
the tower wall. As they descended, the ceiling and inner wall grew
farther and farther away until, in the dim illumination, Wuntvor could
imagine that there were no other walls at all besides the one he ran his
hand against for support.

"Hubert!" the maiden called. "Oh, Hubert!"

With that, the rumbling started anew, much louder than before.
They were approaching light—wild, flickering light, like that of a
dozen torches.

But the flame was not born of wooden torches. It came instead, in
great fiery gouts, from a dragon's snout, which appeared less than a
dozen paces away from the startled Wuntvor.

"Yowp!" the lad cried, but the dragon regarded him in silence.

"There you are!" The damsel clapped her hands in glee. "Hubert
always was one to make a dramatic entrance. Especially now that he is
no longer speaking."

The dragon rumbled and nodded its head, upon which, Wuntvor
noted, the reptile wore a purple top hat.

"Being prevented from talking might be a great burden to anyone whose chosen career is the theater," the damsel continued. "Many an actor could let this turn of events drag him into a despair from which he might not recover. But not our Hubert." She pointed proudly at the giant lizard. "This dazzling dragon has turned Mother Duck's edict into a whole new career direction. Yes, no longer is Hubert a dragon actor. Now, instead, Hubert has become the world's first dragon mime!" She clapped her hands smartly. "What a trouper! Come on, Hubert! Show him your stuff!"

The huge reptile leaned forward, pushing his forepaws against some imaginary wall, while its rear feet seemed to be walking without getting anywhere. Wuntvor frowned. What was this supposed to mean?

"That's right!" the damsel exclaimed proudly. "It's a dragon walking against the wind! What genius!" She turned and looked to the lad for approval.

"Indeed," the lad remarked for want of anything else to say. "But weren't we escaping?"

"Yes, yes, you're right of course. Out there, beyond this tower is a world full of audiences waiting to applaud Hubert's talent. But look!" The damsel pointed once again at the reptile. "Hubert's doing a dragon washing windows! What style! What panache!"

"Indeed," Wuntvor commented again, trying not to get too distracted by the circular motions Hubert was making with his feet. With all this dragon business, the lad was thinking twice about becoming involved with this maiden happily ever after. He wondered if the Brownie would let him re-use a wish. He tapped the damsel on the shoulder, causing her to pause in her gushing praise.

"You wouldn't happen to know where the door is?" he asked.

"Certainly." The damsel beamed. "Just beyond Hubert there."

"Indeed," the lad responded. "What say we go through it?"

The damsel laughed. "And let the world know our little secret?" She skipped merrily toward the dragon, holding her hair back so that it would not trip her. "Oh Hubert, Hubert, we're going on tour!"

The dragon nodded and used its tail to push open the tower door, a door larger than any Wuntvor had ever seen—large enough at least to let a dragon through. With such an easy way out, Wuntvor wondered absently why the damsel and the dragon hadn't left before this. He supposed there had to be some reason, but before he could think of a way to ask about it, the air was again full of rumbling.

He turned to the damsel. "Is Hubert clearing his throat?"

The maiden shook her head. "Oh, dear, no, that isn't the dragon rumbling at all. Listen carefully. That noise has no tone whatsoever, no sense of dynamics. It's obviously totally untrained. Besides, I think it's coming from underground."

Underground? Why was there something about that fact that made the lad uneasy?

"Once upon a time," Wuntvor whispered. "Once upon a time."

The rumbling grew louder, and a great rift appeared in the floor before them. The air became filled with dust, and when the dust cleared, Wuntvor saw that a long table had appeared from the hole in the earth. Seated behind that table were five of the ugliest creatures he had ever seen.

The creature in the center pounded a gavel.

"We claim this land in the name of the Netherhells!"

A gavel? The Netherhells? Thoughts and images raced madly about in the lad's brain.

"Indeed," he managed weakly.

"Wuntie?" the damsel cried in alarm. "Is something wrong?"

The lad managed a choked laugh. "Oh, nothing much. I just wish I knew what was going on here!"

"Granted!" a tiny voice screamed at his side.

SIX

Memory is a funny thing. I can't begin to tell you how many times I have forgotten to keep an appointment with the royal tax collector. This always seems to upset the official greatly, until I mention that perhaps I can make up for my error and help facilitate their inspection of my gold by transforming the official into a sparrow, so that he might fly there directly, or into a frog, so that he might hop quickly from one source of wealth to the next, or—perhaps best of all—into a worm, so that he might burrow beneath the earth searching for hidden assets. Oddly enough, every time we have this conversation, the tax collector forgets to make any further appointments. As I said, memory is a funny thing.

—Wizardnetics: Your Guide
to Total Magical Fulfillment,
by Ebenezum, Greatest Wizard
in the Western Kingdom
(thirty-fourth edition)

That did it. Everything came rushing back at once. It was like getting hit in the face with Hendrek's warclub. I remembered Mother Duck and my quest and companions, and the attacks of the Netherhells and the plight of Vushta and my master and my current situation with Norei and any number of other things.

"Um—," I remarked. "Indeed." I remembered again that I had to somehow convince Mother Duck of the error of her ways. But could I do that while we were being attacked by the Netherhells?

"Wait a second!" the small demon at the end of the table exclaimed in a grating voice. "This isn't Vushta!"

The large demon at table's center pounded its gavel. "What do you mean? You remember our discussions. The remaining magical might of the surface world has concentrated itself in Vushta. You yourself

recall the hundred or more wizards we faced last time we were there."
The demon waved its gavel at the clearing around the table. "Well,
this was where all the magic was emanating from. And we followed
that magic to get here. Therefore, this must be Vushta."

"Point of order!" the small demon objected. "This doesn't look at
all like Vushta."

The main demon waved its gavel even more furiously, as if to dis-
perse the other's objection into the late summer air. "So they've disguised it. Whenever you're facing more than a hundred magicians,
you have to expect clever things like that."

"No, no, no, no, no!" Mother Duck's voice grew in intensity as she
rushed down the hill toward us. "It's all wrong! Why does this sort of
thing have to happen to me?"

"Perhaps," Jeffrey called as he attempted to catch up to her, "things
would go better if you would employ a few talking wolves. Improvisa-
tion is a skill much prized among wolfkind—"

"Hey!" a voice called, close by my foot. "Are you just going to let
me lay here and rust?"

I looked down. It was Cuthbert, my magic sword. I realized I must
have dropped it when the hair had fallen on me.

I knelt and picked the weapon up.

"Much better!" Cuthbert crowed. "The first thing the hero must
learn is the proper care of his weapons. And when his weapon is
something as magical as mmmmpphh!"

I rapidly slid Cuthbert back into its scabbard. I had other things to
think about besides lessons in proper sword care. I wondered how I
might get Mother Duck's attention, but from the way she was glaring
at the demonic newcomers, I had a feeling that reasoned discussion
was one of the furthest things from her mind.

One of the other demons pointed at the rapidly approaching
woman. "I think we may be under attack."

"Is it time to boil blood?" the end demon asked enthusiastically.

Mother Duck shook both her fists as she barreled toward the committee.

"Oh dear," the gavel demon remarked, a slight quaver in its voice.
"Perhaps we are not in Vushta after all."

"What are you doing here?" Mother Duck demanded as she rushed
before the demons. "I certainly hope you're not here on one of your
missions of conquest!"

"Oh! No, no! Never conquest!" the gavel demon insisted. It paused, cowering ever so slightly. When it became apparent that Mother Duck was not going to smite the creature where it stood, the demon wiped its brow and continued in a more moderate tone: "Well, actually, we were on one of our missions, but not to the Eastern Kingdoms—never to the Eastern Kingdoms, I assure you. We simply got a little turned around. . . ." The demon's voice died under Mother Duck's withering stare.

"Anyone could have made that mistake," another of the demons added.

"You see," explained the small, sickly fellow down at the end, "it's dark underground, and the signage isn't all that good either."

"Am I expected to believe—," Mother Duck began slowly.

"No, of course not!" the sickly demon agreed. "We'd never expect you to believe that!"

"There could be another reason why we're here," the gavel demon chimed in, speaking even more rapidly than before. "Say—we missed you. Of course. That's it. Certainly." The demon tugged at its too tight collar. "Uh—you don't know what a trial it's been not to see your face. Right. It's been—well, *hours* since our last encounter, and we were so looking forward to your inspirational—"

"Silence!" Mother Duck commanded.

The demons silenced.

In the sudden absence of noise, I heard other rustlings behind me. I glanced around to see Snarks, Brax and Guxx climbing up the riverbank.

"And don't you try anything, either!" Mother Duck proclaimed, fixing the three with her steely glare. She turned back to the committee. "You remember what happened the last time you tried to boil blood around here?"

All five demons nodded their heads vigorously.

"Certainly, Mother Duck."

"Most assuredly, Mother Duck."

"The survivors are still under the care of the finest physicians in the Netherhells, Mother Duck."

"Very well," the woman stated. "We won't have any more of that sort of thing, will we?"

The five demons blanched noticeably, turning pastel shades of their various fantastic hues.

"Oh, no, Mother Duck."

"Absolutely not, Mother Duck."

"You have it all there in writing, Mother Duck. Would you like us to recite it aloud?"

But before Mother Duck could respond, another gruff demonic voice interjected:

"Begin!"

Brax beat on the drum he had thoughtfully slung from his waist.

> "Guxx Unfufadoo, appalled demon,
> Has had his fill of Netherhells' cowards;
> Will grab them by soft underbellies,
> And feed them to the molten slime pits!"

Guxx flexed his claws as if they could barely wait for the aforementioned grabbing and feeding to begin.

The committee all stared at their former leader, he who had once been Grand Hoohah. Mother Duck was temporarily forgotten. Guxx's pronouncement had clearly upset them.

"Oh, yeah?" exploded the small, sickly fiend at table's end.

"You and what army?" the fellow next to him rejoined.

"Why don't you come over *here* and say that?" something shouted from the other end of the table.

The primary demon pounded its gavel.

"Now, then," it rumbled grimly at Guxx. "Let us get something clear. You were once a power in the Netherhells, but you are a power no more. We now hold the reins of the world below. If you choose to question our might, there will be"—the fiend paused for dramatic effect—"retribution."

"Oh, yeah!" the small, sickly fellow exclaimed enthusiastically.

Mother Duck stepped between the combatants.

"I think not," she said calmly, staring at the five demon committee members. "You will do nothing of the kind. Those already here are under my protection."

I could not believe my ears. Mother Duck, our sworn enemy, was actually defending us! I wondered for an instant what had caused her change of heart, and decided it had to be our obvious sincerity. As we participated in her fairy stories, she was coming to know our true, honest selves. Perhaps it wouldn't be so difficult to reason with her after all!

"But these are demons!" the gavel fiend persisted. "They are ours by Netherhells' common law!"

"Oh, boy! Is it time to boil blood?" The sickly fellow grinned at my three demonic allies as its fellow committee members also turned their collective gaze in the same direction. "Feeling a little hot under the collars, boys?"

Snarks and Brax both quietly retreated behind the greater bulk of Guxx Unfufadoo.

Mother Duck reached a hand inside her woolen vest. She pulled out a sheaf of parchment. "You are perhaps forgetting this," she remarked casually. "This is the contract I signed with the Netherhells after our last unfortunate incident, a contract which supercedes all Netherhells laws, prevents all demonic interference in my kingdoms and is possibly the only reason why the Netherhells still exist!"

"That's telling them!" Snarks cheered, poking his head out to the left of Guxx.

"One should always abide by contracts," Brax added as he peeked out from the right.

I tried hard to repress a smile. Mother Duck seemed definitely to be swinging to our side in this discussion. As soon as this little altercation was over, I resolved to speak with the woman, addressing her as the ally I was sure she would become. I stared at the ground, searching for the exact words. How would my master handle this?

"We certainly don't object," the gavel demon interjected hastily. "We would never object with Mother Duck!" The other committee demons nodded their agreement.

Mother Duck smiled. "I'm glad everyone sees things my way. There will be no more threats against these demons. You are interlopers." She gestured at the committee, then turned and waved in much the same fashion at the rest of us. "Those already here are pawns. They are mine to do with as I choose."

Pawns? Do with as she chose? That wasn't the way one spoke about potential allies. I frowned. Perhaps I had slightly misinterpreted recent events. Maybe I should address Mother Duck as more of a neutral party.

"Consider yourself lucky, demons," the old woman continued. "This time, I will accept your pitiful excuses, and look upon your visit here as an oversight. But listen closely: if I see you again, the Netherhells will pay!"

The demons all began to talk at once:

"Certainly, Mother Duck."

"Our every effort is to please you, Mother Duck."

"We will do whatever you ask, Mother Duck," the gavel demon added. "We ask only one boon. Might you, in your infinite wisdom, be able to point out the way to Vushta and the Western Kingdoms?"

Mother Duck sighed. "Very well, even though it isn't in the contract. I can see no other way to be rid of you for good." She pointed over the demon's shoulder. "That way."

The demon twisted its head around, still perplexed. "That's all you can tell me? That way? You couldn't be a little more specific?"

The other demons nudged their leader.

"That's perfectly all right, Mother Duck," one bubbled.

"Thank you for all the help, Mother Duck," another chirped.

"Don't you think it's time we were going so that we can leave Mother Duck and her pawns in peace?" the sickly fiend asked hopefully.

"Remember the contract!" Mother Duck whispered helpfully.

"The contract?" The gavel demon repressed a shiver. "Very well, Mother Duck. I never meant to question your directions, Mother Duck. Uh—that way." It nodded toward the west. "Back into the earth, fellow demons!"

Grunting and groaning, the committee dragged their table back to the edge of the crevice, and then, with a final heave-ho, toppled it into the pit. The five demons quickly followed.

"At last!" Mother Duck glanced about at the rest of us, clapping her hands peremptorily. "No dawdling, now. Back to work!"

"But—," I began. She didn't even seem to hear me as she marched back toward the hill, the talking wolf in close pursuit. How could I convince her of the wisdom of our cause if she wouldn't even stop and listen?

"Oh, Wuntie!" Alea breathed in my ear. "She called us pawns!"

"Indeed," I replied, wishing that the damsel would not stand quite so close. "I believe she underestimates us. She is so wrapped up in concocting her fairy stories that she ignores us when we are not under her direct control. We must therefore use this time wisely, and complete our escape plans."

The former Grand Hoohah stepped forward, raising both his clawed hands to gain our attention.

"Commence!" Guxx intoned.

I placed a restraining hand on Guxx's shoulder. "Please, no declaiming—" I glanced at Hubert and Alea. "—or singing for that matter—until I'm finished. I fear our time is limited."

"It's even shorter than that!" Snarks remarked. "The old lady's already made it to the top of the hill."

"No, not quite yet," Hubert said, motioning the truth-telling demon to silence. "She's still talking to the wolf. Something about how having hirsute characters in your stories gives those tales a gritty realism. We have a moment yet." The dragon grinned. "Always depend on dragon ears."

Snarks nodded. "I'd rather do that than listen to a dragon's vocal chords."

"Indeed," I interjected. "I fear there is no time for an argument, either. But Snarks's remark about vocal chords reminds me of the way Mother Duck controls us. Each of us falls under her spell through the use of our own voices. I believe we could actually break free of her spell, if only there was some way we could keep from saying those words. All of us must concentrate—"

"Those words?" Guxx rumbled.

"You mean 'Once upon a time'?" Hubert added helpfully.

Something strange happened to the dragon as soon as he framed the question. The huge reptile's eyes glazed over, and he began to totter back and forth.

"Look out!" Alea cried.

The rest of the party rapidly retreated as Hubert finally tottered too far and fell upon his back. When the dust settled, I saw that he was grabbing great handfuls of air with his forepaws while his legs kicked out against an invisible barrier.

"What is Hubert doing?" I asked, already afraid of the answer.

"Can't you tell?" Alea replied, excited despite herself. "It's a dragon doing the backstroke! He's back in the fairy story. But what talent!"

So saying the four words turned Hubert instantly back into a dragon mime. I nodded grimly. "This proves my point. If we can only resist, we may be able to overcome this spell!"

"But how can we resist?" Tap asked urgently. "Her spells are even stronger than Brownie Power!"

"We simply must be very careful about what we say, and never put those four words together in a sentence. Now concentrate with me, so that we might prevail."

I took a deep breath. I had broken into a sudden sweat. Was Mother Duck already attempting to exert her magical control over me? I waved for the others to come closer. "Now listen to me," I began. *"Once* Mother Duck gets us under her control, we are lost, for who

knows *upon* what whim she will once again relinquish her control."
My head was beginning to swim. I bit my lip, willing the pain to clear
my mind. "Now, all we have to do is take her spells one at *a time—*"
      I blinked. Something had changed. What was I saying? What had I
said? Why was everyone around me saying the same thing?
      Had something gone wrong with one of my wishes?

SEVEN

I admit it. I have always had a weakness for damsels with long blond hair. Well, actually, I have a bit of a weakness for brunette maidens as well. Ah, yes—and then there are damsels with hair of fire red! And did you ever notice how attractive women can be when they are totally bald?

—An uncompleted later chapter of
Some Thoughts About Apprenticeship,
by Wuntvor, apprentice to Ebenezum,
greatest wizard in the Western Kingdoms
(a work in progress)

Once upon a time, Wuntvor had thought this whole wish thing with the Brownie might bring him his fortune. Now he wasn't so sure.

"Now where were we?" the Brownie asked helpfully. "Oh, yes, you had just escaped from the tower with the maiden and the dragon, and having used three wishes, were wondering what next to do on your quest for adventure."

Wuntvor frowned. The Brownie's summation sounded fundamentally correct, and certainly went a long way toward calming the confusion that rattled about in his skull. There was only one thing that troubled him.

"Three wishes?" he queried.

The Brownie nodded his tiny head.

Wuntvor shook his in turn, still trying to remember. "I had wished for . . . a weapon. Oh, yes! And to find a woman to be my love. What was my third wish?"

"That you wanted to know everything!" the Brownie replied.

Wuntvor scratched his head. "Then why don't I remember it?"

The Brownie looked at Wuntvor solemnly, then glanced at the hill beyond. "Believe me, you don't want to know."

What? Wuntvor now found himself so confused that he couldn't
even frame another question. He was beginning to suspect, however,
that this whole conversation was a Brownie trick to get him to waste
another wish. Perhaps it would be best to go on to other matters.

"Oh, Wuntie!" the beautiful maiden called to him. How did she
know his name? Had they ever officially been introduced? "We have
great news for you!"

"Once upon a time," Wuntvor murmured as he turned to face the
long-haired beauty, for those words somehow seemed to calm him.
"Once upon a time."

"Hubert and I have been thinking," the damsel continued. "It is
difficult for an unattached man and woman to travel through the
countryside. There are malicious gossips everywhere, and certain people who will always think the worst. Of course, having a dragon along
does help somewhat. For some reason, people are reticent to speak
their worst excesses in the vicinity of a fire-breathing reptile. Still, we
might have trouble if your presence is not properly explained. Therefore—"

She paused while the dragon leapt about from foot to foot in what
could charitably be called a dance. The giant lizard waved its top hat
in Wuntvor's direction.

"Can't you see what Hubert's trying to tell you?" The damsel
cheered. "You're going to become part of our act!"

"Indeed," the lad replied, somewhat startled by this information.
Somehow, becoming part of a touring company with a beautiful damsel and dancing dragon was not his precise definition of "adventure."
Still, he was willing to attempt anything, as long as a lovely maiden
was about. Besides which, he reflected, it was easy to make decisions
of this type if you still had four Brownie wishes to fall back on.

"Indeed," he said again.

The damsel clapped her hands happily. "Oh, we'll have such fun!
And listen, we even have an idea for our first routine. It's an old one,
but that means it's a proven audience pleaser."

The dragon blew an elaborate smoke ring by way of agreement.

"That's right," the maiden trilled. "I'm talking about the Thrilling
Dragon Rescue!" She glanced up at the large reptile apologetically. "I
know that's species stereotyping, but what are you going to do? It's
what they expect out in the sticks. And we are definitely in the sticks."
She smiled at Wuntvor. She was lovely when she smiled. "Are you
ready?"

The lad nodded his head somewhat dubiously.

"Right, here we go," the damsel replied. "First, Hubert will breathe a little fire to set the mood."

The dragon roared above them, flame shooting the length of the clearing.

"Now," the damsel instructed, "it is time for you to stare bravely at Hubert and draw your sword."

Wuntvor did as he was told.

"What's going on here?" the sword demanded, its voice cracking in its haste.

The damsel assured the weapon that it was only needed for a demonstration.

"Oh, really? You're sure about that?" the sword replied, somewhat mollified. "You'll have to excuse me, but in my line of work, it's easy to get jumpy. I mean, here you are, sitting snug in the dark, lulled into complacency by the steady slap-slap-slap of scabbard against thigh, then whizzo, you're out in the sunlight. Wouldn't you find that the slightest bit disconcerting?"

"I had never thought of it from a sword's point of view," the damsel mused. "Still, now that you are in the theater, we should be able to avoid that problem entirely. In our act, you will know exactly when you will be drawn, and precisely what you are supposed to do."

She turned back to me. "Now, Wuntie, point the sword away from you at arm's length, and run straight for the dragon's breastbone."

"Wait a minute!" Cuthbert wailed, the panic back in its voice. "This is just another trick to get me into battle, isn't it?" The sword laughed ruefully. "I know the way it is around here. I mean, I remember what my old uncle used to tell me—he was an enchanted brass headboard, and knew all about these things—he'd say, 'Cuthbert, my boy, never get involved with heroes. Heroes are always hacking or slashing something. Stay away from practical swords and daggers. Go for ornamental, my boy,' he said. But did I listen? Oh, no! Magic latticework was too dull for me! Magic locks and keys didn't get to go places and do things! So I end up becoming a talking sword; nothing but a hero's *tool!*"

"Now, now," the lad reassured the overwrought blade in his hand. "I've always had great respect for my weapons. And I will only draw you when it is time for action."

"I know it," the sword replied bitterly. "Then you'll *use* me! Oh, the trials of being an intelligent inanimate object!"

"Indeed," Wuntvor answered solemnly, wishing to put an end to these histrionics. "Cuthbert, we are acting out a play. There will be no cutting, and no blood."

"No cutting?" the sword quavered.

"Indeed," the lad replied.

"No blood?" Cuthbert asked.

"No blood," Alea reassured the weapon.

"Well, why didn't you say so?" Cuthbert cleared its throat. "Go forth, brave warrior! Your noble sword will lead the way!"

"I'm glad we've got that out of the way," the maiden said. "Motivation is so often a problem in our line of work. Now, Wuntie! Thrust your sword forth and rush the marauding beast!"

"Should I say anything?" the lad asked.

"An excellent idea," the damsel agreed. "A bloodcurdling epithet or two would be perfectly in character."

"Indeed," the lad replied, taking a deep breath before he began his run.

He shouted as he picked up speed, hoping to find an appropriate phrase: "I'll get you—uh—beast—uh—reptile—uh—uh—you'd better watch out uh—I've got a sword here."

"Well, we'll have to work on your epithets," the maiden said as she stepped in front of the dragon. The lad skidded to a halt, his shining sword mere inches from the maiden's massive hair. The damsel smiled. "You are, however, very good at stopping. As you see, the brave hero is brought up short by the appearance of the beauteous maiden. However, the hero does not truly fall in love with the maiden until she begins her song."

A song? Hadn't something like this happened to Wuntvor before? Oh, yes, up in the tower. But he had the feeling that it had occurred many other times as well. The young man looked around. Where was the Brownie when he needed him?

But it was too late. The damsel had already begun to sing:

"If you've got a dragon,
You'll never be cold;
But he will eat you
Before you get old!

"If you've got a dragon,
You'll never get wet,

Unless all that fire
Works up a sweat!

"If you've got a dragon,
I've got a hunch,
Your future is short,
And it's probably lunch!

"Take me from this dragon,
Oh please set me free;
Or I will be flame-broiled
On its rotisserie!

"Now you'll be a hero,
Please don't be a slob!
Or soon I will end up
A damsel-kebab!"

The song ran on, verse after verse. After a time, Wuntvor decided to sit, resting his talking sword gently across his knees.

"We don't get much of a part in this, do we?" the sword remarked.

The lad nodded and sighed. "This acting stuff isn't all that I had hoped. It doesn't seem to be much more than a lot of waiting around." He glanced up at the damsel, who was singing a verse about dragon fritters. "I do wish this could be a little more exciting."

"Granted!" came a little voice from nowhere.

Wuntvor heard heavy footsteps crossing the bridge behind him. He stood, turning so quickly that he almost lost his sword.

A massive warrior stood on the near end of the bridge, holding a huge warclub in one of his very large hands.

"Doom," the warrior intoned. "The time of reckoning has come."

EIGHT

It is difficult for some people to realize that giants, like many other huge magical creatures, are largely misunderstood. Think on it, however. How many times are you going to have a reasoned, caring conversation with a creature from whom you are fleeing for your very life?

—*I'm OK, I'm a wizard: The Magician's Guide to Perfect Mental Health,* by Ebenezum, greatest mage in the Western Kingdoms (fourth edition)

"Let's not get any rash ideas," the sword cautioned.

"Shall we see what this warrior wants?" Wuntvor suggested.

Cuthbert groaned softly. "Oh, I knew this was going to be a bad day. You know what I mean? Did you ever have the feeling that you've gotten up out of the wrong side of the scabbard?"

"Doom," the large warrior rumbled as the lad approached. "Norei is waiting. I was supposed to say that."

Norei is waiting? Hope suddenly sprang in Wuntvor's breast. But that meant that—

"Once upon a time," the warrior and the lad said in unison.

"Doom," the large fellow repeated. "I am the warrior of warning. And I am warning you: The giant is coming."

"The giant?" Cuthbert and the damsel screamed in unison. Even the dragon took a few involuntary steps backward.

"The giant?" the lad replied. "I guess that's bad?"

"The giant can find you, no matter where you hide," the sword wailed.

"The giant knows no mercy!" Alea added.

"Doom!" the warrior of warning concluded.

"I guess it is bad," Wuntvor said. "What am I to do?"

"Hide!" the sword screamed. "All is lost! There is no hope!"

"I fear that your weapon is incorrect," the damsel stated boldly. "Where there is theater, there is always hope! But how best to use your newfound abilities?"

The dragon rumbled overhead. Both Wuntvor and the maiden looked up to see the reptile waving his forepaws in a slow rhythm. When the paws were spread apart, the lizard moved his head back and forth, as if it studied something.

"Of course!" the damsel cried as she applauded. "What genius. It is an honor, Hubert, to be working with you!"

"Indeed," Wuntvor interjected when there appeared to be no explanation forthcoming. "I am sure it is truly a subtle piece of genius. Would you mind giving me a hint as to its exact meaning?"

"Oh, can't you see?" Alea cheered. "It's a dragon mime reading a newspaper!"

A newspaper? Wuntvor frowned. That word was somehow familiar. Didn't that have something to do with a chicken crossing the road?

"Indeed," the lad said at last. "What's a newspaper?"

The damsel pulled a piece of parchment from her bodice. As she unfolded the sheet, Wuntvor saw it was covered with dense script.

"This is a newspaper!" she declared. "To be more specific, a trade newspaper!"

Wuntvor found this new statement no more illuminating than what had been said before. However, he was sure that, if he remained quiet, it would all be explained to him, at least after a fashion.

"I tell you, if you want to move around in this business, you simply have to keep up with the trades." The maiden rapidly scanned the page. "All we have to do is give you a new identity. The giant won't be able to find you if you no longer exist!"

"Indeed?" So that was their plan? Wuntvor was still not convinced.

"Ah!" the maiden called in triumph. "There's a town named Bremen that's looking for some musicians. Opportunities are everywhere!" She shook the parchment in the lad's direction. "See? Here's another place—Hamlin. 'Piper wanted.' All you need is a few simple flute tunes. . . ."

She frowned as she continued to read. "Well, I don't know about that one. Being a musical leader for a bunch of rats isn't everybody's idea of a good time. It always pays to read these things all the way through."

"Doom," the warrior interjected. "You have no time to read. The giant is coming."

The damsel ignored the sword's hysterical screams to stare critically at Wuntvor. "Perhaps we do not have time to give you a new identity, but theater will save you yet! It is time for a quick disguise."

"Indeed?" the lad asked. Well, he had asked for adventure, and now, apparently, he had it. He stuffed his sword back in its sheath so that all he heard was an occasional muffled whimper. Perhaps it was time then to come up with some disguise that would allow him to flee unhindered through the forest; a brave soldier, perhaps, on an unnamed mission from which he could not pause, or a simple woodsman, rushing home after a trying workday. The lad resolved that, whatever the charade, he would act it to make the maiden proud.

The damsel looked about quickly. "We have little enough at hand. We will have to use a length of my hair."

"We will?" the lad queried, somewhat surprised by this turn of events. Should a brave soldier have long, blond hair? Or would it be more appropriate to a humble woodsman?

"Alas, it is all that is available to me," the damsel replied. "Have no fear. I shan't miss it. You wouldn't believe how fast it grows. Hubert! I have need of your claws."

The dragon obligingly knelt nearby, shearing off a length of the maiden's locks with one reptilian forefinger.

The damsel picked up the newly freed mass of hair with a smile. "Now all we need is a length of sackcloth that we can wrap like a skirt to hide your leggings. Hubert, if you could nip back into the tower larder to see what we have?"

The dragon nodded and nipped.

"Now." The beautiful maiden bit her perfectly formed lip as she surveyed Wuntvor's skull. "We will need my sash to serve as a headband to keep the hair in place."

"Indeed?" the lad remarked hesitantly. "If I may ask, what is this disguise to be?"

"You will masquerade as a fair maiden—" She frowned at his face. "Well, at least as a maiden, until you have left the vicinity. The hair is long enough to disguise you above the waist, and the skirt should hide your lower extremities as well. Once you are beyond the Eastern Kingdoms, you can remove the wig and resume your true identity."

"A maiden?" the lad began to protest. "But—"

"Doom," the warrior of warning interjected. "The giant."

"Indeed," Wuntvor replied. "The giant." He stood still while the real damsel adjusted the hair and headband, then wrapped about his waist a long piece of brown cloth that the dragon had brought.

"There," the beautiful maiden said at last. "You'll do. The hair will fall in your face, further masking your features. Just don't let anybody get too close to you."

"Indeed." At least the lad could agree with the last remark. "Now you must excuse me while I make my escape." The sooner he was shed of this silly disguise, the better.

"Doom," the warrior agreed. "Leave quickly."

"But take smaller steps," the damsel coached as Wuntvor moved away. "And hold your head up. Remember, you are a refined maiden now."

Wuntvor didn't respond. He felt more like a refined dustmop with all the hair in his face. And he almost tripped on the long skirt. How did people walk in these things, anyway?

Still, from the way the others had spoken of the giant, this appeared to be his only chance for survival. He had no choice but to ignore how ludicrous he looked and hope he could escape from this place before anything truly embarrassing happened.

"Farewell, Wuntie!" the damsel called as he began his flight in earnest. "Perhaps some day we can act together again, in more intimate surroundings!"

Wuntvor waved a final time, careful not to move his head too quickly, lest he dislodge the mass of hair. Even taking smaller steps, he was soon out of sight of the others, surrounded by the ancient Eastern forest.

"Well, hello there," a beautifully modulated voice spoke from the nearby underbrush. "I almost didn't recognize you."

Wuntvor stopped short. Could this be the giant? He reached for his sword.

But something considerably shorter than a giant stepped from between the bushes. Still, despite its smaller size, it was more wondrous than a giant could ever be.

"A—a unicorn," the lad said aloud.

"Not just any unicorn," the beast replied proudly. "The unicorn. *Your* unicorn. Could you have forgotten me so soon? Oh, of course you could. You're in one of her fairy tales, aren't you?"

"Once upon a time," the lad replied.

The creature sighed magnificently. "This might be more difficult than I thought. And after I've traveled so far to see you again. If not for that certain quality you have—" The unicorn looked at him meaningfully. "You know what I'm talking about. I can't help myself." The beast shuddered gloriously. "And now *this.*"

"Do I know you from somewhere?" the lad replied, for he couldn't remember this beast at all, which was doubly disturbing, since the unicorn was one of the most memorable things he had ever seen.

"I know," the creature said with a profound sadness. "I've got eyes, don't I? I can see what you're doing: Practicing to join one of the forbidden delights as soon as I've gone. You know how desperately I need to rest my weary head! How can you toy with my affections so?" The beast brushed at the lad's blond wig with its lustrous golden horn. "It's even worse when you get kinky!"

"Indeed," the lad said, still uncertain of what the magnificent beast was going on about, but increasingly glad for his ignorance. "I'm sure what you are saying is all very interesting, and I would be glad to discuss it with you at some other time. Now, if you will excuse me, I have a forest to flee."

"Well, if you are in such a hurry," the unicorn remarked coyly, "I suppose I can't tell you about Norei."

"Norei?" Why did that name send a shiver down his spine? Why did the words "one true love" fill his brain? Of course!

"Once up—" Wuntvor clamped his lips tight before he could finish the phrase. This was no time for reassurance. There were serious things to consider. He thought of Norei again, and a young woman's face burned its way into his consciousness. The young witch. His only love. Norei. It took his breath away.

"Are you all right?" the unicorn inquired.

Wuntvor took a deep breath, remembering to stand up straight. "Indeed," he replied.

"That's a relief," the beast remarked. "It seemed you were having a spasm of some sort. I'd hate to lose you now, when we've gotten so close."

"But what of Norei?" Wuntvor asked, wishing to hear more of her. "Do you mind if we walk as we talk? I'm afraid I'm trying to escape."

The unicorn trotted wondrously alongside as Wuntvor began to walk swiftly but casually. Smaller steps, the young man reminded himself.

"Well, of course, Norei's the reason why I'm here." The creature wriggled its splendid eyebrows. "Well, at least that's *one* of the reasons."

"And Norei?" the lad prompted.

The unicorn sighed. "Well, if we must. Norei has a plan for your escape. Now remember these words: Happily ever after!"

"Happily ever after?" the lad repeated.

"Exactly. Said at the proper moment, those words will set you free. Mother Duck will hold sway over you no more."

"Mother Duck?" Wuntvor asked, suddenly remembering her as well. "But how did you escape her control?"

"It is in the nature of being a unicorn." The beast sniffed magnificently. "My coat is so white, my hooves so swift, my horn so blinding in the summer sun, that Mother Duck's spells reflect off me and can do me no harm."

"Indeed?" the lad said, wondering if this information might do him some good at a later time.

"Certainly," the wondrous creature murmured proudly. "Why do you think unicorns appear in so few fairy tales? Mother Duck can't use what she can't catch."

"So Norei—," Wuntvor began.

"Norei, Norei, always Norei!" the unicorn wailed. It paused, pointing its shining horn at the leaf-strewn ground. "No, it is quite all right. Forgive my outburst. I am myself again. What can my longing do but make me a better beast?" The creature looked at the lad with its deep and soulful eyes. "For what is perfect beauty without perfect pain?"

"And Norei?" the lad insisted.

"Yes, yes, of course," the unicorn added hastily. "She will save you, of course, if you simply remember the magic words. Of course. Still—"

The magic creature paused again, its eyes filled with the greatest sadness Wuntvor had ever seen.

"Is there something else you wish to say?" the lad asked.

"Well," the beast began hesitantly, "I was just thinking . . . my head is so heavy . . . and your lap is so near . . . so inviting . . ." The beast shivered wondrously. "I realize you are not entirely yourself and it wouldn't mean quite the same thing—well, a beast can dream, can't it?"

"Indeed," Wuntvor responded, wishing he could find a way to change the subject. "I'm sure we might be able to come to some arrangement, if I weren't in the midst of fleeing for my life—my, did you ever see such a large tree in your life?"

And, indeed, there was a huge tree before them, perhaps twenty times the circumference of any of its neighbors. Stranger still, this tree was not the usual deep brown of the others in the forest, but was closer to the green of meadow grass.

"That's no tree," the unicorn replied. "That's a beanstalk."

"A beanstalk?" The lad rolled the word around his tongue. "Indeed. And what is a beanstalk?"

The unicorn looked at the lad incredulously. "Surely you know what big beanstalks are for. They take you up to where the giants live."

"Once upon a time!" the lad cried in surprise. For, when he looked up the beanstalk, he saw someone descending from far overhead.

An incredibly deep voice wafted down from the clouds.

"Oops!" the voice said.

NINE

They tell you to "always watch your feet." But if you're constantly looking at your feet, how can you tell where you're going?

—*Some Notes on Apprenticeship,*
by Wuntvor, apprentice to Ebenezum,
greatest mage in the Western Kingdoms
(a work in progress)

Something was falling very rapidly from the sky. Something that Wuntvor suspected would be much heavier on impact than a mass of hair.

"I suggest that we move as quickly as possible back into the forest," the unicorn called, already on the move.

"I think I need to do more than that!" Wuntvor exclaimed. "That's the giant I've been trying to get away from."

The unicorn risked a final look aloft. "Well, I fear that this particular giant is going to be very close very soon."

"Indeed!" the lad yelled back, redoubling his speed. "I just wish I had some place to hide."

"Granted!" a small but very chipper voice yelled nearby.

Wuntvor screamed as a pit opened up beneath him.

The lad opened his eyes. He couldn't see a thing. With some trepidation, he parted the mass of hair that had descended in front of his face. He looked at an expanse of light gray rock. He lifted his gaze and saw that he had fallen into a cave of some sort, but it was a well-lit cave, swept and tidy besides, obviously the sort of place someone or something called home.

Wuntvor peered carefully through his disguise. As far as he could tell, there was no one moving about. But didn't he smell food?

Until this instant, the lad had not realized how hungry he was. When was the last time he had eaten? Wuntvor couldn't remember, but then there were so many things he could not recall.

"Once upon a time," the lad murmured as he walked toward the warm food smells. He turned a corner in the cave, and found that the home that he had stumbled upon was not simply a resting place for some creature from the wild. No, there were furnishings here; places to sit and hangings upon the wall, although none of it was quite like anything he had ever seen.

Wuntvor warily circled a trio of stools. They looked much like ordinary stools except that each had a seat covered with some sort of cloth padding. Well, he didn't imagine that padding could hurt him, so perhaps he should try sitting down, especially since the warm food smells came from the table just beyond.

The lad sat first in the tallest stool. But he leapt off in an instant, barely stifling a cry of pain. His posterior stung in half a dozen places. That stool hadn't been soft at all. Rather, the padding seemed to be filled with sharpened rocks. Wuntvor had never felt anything so hard in his life.

The lad tentatively felt the padding on the second stool, wary of further tricks. But this cloth was what he expected, soft and pliable. Perhaps the first stool was a trick of some sort, placed there for unwary visitors. Then again, it could have been built for something that enjoyed sitting on sharpened rocks. Wuntvor fervently hoped for the first alternative.

Still, there were three large pieces of pie on the table beyond the stools, and their aroma was making Wuntvor's taste buds scream for sustenance. The lad decided he would have to try the second chair after all. He climbed the stool and sat gingerly.

Ah, that was much better, Wuntvor thought as he sank into the padding. But shouldn't he stop sinking? There seemed to be no seat under the stuffing. The lad felt he would sink forever. He leapt from the stool as best he could. He never realized anything could be that soft!

Wuntvor stood there for a long moment, waiting for his heart to quiet down. Perhaps he should leave this place before he got into further trouble. If only he weren't so hungry!

Well, there was always the third stool. It was the smallest of the three, so he would be able to easily get away should there be any trouble. And, now that the lad thought about it, neither of the first two stools had caused him any serious damage.

Well, he was here to go on adventures, the lad reasoned, and, considering what had happened thus far, sitting on the small stool qualified. He took a deep breath and sat.

To his surprise, the stool felt wonderfully comfortable. It was like sitting on a pile of new-mown hay, soft yet buoyant. Wuntvor couldn't imagine a better seat.

The lad smiled. It was time to turn his attention to the food. There were three pieces of pie before him, the filling a tempting pinkish-purple. Cautiously, Wuntvor reached for the largest piece.

He pulled his hand back with a stifled cry, stuffing his fingers in his mouth. He had never in his life felt anything that hot! He examined his fingers. There didn't seem to be any permanent damage. And the juice that had clung to his skin had been quite tasty.

Even more cautiously, Wuntvor decided to touch another piece of the treacherous dessert. He pushed gently at the crust of the middle-sized piece. The crust didn't give at all. It was solid as a rock. And cold, too, as if someone had kept it stored in a mound of snow. Never in his life had he felt a dessert that cold.

The lad withdrew his hand. What was going on here? If he hadn't been so hungry, he would have left this strange place at that instant. But here he was, sitting on the smallest, most comfortable stool. As long as he was here, he might as well attempt to sample the smallest of the three wedges of pie.

He gently touched the crust. To the lad's surprise, it was pleasantly warm. He pulled the pie toward him. At last, he could satisfy his hunger. He took the wedge in both hands and brought it to his eager lips, tentatively sampling a bit of the filling with his tongue. It was delicious, just the right mixture of tart and sweet. There would be no more tricks this time.

Wuntvor took a big bite and screamed. He spit the contents of his mouth back onto the table. The pie was full of tiny sharp things, like nettles. A couple had gotten stuck to his tongue and gums, and the lad carefully pulled them out, whimpering softly with the pain. Who lived in this place anyway? Who would be crazy enough to bake a deadly pie?

That's when the lad heard the voices, and the heavy footsteps. Someone, more than one—two or three—they were coming into the cave!

Wuntvor jumped from the stool. Where could he go? Where could he hide? The voices were getting closer. They were just beyond the bend. The lad ran around the table and bolted through an open doorway that led into another room.

He looked quickly around this new space. Besides a small hole in the ceiling to let in light, there were no further openings. Wuntvor was trapped! But wait a moment. On the far side of the room were three pools. Perhaps one of them might lead to safety.

The voices were in the next room! Wuntvor ran to the wall by the door, praying whoever had arrived would not look in here until he had made his decision.

A deep, gravelly voice spoke first:

> "Guxx Unfufadoo, poppa demon,
> Sees that we've had an intruder!
> Sees that someone has been sitting
> In his stool—my rocks are messy!"

"Oh, dear—," another deep voice began, but stopped to cough. "Oh, dear," the same voice repeated, this time in a falsetto, "Someone's been sitting in my stool, too. Look, it's all saggy!"

"Someone's been sitting on my stool, too!" exclaimed a third voice, even more grating than the first two. "And the seat's still warm!"

Uh-oh, the lad thought. They suspected he was still here. If he was going to escape, it would have to be soon. But which of the three pools should he try? From what had already happened in this place, he knew he had to be careful. There could be all sorts of things lurking in those dark waters. As quietly as possible, the lad crept across the room, eager to examine his potential escape routes.

The deep voice spoke again in the other room:

> "Guxx Unfufadoo, poppa demon,
> Sees the stranger has not rested;
> Sees he's disturbed my Sweet Demon
> Pie—he's scuffed its molten surface!"

"Someone has touched my Sweet Demon Pie as well," the falsetto voice answered. "You can see the fingerprint etched in the frost. And I had put in extra brambles, just for you!"

"Someone's gone after my pie, too," said the most grating of the voices, "and—ptuui!—is he a messy eater!"

The voices in the other room were becoming more agitated by the minute. Wuntvor knew he would have to make a decision soon, or it would be too late. He knelt down by the largest of the three pools, trying to see whether it had a bottom.

The water appeared totally opaque. More than that, it looked like it was colored a dull gray. More even than that, Wuntvor doubted it was water at all, but rather some far heavier, more odiferous liquid. He wondered if he should disturb the surface with his hand, but was wary of the great quantities of steam the pool seemed to be producing. After all, he had already been burned once. No, this pool definitely would not do. Perhaps, he thought, he should try one of the others.

He duck-walked over to the next smaller of the three, but noticed that its surface was marred by something solid floating through the viscous liquid. It was only when the cold breeze rose to brush his face that he realized the solid particles were ice.

No, Wuntvor thought, that pool won't do either.

Still, there was the smallest of the three. So far in this household, he seemed to have the most luck with the most diminutive objects he had found. Perhaps his good fortune would hold here as well.

Cautiously, he placed his hand gently in the liquid. It slid down quickly, as if his flesh had somehow grown heavier under the surface. He imagined, if he had not braced himself, that not only his hand but the rest of him would have been drawn into the pool instantly. There was something strange about the feel of the liquid itself, too, somehow slippery and heavy at the same time, like oily oatmeal.

Wuntvor quickly pulled his fist from the pool. His hand was covered with slime.

"Uck!" the lad yelled, quite beside himself.

"Who's that?" three gruff voices called from the other room.

Wuntvor heard three sets of feet heading for the doorway. This, then, was his last chance to escape. He looked back at the mucous-filled pool. If he was going to jump, it was now or never.

Mucous-filled pool? The lad decided it would definitely be never.

He almost reconsidered when three heads appeared in the door.

"Guxx Unfufadoo, poppa demon,"

An incredibly large and ugly bluish-purple creature began,

> Sees the stranger came in this way,
> Sees she looked at all the slime pools,
> Who's been mucking in our pool muck!"

The second demon nodded its somewhat shorter, somewhat grayer head, which caused its long hair to bob about like a gaggle of spastic snakes. That is, if you could call it hair. It looked to Wuntvor more like a mass of tangled seaweed.

"Someone dragged herself past my slime pit as well," the second creature added in its falsetto.

"Somebody's been inspecting my slime pit, too!" the third, slightly smaller creature (who was wearing a lace bonnet) declared as it pointed at the cowering Wuntvor. "And there she is!"

She? the lad wondered for an instant, before he remembered his disguise.

"It's a human!" the lace bonneted demon continued. "And it might be female!"

The seaweed-haired creature waved pleasantly. "Welcome to our home, oh golden locks. As we are civilized creatures, I thought I might introduce the three of us before we eat you."

It pointed at the largest of the three. "This is the poppa demon. And over here is our little baby demon. And I, of course, am the momma demon." The seaweed-haired creature gave Wuntvor a conspiratorial glance. "Should you be interested, in this time of crisis, I also sell used weapons on the side."

With that, the poppa demon sauntered into the room.

> "Guxx Unfufadoo, poppa demon
> Sees our golden-haired intruder;
> Cooks her with a little butter;
> Eats her with a side of cole slaw!"

"Poppa's right," momma demon agreed pleasantly as it, too, entered the room. It was wearing a dress of orange and green plaid. "How fortunate that you have come. We really like to eat golden-haired girls."

"Even golden-haired girls that look like that?" baby demon sneered as it also hopped into the room. Wuntvor thought its diaper looked a little incongruous on one so green and scaly.

"Now, now, baby demon," momma reprimanded. "Diners can't be

choosers." The creature smiled at Wuntvor. "Now, if you would just walk this way, I think I have a pot barely big enough!"

Wuntvor fought down the panic growing deep inside him. These were intelligent creatures, he told himself. Certainly they could be reasoned with.

"Indeed?" he asked. "And what if I was not exactly as I appeared? What if I were, say, an adventurer in disguise?"

"What if you were thrown into a pool of molten slime by an enraged demon?" the baby of the family replied. "It's not nice to fool poppa demon."

"Yes," the momma agreed, "Daddy does have a temper. But you won't have to worry about that, will you?" The creature frowned contemplatively at Wuntvor. "I'd say forty-five minutes at 375 degrees and all your worries will be over."

"Indeed," the lad replied, following the momma demon through the doorway into the other room. He reasoned that, though he would be much closer to the stove, he would also be that much closer to the cave mouth and escape.

"You can just sit anywhere." The momma demon motioned expansively at the glittering countertop before them. "Oh, and as long as you're sitting here, you wouldn't mind helping me peel carrots, would you? Believe me, it will help you pass the time." The creature opened a cupboard door and searched through a pile of large knives. It extracted the smallest of the lot and handed it apologetically to Wuntvor. "It's so hard to get good help down in these caves."

Wuntvor took the knife and began to peel. He wondered if he could use this little tool as a weapon. But what could he do with something this tiny—poke the demons to death?

It was then he recalled he still had a sword hiding under all his hair.

The momma demon chatted on as it minced onions. "I know that this may seem to be an imposition, in that we're going to eat you and all, but could you tell me who does your hair? I mean, look at mine! I can't do a thing with it. Lucky for my sideline. Amazing how a collection of used weapons cuts down on comments on your appearance."

"Uh—indeed," Wuntvor answered, keeping the conversation alive until he could think of a way to escape. "Mine just sort of—uh—comes naturally."

The momma demon sighed. "Well, I guess beautiful hair simply doesn't fall out of the sky. If you've got it, you've got it."

"We want to eat!" the baby demon exclaimed as it rushed into the room. The amazingly large and imposing poppa demon was right behind.

Well, the lad thought, it was now or never. He drew his sword with a scream.

"Oh, no you don't!" he shouted at the startled demons.

"That's right!" the sword added. "You don't. In fact, as of this moment, no one does!"

The lad stared at the sword. "I beg your pardon?"

"I've had enough of being whipped from my scabbard on a moment's notice!" the weapon sniffed haughtily. "From this minute on, I'm on strike! That's quite correct: As of now, I refuse to cut anything, anywhere, for any purpose. Sorry I have to be so blunt about this, but things have to change!"

"But I am about to be cooked and eaten!" the lad wailed.

"Sorry," the sword answered, "but your scare tactics won't work on me this time. You're always about to get killed one way or another. There comes a point when a weapon has to say 'no more'!"

Wuntvor looked up helplessly as the three demons approached.

"Do you have any last requests?" the momma demon asked as she raised her butcher knife.

The lad nodded. "Only one. I wish I could get out of this alive."

"Granted!" shouted a tiny voice from nowhere.

TEN

The practicing wizard will often find himself in stressful situations. Two different clients may expect completely opposite results from some magical situation. The practicing mage must therefore weight each client's case carefully, thinking of the long-term results of his magicks, what part of his spells will best satisfy each client, and how best to leave if one of the parties in question becomes angered by the results. But no matter what the outcome, the practicing wizard must never neglect the first rule of professional wizardry: Always make sure you are paid by both clients well in advance.

—The Teachings of Ebenezum, VOLUME XXI

Wuntvor found himself back in the forest. The Brownie stood beside him.

"See?" the sword in his hands reproached him. "There are always alternatives to violence."

The lad slid his weapon back into its scabbard. He would have to deal with it later.

"So where have you been?" the lad demanded of the little fellow.

"Oh, here and there," the Brownie replied nonchalantly. "I've always been there when you needed me, haven't I? We wee folk have ways of making ourselves scarce. I decided that my presence was getting in the way of your story. It's an area of concern for us magic-producers: You were becoming too wish-conscious."

"My story?" Somehow, the lad had never thought of his adventures in quite that way. Still, why else would he keep saying "Once upon a time"?

"But now it's time for me to come back," the Brownie explained. "It's the Grande Finale. You've only got one wish left. You'd better make this one a doozy."

For a minute, Wuntvor considered wishing for a pudding and getting it over with once and for all. But no, with the way his luck had been running lately, he would probably need the last wish for something serious. He told the Brownie to stick around.

"As you wish," the little fellow replied, adding quickly: "Sorry, just a manner of speaking."

The lad turned from the Brownie to examine his surroundings. He was once again near the huge beanstalk, although now the giant seemed to be nowhere about. In fact, nothing much had changed, save for a sizable depression in the forest floor that Wuntvor had not noticed before.

"Indeed," the lad remarked after a moment's thought. "I think it is time for me to resume my escape."

But he had not gone a dozen steps before a chorus of voices assailed him from the surrounding shrubbery.

"Your mother wears army boots!" the first voice yelled.

"That's exactly like a human," a second voice added. "We come to visit, and you don't even say hello!"

"Oh, wow!" a third voice commented.

Eight very short men stepped from the forest and formed a semicircle around them.

"Indeed?" Wuntvor asked. "Pardon me, but have we met?"

One of the eight stepped forward, and spoke as he wrung his hands. "Oh dear, oh my. Excuse us, please. We didn't realize you were still under one of Mother Duck's spells. We are, of course, the Seven Other Dwarves." He waved to his fellows. "Snooty, Nasty, Touchy, Dumpy, Noisy, Sickly and Spacey. And I am their humble and only barely competent leader, Smarmy."

"You can say that again!" one of the other dwarves shouted. Wuntvor assumed that must be Nasty. Unless he was Snooty?

"And who elected you?" another asked with a tone of moral outrage. Okay, then this one must be Snooty. Unless he was Touchy?

One of the others groaned. Did that mean he was Noisy? Or could he be Dumpy or Sickly? Wuntvor decided that this speculation was getting him nowhere.

"Indeed," he began. "It's been awfully nice chatting with you, but unfortunately, I was in the midst of escaping."

"But that is the very reason we are here!" Smarmy exclaimed, redoubling his hand wringing. "How serendipitous for all of us!"

"Pardon," said the lad, quite surprised. "Are you escaping as well?"

"What a stupid idea!" one of the others, who had to be Nasty, replied.

"If you will excuse the forwardness of my fellow dwarf," Smarmy interjected, "no, escape is the farthest thing from our minds. As magical creatures, we belong in the Eastern Kingdoms. Rather, we have been sent by Norei, to help guide you in your own escape."

Norei? His beloved! The beautiful witch's face came back to Wuntvor in a rush. It was hazy still, he realized with a shiver. What else had he forgotten?

"That is correct," Smarmy continued after Wuntvor had regained his equilibrium. "Now please listen carefully, and may I say that I am honored that one as unworthy as myself was chosen to pass on this information—"

Smarmy paused for a second as catcalls like "You can say that again twice!" and "Yeah, who did pick you to be leader?" emanated from his fellows before he continued:

"You are to go to a hill in the west, and wait there for His Brownieship."

"His Brownieship?" Tap, the Brownie wish-giver, suddenly paled.

"But Norei—," Wuntvor began, desiring to see the young witch as soon as possible.

"I must beg your forgiveness," Smarmy interrupted, "but that is all I know. You must travel to the Western hill."

"His Brownieship?" the little fellow fretted. "Why would he be coming here, when I'm already in charge? I mean, I've been doing my job, haven't I?" The Brownie frowned up at Wuntvor. "Oh, dear. Maybe I haven't. What is this seven wishes thing, anyway?" He hit his tiny cheek with his tiny hand. "Mother Duck! I've fallen under her spells!" He appeared to be sweating. He tugged earnestly at Wuntvor's sackcloth skirt.

"Listen," he said to the lad, "I'd appreciate it if you didn't mention anything that's happened lately when His Brownieship shows up. I mean—buckles and laces!—I'll be demoted to heel sorting!"

"Indeed?" the lad agreed, not absolutely clear himself on all the fine points of what had happened. "What say we resume our escape?" If there was one thing he was sure of, it was that, if Norei had asked him to do so, he wanted to get to that western hill as soon as possible!

"Farewell, then!" Smarmy called as Wuntvor and Tap marched to the west. "And believe me, I can't wait for this to be over so that I can resume my Brownie lessons."

"Oh, that." The Brownie grinned sheepishly. "Perhaps, if it's all right with you, we won't mention that to His Brownieship either." The little fellow groaned softly, shaking his head. "I'll be demoted to bent buckle straightening!"

The Brownie had to hurry to catch up with the marching Wuntvor, who was rushing so fast that he almost tripped over his skirt at least three times. The small steps, indeed, the whole charade was forgotten in the lad's hurry to see Norei again. He had to reach that hill before Mother Duck's spell could reassert itself. He had to! Nothing would get in his way this time!

The day was growing late, the forest around them filled with long shadows. Wuntvor picked the Brownie up so that he might move even faster, heedless of the bushes and shrubs that stood in his way. They came at last to a clearing, but they both had to squint to make out a large shape etched against the glare of the late afternoon sun.

"Is that the hill we seek?" he asked the Brownie.

Tap still squinted into the brightness. At last he spoke, his voice hushed: "Alas, no. It is something even more awe-inspiring."

The Brownie climbed to Wuntvor's shoulder and whispered in his ear. "It is a shoe."

The lad stared at the shape. A shoe that big could mean only one thing—

"Oops!" came from far overhead.

A copse was smashed to splinters directly behind them.

"Now just stand still!" Richard the giant called down to them. "It's not going to do you any good to run. I'm too big to get away from!"

Wuntvor resisted the urge to flee screaming into the forest. He knew the giant was right, and furthermore, he suspected that, the more he might try to escape Richard, the larger the risk would become of falling victim to one of the huge fellow's frequent accidents.

The giant scooped the lad up in one very large hand.

"Ah," his very large voice boomed with satisfaction. "I knew I'd get you sooner or later!" He brought his hand up to eye level, peering intently at the lad. "Not that it's any of my business, but why are you wearing that silly costume?"

Wuntvor couldn't take it. It was the final straw. He would go down fighting! He pulled his sword.

"All right!" Cuthbert demanded hysterically. "What's going on this time?"

"We have to take on a giant," the lad replied.

"A giant?" the sword asked a bit too brightly. "Oh, is that all? Why don't we take on the entire amassed might of the Netherhells, instead? Oh, I forgot. We've already done that! And, speaking of forgetting, I suppose you don't remember our conversation from the last time I was out of the scabbard?"

The lad's brow crinkled with thought. "That was when we were with the demons?"

"Bravo," the sword replied sarcastically. "There's something about constantly being trapped in these fairy tales. It sure wreaks havoc with the continuity!"

"Indeed," Wuntvor responded. "I fear we have no time for continuity, or naught else but battle!"

"See?" the sword cried with a note of triumph. "You don't remember! Well, I guess I'll have to fill you in again. I'm on strike!"

"Pardon?" the lad inquired.

"I quit," Cuthbert affirmed. "My life should be more than hacking and slashing. I must have complained to you about this a hundred times, and still you wouldn't listen. Well, there comes a point when a magic sword must take a stand. As of this moment, my fighting days are through. Not another cut! Not another parry! And riposting is completely out of the question."

The lad stared at the sword. "Indeed? Well, if that is the way you feel."

"Who are you talking to?" the giant rumbled, peering at the tiny man in his hand.

"Oh, nothing. Something completely beneath your notice."

"What?" Cuthbert demanded. "I expected you to negotiate. Instead I become nothing?"

The lad shrugged. "How do I explain a sword that won't cut or parry? It seems to me that the object in question ceases to be a sword."

"You are too talking to something," the giant rumbled.

"Well," Cuthbert said, considering the lad's words, "perhaps my reaction has been a little extreme. I suppose I could agree to a concession or two. I mean, I'm a reasonable sword. Say, I might consent to a little dueling here and there—you know, in demonstrations and charity jousts—things like that."

"No, no, I assure you," Wuntvor insisted to the giant. "This whole thing is beneath your notice."

"Beneath his notice!" the sword wailed. "Oh, you're a tough negotiator. All right, because we've been together so long, I'll even do a *real* swordfight once in a while, one-on-one, duels of honor between gentlemen, as long as there's no bloodshed."

Richard frowned. "Won't you tell me, please? I'm tired of missing things beneath my notice. Being a giant, you miss a lot of the nitty gritty."

"All right! All right!" the sword blurted. "All right, perhaps even a little blood now and then, as long as you clean me quickly. Only, no ichor! I refuse to do ichor!"

"This is my magic sword," Wuntvor told the giant.

"Thank you," Cuthbert commented.

Richard flinched. "That isn't anything like a magic toothpick, is it?"

"Well, a bit. Except a sword is, of course, much more powerful." He had disabled the giant with a magic toothpick once before, he remembered. But he neglected to mention that, unlike the toothpick, the sword lacked the ability to grow to a size large enough to bother the giant.

"I don't know if this is fair," the big fellow complained. "You have to promise not to use that thing."

Wuntvor shook his head. "I don't promise anything, unless you put us back down."

The giant's frown deepened even further. "Put you down? I don't think Mother Duck would like that."

"Indeed?" Wuntvor replied regretfully. "I may have to use the sword. . . ."

"Now wait a minute—," Cuthbert began.

"That is," Wuntvor whispered, "if I had a sword."

"Use the sword! Use the sword!" the weapon insisted.

"Hey!" Tap called, still perched on Wuntvor's shoulder. "Don't forget you have another weapon."

"More voices," Richard grumbled. "Why do all you people have to be so small?"

Wuntvor glanced over at the little fellow. "Tap," he whispered, "do you really think you could work some magic on this giant's shoes?"

"You mean those?" Tap pointed at the footwear far below. He looked back at Wuntvor, wonder in his eyes. "If I do this right, it could be my masterpiece!"

"You're not answering my questions!" Richard rumbled. "Giants are not used to being ignored. Not that I want to provoke you into using your sword—anything but that. It's just that someone as large as I am expects civil conversation from my victims."

Tap concentrated, a terrible frown on his tiny face.

"What?" the giant demanded. "What's happening to my shoes?"

The Brownie began a slow dance from Wuntvor's collarbone to his shoulder socket.

"Hey!" the giant cried. His tone had become threatening. "You remember Mother Duck's ovens, don't you? What's happening to my laces?"

Tap's dance became more sprightly. Wuntvor winced at the pounding of tiny feet, but did his best not to move. Brownie Power was their only hope.

"My shoes! My shoes are moving!" The giant swallowed, a distant booming sound, as he tried to regain his composure. "Yes, the ovens! The ones where she bakes heroes into bread?"

Tap redoubled his jumping about, adding rhythmic hand gestures.

"Well—," the giant gasped, rivers of sweat now exploding from his enormous brow. "Well, you're about to become a hero sandwi—" The huge fellow breathed in sharply. "I can't stand it anymore! I've gotta dance!"

And with that, Richard began leaping about, clumsily mimicking the Brownie's movements. Wuntvor fell into the giant's palm, clinging for dear life.

"Oops," Tap gasped, clinging in turn to Wuntvor's wig. "Perhaps I overdid it."

"Indeed," Wuntvor agreed, watching the scenery move wildly as the giant swung his hand from shoulder level up above his head. "I suppose you can't undo this?"

The Brownie shook his head, miserable. "I'm afraid not. I mean, how can you undance?"

The lad looked below them, his expression grim. "Then we're going to have to jump."

"Jump?" the Brownie wailed.

Wuntvor pointed at the huge head below. "Into his hair! Now!"

Both lad and Brownie leapt. The hair bounced beneath them, breaking their fall. Wuntvor slid down a thick strand, waving for Tap to follow.

A moment later, they had both planted their feet firmly on the giant's skull. Wuntvor looked about him. From here, Richard's hair looked like a dense, dark forest, save that the hair had a much rougher exterior than any tree bark, and was covered with a thick, moist substance.

Tap inspected the moisture more closely, wrinkling his nose. "Hair oil."

"Indeed," the lad replied as he caught his breath. The giant continued to jump around beneath them. "Pray tell me, Tap, what will happen when the dance is over?"

"Why," Tap replied proudly, "the dance is never over. The recipient of the dancing spell dances on and on, until—"

The Brownie paused, a look of horror on his tiny countenance.

"Until?" the lad prompted.

"Exhaustion!" the Brownie whispered.

The skull lurched wildly beneath them.

"Quickly!" Wuntvor cried. "Into my pocket, Tap! We must anchor ourselves." He pulled forth his sword.

"What is it *this* time?" Cuthbert screamed.

"No blood!" the lad called back. "We just need to stick you in this giant hair follicle."

"That oily thing? Yu—" The weapon's voice died as its point gushed into the spongy strand. The Brownie leapt for the protection of the lad's vest.

Richard swayed a final time, then stumbled to his knees. Wuntvor swung wildly about, but the sword held.

"Gotta—," the giant managed, his labored breath as loud as the wind between two mountaintops, "—dance." And with that, the giant collapsed, falling face first to the earth far below.

"Oops," Richard mumbled, his nose and brow pressed against the shattered pine trees. Then he began to snore.

Wuntvor stood, shaken but still more or less in one piece. He pulled Cuthbert free from the oily stalk.

"—uck!" the sword concluded. "I had thought there was nothing worse than ichor. Apparently I was wrong."

Wuntvor sheathed the weapon before it could complain further. He climbed carefully down from strand to strand, careful not to slip on the moist hair. He breathed a sigh of relief as his feet finally touched the ground.

Tap peered out of the lad's pocket.

"Are we down yet?"

Wuntvor nodded, still catching his breath.

"Totally off the giant?" Tap asked. "Completely on the ground?"

"Indeed," the lad answered.

Tap leapt from Wuntvor's pocket with a flourish. He did a little dance as his tiny feet hit the earth, waving at the fallen giant. "I tell you, was that Brownie Power or what?"

"Indeed," Wuntvor said again, rather than what he was really thinking. "I wonder if we have gotten any closer to the western hill?" In fact, Richard's head seemed to have crashed into a rise of some sort. It was so hard to tell. The giant's head was so big, it made everything else seem disproportionately small.

There was a small explosion directly in front of them.

"His Brownieship!" Tap exclaimed.

"I'll deal with you later," the newcomer replied. For it was, indeed, the King of the Brownies, complete with his leather crown. Tap moaned softly, fearing the worst.

"But first," His Brownieship announced regally, "I have a message. And I am better at delivering messages than some Brownies I know." Tap moaned again, covering his tiny head with his tiny hands.

His Brownieship looked up at Wuntvor. "There are shoes in your future."

"Indeed?" the lad queried.

The King of the Brownies nodded nobly. "Very big shoes."

"You might be a little late." Wuntvor pointed down at the other end of the giant. "Would those be the shoes you mean?"

His Brownieship frowned, then leapt up to Wuntvor's shoulder to get a better view. He stared for a long moment, speechless.

The Brownie king tore his gaze away at last. "No, those are not the shoes." His head turned once again toward the giant. "Still, they may require further study—" His Brownieship shook himself. "But this is not the time. I have told you what I dare. In the Eastern Kingdoms, Mother Duck is everywhere. You will know the shoe when you see it. Norei and I will attempt to distract—but I have already said too much. Just remember—Happily ever after!"

Happily ever after? The unicorn had told him about that, too, but what with all the excitement in dealing with Richard, the phrase had slipped the young lad's mind.

"Indeed," Wuntvor agreed.

"And now," His Brownieship continued, turning his attention to Tap, "as to what we will do to certain Brownies who apparently find it impossible to follow orders . . ."

"Buckles and laces!" Tap pleaded. "But, Your Smallness, there were extenuating circumstances!"

"Circumstances that led you to completely forget you were supposed to wait for me in Vushta?" His Brownieship demanded.

"Well—uh—yes," Tap replied somewhat unevenly. "You see, there was this quest, and this demon, Snarks, whom I was supposed to teach the wisdom of the Brownie Way, and then these Seven Other Dwarves—"

A horrible, deep rumbling noise drowned out the Brownie's excuses. It took Wuntvor a moment to realize what the noise was: Richard had groaned.

"And I suppose," His Brownieship spoke to Tap as if the giant wasn't even there, "you also completely forgot the Brownie Code when you got wrapped up in this silly seven wishes thing?"

"Well, you see, then we ended up in the Eastern Kingdoms," Tap continued hurriedly. The little fellow seemed to be perspiring even more heavily than he had during his giant-controlling dance. "You can't imagine how powerful Mother Duck is. And then there was this giant, see—"

The earth moved as the giant sat up.

"Oops," Richard intoned. "I didn't mean to fall down like that. But at least you weren't so foolish as to run away. Nobody can run away from a giant."

Wuntvor drew his sword.

"Don't I get any rest at all?" Cuthbert wailed. "It's bad enough that I'm still all slimy from hair oil!"

"I'm still waiting for an answer," His Brownieship said to his subordinate.

"All right now," Richard remarked as he shifted his weight. "I want you all down there to stay calm. Let's make this capture as painless as possible."

"Indeed," Wuntvor remarked. "Tap, perhaps your best answer would be to repeat the Brownie Power dance that defeated the giant before."

"Buckles and laces!" Tap exclaimed, looking anxiously at His Brownieship. "Would that be all right?"

"Of course," Richard continued, "I can't guarantee you a painless future. Who knows what Mother Duck has in store? After all, bread may be your destiny."

"That would be better than being stuck in a scabbard when you're covered with slime!" Cuthbert commented. "And after all the service I've given you. Don't you ever think of cleaning your weapon?"

Richard frowned. "That's that magic sword again, isn't it? I warned you about that magic sword!"

"Yes," Wuntvor hissed to Tap. "I think it is once again time for Brownie Power!"

"Is it?" Tap whimpered to His Brownieship.

"Perhaps," the Brownie king replied coolly. "After you have given me an account of all your actions."

"Is there anything in Brownie Power that can clean off hair oil?" Cuthbert asked hopefully.

"You've heard my warning," Richard rumbled. "Here I come."

Tap stared at the descending hand, then turned wildly to the others.

"Do something!" Wuntvor pleaded.

"Explain!" His Brownieship demanded.

"Do nothing!" the giant warned.

"Clean me off!" the sword moaned.

"That's it!" Tap the Brownie shrieked. "I can't take it anymore! Once upon a time. Once upon a time!"

A glazed look came over the Brownie's countenance. The worried, perspiring Tap was gone. Wuntvor realized that in his place was a calm, collected little person, totally under the control of Mother Duck.

"What's happening here?" His Brownieship demanded. Tap didn't respond. The Brownie king turned angrily to Wuntvor.

"If I don't get this oil cleaned off me, I'm going back on strike," Cuthbert complained. "I demand decent working conditions!"

"Now I want you to stay perfectly still," Richard said quietly. "We don't want any accidents. You know how easy it would be for me to squeeze just a little too hard." The giant made a *tsk*ing sound that resembled distant thunder. "You'd be turned into pumpernickel in no time."

"I'm warning you!" The Brownie king shook his tiny fist at Wuntvor. "I need to know what happened to Tap. His Brownieship does not like to be fooled! I demand an answer!"

"So do I!" echoed the sword.

Wuntvor was beginning to realize the feelings that had driven Tap to his present state

The giant's hand was almost on top of him.

"Very good," Richard the giant rumbled. "No resistance at all. That's a good victim."

Wuntvor was almost beyond his wit's end. He had to say something.

"Enough!" he screamed. "I wish I didn't have to deal with any of you people!"

"Granted!" Tap the Brownie shouted with finality.

Wuntvor knew immediately that he had made a mistake.

ELEVEN

S *is for the sole that goes on forward,*
H *is for the heel that rearwards be,*
O *is for the oxen-leather stitching,*
E *is for the eyelets, don't you see?*
Put them all together, they spell SHOE-oo,
And that means an awful lot to me!

—*The Brownie Creed*, Stanza 603

I knew I was in trouble the moment I opened my eyes. Without thinking, I had wished myself away from all the others, and apparently, completely out of Mother Duck's control. But where had I wished myself to?

I still was in a forest, perhaps in another part of the Eastern Woods. But it was different here, far darker than the clearing where we had met the giant. The trees were much taller and broader, towering far overhead, their great shadows keeping the sunlight from the forest floor. Their bark was dark gray as well, almost the gray of the shadows, and for a moment I imagined I had wished myself to a place that held no color, but only shades of shadow.

I tilted my head back as far as I could, trying to see the tops of those monstrous trees. There, high overhead, I could see some small patches of blue. But the color gave me no comfort because of what else I saw above me.

Here it was, the end of summer, and none of the trees had leaves. Their branches were barren, shaking in the wind high overhead, rattling against one another like skeleton bones. All the trees were dead.

That same breeze whipped against me with an unexpected suddenness, blowing Alea's borrowed blond hair from my head. I let it go. The giant had seen through my disguise in an instant. I pulled the sackcloth skirt up about my shoulders, hoping the extra fabric would provide me with some protection against the sudden chill.

I did not like this; it was all too familiar. I had been in a forest like this before.

I thought I heard a dry chuckle carried by the wind.

I turned and saw a robed figure regarding me from between the trees. Even before I could see his face through the shadows, I knew what to expect; the darkened sockets, the skull-like grin, the hands that looked like whitened bones.

"Greetings," the sepulchral voice of Death announced as the spectre approached. "It has been quite some time, Eternal Apprentice, since we have had a chance to speak alone."

I stood my ground as Death drew nearer, floating toward me as if he was carried forward by the howling wind rather than anything as simply mortal as legs and feet. Death seemed to think there was something special about me. That was why he called me the "Eternal Apprentice," a soul that managed to elude Death's grasp by constantly being reborn in new forms, a soul destined to always aid, however clumsily, true heroes, with the assistance of multiple companions.

I had no idea if there was any truth in Death's claim. But it didn't seem to matter what I thought about it. Death had decided that I had somehow escaped his kingdom many times in past lives, and because of that he was willing to bend the rules of life and death, and steal me away as soon as I was alone.

As I was now. All alone with Death, without even my cowardly sword to protect me.

Death grinned at me, and held out his hand. "You cannot imagine how I have longed for this moment. To at last possess the one who has forever been beyond my grasp!"

He threw his head back and laughed, a high-pitched, frightening sound, like nightbirds falling from the sky with broken wings.

"Indeed," I responded, concentrating mightily to keep my voice from cracking in terror. Death would take me now; he had made his desire for my Eternal Apprentice soul abundantly clear in my last two narrow escapes. But I could not succumb to the emotions that raged inside me, threatening to block my windpipe, to stop my heart. Perhaps, I reasoned instead, if I could get Death to talk, he might betray some weakness and inadvertently show me a way to save myself.

"Indeed?" Death replied, a bit surprised.

"Indeed," I said again. "I think not."

Death chuckled, the sound of black beetles being ground underfoot. "Pitiful human," the spectre whispered. "Resistance is useless against a force such as Death. Still, you know my fondness for games. Come! Try your best to keep me from taking you to my kingdom of darkness, and I will thank you for giving me my sport."

I took a step away. Somehow, though I did not see him move, Death seemed no farther away than before. If anything, he was closer; his outstretched hand now almost touched my shoulder.

"You will not escape that way," the spectre said. "Death is everywhere." He flexed his bone-white fingers. "Come now. Take my hand. It will be so simple."

Was this, then, the end? I could feel panic shooting up my spine. Before, my companions had always rushed to my aid, presenting Death with far too many souls to dispose of, thus defeating his deadly plans. Now, though, I was completely alone, far from everyone I knew. I had even lost my trusty ferret, in an earlier altercation with the giant. The silence of the dead forest seemed to close in around me. Oh, if I could only hear that reassuring "Eep-eep-eep" which had saved me from Death before.

Death's bony fingers brushed the cloth at my shoulder.

"No!" I cried. "I am not ready!"

Death guffawed, the sound vultures make as they circle their prey. "Ready? You don't have to be ready for Death. It simply happens. Come now. I have plagues to spread, disasters to provoke. Death can never rest."

His hand reached for me again. "Come! No one can resist me!"

I am not precisely sure what happened next. The soft, barren earth beneath my feet seemed to give way as I kicked back from the reach of Death. The ground appeared to slip one way, my boots another. Whatever the cause, I lost my footing. I looked up to see Death grasp the empty air where once my head had been.

"I have never seen anyone so clumsy!" the spectre raged. "And you would dare to deny you are the Eternal Apprentice!"

I rolled away, scrambling to my feet.

"Indeed," I remarked, searching for some words that might further distract the angry spectre.

"What is that?" Death whispered in a voice as cold as Midwinter Night.

I stopped, and in the stillness I, too, heard something cry, an animal of some sort, coming toward us!

"Eep!" the animal sounded. "Eep! Eep!"

I knew what it was even before I saw its gray form streaking between the trees.

It was my ferret.

"Eep!" the ferret cried, overjoyed to see me. "Eep! Eep!"

Death stared at the ferret in disbelief. "That is impossible. We are in the most destitute part of the Eastern Woods, miles from life of any kind. And yet, you are sought out by this animal companion. And still you doubt that you are the Eternal Apprentice?"

The ferret leapt up into my arms. I, too, believed it was a great coincidence that my pet could find me, out in the midst of these barren woods. But then again, this was one of my magic ferrets, produced from an equally magic hat I had taken with me to the Netherhells. Perhaps, because I had conjured them, the ferrets were somehow connected to me. Could it be, then, that all I had to do was think of them, and they would come?

Death glowered at the ferret, spreading his arms wide as if he would encircle me in a skeletal hug.

"Before, I would have contented myself to merely touch you," the spectre leered. "But no, you choose to elude my deadly grasp. Now, I will be forced to wrestle you to the ground. I will take your soul, and the life of that ferret, too! Submit, mortal! No one can survive the grip of Death!"

I am also not entirely clear on the exact sequence of subsequent events, but I do remember Death lunging for me again and the ferret streaking between us, and my arms flailing to get out of the way, but despite my best efforts somehow getting caught up in Death's robes, and the spectre flying over my head, falling to the ground with a rattle of bones. I tried to scramble away, only to have my feet get caught by the robes' coarse material.

Death managed to roll away at last, freeing his ripped robes from my heavy boots.

"This cannot be happening!" the spectre screamed. "I can see it all now: You will stumble around, barely eluding capture, until the entire world happens to wander into this corner of the forest!" Death laughed ruefully, the sound of forest bears being slowly strangled.

There was another noise behind us.

"What was that?" Death shrieked as he whirled about. For some reason, he seemed to be losing his composure. "It can't be!"

I turned to look as well. It was a shoe that had made the noise. A

very large shoe. For a moment, my heart stopped. Then I saw that it
was perhaps not as large a shoe as it would take to fit a giant, but a
shoe big enough to hide a mortal man.

"Indeed," the shoe stated.

"A shoe?" Death whispered. "More than that, a talking shoe? It
cannot be, and yet it is." The spectre turned back to me, its voice
gaining power with every word. "But, no matter what its true nature,
I will not be foiled. I have come to take you this time, Eternal Apprentice, even though I may be tempting the forces of chaos to do so. It
will be simple enough to take the ferret, too. And even though I am
not quite sure what it is, the talking shoe is mine as well!"

"I think not," the shoe replied, as two hands emerged from the very
large footwear's very large eyelets. The hands set themselves into
prime conjuring position.

"A talking wizard shoe!" Death stared, and his voice was tinged
with wonder. "Every once in a while, there is something that can
surprise even me. But I will have all the time I desire to examine it,
once it is mine. And I take the Eternal Apprentice, too!" The spectre
chuckled once again. "What a day this will be for Death."

But the hands in the shoe had already begun to conjure, and, as they
moved, a small, intensely dark cloud appeared over the spectre.

"How can you stop me?" Death asked in amusement. "Magic holds
no power over me."

The hands waved again, and a great, jagged bolt of lightning
streaked down upon the robed spectre, followed by a crash of thunder
that almost shattered my ears.

I blinked, trying to regain the totality of my sight after the brightness of the lightning. A great cloud of dust had risen about where the
spectre had once stood.

Then the chill winter wind howled all about us, blowing the dust
away. Death stood there still. And his grin was, if anything, broader
than ever.

"Is that all your pitiful magic can do?" The spectre waved at the
dissipating cloud overhead. "You try to turn my own tools against me.
I use the lightning for my sword, and the thunder heralds my approach. Foolish mortals, you will never defeat me that way!"

"Indeed?" the shoe remarked, obviously not impressed.

Death screamed at the impertinence.

"Wuntvor!" the shoe called. "Run to my side!"

I did as the shoe asked, for I knew that powerful voice. My master, the wizard Ebenezum, greatest mage in the Western Kingdoms, was inside. I turned around to look at Death, my back pressed reassuringly against the dark brown leather. The ferret, with a glad "eep," climbed to my shoulders.

The spectre approached, arms opened wide, as if he would lift us all to his dark kingdom.

"Why do you bother to run? Why do you bother to conjure? All your plans, all your spells are as nothing to the Power of Death."

Death was coming fast. Surely my master could do something. I wondered if it would be better if I moved to the other side of the shoe, away from the ensuing battle. But when I stepped toward the heel, I saw a bone white hand before me. Death blocked my way. I was trapped against the shoe!

"At last," Death snickered, the sound of butterfly wings being torn apart by knives. "I have been waiting for this moment for ever so long."

"Oops!"

A large portion of the dead forest came crashing down nearby. Richard the giant had arrived.

"So here you are," Richard rumbled. "I wondered what all that noise was about."

"No!" Death screamed, the sound of a million souls in agony. "I will not be thwarted again. Though it will task my powers of attrition and decay, I will take all of you, shoe and giant, apprentice and ferret!" He smiled fiercely as he looked at all the living. "Prepare to die!"

"See?" a voice called overhead, accompanied by the heavy flapping of dragon's wings. "I knew with all that noise, there had to be something interesting happening."

"Yeah!" a woman's voice answered. "And Wuntie's here, too!"

There was a small popping sound close to my foot. "Hey!" a tiny voice said. "That explosion was almost louder than Brownie Power!"

"Nooooooo!" Death wailed, the sound of a hurricane laying waste to everything in its path. And then the spectre was gone as well.

"No, no, no, no, no!" Mother Duck rushed into our midst, followed closely by Jeffrey the Wolf. "This has gotten totally out of hand!"

"Well," Jeffrey added, "if you just would have taken my simple suggestions about the use of wolves . . ."

"I don't want to hear any more from you, either," she snapped. "I had no idea, in dealing with the Eternal Apprentice, how complicated things could become!" She paused to smile. "Now, though, that I see the scope of the situation, I can *really* put you in a fairy tale!"

"Indeed," I said, stepping forward. "I think not." I found I had a new confidence, now that my master was here. "We have ways of dealing with you."

"Oh, really?" Mother Duck replied, already humbled by these new circumstances. "And what might they be?"

I waved behind me. "Well, for example, take a look at this shoe."

Mother Duck frowned. "What shoe? Are you standing on it or something? Shoes aren't all that big, you know."

What did she mean, "What shoe"? Was this one of Mother Duck's tricks? I spun around.

There was no longer a shoe behind me. In fact, the enormous footwear was nowhere to be seen.

My master was gone.

TWELVE

When you wish upon a star,
Wish for song and dance, and you'll go far.

—*The Damsel and Dragon Songbook*
(still seeking publication)

"There, there, now," Mother Duck spoke soothingly to my confusion. "I'm not surprised that you are a little addled, not after all that has happened. Don't worry, Mother Duck will not be cross with you. Especially since you have to work again so soon."

"Doom!" a deep voice echoed through the trees. "What have I missed?"

Mother Duck sighed as Hendrek bounded into our midst. "Apparently, everybody in the immediate vicinity will be arriving here shortly. I am quite in awe of the drawing power of the Eternal Apprentice." She patted me graciously on top of the head. "I've never gotten to use the spectre of Death in one of my fairy stories before. It's very impressive, the supporting cast that comes with you. And how you get out of these things! Someday, you'll have to explain to me exactly how you made that sound."

It occurred to me then that Mother Duck did not know about my master's arrival. Perhaps it was best kept secret, at least for now.

"Indeed," I said at last, for I felt the old woman expected an answer. "Perhaps I shall, when I am given more control over my own destiny."

"Oh, but I have been giving you more control." Mother Duck grinned congenially at me. "You and your companions had been fighting against me for so long, I decided to loosen the reins a wee bit. And when I did, I was rewarded by the occurrence of even wilder events.

Of course, those events were almost completely out of hand, but we can fix that when we fine-tune the fairy tale later."

"Fine tune?" I asked, being unfamiliar with the term.

Mother Duck nodded enthusiastically. "It's a phrase we use in the fairy tale business. Fine-tune—fine-tuning—" She looked heavenward, as if searching for the precise words. "Yes, you know, improvements we add to the fairy tale as we continue to rehearse it, over and over, until we get it just right. It's going to take a bit longer than usual with all the variables. Still, I think thirty or forty run throughs should start us in the right direction."

"Thirty or forty?" I asked, afraid to further inquire just what constituted a "run through."

"Doom," Hendrek added.

"See how much easier it all becomes when you cooperate?" Mother Duck enthused. "With my fairy tale experience, and the incredible number of things that happen to you, I think we can make storytelling history here. That is why I gave you your own way a little more as we went along, while of course still supervising the action in case I might again need to take control."

My own way? Taking control? Now that she mentioned it, I remembered how odd I had felt trying to escape the giant, as if I was somehow reading or hearing a story, rather than participating in it. It was only when I once again confronted Death that I truly felt my destiny once more under my own power.

Now, I realized that my taking charge of my own life was but a happy accident, and one that Mother Duck would soon rectify so that I might repeat the events of the past few hours another three dozen times. I also realized, with a new clarity, how important it was for Norei and Ebenezum to rescue me. If something didn't happen soon, I feared that I would spend the rest of my existence doomed to constantly relive a fairy tale full of seven Brownie wishes.

"It's about time we found you guys!" an incredibly grating voice called out as the three demons, who had apparently left their fairy tale bonnets and seaweed wigs behind, emerged from the trees.

"Might I make a suggestion?" Snarks called out as the three approached. "If you're going to blow up something to get our attention, next time why don't you do it a little closer to civilization?"

Get their attention? It was only there, in the midst of the crowd, that I realized my master's true intention in conjuring up the thunderstorm. Not to defeat Death with the lightning, but rather to overwhelm him with the crowd that would be attracted by the sound. I marveled at my master's foresight. He truly was the greatest wizard in the Western Kingdoms! I wondered in what clever way he would strike next.

Snarks looked around at the dead and broken trees. "Boy, you sure can pick some scenic spots to hold a meeting. Reminds me of some of the prime areas of the Netherhells; you know, urban renewal zones, sites of major industrial accidents."

"Begin!" Guxx Unfufadoo intoned. Brax hastily retrieved his drum from his ever-present sack.

> "Guxx Unfufadoo, angered demon,
> Wants no more of fairy stories,
> Warns the Mother if she uses
> Demons more it will get gor—"

The large demon fell to the ground, overwhelmed by a sneezing fit.

"Such a shame," Brax murmured as he watched his indisposed leader roll about in the dust. "Such a natural rhyming talent, gone to waste."

"What?" Mother Duck stared at the thrashing demon. "What is going on here?"

"Indeed," I replied, trying to concoct a reasonable, but false, explanation. For it had occurred to me that not only did Mother Duck not know that my master, the great wizard Ebenezum, had magically traveled to her kingdom, she also did not know of my master's malady, similar in nature to that of the sneezing demon now rolling about before us. "Indeed," I therefore repeated, stalling for time. "Alas—uh —the poor demon tends to sneeze—uh—when he is—uh—over-wrought."

"Really?" Mother Duck marveled. "From what I have seen, I thought he spent his entire life being overwrought. Still, that is useful information. I may be able to use it in one of my fairy tales."

"Indeed," I added for a final time. I looked about at my companions, urging them to complicity in my deceit. While the situation seemed to make the truth-telling Snarks uncomfortable, both Brax and Hubert nodded knowingly.

"What the demon needs to do is relax!" the dragon announced. "And what better way to relax than appreciating song and dance! Hit it, damsel! Number 703!"

"Always a winner!" Alea agreed. She made gentle shooing motions with her hands. "If all you folks would give me a little space to perform?"

"Wait a second," Mother Duck protested. "This is not what I had in mind."

But the damsel had already launched into song:

> "Do you have a friend who's feeling down?
> Who's cold and has a chill?
> If you need a cure to come around
> That's better than a pill
> Good song and dance then must be found
> And Damsel and Dragon will!"

Mother Duck looked from the performers to me, her gaze an odd mix of disbelief and nausea. "They do this sort of thing all the time, don't they?"

"Indeed," I answered, this time truthfully.

"Pardon us."

I looked down to see that we had been joined by Smarmy and his fellow dwarves, who had entered our group unnoticed, thanks to the nearby performance.

Smarmy wrung his hands as he looked up apologetically. "We thought we were coming to rescue someone—" He glanced apprehensively at the dancing dragon "—but maybe we should have stayed away."

I sympathized with the dwarf, for at that moment, Damsel and Dragon began another verse.

> "Do you know someone who's feeling low,
> Near the end of his life span?
> And they need a pick-me-up to go
> So they don't feel like an also-ran?
> They need song and dance that's fast, not slow
> And Damsel and Dragon can!"

"We came out of the woods for this?" Nasty complained.

"Pay no attention," Snooty admonished. " 'Tis naught but entertainment for the rabble."

Sickly coughed contemptuously.

"Hey!" the Brownie demanded. "Who are you calling *rabble?*"

"Not me!" Touchy insisted.

"Although he would have if he'd thought of it!" Nasty sneered. Dumpy moaned in agreement.

"What's going on here?" Snarks demanded, stepping between Tap and the dwarves. "Did I hear someone criticizing the dancers?"

"Do you hear anyone *not* criticizing the dancers?" Nasty retorted.

"Oh, wow," Spacey agreed.

"They were making fun of us, too!" Tap interjected. "They called us rabble!" He stopped for an instant, so upset he could barely breathe. "They're making fun of Brownie Power!"

"Doom," Hendrek remarked as he pushed his great bulk amidst the throng. "Is someone here causing trouble?"

"I suppose you never cause trouble!" Touchy demanded. "I suppose you never criticize anybody!"

Tap and Hendrek both looked at Snarks.

"Well, it's different for me," the truth-telling demon replied hurriedly. "And look, a little constructive criticism never hurt anybody. So I get to call them awful once in a while. They're my companions, after all. They expect it of me!"

"Doom," Hendrek added. "It pays to be polite."

Tap nodded. "That's what Brownie Power's all about!"

Nasty looked to his fellows. "So that means we have to be polite to this rabble?"

Snarks stared grimly at the upstart dwarf as Hendrek hefted his club and Tap did a few tentative dance steps.

"Doom," Hendrek remarked.

Brax stepped between the combatants. "Pardon me for butting in, but is anyone here in the market for a previously owned weapon?"

But just then, Damsel and Dragon launched into another verse:

"So if you know someone who's feeling bad,
And you want to make them well,
We've got an answer, so don't be sad,
For soon they'll be feeling swell!
Song and dance'll be the best time they ever had,
And Damsel and Dragon shall!"

Guxx's sneezes redoubled as he rolled about in the dirt.

"Do you have the feeling this is getting out of hand?" Mother Duck inquired.

I did not answer her for fear that, if I agreed, she would again put us all under her spell.

"Perhaps this is too big a challenge for me, after all," she murmured, more to herself than to me. "Perhaps I'd be better restricting my fairy tales to golden geese and blind mice?"

Alea began an elaborate tap dance across Hubert's wings.

"If only I liked my name better," the old woman continued. "Having a name like Mother Duck sometimes causes one to lose confidence. But I've told you about that, haven't I?"

The Seven Other Dwarves and my companions in the quest glowered at each other.

"Oh, yeah?" the dwarves shouted.

"Doom," my companions replied.

The situation was getting tenser by the minute. But if I asked Mother Duck to intervene, she would control us all, robbing me of my free will!

"Mother Robin?" the old woman mused, then shook her head. "Entirely too singsong. How about Mother Bluebird?" She pursed her lips, then frowned. "Too much alliteration. Mother Red-Winged Blackbird?" She sighed. "Altogether too long. How would they fit in on my books? Oh, I know I shouldn't grouse—wait a minute, that's not bad at all." She looked at me in triumph. "Mother Grouse! Well, perhaps it's not perfect, but it certainly sounds better than Mother Duck, don't you think?"

"Indeed," I replied, mostly to keep the conversation going. Mother Duck seemed to handle chaos badly; it was also the only time she chose to talk to me. I had failed before in persuading her to join our cause. I wondered if there might be some other way I could turn this situation to my advantage.

Damsel and Dragon had slowed their dance to a shuffle.

"Tell me, Damsel," Hubert began.

"Yes, Dragon?" Alea answered.

"How do my fellow lizards build their homes?" the dragon asked.

"Oh, that's easy," Damsel chorused. "With Rep-Tiles!"

"But I understand you can really swing," Alea continued after the groans had subsided.

Hubert wiggled his posterior. "Sure can. But that's another tail altogether!"

The crowd reaction to that one was even worse.

"But enough of clever patter!" Hubert shouted over the din. "Now here's a number that really makes me want to shed my skin!"

"I think not!" Mother Duck exclaimed, raising both her hands. "No, this is too much. Total confusion is one thing. That I can handle. The way chaos constantly settles around the Eternal Apprentice is interesting, to say the least. Vaudeville humor, on the other hand—" She did not quite suppress a shudder. "I'd better put everyone back under my power before something else happens."

Jeffrey the Wolf waved his green cap at the old woman. "May I make a suggestion?"

Mother Duck sighed. "If you must."

"You worry about your fairy tales becoming too chaotic," Jeffrey added quickly. "Well, I have a solution to your problems." He thumped his chest for emphasis. "We talking wolves are fairy tale professionals! Just put me in your next story, and my tried and true enchanted tale experience will guarantee a classic!"

"Perhaps," the old woman said warily.

"You won't be sorry," Jeffrey promised.

"Mother Duck is never sorry. But you might be." She shook her head smartly, as if the contents needed to be slightly rearranged. "All right," she agreed wearily. "Heaven knows I've tried everything else."

She surveyed the whole group before her. "Now, everyone repeat after me: Once upon—"

The earth began to shake. We all backed away quickly as a crevice yawned in our midst. As usual, there was a cloud of dust, and when it cleared, we saw a table with five demons.

"We've got you now!" the gavel demon cried in triumph.

It was the Netherhells again.

THIRTEEN

"Guxx Unfufadoo, concernèd demon,
Asks you why you read quotations,
When you know Wuntvor's in danger;
Says you should get on with chapter!"

—The preceding was provided by
The Equal Time for Demons Act,
Vushta common law 77034
(recently repealed)

"This time," Mother Duck remarked, "you're in trouble."

All five demons caught sight of the angry old woman. All five demons blanched noticeably.

"Oh, dear!" the gavel demon exclaimed, attempting a smile. "We've made a mistake, haven't we?"

Mother Duck nodded. "Your last mistake."

"But we were sure this was Vushta!" the small, sickly demon at the end broke in.

"Maybe it's Vushta in disguise!" another committee member suggested.

"Yeah!" the demon in the flowered hat added. "Maybe Mother Duck is in league with the wizards!"

"How dare you suggest such a thing?"

The demons all looked up, startled at Mother Duck's tone, for her voice had slid from heated anger to coldest rage.

"What do you think of me?" the old woman continued. "Consorting with wizards? From Vushta? What sort of a person do you think I am? Next, you'll have me taking tea with one of those grubby mages from the Western Kingdoms!"

The demons all began to talk at once.

"Oh no, Mother Duck."

"So sorry, Mother Duck."

"How could we have been so tactless as to make that mistake, Mother Duck?"

"You are demons," the old woman reminded them. "It is in your nature. What I cannot excuse, however, is your trespassing once again in the Eastern Kingdoms!"

"But the magic, Mother Duck—"

"It led us here, Mother Duck—"

"Oh, this is embarrassing," the gavel demon interjected. "Here we are, an elite corps of Netherhells mercenaries, and we can't even find Vushta. You'd think there'd be *some* magical activity going on there, wouldn't you? It is Vushta, after all. I mean, how else are they going to get those forbidden delights?"

"I am not interested in your problems," Mother Duck replied. "My only concern is that you are here again, interfering with the order of my fairy stories! If you cannot tell the difference between fairy magic and wizard magic, well—" She glanced meaningfully at Richard. "—I think it might be time to bake some bread."

"But Mother Duck, there was—"

"—Definite wizard magic, Mother Duck—."

"Please, Mother Duck, *any* demon can tell the difference between wizard magic and fairy tale magic!"

"What?" Mother Duck demanded. "Wizard magic? In my kingdom? Well, my demon committee, if what you say is true, you may have earned yourself a reprieve. Richard?"

"Oops!" the giant replied. "Didn't see that crevice there. I almost tripped. What do you wish, Mother Duck?"

"Look about my kingdom. Do you see anything strange? Anything that looks out of the ordinary? Anything that might be a wizard?"

The giant shielded his eyes from the glare of the sun and looked east. "No, nothing there." He looked south. "No, nothing there, either."

He turned about to look north. "Oops. Darn it. I wish they wouldn't grow those trees so close together. But there's nothing out here, either."

At last, he turned west. "No, there's nothing this way, either. Well, there's that giant shoe, but that doesn't look anything like a wizard."

"Pardon!" Mother Duck peered up at the giant.

"It's a shoe," Richard repeated. "A very large shoe." He knelt down to touch his own. "Not as big as mine, maybe—"

He swung his shoe forward so that Mother Duck could get a better view. "Oops! Well, we probably didn't need that hill there, anyway. But it's still a pretty big shoe."

"Really?" Mother Duck stared thoughtfully at the committee. "I haven't made any giant shoes, at least not recently. Demons, you are correct. There is wizardry afoot!"

The five demons all fell to their knees.

"Thank you, Mother Duck!"

"Bless you, Mother Duck!"

"We knew you could recognize the truth, Mother Duck!"

At the moment, Mother Duck was content to watch the demons grovel, but I had to use the brief respite to think. My master had come to the Eastern Kingdoms to save me, but he had already been discovered by Mother Duck. Even worse, I had heard what she thought of western wizards. If she cornered the shoe, I knew my master was in real trouble! There had to be some way I could distract her and stop her from investigating.

"Indeed," I began, trying desperately to think of something that might delay her.

Mother Duck glanced down at me, a bit surprised. "Oh that's right! I haven't completed my controlling spell. Well, why don't you just sit here for a bit, like a good pawn, while I take care of this little difficulty?"

She turned back to the giant. "Richard, what say we visit this big new shoe?"

"Oops!" Richard replied.

Mother Duck scowled. "What's the matter now?"

The giant cowered at her tone. "The shoe is gone, Mother Duck. It is no longer on the western hill."

"A phantom shoe?" She rubbed her chin in thought. "How interesting. Perhaps we have an adversary worthy of Mother Duck. For I have a feeling we will be seeing that shoe again."

She turned back to the committee. "The information you've given me will be very useful. In fact, it will guarantee your continued existence. But make no mistakes! The Eastern Kingdoms are off limits to the Netherhells, now and forever. Come back again, and no excuse will be good enough!"

The five demons shouted assent as they pushed their table back toward the crevice.

"Yes, Mother Duck."

"Certainly, Mother Duck."

"Your mercy is astounding, Mother Duck."

"And what will happen to you if you come back?" She looked about at the rest of us, then smiled at the demons. "I don't really want to upset the others. I'll come over and describe it in detail."

"Must you, Mother Duck?"

"Can't we leave it up to our imagination, Mother Duck?"

"The last group you warned is still under the finest mental care the Netherhells can provide, Mother Duck."

But the old woman would not be stopped. She marched over to the committee and addressed them in low tones. An occasional word or two drifted my way on the breeze:

". . . pummel . . . dice . . . bake . . . julienne . . ."

"Pardon me," a voice said at my hip, "but can we talk?"

I looked down to see Smarmy wringing his hands.

"Indeed," I answered.

"Good," Smarmy replied, nodding toward his fellow dwarves, who had gathered in a semicircle around us. "Some of us, humble as we are, feel that it was only because you threw your lot in with us that you got captured by Mother Duck. We sort of got you into this and well, we'd like to get you out."

"Indeed?" I responded. "Do you have a plan?"

"Well, no," Smarmy admitted. "Not precisely. But, since it seems that Mother Duck is never going to use us again in her fairy tales, we have a lot of time on our hands. We'll come up with something."

"Yeah!" Nasty agreed. "Anything to get rid of those friends of yours!"

"That's correct," Snooty asserted. "The neighborhood used to be so nice, before you moved in."

Dumpy moaned. Sickly coughed. Noisy dropped something. So the dwarves were all in agreement.

"And I mean it this time!" Mother Duck called after the retreating demons. Calls of "Yes, Mother Duck!"—"Wouldn't have it any other way, Mother Duck!" and suchlike rose through the cloud of dust.

But I had other things to consider. The Seven Other Dwarves were going to help us escape. As were Norei, and His Brownieship, and the unicorn, and my master, the great wizard Ebenezum. Perhaps our situation was not as bleak as it seemed. With all these allies, our escape plans could not possibly fail. Could they?

But then there was Death. Somehow, the spectre had developed an obsession with me, and if I was ever left truly alone, whether I was under Mother Duck's control or not, I knew that Death would find me. Perhaps my master would find me, too, and rescue me again before the spectre could take me to his kingdom. That is, if my master could continue to elude Mother Duck's grasp. I sighed. Why did life have to be so complicated?

If only, I thought, I could keep some shred of self-control under Mother Duck's spell. I considered Norei's message, something about remembering three words: Happily ever after. I whispered them to myself now, as if they might be an antidote for what was to come.

"And now," Mother Duck remarked as she turned back to the rest of us, "what to do with all of you? For I think I was a trifle hasty a moment ago, when I tried to put you back into my spell. We need to consider a few things if we are going to create my masterpiece!"

She pointed at Hubert. "Firstly, I have insubordination to deal with. Perhaps the dragon did not recall certain prohibitions I made about singing in my presence?"

"Oh, that?" Hubert did his best to laugh jovially. " 'Twas but the theater in my blood, bubbling over. You know what they say: Gotta sing, gotta dance?"

Mother Duck frowned at the dragon. "No one has 'gotta do' anything in my domain, at least anything that I do not decree. Therefore, as long as you are in my kingdoms, you will never speak again." She snapped her fingers three times.

"But it was only my acting exuberan—" Hubert's nostrils shook, smoke coming from his mouth and ears. "—urrgghh—but I mean—grahhh—couldn't you—unhhh." And the dragon was silent.

Mother Duck turned to Alea. "Be thankful that I need you to speak in your fairy tale role, or you would share your companion's fate. I mean, 'Damsel and Dragon shall'? There is only so much a professional storyteller can stand."

Alea looked up at Hubert, who kept opening and closing his mouth, all in the complete absence of sound.

"Yes, Mother Duck," she said nervously.

"Good," the old woman replied. "Then let that be a lesson to you all. Mother Duck must be obeyed!"

"Yes, Mother Duck," a number of my company replied quickly.

"Now, let's get on to specifics," she continued, satisfied with the response. "Mr. Wolf, you have volunteered your services?"

Jeffrey replied that he had.

"Well, that's fine, except—You don't want to do the one about the red riding hood, do you?" Mother Duck said with obvious distaste.

"Certainly not, Mother Duck," Jeffrey reassured her. "I have another story with even more drama, and an even bigger part for talking wolves."

The old woman nodded. "You never miss an opportunity. This should be interesting. In addition, I anticipate using all our characters this time—that might change your story a bit. And, as always, I will be supervising the action. I trust now that everybody understands their function?"

"Yes, Mother Duck," came the chorused reply.

"Good." She smiled. "That's what I like. One happy family. Jeffrey, if I might speak with you for a minute?"

"Excuse us, Mother Duck," the Seven Other Dwarves chorused in turn.

"Yes?" she answered, her expression halfway between annoyance and amusement.

"Pardon us for interrupting," Smarmy replied, "but did we hear you say that everyone will have a part?"

"Certainly." Mother Duck was all smiles again. "Oh dear, I have been ignoring you, my dwarves, what with all this new blood. Don't worry. You'll have a very important part."

"A very important part?" Snooty sniffed.

"Oh, wow," Spacey commented while Noisy cheered.

Mother Duck nodded at the wolf. "Jeffrey, if you don't mind?" The two of them retreated behind a stand of dead trees and conversed in hushed tones.

"Indeed," I whispered to Smarmy. "We must plan now. I fear our time is running out."

"Plan?" Smarmy chirped. "What do we need to plan? We've got a part!"

"A very important part!" Snooty added.

"You remember," I insisted. "What we were just talking about. My escape!"

"Escape?" Smarmy said the word as if he had never heard it before. "Oh, that. Well, I think escapes will simply have to wait. That is, unless they're part of the fairy story."

"A very important part!" Snooty elucidated.

"Indeed," I replied. Apparently, my escape plans had received a temporary setback. Now that the dwarves were included in Mother Duck's plans, they could think of nothing else.

"It will make a great beginning!" Mother Duck announced, shooing Jeffrey the Wolf back into our midst. She waved to the rest of us. "I will leave you a few moments of peace as I return to my hilltop observatory."

This time, Mother Duck marched off alone.

Jeffrey wore a big, wolfish grin as he walked toward us.

"This is going to be great," he assured us. "I tell you, we're going to see talking wolves like they've never been seen before!"

"Tell me," Brax inquired. "Have you ever considered a future selling used weapons? Franchises are available."

But I had no time for idle chatter. The fairy story would once again begin in earnest. I repeated the words Norei had given me, hoping against hope that they held some power:

"Happily ever after. Happily ever after. Once upon a time."

Everyone said that last sentence in unison with me.

FOURTEEN

Fairy tales can come true, it can happen to you, if you're stuck in Mother Duck's kingdom.

> —*Some Notes on Apprenticeship,*
> by Wuntvor, Apprentice to Ebenezum,
> greatest wizard in the Western Kingdoms
> (a work in progress)

Once upon a time there was a lad named Wuntvor, who had two good friends. One of the friends was large, both in height and width, and always carried an equally large club. The other friend, however, was just plain small, and tended to talk a lot about shoes. Still, the three of them got along famously, except for an argument here and there.

One day, Wuntvor remarked: "I heard there is a wolf skulking about the neighborhood."

"Doom," his large friend, whose name was Hendrek, replied. "You worry too much about these things."

"That's right!" the small fellow, who was known as Tap, chimed in. "Why worry about wolves when you can talk about shoes!"

Wuntvor thought the two of them were probably right. It was such a fine, sunny day, after all, and Tap could speak for hours about the intricacies of eyelet placement.

"Still," the lad said to the others, "you can't be too careful about these sorts of things. It is best to take precautions."

The other two laughed at his serious nature on such a sunny day, and went on to talk of other things. But little did any of them know that they were being watched at that very moment by the very wolf Wuntvor had mentioned!

Yum-yum, thought the wolf, whose name was Jeffrey. What tasty morsels these three would make. True, the little fellow would serve as not much more than an appetizer, but the enormous one could feed him for a week. And as for the young lad, well the wolf thought he just might be the right age and tenderness to make the most wonderful meal imaginable. Perhaps sauteed would be best, the wolf thought. But he had to be careful, for if he became too excited by the thought of his impending dinners he might reveal himself prematurely, and thus waste that all important element of surprise.

"Well," Wuntvor said at last, "it certainly has been pleasant whiling away an hour with the two of you, but I think it's time we got back to work."

"Doom," Hendrek agreed.

"Watch out for skulking wolves!" Tap cried over his shoulder with a laugh.

And then Wuntvor's two friends left and went their separate ways, for all three were in the construction business, and by odd coincidence, all of them were working on new homes for themselves.

Ah, thought the wolf. This is better than ever. Divide and conquer is always the best strategy. I shall pick them off one by one, and have enough tasty morsels to last me for weeks.

But where to start? The wolf frowned for a moment, but the answer was obvious. You always ate the appetizer before the main course. With that in mind, the hungry wolf skulked after the little fellow.

Jeffrey soon came to the edge of a clearing. He carefully hid in the bushes and watched the little fellow for a moment as Tap casually put the finishing touches on his house.

"I think the big boot should go here," Tap said to himself, placing an enormous brown boot at the peak of the roof. "And I can use these ten pairs of sandals as a walkway."

The wolf squinted to get a better look at the little fellow's handiwork, for the house he was building was different from any Jeffrey had ever seen. To call the structure ramshackle would be kind, for the house seemed to be made from hundreds or even thousands of small brown and black objects with all sorts of tones and textures. It took the wolf a long moment to determine the building material, for it was too dark to be mud, and too smooth to be brick.

And then he realized that the house was made entirely out of shoes.

Jeffrey the wolf was taken aback for a moment or two. Shoes? How could you make a house out of shoes? Not very well, was the only answer he could come up with. But then, the little fellow's badly built

house fit right in with the hungry wolf's dining plans, for, when Jeffrey confronted Tap, the small one would have no safe place to go to.
The wolf skulked silently from his hiding place.

"Oh, a boot goes here," Tap sang to himself, "a slipper there, boot here, slipper there, shoes shoes everywhere—Who are you?"

Tap had seen the wolf! Jeffrey, however, put on his very best smile and stood up somewhat straighter than his skulking position.

"Hello, neighbor!" Jeffrey said cordially. "I just thought I'd drop by to admire this house you're building."

The little fellow beamed at that. "Yes, it is a fine house, is it not? Built of the finest shoe leather available."

"No doubt," the wolf replied, but he looked at Tap and not the house. Yes, he was quite sure of it now. He would be able to swallow the little fellow in a single gulp, perhaps after dipping him in a suitable sauce. Now, if only Tap did not move for another moment.

"What are you doing?" Tap demanded.

"Why, looking at your fine house," the wolf replied innocently.

"You were not!" the wee one insisted. "You were skulking! My friend Wuntvor warned me about creatures who skulk! And you're a wolf besides!"

And with that, Tap ran inside the house and slammed the door.

Jeffrey chuckled to himself. He was not upset in the least. In fact, the wolf always loved this part best of all. He removed his cap, cleared his throat, and said in a loud voice:

"You should let me in and I'll know what to do!"

But Tap replied:

"Not by the laces of my shoesy-shoo-shoes!"

Jeffrey grinned even wider, and added:

"Then I'll huff and I'll puff and I'll bloooow your house down!"

The wolf took a very deep breath, inhaling for fully half a minute. Then, with lungs bursting, he positioned his snout for the very best velocity and trajectory, and blew. The ensuing gale easily destroyed Tap's house of shoes.

"Buckles and laces!" the little fellow exclaimed. "What have you done?"

Jeffrey's grin was so wide now that it showed every one of his long, pointed teeth. "Just gotten a little obstacle out of the way, so that we can get down to the serious business of dinnertime!"

"Oh, no you don't!" And the little fellow began to dance. And the fallen shoes around him began to dance as well, leaping higher and higher into the air. And closer and closer to the wolf, Jeffrey noticed in alarm. He backed away, but the shoes were faster. They jumped all about him, raining down on him in a merciless mass of shoe leather. The wolf fell to the ground, covering his head as best he could.

It seemed like hours before the footwear stopped moving. Jeffrey groaned as he climbed out of the pile of shoes. Something, it seemed, had gone wrong. He couldn't remember the story going this way. He moved a particularly nasty mound of boots away from his face, gasping for air. But he forgot to breathe, for the first thing he saw above the pile was another shoe, far bigger than all the rest, big enough even for a man or a wolf to hide inside.

"Indeed," the shoe remarked.

Jeffrey fell backward in alarm, slipping down again into the loose jumble of footwear. He struggled back to the surface quickly, but when he once again broke free of the sea of soles and heels, the giant shoe was gone.

It must have been some sort of hallucination, Jeffrey rationalized. It was all perfectly explainable. It was some sort of reaction to being attacked by so much footwear. After all, what other reason would there be for a shoe of that size to even exist? The wolf decided he was better off not even thinking about it.

But the little fellow had escaped as well. And the wolf realized, now that he had started thinking about food, that he was ravenously hungry. Whose house should he blow down next? With an appetite like his, there was really no choice.

"Once upon a time," the wolf whispered, and went about his work.

If anything, Jeffrey the Wolf was even hungrier now. It was making him lose his judgment. He had startled a unicorn just beyond the house he sought, and the wolf hadn't even thought to chase it. But the unicorn no longer mattered, for Jeffrey had at last located the object of his desire, a meal large enough to sate even his enormous appetite.

"Doom doom," Hendrek hummed tunelessly as he built a wall out of what seemed to be random objects, although many of them were long and shiny. "Doom-de-doom-doom-doom."

It was then that the wolf realized that Hendrek was not alone. Well, Jeffrey thought, all well and good, for every diet needs a little variety. Or at least he thought that until he got a good look at the assistant, who was busy handing Hendrek his building materials. The other fellow was short and squat, and sort of an unhealthy grayish-green in color, besides which he had the most horrendous taste in clothes imaginable, wearing some sort of orange and purple checked coat. Perhaps, the ravenous beast considered, the large fellow would be more than enough for dinner. After all, even a wolf as hungry as Jeffrey had some standards.

The wolf left the concealing bushes to get closer to the object of his hunger.

"Doom," Hendrek noted. "We have a visitor."

His assistant looked up. "Oh, you mean that guy skulking over there?"

Jeffrey chose to ignore that remark, instead standing up straight and doffing his cap.

"And a good day to you, too, neighbors," he greeted them cheerily. "What a fine house you are building!"

"Doom," Hendrek agreed.

"Made out of the finest previously-owned materials available," the incredibly ugly assistant added. "My previously owned materials."

"Doom," Hendrek replied, lifting an imposing looking warclub.

"Of course, most certainly!" Brax added hurriedly. "We have an arrangement."

"Doom." Hendrek nodded. "The arrangement is he lends me his previously owned materials, or I use Headbasher."

The wolf nodded pleasantly, although he was not really listening. Instead, he wondered what would be just the right method of attack to quickly subdue this large and certainly tasty Hendrek. Perhaps, Jeffrey decided at last, if he strolled around a bit behind him. He pictured the large fellow coated with a thin honey glaze.

"There he goes," the assistant remarked, "skulking again."

"Doom," the large fellow added, "he also appears to be a wolf."

"Are you going to hold something as small as that against me?" Jeffrey tried to smile innocently.

"You know, Hendy baby," the assistant replied as he looked closely at the wolf's long and pointed teeth, "perhaps it's time we went and worked on the interior of the house, with the front door securely closed and locked?"

"Doom," Hendrek agreed.

The two of them retreated inside. But all the wolf did was smile even more, for they had gotten to his favorite part of the story once again. He took a deep breath and called out:

"Come on and let me into your front room!"

But Hendrek boomed back:

"Not by the hair of my doom-de-doom-doom!"

Jeffrey chuckled. Now was the moment for the really good part. And this time, there weren't any of those nasty shoes around here to ruin it for him.

He took a bigger breath: "Then I'll huff and I'll puff and I'll blooooooow your house down!" And he took the biggest breath he possibly could, feeling as though his lungs would burst right through his hairy chest. He quickly positioned his snout once again for maximum effect, and blew.

Hendrek's house didn't stand a chance. It came apart with a clatter. Hundreds of shiny things flew into the air.

And then they started to fall down. Jeffrey looked up in the sky and realized with a horrible sickening certainty exactly what Hendrek had built his house with. For spread overhead, but descending quickly, were spears and arrows and knives and scimitars and broadswords, and any number of other long, sharp and pointy things.

And they all seemed to be falling toward Jeffrey.

The previously owned objects Hendrek had built his house with were all weapons. What sort of person built a house out of weapons? By now, Jeffrey was quite certain this was not the way the story was supposed to go. But he was even more certain that if he stood his ground he would be skewered at least a dozen times.

Jeffrey ran back into the woods with a howl. The wolf knew he would have to look elsewhere for dinner. But it would be the tenderest dinner of all.

Wuntvor worked diligently on his sturdy, new brick house. As nice as it was to discuss shoes and the issues of the day with his two good friends, it was even nicer to be alone for a change.

But wasn't the day growing suddenly cold? Perhaps it was only that chill wind that had sprung up so suddenly. It was an amazingly ferocious breeze, stripping the leaves from the surrounding trees. Wuntvor was glad he would soon have a nice, warm house to protect him from the weather. And then he heard another sound, a dry, hollow chuckle, as cold in its way as the wind that had preceded it. Wuntvor looked up. He thought he saw a dark figure walking between the trees.

Was someone coming?

FIFTEEN

There is another saying among those mages I am always talking about: "If a man can stand tall and proud, he will not be afraid." And perhaps there is some truth in this statement, for if a man can stand tall and proud, with a good weapon or two in his hands, a trusted banishment spell upon his lips, and his back against the wall, then his fear might diminish considerably. Even better is the scenario where he has two or three hundred trusted allies at his side, a nearby trap door for hasty escapes, and no enemy approaching for miles around. It gets better still when you add a tidy sum stashed away in a handy retirement account, the love of a good woman and a hiding place that no one else has discovered in hundreds of years. Under such circumstances, fear could conceivably be controlled. But don't count on it.

—*The Teachings of Ebenezum,* VOLUME LV

Wuntvor was suddenly afraid. There was something about this sort of weather, something about that mysterious figure, that he should remember. Everything around him seemed like ice. Even his clothes were cold against his body.

Somebody coughed.

Wuntvor jumped. There was a rustling in the bushes.

"Oh, wow," another voice said.

"Aren't you going to say hello?" yet another voice demanded. "It's getting cold out here!"

"Beg pardon?" Wuntvor replied as eight fairly short men emerged from the shrubbery. He looked up as a distant scream echoed eerily through the forest, as if a hundred lost souls cried their death agonies. But then the day warmed again as suddenly as it had cooled, and the late afternoon sun once more shone through the treetops.

"Weird weather patterns you have around here," one of the short fellows muttered as he wrung his hands. "But that's not why we're here."

"Indeed?" Wuntvor replied, somewhat dubiously. "Have we met?"

"Must he always say that?" one of the dwarves complained.

"Don't mind Touchy, there," the hand-wringer quickly added. "You would recall us, if you were not under one of Mother Duck's spells."

"Indeed?" Wuntvor wasn't really trying to comprehend what these short people were talking about. There was something about the cold wind and the mysterious figure which somehow seemed much more important.

"I'm sorry," he added at last. "I don't remember."

"Of course not!" the hand-wringer agreed with him jovially. "You're in a fairy tale. The very tale in which we have been promised a major role!"

"This doesn't seem very major to me!" one of the others sniffed.

"Of course not, Snooty," the hand-wringer answered. "Our major role hasn't started yet. This is more of a cameo appearance." He turned back to Wuntvor. "But, we came to admire your new home!" He added in a lower voice: "I'd introduce everybody, but what's the use? The way things have been going lately, Mother Duck will have to start this whole thing over again in a minute, anyway." He continued in his louder, more forceful conversational style: "My this certainly looks like a sturdy house. We were awfully glad to get the opportunity to see it!" For some reason, the short fellow glanced at his wrist. "Look how late it's gotten to be! Well, we have to run!"

The speaker waved as he and his fellows turned to go.

"That's it?" Wuntvor asked. "That's all you came here to tell me?"

"Why, of course!" the hand-wringing fellow called back over his shoulder. "Still, if our appearance here serves to remind Mother Duck that we're still around, eager to begin our part in this drama, that couldn't hurt, either."

"Wait a minute!" Wuntvor called, desperation rising in his voice. For he had suddenly remembered that that mysterious figure wanted to capture him, but could only do so if he was all alone.

"What is it this time?" one of the others barked.

"Um—," Wuntvor fumbled, trying to think fast. "Wouldn't you like to see the inside of my house?"

"If it's as boring as the outside, no way!" the same fellow added.

"It's enough that we have to go along with Smarmy's publicity ideas here—"

"But we all agreed—," the hand-wringer interrupted.

"Only so that we didn't have to put up with your whining—"

"Oh, wow."

Somebody moaned. Somebody else coughed. A third somebody dropped something, very loudly.

"Oh, dear," the hand-wringer said at last. "Well, if it's that way, I'm afraid our humble selves really must be going."

Then they were still leaving? Wuntvor fought a panic that seemed to sweep over him from nowhere. How could he make them understand?

"But I'm all alone!" he wailed.

The brashest of the fellows snickered. "Sure you're all alone, except for that guy skulking over there in the bushes!"

The wolf stepped out from his hiding place. "Skulking? Me? Never. I just feel it is impolite to interrupt."

All eight of the short fellows laughed as they walked away.

"Nevermind them," the wolf scoffed. "I've come to look at your fine new home."

Nevermind them? Wuntvor didn't even understand them. He had no idea why those eight short fellows had shown up. "Once upon a time," he muttered under his breath, turning his attention to the furry fellow with the green cap, who seemed quite a bit closer than the last time Wuntvor had looked. At this distance, he couldn't help but notice the size of the beast's incisors.

"Is something the matter?" the wolf inquired smoothly.

"Um—," Wuntvor began, trying to phrase his observation as politely as possible. "My, what big teeth you have."

The wolf shook his head peremptorily. "No, I'm sorry, that's another fairy tale altogether."

The lad looked down at the ground, trying to think of a suitable apology. But when he looked up again, the beast was almost on top of him.

The wolf licked his chops. "Speaking of appearances, you'd look particularly good in a light cream sauce." The wolf wiggled its shaggy eyebrows. "But perhaps others have told you that."

Wuntvor frowned. Come to think of it, somebody or other *had* told him that once, somewhere or other. Or at least Wuntvor thought they had. Didn't he? But what did it all mean?

"Doom," came a deep, booming voice from the bushes.

"You'd better watch out," a much smaller and higher voice added. "Or it'll be time for Brownie Power!"

The wolf frowned. This was *definitely* not the way this story was supposed to go. After all he'd promised Mother Duck, his fairy tale was getting out of hand as well.

"That's right!" Wuntvor declared, as if a veil had been lifted from his eyes. "That's what you were doing when you snuck up on me. You were skulking!" He pointed at the beast's open mouth. "That must mean that you're the wolf!"

"Doom!" Hendrek exclaimed as he charged from the bushes, his warclub high above his head. Tap cheered from where he clung to the large fellow's shoulder.

"Hey!" the wolf protested, covering his head. "Give a guy a break. I'm only trying to make a living!"

"Doom!" Hendrek replied, grabbing Wuntvor by his shirt. "Into the house!"

And the three friends ran inside, slamming the very heavy oak door behind them.

Jeffrey uncovered his head and stared at the thick door. This fairy tale had gotten so far off course that even he could barely recognize it. He decided not to even try the next part, with the huffing and puffing. The wolf was a realist, after all. He knew all about his luck with brick houses.

But there were other ways of getting food. The wolf laughed rue-fully at the closed doors. All right, my dinner delicacies, he thought. If that's the way you want it, that's the way it's going to be.

They had tricked him with houses made of shoes and weapons. Well, there was more than one way to end a fairy tale. He'd show them that a wolf could improvise as well!

And with that, the wolf skulked back into the forest.

In the meantime, the three friends huddled within Wuntvor's brick house.

"Doom," Hendrek remarked. "Isn't it a little dark in here?"

"Yeah!" Tap added. "The only light's coming from that little hole overhead!"

"Indeed." Wuntvor looked up at the small portal that still showed the early evening sky. "That is the only part of my house that I haven't finished."

"Doom," Hendrek commented. "Don't you think you should have put in windows?"

Wuntvor considered, then shook his head, a motion that was almost lost in the gathering gloom. "Windows wouldn't have been wolfproof. I had a singleness of purpose when I built this house. Still, this place isn't much good for anything but hiding, is it?"

They opened the door and peered out. The sun had sunk far below the trees, and deep shadows stretched across Wuntvor's lawn, as if the night had already claimed the ground and was working on the sky. It was difficult to see anything in the gathering dusk, but they all heard a great crashing and tearing that was coming closer.

"Doom," Hendrek whispered. "What could that be?"

"Indeed," Wuntvor added. "It doesn't sound like a wolf."

Tap jumped boldly from Hendrek's shoulder. "I am small and will be difficult to see in the shadows. I will go investigate."

And before either of his friends could protest, he was gone.

The crashing grew louder still, and was accompanied by bestial laughter.

"Tap?" Wuntvor called softly into the night. "Can you see anything? Is there something we should do?"

The little fellow's answer was to run back inside and hide behind the lad's leg.

"Close the door!" Tap yelled. "Close the door!"

"But what did you see?" Wuntvor inquired.

"Big . . ." the little fellow gasped. "Scaly . . . Fire-breathing . . ."

"Doom," Hendrek rumbled. "The wolf has brought a dragon."

"A dragon?" Wuntvor wondered. "What could he do—"

But his conjecture was cut short by the wolf's call:

"Open your door or I'll vent my frustration!"

"Indeed?" Wuntvor whispered to the others. "Maybe this isn't as bad as we think. Maybe there's some way we can talk this out." He called back to the wolf:

"Is this request open to negotiation?"

The wolf could barely restrain his laughter as he yelled: "Then we'll huff and we'll puff and we'll blllooooooowww your house down!"

"Duck!" Wuntvor called as a great roaring sound came from without.

Wuntvor and the others fell to the earthen floor, covering their heads to protect them from flying bricks. But the house was so well put together that the dragon's breath picked it up as a single piece and sent it soaring into the night sky.

Wuntvor stood, looking out at the clearing still lit by dragon fire. The wolf smiled and licked his chops.

"This will all be so much simpler if you just stand there," the beast remarked, stepping forward. "And don't worry at all. The light cream sauce is quite tasty."

"Doom." Hendrek shifted his warclub from hand to hand.

"Buckles and laces!" Tap tried out some tentative dance steps.

"I'll get around to both of you later," the wolf replied, advancing on the lad.

Wuntvor felt helpless. He knew his friends would do the best they could to protect him. Still, he would feel much better if he had some way to protect himself, a weapon with which to smite the beast.

"That's a good meal," the wolf consoled. "It'll all be over in a few seconds. I'm a very speedy eater."

"Oh, no you don't!" shouted a magnificently modulated voice from the other side of the clearing.

"What are you doing?" another voice complained. "Where are you taking me?"

Wuntvor looked in the direction of the commotion. There stood a magnificent beast, the color of moonlight, with a pale horn in the middle of its forehead. And in its mouth, it held a shining sword.

"So are you going to let me down, or what?" the sword whined.

"I am returning you to your rightful owner," the unicorn replied haughtily, somehow enunciating perfectly even with a sword in its mouth. It laid the sword at Wuntvor's feet, then looked up at the lad with its large, soulful eyes.

"I hope that you will be properly grateful," the beauteous beast whispered.

"Indeed," Wuntvor replied. "Perhaps we can discuss it some time, when we are not in the midst of a crisis." He knelt down and picked up the sword.

"Sure, you guys can talk!" Cuthbert continued. "Don't even give a thought to the trusty weapon who just spent half an hour stuck in that beast's mouth. I mean, my entire blade is covered with unicorn saliva! Yuck!"

"There is no more beautiful saliva upon the face of the earth," the unicorn retorted, shaking its moonlit mane to breathtaking effect.

"I am sure there is not," Wuntvor agreed, "but if you'll excuse me, I have a wolf to fend off."

"Oh, so that's the way it is, huh?" The wolf's teeth set in a grim smile. "Well, you may have a unicorn on your side, not to mention a talking sword and a big fellow with a club and a little fellow who does funny things with shoes. But I have a dragon!" He looked back at the imposing fire lizard. "Isn't that right?"

The dragon stared back at him silently.

"Hey!" the wolf insisted. "I thought we had a deal!" He took a step toward the dragon.

The dragon took a step away.

"Oh, no you don't!" the wolf yelled. "An arrangement is an arrangement!" The wolf took two steps forward.

The dragon took two steps away. And, being as the dragon was perhaps twenty times the size of the wolf, the giant lizard's steps were perhaps twenty times that of the green-hatted beast. In fact, the dragon had already backed completely out of the clearing.

"Is that so?" The wolf shook both his forepaws at the distant reptile. "I'll show you what I do to welchers!" He ran toward the dragon. The dragon retreated even more quickly. In a matter of seconds, both were out of sight.

There were twin explosions, one to either side of Wuntvor. The lad jumped back, startled. To his left was a little man, about the same size as Tap, although the newcomer seemed to be wearing a leather crown. And to his right was a huge shoe.

"Good," the shoe remarked. "Now we can talk."

SIXTEEN

There is an explanation for everything. It is a pity that many of those explanations make no sense.

—The Teachings of Ebenezum, VOLUME LXIX

I blinked. It was my master Ebenezum, come to rescue me once again.

"Indeed," he said. I realized I was staring.

"It must be very disconcerting for you," my master inside the shoe continued, "popping in and out of fairy tales like this."

"Um—," I replied. "Indeed."

"Well," my master continued, "I believe our dragon distraction has given us a few minutes. But we must talk quickly."

I nodded, trying to blink away the cobwebs that filled my brain.

Ebenezum explained: "Ever since Norei learned you were a prisoner of Mother Duck, we have been working together to set you free. And when His Brownieship was nice enough to reconstruct this magic shoe, I was able to enter the fray."

"That's Brownie Power for you!" His Brownieship added.

"I've been telling them that all along!" Tap replied.

His Brownieship looked balefully at his subordinate. "I don't think you should be talking to anybody."

Tap paled. "Heel sorting!" he whispered.

"Indeed," Ebenezum continued. "Before I came here, I was able through the protective powers of this shoe to study some of the learned books in Vushta concerning the Eastern Kingdoms. We have come up with some very important facts."

"Bent buckle straightening!" Tap moaned.

"Firstly, whenever you say 'Once—'" Ebenezum stopped himself abruptly. He cleared his throat and began again. "Well, you know those four words that always start the tales, and put you under

Mother Duck's spell. There are three other words that end them, and close the loop, so that the fairy tale becomes fixed, with exactly the right ending."

"Happily ever after," Wuntvor whispered.

"Precisely," the wizard replied. "We are now concocting a scheme by which you, as the tale's primary participant, say exactly those words at exactly the right time." My master chuckled. "If we can plan this correctly, Wuntvor, this is your last fairy tale."

"Indeed?" I replied, fresh hope filling my heart. I knew my master would not let me down!

"Truly," he continued. "All we had to do was somehow find a way to inform you of our plan. Unfortunately, when I first arrived, we had to deal instantly with Death. And since that occasion, I have been trying to keep a low profile. If Mother Duck discovers our plot too soon, we will fail. I have tried instead to feed you hints, snuck into the corners of the fairy story. But that method has not been fast enough."

"So we had to create a diversion!" His Brownieship explained. Tap wouldn't look him in the eye.

"Indeed," the wizard resumed. "We needed to get the wolf out of the way. What you were just in, you realize, was *his* fairy story. Frustrated at the lack of control she has had over her own tales, Mother Duck gave the wolf a chance to see if he could do any better. Once we found out about this, we knew it was our chance. Anyway, it was His Brownieship's idea to add the dragon and the unicorn as a bit of a distraction. Now all we have to do is hope Mother Duck watches the wolf for a moment so we can talk."

There was one question he had not answered. I could not help myself—I had to ask it!

"But master!" I cried. "What of Norei?"

"Norei cannot be here. She is using her powers to watch Mother Duck, to make sure we are not discovered. She was also the one to see the opportunity in the wolf's tale."

My master paused. I imagined him stroking his long white beard deep within his shoe. "In addition, she is one of the few people with magical abilities to still escape my malady. She needs to stay hidden, safe from Mother Duck's power, until we finally put our plan into effect. Listen carefully, Wuntvor, for when we give you a prearranged signal, you must shout out those words."

"Happily ever after," I repeated once again.

"They have a satisfying ring to them, don't they?" His Brownieship smiled. "Sort of like Brownie Magic!"

Tap could hold it in no longer. "B-but my King of Sole!" he stuttered. "Won't you listen to me? I have always been true to Brownie Magic!"

His leader looked condescendingly down his royal nose. "Like those seven Brownie wishes?"

"But your smallness, once you hear—" Tap paused, as if struggling to pick the right words. "Once you—Once upon a time." His voice fell to a monotone, his eyes free of expression.

His Brownieship scowled. "The weak-willed always go first."

"She is reasserting control!" the wizard exclaimed. "Quickly, Wuntvor! There is one more thing I must tell you."

"Once upon—," His Brownieship began. He clapped his tiny hands over his mouth. I felt the pressure, too; those four words pounding in my brain, welling upon my lips. I had the feeling that speaking those words was as important as life itself. But I must fight it! I looked quickly to my companions, and saw from their distress that, now that my master had explained the true nature of the magic, they were battling the spell as well.

"We must go!" the wizard called. And both Ebenezum and His Brownieship disappeared in twin puffs of smoke.

"But master?" I asked the empty air. "What else must I know?"

"Doom," Hendrek remarked. "Ebenezum is resourceful. I am sure he will find some way to tell us."

But the Brownie was back in the fairy tale trance; a spell that any of the rest of us could fall victim to at any moment. That meant that Mother Duck's eyes and ears were with us as well. How could my master give us his message without her finding out?

I looked up in the sky. Something had blotted out the moon. I heard the sound of great wings, descending rapidly. Even in the darkness, I knew it had to be Hubert.

"Here we are again!" Alea's voice called from Hubert's back. "It's the duo who will pull you through-o, the act of acts with all the facts!"

"The pair so slick that they'll make you sick!" another, incredibly annoying voice called from the edge of the clearing. I squinted into the darkness. Anyone wearing that many robes had to be Snarks.

"I had to come and see what would make this much noise," the demon explained. "Guxx is out there somewhere looking for his drummer. I imagine they will both be along presently."

"Indeed," I replied, careful to choose only the safest words possible. Now that I was searching for it, I could feel a subtle pressure within my skull, something there that wanted me to forget, perhaps to sleep. It was a powerful magic that I would have to fight if I wished to discover the rest of my master's message.

"Once upon a time," Tap interjected.

"Doom," Hendrek said, his brow furrowed as he studied me critically. "Then you feel it, too?"

I nodded. "I wish there was some way my master could hurry."

"Oh," Alea said brightly as she jumped from the dragon's back. "That's why we're here. Hubert knows!"

"Indeed?" Hubert knew the final secret my master wished to impart to me? But then I realized the terrible irony of the situation. "He cannot speak! How can he tell us?"

"Simple enough," the damsel reassured us. "It will be difficult, but Hubert can do it. He will have to utilize an ancient art among his kind: Dragon charades!"

Alea quickly outlined the rules of this ancient reptilian art as Hubert silently prepared himself. It seemed that the dragon would pantomime Ebenezum's secret, and those of us assembled here would have to guess the dragon's meaning. When one of us got it right, Hubert would nod and point, and the truth would be revealed to us.

"Simple enough," I announced. "Shall we begin?"

The dragon nodded, blowing controlled bursts of flame to better illuminate his actions.

Alea ran over to join the rest of us.

The dragon snapped his mouth open and shut repeatedly.

"It's a saying!" Alea exclaimed. "That's what Hubert's telling us. The wizard's message is a saying."

So Ebenezum had tried to tell me some ancient truth?

"What kind of saying?" I asked Alea.

"Once upon a time," Tap suggested.

"Watch Hubert and find out," she replied. "What a performer!"

I turned my attention back to the dragon.

"What's the saying about?" I called.

The dragon pointed downward. "The ground?" He shook his head. "The Netherhells?" His headshaking redoubled. I realized then that he was actually pointing to his lower extremities.

"Your feet?" I queried.

The dragon shrugged, then nodded. What did that mean—maybe?

The dragon lifted one foot, then bent over so that he held both his forepaws just below his toes. With great care, he pulled the forepaws back toward his heel.

"Doom," Hendrek conjectured. "He is putting something over his foot."

"Like a shoe?" I asked.

The dragon nodded, thumping his tail enthusiastically.

"So the saying is about a shoe?"

The dragon nodded again.

"Doom," Hendrek added. "We have an expert about shoes."

"Once upon a time," Tap replied.

"Yes, but the Brownie is under Mother Duck's spell," I reminded the warrior. "She has taken over his mind."

"Doom," Hendrek acknowledged. "Perhaps I can remedy that."

"Once upon a time," Tap replied.

The warrior lifted his great warclub Headbasher, cursed to steal the memories of men, and gently bopped Tap on the noggin.

"Once upon an—urk!" Tap exclaimed. "Hey, watch out with that thing! We Brownies crush pretty easily."

"Indeed!" I cheered. "You have broken Mother Duck's spell."

"Doom," Hendrek agreed.

"Spell? I was under Mother Duck's spell?" Tap paled. "Where's His Brownieship?"

I told Tap that his leader had to flee to escape Mother Duck. I also told the Brownie that there might be a way he could redeem himself. All he had to do was figure out the famous saying about shoes that Hubert was trying to give us via sign language.

"Shoes?" Tap laughed. " 'Twill take but a moment for an expert like myself. Show me this pantomiming dragon!"

Hubert waved, then went back through the motions of putting on the shoe.

"Simplicity itself!" the Brownie exclaimed. "The saying is: A shoe in the hand is worth two in the bush."

The dragon shook his head.

"No?" Tap replied, clearly astonished that he had been incorrect. "Then it must be 'A rolling shoe gathers no laces!'—right?"

Hubert shook his head again, resorting once more to the putting-on-the-shoe pantomime.

"Too many Brownies spoil the shoe?" Tap tried again. "It just has to be!"

The dragon shook his head one more time as he tucked his foot into the imaginary footwear.

But that was it, I thought. Could it be?

"If the shoe fits, wear it!" I called.

Hubert nodded and pointed.

"If the shoe fits, wear it?" The Brownie scratched his tiny head. "I've never heard of that one. Doesn't seem to have much pizzazz, does it?"

Well, it might not have much "pizzazz," as the Brownie put it, but since it came from my master, I was sure that it was fraught with meaning. But what could that meaning be?

"Aha!" yet another voice called from the edge of the clearing. "There you are!"

The speaker approached Hubert's flickering nose light. It was the wolf.

"Thought better of running away from me, did you?" the wolf asked superiorly. "Well, I'm glad we're back where we can get something done. On with the story!"

"No! No! No! No! No! No! No!" Mother Duck ran rapidly down the hill.

"What do you mean, no?" Jeffrey the Wolf complained as the old woman burst into our midst. "I was so close."

"Close to total chaos, you mean?" Mother Duck retorted angrily. "I knew I should never have listened to you."

"But I've almost gotten to the best part!" Jeffrey objected. "Where I get to eat everybody!" He turned to the dragon. "Now, if you'll just quick-fry all these characters over here—"

"Oh, no, you don't!" Mother Duck interrupted. "I'm taking back my fairy tale, as of now!"

She smiled at the assemblage.

"Once upon a time," we all said as one.

SEVENTEEN

"Everybody needs their rest."

—Yet another quote attributed to Ebenezum,
greatest wizard in the Western Kingdoms,
when he was once again discovered upon
the royal bed and in the arms of the
obviously enthusiastic Queen Vivazia
by her husband, King Snerdlot the
Vengeful. Luckily for the wizard, the
king was exhausted by endless hours of
Ebenezum-hunting in the hidden corridors
of the castle, and so was easily fooled
by the mage's temporary confusion spell,
which somehow got Snerdlot thinking that
he had wandered by mistake into the
wrong castle altogether, thus allowing
the wizard to escape back into the
hidden corridors during
the king's lengthy apology.

Once upon a time there was a handsome prince named Wuntvor, who
lived far out in the woods with his good friends, the Seven Other
Dwarves. Now the Seven Other Dwarves warned Wuntvor to beware
of strangers, for it was rumored—

No, no, no. That didn't sound at all right. Perhaps if he rephrased
it.

Once upon a time there was a very confused young man named
Wuntvor, who could have sworn there was something that he was
supposed to remember. And he also could have sworn he should have

known all the various people and beasts that surrounded him in the clearing.

"Once upon a time," everyone said in unison, including Wuntvor. But why? Wuntvor had no idea. Wasn't he supposed to say something else instead?

"Are you just going to let me drag on the floor all day?" a voice complained from just below his right wrist.

Wuntvor lifted the object he held in his right hand. It was a sword.

"Much better!" the sword remarked.

"A talking sword?" Wuntvor almost dropped the weapon in surprise.

"Oh, we're not going to start this again!" the sword admonished. "You're in another one of Mother Duck's fairy tales, where she wipes out everyone's memory so that you can be empty pawns that she can use at her whim. But you're nothing of the sort." The sword sighed. "I suppose I'm going to have to go through this whole thing once more. So listen:

"You are Wuntvor, apprentice to Ebenezum, sent here to try and enlist Mother Duck in your cause. Unfortunately, Mother Duck is a stubborn, willful woman, and will not even listen to your pleas. Therefore, you were in the midst of escaping when the old woman once again got you under her spell."

Wuntvor blinked. "You're right. I'm starting to remember. How can I ever thank you?"

"Think nothing of it," the sword assured him. "It's totally self-preservation. Once these fairy tales get going, you always end up whipping out your sword—that's me—for one thing or another. It always ends in blood." The sword shivered in the lad's hand. "Or worse than blood."

"Worse than blood?" the lad asked, intrigued despite his confusion.

"Ichor," the sword explained miserably. "Hair oil. Unicorn saliva."

Wuntvor nodded. He was beginning to recall some of those incidents as well. He closed his eyes, trying to will the last remnants of the spell away.

"Once upon—" He clamped his mouth shut. Those words had come to his lips unbidden.

"Mother Duck's controlling spell," the sword explained. "You must refrain from saying those words at all cost, or you will be under her power forever. But come. Let us try to free the others."

Wuntvor looked to the rest of those in the clearing, all wandering about, mumbling over and over those four fateful words.

"Indeed," the lad asked his weapon as they approached the others, "if this woman's sorcery is so powerful, how did you manage to escape?"

"By my very definition," the sword patiently explained. "I'm a magical device. Spells bounce right off my shiny blade."

"Indeed," the lad responded. Why did that explanation sound so familiar?

"Quickly, now," the sword cautioned, "we have to awaken the others and flee. I want to be done with this as soon as possible, before any —" The sword paused, as if it found it difficult to say the next word. "—bloodshed begins."

"Very well," Wuntvor agreed. But before he could take a dozen paces, he heard a strange, high-pitched laugh emanating from the edge of the nearby forest.

"Hee, hee, hee! Hello, my dearies," the strange voice continued. "I've come with a present for Wuntvor."

The others in the clearing all turned toward the voice.

"Doom?" said one particularly large fellow.

"Buckles and laces!" exclaimed one who was particularly short.

"Yes," the old lady continued as she stepped into their midst. "Hee, hee, hee! I've brought a special basket of apples for my special Eternal Apprentice."

"It's Mother Duck!" the sword whispered.

The old woman smiled as she caught Wuntvor's eye. The lad took a step away, not knowing what to expect.

"Now, now," the woman said reassuringly. "There's no reason to be afraid. I've just brought you all some food."

She pulled back her dark shawl to reveal a basket of apples she had hung on one of her arms. They were unlike any apples Wuntvor had ever seen. In fact, they glowed bright green in the darkness.

"Don't they look delicious?" Mother Duck asked encouragingly. "So plump, so crisp, so sweet. Hee, hee, hee! Wouldn't you like to be biting into one right now?"

Wuntvor swallowed and backed away again. He wasn't sure he wanted to eat any fruit that contained its own light source.

A wolf in a green cap ran up to the old woman. "Hey," the beast said, "if I can't eat anything else, at least one of these will stave off my hunger." He snatched a piece of fruit from the basket.

"How dare you!" Mother Duck began. Wuntvor flinched at her anger. Glancing apologetically at the lad, she spoke to the wolf in more soothing tones. "Oh, I suppose it's all right. You must be hungry. I've neglected to put any meals in any of today's fairy tales, haven't I? We just have to make sure that Wuntvor gets one." She waved the basket in the lad's direction. "Not that there's anything special about these apples. No, no, except that they are especially delicious! Hee, hee, hee!"

"Doom." The large fellow lumbered over to the basket and extracted an apple. "I am famished."

"Buckles and laces!" The very small fellow jumped into the basket, deftly pushing a piece of fruit over the rim. "Brownies need to maintain their strength!" He leapt after the falling apple.

Mother Duck stopped short. In the strange, green light of the apples, she looked very upset.

"If another of you touches my apples, I will smite—" She paused when she noticed that Wuntvor was rapidly backing away once again.

"Oh, dear," she said after a moment, her voice much kinder. "Hee, hee, hee! I'm afraid I'm unnecessarily cross. Mother Duck shouldn't stay up so late. It's after her bedtime!" She once again pushed the basket toward Wuntvor. "There's more than enough fruit to go around. But everyone should wait until Wuntvor gets an apple of his own. It's only polite."

The wolf took a noisy bite from his apple.

"Ummmm!" he exclaimed. "That's delici—"

He fell on his face before he could finish the sentence and began to snore loudly.

"Speaking of inappropriate manners!" Mother Duck exclaimed, pointing disdainfully at the sleeping beast. "He eats before everyone is served, and then immediately takes a nap! The nerve of some creatures! He'll never get to be in any more of my fairy tales, let me tell you!"

She took another step toward Wuntvor. A fair damsel sneaked up behind her and lifted an apple from the basket.

"Hee, hee, hee! Now, my dear, sweet boy. I've brought these apples just for you. I know you've been stubborn, not wanting to say certain words. But Mother Duck isn't angry. Oh, no. Hee, hee, hee. And to show you how pleased I am with you, I just want you to take one tiny little bite out of one tiny little apple. Mother Duck will feel so much better if you do."

"In-indeed," Wuntvor managed, "I do not wish to."

The old woman stood there for a moment, staring without expression at the youngster. A shortish fellow hidden within a huge robe reached out and took a piece of fruit.

"You do not wish to?" she asked at last, the sweetness in her voice evaporating with every word. "You are in Mother Duck's kingdom, and you do not wish to?" She laughed again, but it had a darker sound than before. "You come here, unannounced, unasked for, because of some stupid quest far beneath my notice. And now you refuse to obey my wishes? Oh, I'll grant you that you've brought along some interesting fodder for my fairy tales, but that is not enough! There are orders that must be obeyed! There are apples that must be eaten!"

She thrust the basket forward. Wuntvor could smell the apples now; they were almost beneath his nose. They smelled very sweet, almost sickeningly so, as if their green skins were made of sugar. As sweet as they were, though, he wanted one. He couldn't remember the last time he had eaten. Then again, he couldn't remember a lot of things.

His mouth started to water.

"Why don't you take an apple?" the old woman demanded. "Just one small bite, a few seconds, and it will be over. I think I deserve at least that much, after all I've done for you." She tried to smile encouragement. It didn't work.

She sighed, a scowl once again dominating her face. "You force me to become personally involved in one of my own fairy stories, just so I might rescue my kingdom from the damage this sleeping wolf has done! I have never spent so much time fooling around with my stories —and you know I am a Fairy Tale Professional!" She paused, doing her best to control her temper. "I suppose you have done things for me as well. Heaven knows, you have opened new vistas, new possibilities in which I might ply my traditional tales. I am grateful for that much. Heaven knows I've never been able to call upon Death the way you seem able to. But I think it is time for those possibilities I keep seeing to become fairy tale reality—Now!"

She stared at the lad, and her eyes seemed to glow with a cold, green fire, much the same color as the shining apples.

"Think handsome prince," she whispered.

Wuntvor began to sweat.

"Um—," he managed. "Indeed?"

Mother Duck laughed sourly. "Still you resist me. Can't you see that it is hopeless? I am the supreme ruler of all I survey. Once you enter my kingdom, you are mine. For as long as I want you, you are mine, even if that is the rest of your life."

The green glow in her eyes intensified. Wuntvor couldn't look away. He found his lips and tongue moving of their own volition.

"Once upon—," the lad began. "Ow!"

Somehow, his sword had slapped him in the thigh. Wuntvor looked down at his weapon.

"Don't look at her!" the sword demanded. "I guarantee you, it'll lead to bloodshed!"

"That does it!" Mother Duck raged. "You seem to have some sort of incredible dumb luck that always saves you. Well, it won't save you this time! Eternal Apprentice or no, you are going to eat one of my apples!"

She swung the basket behind her, as if getting ready to fling the fruit in Wuntvor's face. So intent was she on her retribution, though, that she did not notice that the dragon had somehow maneuvered his great bulk directly behind her. The great reptile caught the swinging basket deftly between his formidable teeth, tipping the wicker just so, allowing the five remaining apples to slide down his gullet.

"What?" Mother Duck stared at her empty basket in disbelief. "Gone? Every one of my delicious, very special apples gone?" She glared at Wuntvor. "You will not escape my wrath this easily! Wait right there! I will be back as soon as I reload!"

There was a substantial crash as the dragon fell behind her. The huge reptile began to snore loudly. Mother Duck grumbled under her breath as she stormed off around the sleeping lizard.

"Well," the sword in Wuntvor's hand said, "I guess we showed her."

"Indeed," the lad answered, still not quite sure what he had done. "What do we do now?"

"Hmmm," the sword considered. "Well, now that Mother Duck's gone, I suppose I can resume the introductions. I, incidentally, am called Cuthbert. In case you forget again, my name is tastefully inscribed on the side of my blade. You had forgotten, hadn't you? We definitely have to get you out of this fairy tale business. Now, swing me around toward the others, and I'll reintroduce you, let us hope for the last time."

Wuntvor did as the sword bade, turning the blade toward his companions, who all seemed to have fallen to the ground.

"Oh, dear," the sword moaned. "Everyone seems to be asleep. How can we escape when everyone is asleep?"

Wuntvor frowned. Cuthbert was correct. The entire company was quietly snoring, surrounded by half-eaten apples.

"Oh, well," Cuthbert continued. "I suppose I'll identify them all anyway. It'll save time when they're done with their nap. Point me from left to right, will you? Yes, there's Hendrek the warrior and Snarks the demon, and Alea is the damsel's name. That large reptile in the middle is called Hubert. Oh, yes, and the wolf's name is Jeffrey, but you don't have to worry about him. I'm afraid he wouldn't make much of a companion. His appetite would get in the way.

"Oh, dear." Cuthbert hesitated before speaking again, his voice much less certain. "I'm afraid I don't recognize the gentleman standing over on the far right." The sword glowed faintly, as if it might illuminate the stranger. "If you might come a little bit forward, sir? I'm afraid we swords don't see all that well in the moonlight."

"Gladly," replied a voice that sounded like dead leaves blowing in the wind.

"Oh, dear," the sword remarked. "I believe I recognize him now."

So did Wuntvor.

EIGHTEEN

A wizard always attracts a crowd. The minute magic starts, huge quantities of people are attracted, all asking questions and jostling for a better view. It is not considered good form, however, to use your magic to banish these masses and give yourself quieter working conditions. Rather you should accept your lot, and consider the publicity value of spells performed before a large and grateful public. And of course, performing magic becomes even more fulfilling when you have already charged a nominal admission fee.

—*The Teachings of Ebenezum,* VOLUME V

I came to my senses all at once. It was amazing the way Death could do that for me.

The spectre walked forward to meet us. The night had, of course, grown suddenly cold.

"At last," Death whispered, "I have you alone, in a situation where I think we shall not be interrupted."

What was Death talking about? "But I am not alone!" I waved to the cluster of sleeping companions that surrounded us. "We are in the middle of a crowd."

The spectre laughed, the sound of small songbirds drowning in a whirlpool.

"Yes, a crowd—a sleeping crowd," he told me gently. "You do not know very much of Death, do you? Well, of course you wouldn't—you are the Eternal Apprentice, who has cheated me at every turn. You are the Eternal Apprentice, who always manages to elude me despite my best efforts, instead constantly being reborn to another bumbling life! You are the Eternal Apprentice, whose very existence makes a mockery of all my works and all I stand for—" The spectre stopped himself. "Pardon. There is no reason to be upset. I have you at last. There is no escape. I will show you that Death is a gentleman, and answer your question."

He waved at the crowd with a skeletal hand. "Your companions sleep, a deep, drugged slumber. They cannot help you now, for as long as they sleep, they are half in my kingdom already, and I will assure their continued somnambulance." Death sighed, the sound of dead grass blown by the winter wind. "It is nice of us to meet at night, for this is the time Death feels most comfortable walking through the world. It is fitting that I should take you now, at my leisure, after I have stalked you for so long."

"Indeed," I commented, trying to determine some way to stay alive, if only for a few more minutes. I sidled over to the deeply snoring Hendrek and kicked him gently in the breastplate. Hendrek didn't react. I kicked him harder.

"Ow!" I had managed to hurt my big toe in the process. Hendrek still did not respond, not even a muffled "Doom." He snored on, oblivious to my predicament.

Death laughed drily, the sound of beetles eating at a rotting carcass. "You see now that I have won."

"I am not yours yet!" I yelled, backing away from the spectre.

"That's telling him!" Cuthbert shouted encouragingly. "Now what say we get out of here?"

"Must we be tiresome?" a voice said behind me. I whirled around to see Death barely an arm's length away. "I have told you before that escape is impossible. Death is everywhere. I am inevitable."

The spectre spread his arms wide, pointing to a pair of trees on either side. A wind came from somewhere, perhaps even from inside the spectre's bonelike fingers. Leaves whipped about in the gale, curling inward like small animals in pain. The wind seemed to leech the color from them as well, turning green to yellow to driest brown, the leaves at last ripping away from their branches to be carried away by the death wind until all the tree limbs were bare. But the trees were changing as well. Where once they were young and vibrant, only a few years beyond saplings, now they became twisted and gnarled, filled with a crawling rot that seemed to spread from the inside out, causing limbs to fall and bark to decompose before my eyes until, where once two strong trees had stood, now there was nothing but stumps and dust.

Death's laughter boomed through the forest, the sound of a thunderstorm that would destroy everything in its path.

"Maybe it's time for me to go back in my scabbard," Cuthbert suggested.

"Yes," the spectre chortled. "You can run. You can hide. It will do you no good. It won't do anybody any good. As of now, Death will take anybody he wants, at any time he wants. And that includes the Eternal Apprentice!"

He reached for Wuntvor. "Come. Take my hand. You entered this world alone, but you will leave it with me. As long as I have savored this moment, still I promise you, it will be over in an instant."

"Oh, no, it won't!" a wondrously mellifluous voice interrupted.

"Who is that?" Death raved. "Who disturbs my ultimate moment?"

"I do!" And the unicorn cantered forward. In the darkness, the wondrous beast's coat looked as if it were made of moonlight. It waved its shimmering horn in my direction. "You cannot take him. The lad and I have—" The unicorn paused significantly. "—unfinished business."

"I should have known." Death's voice rose like the howling gale that brings a hurricane. "I come here to find all his companions unconscious, leaving the Eternal Apprentice alone, without aid. I should have taken him in that instant, but no, I was too confident, too willing to gloat over my victory. I am Death, after all, used to having my way with all normal, mortal creatures. But I forget that the creature I want now may not be mortal, and certainly isn't normal!"

"Indeed," I replied, seeking a way to further demoralize the spectre. "Come here, O noble unicorn. To my side!"

"To his side?" the unicorn whispered, its soulful brown eyes filling with tears. "He wants me by his side. You don't know how long I've waited to hear those words."

Slowly, carefully—as if the beast feared that, should it move too quickly, it might wake from its newfound dream—the unicorn trotted to my side.

The spectre made a noise halfway between a moan and a snicker. Death seemed to be trembling.

"Do not think for an instant—," he said at last, each word hissing forth as if spoken by a snake about to strike, "do not think I am not prepared for this eventuality. So it is the middle of the night, when most intelligent creatures do not venture forth. So it is a very special night, when most of your companions rest here in a drugged sleep, unable to help their beloved Eternal Apprentice. Still, I knew my conquest might not be easy, that somehow, some way, you would find a method to try to thwart your destiny."

The spectre's bony hand pointed shakily at the unicorn. "Notice that I said you might *try* to thwart your destiny! For, as surely as I have claimed a million billion souls, I swear this night that I shall add the Eternal Apprentice to my collection, no matter what the obstacles!"

"Eep eep!" came a cry in the night.

"What was that?" Death shrieked, pulling his robes close about his skeletal form.

"Indeed?" I said, surprised by the spectre's reaction. "It is only one of my ferrets."

"Only one?" Death whispered. "Then why have I heard that cry, over and over, ever since that small brown creature attacked me when we met earlier today?"

"Indeed?" I thought fast. That would have been at least a couple of attempts on my life ago, when I had thought fondly of my ferret, and it had appeared.

"Eep eep eep!" the ferret called.

"What is this creature?" Death demanded. "You must tell me!"

I shrugged. "He is naught but a magic ferret."

"Magic?" Death stared wildly out into the night. "How could a ferret be magic?"

"I conjured him, using a magic hat—," I began.

"A ferret, created by the Eternal Apprentice?" Death shook so violently I could hear his bones rattle. "I should have known! Only a ferret created by an immortal could follow Death into his kingdom! Well, this will happen no more! I will end this haunting once and for all. I will take you, and the unicorn, and the enchanted ferret as well. Death will win this night!" The spectre chuckled, his confidence returning. "But then, Death always wins."

I felt the unicorn's soft pelt against my leg.

"If we have to go," the beast moaned magnificently, "at least we go together. I wouldn't want it any other way."

"Indeed?" I remarked, because I was beginning to formulate a plan. "Ferret, to my side!"

"Eep eep eep!" the little creature cried as it streaked across the clearing. I saw Death flinch as it passed.

"Yes," I said to the small animal as it nuzzled my shoe. "We might as well all be together, as Death has suggested."

Death grinned, pleased at my acquiescence. He stepped forward to take all three of us.

"After all," I continued, "being together like this makes it so much easier to call the others."

Death stopped. "The others?"

I nodded. "This is not my only ferret."

Death took a step back. "It isn't?"

"No," I answered. "It is only one of hundreds."

"Hundreds?" Death whispered. "You have hundreds of magic ferrets? Look into my eyes, Apprentice. It is impossible to lie to Death!"

I did my best to gaze into the spectre's deep eye sockets. For I was not lying. I did have a virtually limitless supply of ferrets. Of course, all but one of them were still back in Vushta, with no way to join us here. But I did not intend to tell Death that particular fact.

"You do have hundreds!" Death moaned. "Hundreds of ferrets, overrunning my peaceful kingdom?"

My plan was working. Death's sudden panic at my magic ferrets entering his kingdom had unnerved him enough so I was sure that he would think twice about taking our lives.

"But, no," Death said, shaking himself. "I am overreacting. There is only one ferret here. If I take you quickly, perhaps you would not have time to call the rest of them. And even if you could, perhaps it would be worth it to have hundreds of eeping ferrets in my kingdom, if I also had the Eternal Apprentice!" He reached out both his arms to take us all. "For, no matter what happens, I have sworn to take you tonight."

"Indeed?" I said, more than a bit upset at this turn of events. It had not taken him long to think twice. Unfortunately, my plan went no further.

"And what exactly is going on here?" a commanding female voice called from behind me.

Death looked past my shoulder. "I knew it would happen like this! I've had any number of chances to take the Eternal Apprentice. But do I? No, I end up talking with him, instead. Discussing ferrets! And then, who shows up, but yet another companion that I must take to my dark domain."

"Another companion?" the female voice asked.

"Do not deny it!" Death shrieked. "The Eternal Apprentice draws companions the way rotting meat draws flies!"

"It's bad enough that Death is going to get us all," Cuthbert wailed. "Do we have to listen to his metaphors as well?"

"How dare you call me a companion!" the voice demanded. "I am Mother Duck! I was simply bringing Wuntvor his apples."

"No matter who you claim to be," Death replied, "I must take you. For to take the Eternal Apprentice, I am risking chaos. I can leave no living witnesses."

"You will do no such thing!" Mother Duck exclaimed, walking forward so that she stood between me and Death. "This is my kingdom, and whoever enters it acts only on my command!"

Death laughed again. I did not like the way he was regaining confidence. "You, then, are the legendary mistress of fairy tales who rules the Eastern Kingdoms? You will be a welcome addition to my domain. Concocting fairy stories seems very much like a game. Have I told you that I am very fond of games?"

"You seem awfully sure of yourself for an interloper," the old woman complained, "but we'll soon take care of that. Look into my eyes."

"Ah. That sounds like a fine game." Death smiled and did as she wished.

Nothing happened. Mother Duck turned away in frustration.

"How can I bend you to my will when you don't have any eyes to stare into?"

"Death is beyond the petty concerns of mortals," the spectre replied casually. "But come now. I have dawdled enough with all of you. You must join with me, before there are any further distractions."

"See?" a voice came from the forest. "They are so having a party, and they didn't invite us!"

"Really, Touchy," another voice chided, "we should be above that sort of thing."

"Oh, wow," a third voice added as the Seven Other Dwarves strode into the clearing.

"I don't believe this," Death whispered, the sound of ice freezing forever.

"Oh, look," Smarmy said, reading from a piece of parchment. "It is our good friend, the handsome prince. But look again! He has fallen asleep."

Smarmy looked up at me and frowned. "Oh, my. Excuse me if I'm wrong, but aren't you supposed to be the handsome prince?"

"He's the handsome prince?" Nasty asked sarcastically. "Pardon me, but is there a new definition of the word *handsome?*"

Smarmy looked about at the bodies littering the clearing. "But it appears that everybody else has fallen asleep instead!"

"Oh, it just figures that *our* fairy tale would go wrong—" Touchy hesitated. "Why, Mother Duck!"

"Mother Duck?" Smarmy dropped the piece of paper to wring his hands. "Why, so it is. I'm sure Touchy didn't mean anything by his fairy tale remark, Mother Duck."

"Certainly not, Mother Duck," Touchy hastily added.

"Always a pleasure working for you, Mother Duck," Nasty chimed in.

"Oh, wow, Mother Duck," Spacey remarked.

"And may I humbly say what a great pleasure it is to see you, Mother Duck?" Smarmy continued. "As you can see, we were following your instructions to the letter."

"Yes, you were, my most excellent dwarves," the old woman replied with a smile that evaporated when she turned to look at me, "unlike certain others I can name!"

"This must end," Death intoned with a force that stopped all other conversation. He then turned to look at me as well. "You are almost beyond belief. I'm sure I could meet you in the most desolate place on earth, and it would immediately become as crowded as Vushta on market day! Well, the walls of chaos may rip asunder, and I will be so tired that no one will die for a week, but I will take you all."

He walked toward me, holding out both his hands. "I have long ago stopped doubting that you were the Eternal Apprentice. Now, I only wonder at what a grand addition you will be to my kingdom. But come, we have dawdled long enough—"

He paused. The clearing was filled with the beating of a drum.

> "Guxx Unfufadoo, curious demon,
> Wants to know what's going on here,
> Wants to speak to his friend Wuntvor,
> Wants to go on back to Vushta!"

"No!" Death screamed in frustration. "No, no, no! This gets worse with every passing second!" The spectre shuddered. "But I will *still* take all of you. The paperwork will be staggering, but while the declaimer is an imposing fellow, the one beating the drum is small enough. I think I can still fit both of them in. Come now! I will not wait another—"

There were twin explosions in our midst.

"Indeed," remarked the shoe that had just appeared.

"It's really time for Brownie Power!" His Brownieship added.

"It's the talking shoe again?" Death seemed overwhelmed. "What can you do with a talking shoe?"

"A lot of things!" Mother Duck replied, obviously intrigued. "For one thing there's this old lady I know who keeps having these kids and doesn't know what to do with them—"

"I was speaking rhetorically," Death informed her drily. "I know what I will do with this shoe, and the little person who has arrived as well. I will take them to my kingdom. I will take you all to my kingdom, though it shall tax my powers to the utmost." He looked to the heavens. "Come storm! Come wind and thunder and rain! Give me your energy, for I have many to kill!"

The howling was faint at first, as if it came from a great distance. But it grew quickly, doubling in intensity with every heartbeat, until it sounded like the anguish of a million souls. Black clouds rushed overhead, blotting out the moon and stars, making the dark night darker still. There was a rumbling in the distance.

Death laughed.

"I have you now!" he roared. "Although it will take all my resources, I will gain the strength to transport every one of you to my kingdom in an instant."

The clouds crashed together overhead. The distant rumbling was coming closer, gaining definition so that it sounded like someone beating the world's largest drum.

"Odd." Death paused, as if even he were startled by the noise. "But it does not matter. Perhaps it is some manifestation of my power that even I am not yet aware of." He returned his gaze to the sky.

"Come lightning!"

The clouds above crashed together with resounding force, sending out bright white flashes where they met. Death's laughter doubled.

The booming sound was coming closer, too.

There came a crash overhead so great that I fell to my knees and covered my ears. A bolt of lightning streaked from the clouds, straight for Death.

I could feel the booming sound. It shook the ground where I knelt.

Death's laughter became as loud as the thunder as he was bathed in the white fire. Then the lightning was gone, but Death glowed from within, his bonelike face so bright that you could not look at it for more than a second.

"Now," Death whispered in a voice far louder than a shout. "The time is—"

The booming sound intensified, now as loud as Death, shaking the whole clearing with every thundering beat.

The booming stopped.

Death looked up. A single word came from on high.

"Oops!"

And Death screamed.

NINETEEN

Any working magician will encounter situations which are potentially embarrassing, such as being trapped at a party with your spouse's relatives, or potentially deadly, such as finding yourself in front of a murderous crowd when a very important spell has backfired, or even both, such as being trapped with a crowd of your spouse's murderous relatives. It therefore behooves the mage to always have a couple of escape spells handy so that he might quickly exit these situations. But the truly professional wizard will go one better, devising another spell (and this is especially important with spouse's relatives) that proves he did not go into those situations at all.

—The Teachings of Ebenezum, VOLUME XXII

Death was gone. And dawn was breaking over the Eastern Kingdoms.

Mother Duck groaned. "That was quite a night. With you around, I doubt I shall ever get any sleep. But there are newcomers to my kingdom I must greet. Now what have I done with my apples?"

"Breakfast," Richard remarked, turning the basket over so that all the green, glowing apples fell upon his tongue. He swallowed them with a single gulp.

Mother Duck groaned again, flinging her hands up toward the heavens. "What else can happen to me now? Oh, Richard!" She sat down heavily upon a tree stump. "I would be more upset with you if I was not so exhausted."

"Oops!" Richard replied. "Have I done something wrong?" And then he burped.

But Mother Duck waved him to silence as she stood again and walked over to my master, still hidden within his shoe.

"Welcome to my kingdom, oh talking shoe," she greeted Ebenezum. "I will have to find a use for you."

"Indeed?" my master replied. "Well, I shall have to return once you have made up your mind."

And with that, both my master and His Brownieship disappeared.

"Richard!" Mother Duck screamed, suddenly furious.

"Yes, Mother Duck?" the giant said with a yawn.

"That talking shoe is trying to escape me!" she replied. "No one escapes Mother Duck!"

"Yes, Mother Duck," a chorus of voices added all around me.

"Track down that shoe, Richard," Mother Duck commanded, "and bring it to me!"

Richard yawned again. "Couldn't I take a nap first?"

"No sleeping on the job!" the old woman snapped. "Bring me that shoe *now!*"

"Yes, Mother Duck." Barely able to keep his eyes open, the giant staggered off into the woods.

"Now I will have to see what I can do with the rest of you." She looked at me first. "Since you seem destined never to eat one of my special apples, we will have to revise the plot slightly."

The wolf moaned in his sleep. The dragon shifted, his tail propelling the heavily robed Snarks a dozen paces. Alea sat up and rubbed her eyes.

Mother Duck nodded sagely. "The effects of my special sauce seem to be wearing off. We'd better get to work!"

"Happily ever after," I whispered. I had been able to avoid Mother Duck's control for hours now. Still, I wondered if I could survive a direct confrontation. I concentrated hard on anything I could think of besides those four words: Norei, my master, the crisis in Vushta, the threat of the Netherhells. Once—no, I didn't want to think of that word! My mind had to dwell on other, more intricate things: Snarks's worst insults, Guxx's most elaborate poetry, Damsel and Dragon's production numbers.

That seemed to work, at least for a moment.

Mother Duck frowned. "Wasn't there a unicorn around here a minute ago?" She covered her mouth as she yawned. So she was tired, too. It seemed to be affecting her concentration. I felt the pressure lift from my skull.

All the sleepers were stirring now. Alea had gotten to her feet, while the wolf sat up and stretched and Hubert tentatively flapped his wings. Snarks rolled around on the ground, somehow lost deep within his voluminous robes, while the Brownie seemed to have embarked on some sort of a morning exercise program, leaping from place to place with a great deal of shouting and arm waving.

I sat down on the hard-packed earth. I realized it had been a long time since I had slept. All this stretching and yawning was making me feel even more exhausted. My eyes were heavy, but I wouldn't let them close. I was still afraid of Mother Duck's powers, and what might happen if I let my concentration slip, even for an instant.

"Look!" Mother Duck called triumphantly. "The handsome prince is getting drowsy! Perhaps we can get this fairy tale moving after all!"

Handsome prince? What handsome prince? I tried blinking, but for some reason my eyes, while willing enough to close, did not wish to open again.

"We'll have to start right now!" the old woman exclaimed. "There's no time for me to cast any spells." She barely repressed another yawn. "Also, I do not know if I have the energy. I don't want things going wrong once more. You'll just all have to be on your best behavior."

I breathed deeply. There was something about this handsome prince thing that seemed familiar. Wait a minute. Didn't that have something to do with me?

"First, you see," Mother Duck instructed, "is the kiss to wake him."

Oh. I breathed more easily, and stopped struggling to open my eyes. Kiss to wake me? That didn't sound so bad.

"And then, of course," Mother Duck continued, "the prince will begin his terrible trials of violence to rescue his kingdom from the evil curse."

"Terrible trials of violence?" a voice squeaked nearby. Something whipped sharply against my side. "Hurry up! It's time to wake up! It's time to get out of here!"

"Ow!" I exclaimed, my eyes opening so suddenly that I had difficulty focusing on my surroundings. I managed to blink more normally. The bruise on my thigh had brought me back to wakefulness.

"Well, are we getting out of here or not?"

I looked in the direction of the voice and saw that I still held my sword in my limp fingers.

"Oh, drat!" Mother Duck yelled. "He's waking up. Well, we'd best start the fairy tale *now!* Let's see—um—Once upon a time there was a handsome young prince, who had been put to sleep by a poisoned apple given to him by an evil witch. Now this witch wanted to rule the prince's fair kingdom, and so brought forth three terrible trials upon the land. The people despaired—um—that is, all except—um—one fair damsel, who knew if she could wake the prince, all could still be saved." The old woman clapped her hands. "There. Not bad for off the top of my head. Always get the action going quickly—that's what I always say. So where's the beautiful damsel?"

Alea pointed to herself. "Do you mean me?"

Mother Duck tapped her foot impatiently. "No, I mean all the other beautiful damsels who are sitting around this clearing. Hurry up and kiss the prince!"

"Wuntie?" Alea asked tentatively.

"Do I have to cast a spell?" Mother Duck inquired darkly.

"Oh, no!" Alea replied, dimpling prettily. "I like kissing Wuntie!" She skipped happily in my direction.

"Wuntie!" she called, getting into her role. "I am coming to kiss you awake!"

"Pardon me," I apologized to my sword as I sheathed it. I often was not at my best around Alea, and I thought it prudent to avoid any accident. Still, I supposed I would have to let her kiss me, even though my heart still belonged to Norei, my own true love. After all, I reasoned, a kiss like this was a small thing, and there was no reason to needlessly anger Mother Duck before I could find some opportunity for me and my company to escape.

I therefore stood my ground and puckered, fully ready to take the consequences.

"Kiss him now!" Mother Duck commanded. "Remember, this is the beginning of the story, so make it a good one!"

Alea ran forward, flinging her arms wide.

I am not precisely sure what happened next. Perhaps it was that I was still not fully awake. Whatever the cause, I managed to misjudge Alea's approach. Somehow, my right arm got in the way of her face.

"Ooh!" the damsel exclaimed. "Watch the fingers, Wuntie!"

I pulled both arms back, trying to stammer an apology. It was then that I lost my balance.

"Kiss him!" Mother Duck demanded. "The story can't start unless you kiss him!"

But Alea's arms, seeking to hug me, instead embraced the empty air. I had fallen rather ungracefully to the ground, knocking the breath from my lungs.

"Exhaustion or no exhaustion, Mother Duck is becoming annoyed," the old woman announced. "Kiss him now, or I cast a spell."

I realized that, no matter what happened, our chances were far better as long as our lives were still under our own control. Therefore, winded though I was, I struggled quickly to my feet. Unfortunately, Alea seemed in as much of a hurry as myself and was rapidly bending down toward me, her lips puckered and at the ready.

Her jaw hit my forehead with a sharp crack. Both of us recoiled at the sudden pain. Just before the blow, however, I had felt Alea's lips brush across my forehead.

"Kiss him!" the old woman demanded. "Or you will feel the wrath of Mother Duck!"

"I did!" Alea protested, massaging her chin. I helpfully pointed to where her lips had brushed my scalp.

Mother Duck shook her head disapprovingly. "That's no way to start a fairy story. We want a real kiss. We want passion. You're an actress. Act!"

Alea stopped stroking her jaw and managed a smile that still contained a bit of a wince.

"Oh, Wuntie," she emoted. "I have waited for this moment for so long."

"That's better," Mother Duck encouraged.

"Oh, Alea," I replied, for I felt something was expected of me. "Um —How pleasant it is to see you."

"Not so good," the old woman murmured. "But we'll let it pass. It's time for the hug."

Alea grabbed me. Her face was very close to mine, her curly blond hair brushing against my nose. It was getting very hot around here again.

"That's fine," Mother Duck commented. "So kiss him, and kiss him good. Now, let's see some tongues!"

"What is going on here?" another woman's voice cut through the morning air.

My heart leapt, as if it wished to escape from my ribcage and run to my beloved. For I recognized that voice.

It was Norei.

I pushed away from Alea with such suddenness that both of us fell in opposite directions.

"Who is this?" Mother Duck asked, her surprise temporarily conquering her annoyance.

My beloved surveyed all those in the clearing, her arms folded before her. Her gaze paused on the fallen Alea. "There is only so much a maiden can stand."

"If you say so," the old woman replied. "May I ask who you are?"

"I am Norei," my beloved replied, "daughter of one of the most powerful witch families in the Western Woods."

"A witch family? This gets more and more interesting with every passing minute," Mother Duck remarked. "Perhaps I will dispense with my control spells altogether. Who knows who, or what, will show up next?"

"Indeed!" I called, jumping up from the ground and drawing my sword in one more or less fluid movement. Ignoring Cuthbert's startled cry, I rushed quickly to my beloved's side. I had been a prisoner in Mother Duck's kingdom long enough to know the true duplicitousness of her nature. I would protect Norei from the old woman's spells any way I could, though it might cost me my very life.

"Wuntvor?" Norei stared at me in delightful surprise, startled I am sure with the speed with which I reached her side. Her green eyes were opened wide, her beautiful lips slightly parted. I could not help myself.

I kissed her.

"At last!" Mother Duck exclaimed. "Let the fairy tale begin!"

TWENTY

When you are with your beloved, nothing can go wrong. Well, actually, some things can go wrong, I'm afraid I know that from experience —really, I guess, now that I think of it, all sorts of things can go wrong —Norei! Where are you going?

—*Some Thoughts on Apprenticeship*, by Wuntvor,
apprentice to Ebenezum,
greatest wizard in the Western Kingdoms
(a discarded early draft)

Norei and I clutched each other as the world around us was suddenly filled with smoke. Somewhere, far away, I heard Mother Duck's laughter.

"Oh, Wuntvor," my beloved whispered in my ear. "I know I shouldn't have shown myself. At least not yet. It's simply that you have been put through such indignities by that Mother Duck person. It was almost impossible to stand by when your life was repeatedly in danger. And then, when that Alea—" She paused, unable to continue.

"Do not worry, Norei," I replied with a conviction that I did not truly feel. "Now that we are together, we have to win."

"Well, I hope so," she replied, not wholly convinced herself. "Heaven knows why I get into these things with you, Wuntvor. You can be the most exasperating man in the world."

I looked as deeply into Norei's eyes as the dissipating smoke would allow. I knew, when she talked to me that way, that she truly loved me. Sometime, when we were not in the middle of an ongoing crisis, I would have to prove to her how much that love meant to me.

"Doom." The word echoed all around as a large shape loomed before us in the clearing. A summer breeze sprang up, whisking the remaining smoke away in an instant.

Norei whistled. "This Mother Duck likes her special effects, doesn't she?"

"Doom." The large warrior Hendrek appeared before us, the cursed warclub Headbasher at his side. "I am the first trial."

"Hendrek?" I asked my large friend. "What trial?"

But the large warrior continued to advance on us, his only reply another muttered "Doom." I tried to catch his eye, but his face was without expression. I understood at once. Apparently, Mother Duck was still exerting her control on some of us.

I lifted my sword before me. "Hendrek, think what you are doing. Don't force me to use this."

"Just what are you suggesting?" Cuthbert demanded. "Oh, no matter how many times you have reassured me, I knew this would happen! There's going to be blood!"

"Your sword is no match for this." Hendrek smiled unnaturally, lifting his club.

"He's right, you know," Cuthbert interjected hurriedly. "Other methods are called for. Methods that don't involve swords."

"Come," the warrior beckoned, "and let me add you to my list of victims."

"Oh, no you don't!" my beloved interjected. "If you attack Wuntvor, you must attack me as well!"

What was Norei saying? I thrust my sword even farther forward, ignoring the blade's whining pleas. I had to protect my beloved!

"Doom," the warrior replied with a frown. "If that's the way you want it." Taking a final step in our direction, he lifted Headbasher high over his head.

Norei spoke a quick string of arcane syllables, snapping her fingers twice.

The warclub reversed direction and hit Hendrek's helmet with a resounding clang.

"Do—urk!" the warrior remarked as he crumpled to the ground.

"Simple violence-reversal spell," the young witch explained.

"I don't know if it should be going this way," an older woman's voice complained somewhere out in the forest.

"Now you know how I felt!" a gruff and wolfish voice replied.

"Mother Duck will not be defeated. It is time for the next trial! And —," she added, raising her voice, "if anyone uses magic to save the handsome prince, it will be their last act!"

"Norei!" I cried, frightened for my beloved.

But the young witch only smiled at my concern. "Do not worry, Wuntvor. As you said, we are together. We will think of something."

Once again, from out of nowhere, smoke surrounded us. It cleared even more quickly this time, to show us two demons, one of whom was already beating a drum.

The other demon seemed to hesitate. After a moment he started, as if he had been asleep on his feet, and cleared his throat, a truly horrendous sound. He spoke:

> "Guxx—uh—Unfufadoo—er—hypnotized demon,
> Um—Sees a prince who's ripe for beating,
> Sees a prince who's—uh—ready to topple,
> Sees someone who—um—will make an okay meal!"

Norei frowned. "Guxx!" she demanded. "The rhythm on that is terrible! Do you expect us to quake in fear with verse like that?"

"Um," Guxx replied, for he, too, seemed to be suffering from one of Mother Duck's spells. "I suppose not. Um—" He frowned, his oversized fangs making small marks in his lower lip and chin. "What do you suggest?"

"More active verbs," Norei suggested. "I mean, what do you do with your meals?"

"Oh, I see." The demon's hideous green tongue stuck out of the corner of his mouth as he was temporarily lost in thought. He mumbled: "Guxx Unfufadoo, dada demon,/Sees a prince dadada beating,/Sees dadada dada topple—"

Guxx paused and smiled. "Yes, that's much better." He raised his voice and enunciated every word: "Sees a prince who's good for eat—"

Guxx Unfufadoo began to sneeze.

"A natural rhyming talent!" the drum-beating Brax proclaimed as the larger demon fell to the ground, the sneezing fit getting the better of him.

"There we go," Norei announced. "You've conquered your second trial. And without a bit of magic!"

"This is all wrong!" Mother Duck wailed from her hiding place. "Where have I failed?"

"You didn't put any talking wolves—," Jeffrey began.

"I know what it is," the old woman interrupted summarily. "I've been warned about it. It's Fairy Tale Fatigue. We storytellers always have to be aware of the syndrome." She heaved an exhausted sigh. "I had always thought myself beyond it—until now—until I met—these people."

"Think how much easier it would have been though," Jeffrey interjected, "if you had had the buffer of a talk—"

"One more word out of you—," Mother Duck screamed, "—and you're pumpernickel!" She called out to the rest of us: "I remind you, this is the handsome prince's story. Anyone who interferes with the third trial in any way will have to answer to me!"

And with that, we were once again surrounded by smoke.

"Norei!" I called to my beloved. "Behind me. I must face this trial alone."

"Wuntvor—," she began, but the protest died in her throat. She knew I was right. Our chances of escape, even victory, were far greater so long as we did not incur the wrath of Mother Duck.

I heard a great rumbling through the impenetrable fog before me. I knew, even before the smoke cleared, that it was the dragon.

"I have a question," Cuthbert's voice quailed from where I still held it before me. "If you're going to face this menace alone, isn't it time you sheathed your sword?"

"Perhaps you are right," I replied, for I had thought of a plan.

"I'm right? I'm actually right? There's not going to be bloo—" The sword's cries of jubilation were lost once he was back in the scabbard.

I looked up to see that the smoke had cleared. There, before me, the size of a castle or a medium large hill, was the fire-breathing reptile—the dragon that I was sure was under Mother Duck's spell.

Thick smoke curled from the dragon's nostrils as the lizard's tongue darted forward, searching, I was sure, for my oh-so-edible scent. The dragon breathed in, preparing to fry me where I stood.

It was now or never.

"Hey!" I cried aloft. "It's showtime!"

The dragon paused. I had to think fast.

I started to sing:

"What do you say to a dragon,
When he's stomping you into the ground?
I know my answer for certain,
Dragon, I'll see you around!"

Hubert exhaled, but it was smoke, not fire. He shook his head, as if trying to throw off the rigors of Mother Duck's magic. I decided to try another verse.

"What do you say to that reptile,
When confronted by old dragon fire?
You tell the lizard you're sorry,
But you just have to retire!"

Hubert's tail started to swing in time to my singing. I had him now! I quickly continued.

"What do you say to a dragon,
When he waits for battle so hard?
Well, it seems that you just have to travel,
But maybe you'll send him a card!"

Hubert's whole body was swaying by now. It was time to finish it. "Take it, dragon!" I screamed.

And Hubert began to dance, bounding happily back and forth across the clearing as I sang the verses once again. As I had hoped, theater was too strong in his blood. With luck, I had found something Mother Duck could never conquer.

"No, no, no—," the old woman began, bounding out from her hiding place behind the trees. She stopped to consider. "Well, I suppose it will have to do, at least for this run-through. Now, though, we have to find a suitable conclusion."

"Oops!" came a voice from high overhead.

"Richard!" Mother Duck looked up, infuriated. "Your timing is terrible. Can't you see we're busy?"

But the giant would not be deterred. "See what I've found!" Richard had the shoe.

"Really?" the old woman's anger vanished. "What a good giant. Quickly, Richard, tell me what's inside."

"Oops," the giant replied as he stuck his index finger in the shoe. He shifted the footwear around to peer inside.

"Uh," he answered at last, "leather, mostly."

"I know about the leather!" Mother Duck replied, exasperation once again entering her voice. "But there's something else in there, too. What is it?"

"Oh." Richard turned the shoe upside down and shook it. He looked inside one more time, then frowned miserably down at Mother Duck.

"Nothing," was his answer.

Nothing? What had happened to my master?

"Nothing?" the old woman demanded. "That isn't possible!"

And then the earth began to quake.

"It cannot be!" Mother Duck raged.

But it was. I recognized all the signs: the violent tremors, the great clouds of dust, the sudden appearance of crevices in the earth.

And then the shaking stopped, and the dust cleared. There was the table with the five demons.

"Vushta!" the gavel demon cried in triumph. "We have you at last!"

But the demons' cheers died when they saw the old woman.

"Uh-oh," the gavel demon remarked.

"That's it," Mother Duck replied, all too casually. "You will never see the Netherhells again."

The demons all started talking at once.

"But Mother Duck, there was wizard magic—"

"Lots of it, Mother Duck—"

"And witch magic, too, Mother Duck—"

"Richard?" the old woman called to the giant. "I need your assistance."

"Oops!" The giant dropped the shoe and lumbered toward the committee.

"I see your master's plan!" Norei clapped me on the shoulder. "Oh, how brilliant!" She grabbed my hand and pulled me toward the fallen shoe. "Quickly, Wuntvor, we must get inside!"

I knew there was no time for questions. I did as my beloved bade.

At the far end of the clearing, Mother Duck and Richard faced the committee.

"Please, Mother Duck—," the demons pleaded.

"There's no other magic going on *anywhere,* Mother Duck—"

"We'll make a deal with you, Mother Duck! You show us where Vushta is, and we'll split it with you, fifty-fifty." The demon tried to smile ingratiatingly. Richard lumbered another step. "Uh, sixty-forty?"

But the old woman was unmoved by their pleas. "I do not want Vushta. I want my kingdom demon-free!"

We reached the shoe. Norei turned to the others in the clearing.

"All of you," she called, "flee now, while Mother Duck is occupied. It is part of the wizard's plan!"

All those in the clearing fled. Norei scaled quickly up the shoe, using the eyelets for handholds and footholds. I followed as soon as she had dropped inside. I took a final look at the combatants before I, too, entered the footwear.

"Don't force us to get rough, Mother Duck—," one of the demons wailed.

"You'd better watch out, Mother Duck—," another added.

"We can boil blood, Mother Duck—," the demon in the flowered hat insisted.

The old woman sneered at their threats. "I don't think there's going to be any boiling around here. I think it's time to bake, instead. Richard?"

Norei pulled at my pants leg. I dropped down inside the shoe. The interior, while large enough to fit my master, seemed a little snug for two. I felt myself being pressed close to Norei.

"Quickly, Wuntvor!" my beloved insisted, gently pushing me away. "The words!"

Oh, that was right. The words! Now what were they? It was hard to breathe in these close confines. I managed to inhale anyway, and spoke:

"Happily ever after."

Nothing happened.

I saw Norei frowning in the dim light, her lips beautiful even in concentration.

"Why didn't they work?" she wondered. "They must have been muffled by the shoe leather. Poke your head out and try again. And say them slowly and distinctly."

I did as my beloved bade, climbing up so that my mouth was just above the top of the shoe. I was more exposed this way, though. I knew I would have to speak quickly, before Mother Duck could act.

"Happily—," I began.

"What's that?" Mother Duck asked, turning her head.

". . . ever—," I continued.

"Oh, no!" the old woman screamed. "The fairy tale! I didn't stop—"

". . . after!" I concluded. There was another puff of smoke. I was thrown back inside the shoe. Norei grabbed my hand as the giant footwear lurched off the ground.

We seemed to be flying.

TWENTY-ONE

"At least that's over."

—Final remarks made by Ebenezum, greatest mage in the Western Kingdoms, upon at last discovering an exit from the secret passageways that actually led outside the castle of King Snerdlot the Vengeful. Rumor has it that, despite the rigors of the night, the wizard managed to stagger clear of the castle and its surroundings, tactfully ignoring the dozens of love notes thrown by Queen Vivazia and her handmaidens until he had reached the safety of the forest.

When we came out of the shoe, there was a rainbow overhead.

His Brownieship beamed up at us. "Is that Brownie Power or what?"

Norei had explained my master's plan as we had flown. At the first likely diversion during Mother Duck's tale, he and His Brownieship would find a means to transport me beyond the ruler of the Eastern Kingdom's power. The shoe was an ideal vehicle for that transportation, and when Ebenezum stayed around within it long enough to engage Mother Duck's curiosity, he guaranteed that it would be brought, without even having to use magic, back to Wuntvor by Mother Duck's minions. Then, once I was inside, all I had to do was shout three words to end the fairy tale, and His Brownieship did the rest.

I smiled down at the small fellow in the leather crown.

"Indeed," I replied, trying to place our exact location. We were still

in the Eastern Woods, but in one of the clearings we had visited earlier, where we had first destroyed one of the dwarves' warning signs. I
could still hear the sounds of distant battle, and I discovered that, if I
craned my neck, I could see the top of the giant's head.

"We should move quickly," I announced. "We need to get out of
here before the battle ends."

"Oh, it'll take them awhile," Smarmy announced as he and the
other dwarves entered the clearing.

"It always does!" Snooty added.

"Indeed?" I replied. "This has happened before?"

"Regularly!" the dwarves answered in unison.

"This could take weeks!" Nasty shouted.

"And what do we get to do?" Touchy chimed in. "Sit on our
hands!"

"Wuntvor?" my beloved interjected. "I still think it might be better
if we returned to Vushta and the Western Kingdoms with all due
speed. Even though Mother Duck appears to be fighting our battle, we
still have a war."

Norei was right, and I told her so. We would leave as soon as all our
party had gathered together.

The dwarves and His Brownieship were already here. The beating
of a drum heralded the arrival of Guxx and Brax, and Snarks arrived
shortly thereafter, complaining about the conditions of his robes.
There was a flapping of wings overhead, and Hubert landed in the
middle of the clearing, Alea astride his back. The unicorn galloped
into our midst and proceeded to gaze moodily in my direction. Hendrek was next, using his great warclub to smash through the underbrush. I saw, as he approached, that he carried Tap upon his shoulder.
And, fast upon his heels, I heard a joyous eeping as my ferret bounded
forth to greet me.

We were almost all here, then. All save my master. But where was
Ebenezum? Where might he have hidden when he gave up the shoe?

There was a rustling in the bushes behind me.

"Master?" I called.

But it was not Ebenezum, but instead Jeffrey who skulked into our
midst.

"Anybody know of any openings for talking wolves?" he asked
hopefully.

I had no time to answer his query. I looked down at His Brownieship.

"But where is my master?"

A wind as cold as winter sprung up before His Smallness could answer. I spun about as I heard that familiar dry chuckle. But why would he be here now, when all my companions were about me?

I looked into the face of Death.

"Greetings," the spectre whispered, the sound of snow falling over frozen tundra. "I usually don't speak before such a large audience. At least not an audience of the living."

Norei grabbed my arm. "What are you doing here?" she demanded. "There are too many of us. You cannot take Wuntvor now!"

"I do not need Wuntvor—now." Death grinned. "I have another new addition to my kingdom." He paused, and stared straight at me. "A wizardly addition."

"My master?" I blurted.

Death nodded. "The wizard Ebenezum. I found him, all alone in the forest. But he has joined me now."

"No!" I screamed. "You cannot take him!"

The spectre shrugged. "True, it is not yet his time. But Death takes who he wants, when he wants."

I could stand no more of this. With a scream of rage I drew my sword and ran for the spectre.

Death did not move, except to extend his hands toward me. He laughed at my approach, the sound of thunder above a forest fire.

I stopped, realizing that even now I dared not risk the spectre's touch. Killing myself would not save my master.

"You hesitate?" Death asked. "Then perhaps we can negotiate. The wizard might yet again walk the earth. I would release his soul on certain conditions."

The spectre pointed a single bone-white finger at me.

"I would consider a trade."

"Wuntvor! No!" Norei cried.

"Oh, I don't want to be hasty about this thing," Death quickly added. "I will let the Eternal Apprentice consider his options. Remember, Death has all the time in the world. When you are ready, Wuntvor, all you have to do is say my name."

The spectre vanished, his laughter hanging in the air for a moment before it, too, faded away.

I turned back to the others. Death had my master. What should I do?

My companions were talking all around me. Norei looked at me, her face full of concern. She might have asked me a question. I did not know.

All I could hear was Death's laughter, ringing in my ears.

A
DISAGREEMENT
WITH DEATH

ACKNOWLEDGMENTS

Uh-oh. Here we are at the end of another trilogy. This time, I'd like to thank those people and things that made me The Way I am Today, specifically: Jay Ward and Bill Scott's *Rocky and Bullwinkle,* Walt Kelly's *Pogo,* Carl Bark's *Uncle Scrooge* and anything made by Chuck Jones; the writings of Robert Sheckley, Jack Sharkey and L. Sprague de Camp (often with Fletcher Pratt); Preston Sturges's movies; Stan Freberg commercials (who put those eight great tomatoes in that itty-bitty can?); Danny Kaye in Frank and Panama's *The Court Jester* (a partial prototype of Wuntvor—the vessel with the pestle holds the brew that is true); and almost anything made by those Monty Python people. In addition, much of these books was written while listening to the recordings of Louis Jordon ("Beware, Brother, Beware") and Kid Creole and the Coconuts ("Annie, I'm Not Your Daddy"). You have been warned.

The usual round of thanks must also go to my stalwart and long-suffering friends, including Jeff, Richard, Victoria and Mary (a.k.a. Team Cambridge), who critiqued this whole thing as it went along, and the lovely Elisabeth, who puts up with me wandering around the apartment chuckling at my own jokes. And then there's those New York people, like my Superagent, Merrilee Heifetz, and the entire friendly and helpful staff at Writers' House; and also my Supereditor, Ginjer Buchanan, who almost always changes stuff back when I yell and scream, and everybody else at Berkley/Ace (Hi, Susan! Hi, Beth!).

Lastly, I would like to dedicate this, the last of the Ebenezum books, to the memory of my grandfather

Walter W. Shaw

who introduced me to the world of art

and a world of wonders

ONE

There is one fact that every magician must accept: Sorcery is not a stable science. Quite the contrary, magic is ever-changing, and the nimble mage must learn to change with it. Magic is never done. It goes on forever and ever, constantly new, impossible to categorize or summarize. The magician must never consider a spell complete and successful until he or she sees the results. He must realize as well that every spell has a counterspell, and, in a world where magic rules, all things are possible. Using magic becomes a lifetime's work, as the mage discovers that all the spells and conjurations grow together into a force beyond the magician's simple goals, and further join with all the other spells, of all the other wizards, past, present and future, becoming an ever-changing tapestry beyond mortal ken, a force that no wizard can ever completely understand. Or completely take for granted.

That's magic in a nutshell. And that's my final word on the matter. I think.

—From *Spells That Hate Wizards,
and the Wizards Who Love Them*, third edition,
by Ebenezum, greatest wizard in the Western Kingdoms

"Wuntvor?"

I looked up. I realized that someone was calling my name, and perhaps had been doing so for quite some time.

"Wuntvor?" the young woman's voice repeated. It was the voice of my beloved, the witch Norei. "Do you want to talk?"

I shrugged. I did not care. After what had happened, I didn't care about much of anything. My master, Ebenezum, the greatest mage in the Western Kingdoms, was gone. He had been taken by Death. Worse still, Death had taken the wizard because the specter could not take me, whom it wanted because of some nonsense about my being the

Eternal Apprentice, always instantaneously reborn into another apprenticing form, forever bumbling, forever helping heroes throughout eternity, and therefore forever beyond Death's grasp. And for this very reason—my supposed unobtainability by the creature to whom all came in time—Death desired me. The specter coveted my soul, and would go to any lengths to obtain it.

Norei squatted by my side, so that her face was even with mine. She gripped my chin with her cool, delicate fingers.

"Are you going to sit there for the rest of your life?"

When I did not reply immediately, she pulled her hand away. I blinked, glancing down at the dirt and grass between my knees, then looked up again at Norei's concerned expression. I sighed. I shrugged. Death had taken my master. What did it matter?

Norei whistled softly. "Alea was right."

"Alea?" I murmured. Had Alea been here?

Norei nodded, more to herself than to me. "When she told me that she had embraced you, and nestled her cheek tenderly next to your own, and promised you she would do anything, anything at all, to break you from this mood, and that, to all of this, you showed not the slightest reaction, I doubted her. Until now."

Alea had done what? I did not remember an embrace, and Alea was the sort of person, what with her long blond hair and trim actress's figure, with whom an embrace would be memorable. And there had been cheek nestling as well? And she had promised to do anything?

Anything? Well, not that I would have done *anything*, because, after all, I was promised to my beloved Norei. But still. Anything?

And I didn't remember any of it?

Norei frowned at me. "There must be some way we can get you out of this state."

I frowned back at her. I hoped that there was. Obviously, from what Norei had told me, the depression I was in was more serious than I had thought. I furrowed my brow, but the memory of Alea was lost to me.

Anything?

Norei reached out her arms to me and clasped me firmly.

"I think this calls for drastic action," she whispered, a grim half-smile upon her lips. She leaned in my direction.

What was she doing? My master was gone! I didn't have any time for such foolishness. Her full lips were much too close. I wanted to turn my head away.

For some reason, I did not.

I closed my eyes, and we kissed.

The kiss lasted for quite some time. I felt a tingling warmth in my chest, which spread outward as the kiss continued, until it heated me from the top of my head to the ends of my toes. And the true center of the warmth emanated from Norei's soft lips, the sweetest lips anyone had ever kissed.

The kiss ended at last. I gasped for breath. I opened my eyes.

Perhaps, I reconsidered, there was hope, after all.

"Now," my beloved said again. "Would you like to talk about it?"

I nodded, not yet able to speak.

"Ebenezum is gone," Norei summarized. "Death has taken him. But Death really wants you."

I nodded again. I marveled at my beloved. How could she be so clearheaded after such a kiss?

"And Death would be glad to trade your soul for Ebenezum's?"

I sighed. "I'm afraid so. That is, if we can trust Death. The specter is too fond of its games and tricks. I fear that, instead of releasing Ebenezum from its kingdom in exchange for me, Death may try to take us both."

"Humans!" an excruciatingly annoying voice exclaimed behind us. "Don't you know anything?"

I whirled to see the truth-telling demon Snarks, attired as usual in his monkish robes of somber gray; robes that, despite their neutral hue, still seemed to clash with the demon's bright green complexion.

I glared at the smirking Snarks.

"How long have you been here?" I demanded.

"Oh, long enough. Your kissing's not bad." The demon nodded pleasantly at Norei before turning back to me. "After we're alone, of course, I'll be glad to give you one or two pointers to improve your technique."

"Snarks!" I began, pointing back toward the clearing where the rest of our party rested. "If you don't—"

But my beloved put a restraining hand upon my elbow, stopping my tirade before it could properly begin. "No, no, let the demon be. I believe he has a point."

Snarks nodded his agreement. "Actually I have a number of them, but they're covered by my robes."

I was horrified. Norei and Snarks agreed about me? I could barely bring myself to look at my beloved as I asked: "You mean he's right about me having to improve my technique?"

Norei laughed softly. "No, no, your technique needs no improving whatsoever. Not to say that we both couldn't benefit from additional practice, whenever and wherever we can find the time." She kissed me gently on the cheek. "But I think he is correct when he implied that there might be more than one way to fight Death."

I didn't remember Snarks saying that. Still, after a prolonged bout of kissing, I had a tendency not to remember much of anything. What would my master have done in a case like this? After a moment's consideration, I nodded sagely and waited for one of the others to continue.

Snarks waved a sickly green finger at Norei. "The young witch is very perceptive, especially for a human. When I came upon this cozy little scene, you were bemoaning the fact that Death seemed to control the situation. Typical limited human thinking." The demon paused to shrug his heavily robed shoulders. "But then, you were not blessed with an upbringing spent in the devious byways of the Netherhells. One's thoughts flow much more freely when they're covered with a bit of slime."

I listened intently to the small demon, for, although Snarks somehow always managed to phrase things in the most irritating manner imaginable, still much of what he had told us in the past had been of great use. The small demon had developed an odd clarity of vision, based in large part on his overwhelming compulsion to tell the truth in all things—a reaction, apparently, to an experience Snarks had while still in the womb, when his mother was badly frightened by a group of demonic politicians.

"So here we are," the demon continued, "in the middle of a brand-new game, and Death appears to be holding all the cards." Snarks smiled. "But I think that the game we're going to play won't use any cards at all. Who says we have to play by Death's rules? You have a crowd of allies only a few feet away, some of whom have very interesting powers. I think that, with a little thought, we will come up with a game that will actually put Death at a disadvantage." The demon clapped his hands enthusiastically. "We can win this!"

"That's right!" a tiny, high voice said from the vicinity of my ankles. "You can't help but win with Brownie Power!"

Snarks paused mid-clap to make a face even more unpleasant than usual, as if something he had eaten recently was interfering with his digestion. He had also managed to turn an even deeper shade of green.

"Then again," he added a moment later, his stomach apparently once more under control, "perhaps there are some of your allies who might be better excluded from further assistance."

"Nonsense! Brownies need no rest. We thrive on conflict!" Tap the Brownie performed an impromptu tap dance as he spoke. "Especially if that conflict has something to do with shoes!"

"I've got you there!" Snarks replied triumphantly. "I don't think Death has anything at all to do with footwear!"

"Nonsense! A being of Death's stature, not wearing—" Tap paused, doubt spreading across his tiny face. "Oh, my. The specter's robes are rather long, aren't they?"

Snarks nodded triumphantly. "There's no way to tell if Death wears shoes. There's no way to tell if Death even has feet."

Oddly, the dismay seemed to vanish from the Brownie's countenance, replaced by a faraway look in his eyes. "Then Death may have spent millennia wandering the cosmos shoeless?" Tap spoke in a voice barely above a whisper. "Then—could it be—the first pair of shoes Death wears might be made by me?"

"Indeed," I interjected, for the conversation seemed to have wandered a good distance from our original topic. "Perhaps, before we consider Death's footwear, we should give a little more thought to the predicament of my master—"

"Exactly what I was going to do." Snarks interrupted, "before this shoe fanatic butted in."

"Shoe fanatic!" Tap blurted. "Well, if caring passionately about one's footwear makes one a fanatic—if it makes a difference to you about the proper heel size, and the quality of the leather, and the aesthetic roundness of the toe, and the elasticity of the laces, and the color of the leather, using of course only true browns from nature, and the correct eyelet placement, taking into account the proper mathematical proportions, and the absolute best angle for stitching the seams, and—well, ten or twelve other factors equally important, then I guess you could call me—"

I tugged on Snarks's sleeve, drawing him a bit farther away from the declaiming Brownie.

"My master," I repeated.

Norei walked up behind us. "We must find out what Death has done with him. If the creature will tell us."

I smiled back at my beloved. Discussing my predicament with her and Snarks seemed to be restoring both my confidence and powers of thought.

"Why not?" I replied. "Death feels above us. I am sure we can get it to boast of my master's capture with no bother at all."

A green, scaly hand patted me briskly on the back. "Thinking worthy of the Netherhells!" Snarks exclaimed. "If you keep up this clever planning for—say—another three or four weeks, I may have to revise my opinion of humankind."

"But to make Death's shoes!" Tap shouted behind us. "I'd go down in the Brownie Hall of Fame! I can see the plaque now, made of that fine silver we use for our very best buckles: 'First footwear for lord of the dead, with heels designed to walk upon a billion souls. Designed by the humble—ME!' " Tap applauded his conjecture. "His Brownie-ship would have to forgive me then!"

Snarks looked back at the Brownie with some distaste. "Perhaps we should move even farther aside," he remarked, "say, to an entirely different clearing?"

I chided Snarks for his remark. After all, our tiny Brownie ally had been through a lot lately, what with his somewhat impetuous actions coming under criticism by his Brownie superiors, simply because he forgot he was supposed to wait for one of those superiors, and rushed to my aid instead. Now the head Brownie of them all, His Brownie-ship, was making noises about disbarring Tap from all future Brownie activity, which meant no more making shoes. In a situation like this, Tap was bound to be distraught. He deserved a little understanding.

Snarks nodded grimly when I was done. "Oh, I understand him all too well. But do I have to listen to him, too?"

The Brownie walked petulantly toward us. "You may scoff, but my whole future is at stake. I can't wait to meet Death and discuss footwear!"

In that instant, the sun disappeared behind a cloud. A wind sprang up from nowhere to remind us that summer was almost gone. And then the wind, too, was gone, replaced by a chuckle drier than a stone in a desert after a thirty-year drought.

"Somebody called?" the newcomer's voice rasped.

Tap began to tremble as he looked up at the newcomer's rotting robes. "On second thought, I might want a little more time to prepare for my discussion—" He paused as he backed hastily away. "Say, forty or fifty years?"

Death nodded at the Brownie. "Ah, yes. But we will talk, my little friend. Sooner or later."

The specter turned to me, the skull-like face beneath its hood showing all its teeth in a perpetual smile. "Ah, but there is no reason to be upset. This is naught but a courtesy call. As I recall, we have business to discuss. Something to do with an exchange of souls?"

I glanced at both Norei and Snarks, then stepped forward. I would have to handle this somehow. "Indeed." I tried to smile, but my lips would not refrain from trembling. "Do you have a proposal?"

Was it my imagination, or did Death's grin become even wider? "Oh, I have any number of them. But I don't think it's proper that proposals should come from me." Death's voice quickened, rising with every word. "After all, I am dealing with the Eternal Apprentice, the one being in the entire cosmos forever beyond my grasp!"

It stopped itself for a minute to smooth its dark, rotting robes. "At least, that is, until now," it added in a much more reasonable tone. "I therefore think it only proper that the initial proposal come not from me, but from the Eternal Apprentice."

"Indeed?" I replied. Death was taunting me, flaunting its advantage. Looking at the specter's smile, I felt the fear drain away, to be replaced by a building anger. If Death was going to play with me, I would play right back.

"You want a proposal, then?" I asked, managing a firm smile at last. "You give Ebenezum back to us and we would forget all about it."

Death made a strangled sound, deep in whatever it had that passed for a throat. "You dare—" it whispered. "When I could reach over and snuff out—" The specter paused again and stood up straight, regaining its skeletal composure. It laughed. "But I misunderstand. You wish to bargain. I apologize for my outburst, but I fear I am a bit too emotionally involved in these proceedings. I will go along with your game, of course. I am the master of games."

Death's knuckles clacked together noisily as it stroked its chin. "You have made an offer. It is, of course, unacceptable. However, I generously agree to make a counteroffer; say, let's forget all about the foolish wizard, and allow me rather to end this nonsense once and for all by taking you and your companions here to the Kingdom of Death for the rest of eternity."

Snarks sidled over to me. "I don't think this is working."

"Come, now," Death insisted. "I am waiting for your counteroffer."

"Indeed?" I answered, stalling for time. What could I bargain with next? I knew there was only one offer that would satisfy Death, and that was the possession of the Eternal Apprentice's soul. *My* soul.

Tap jumped across the clearing, landing on my shoe. "You'd better speak up. I don't think this guy is long on patience!"

"For once, we are in agreement," Snarks said, then added, "Why don't you offer the creature one of your companions in exchange for the wizard? Somebody with a useful skill, like making shoes."

"Then again," the Brownie reconsidered, "perhaps it is time to give this matter more thought. Perhaps fifty or sixty years more thought?"

"I await your answer," Death intoned. "Quickly, now! I have souls to collect!"

"Doom!" answered a deep voice behind me.

"Oh, here we go again," Death remarked fatalistically. "The longer we talk, the greater the number of companions to the Eternal Apprentice that will arrive. How many are there now? A dozen? Two dozen? May I suggest that we conclude our business before there are hundreds?"

"Indeed," I replied. "You will excuse me for a moment, but I need to consult with my fellows."

"Doom," the warrior Hendrek agreed as he walked forward to stand by my side.

"Of course," Death said with a sigh. "How could I expect anything else?"

Norei walked to stand by my other side. I motioned my companions to huddle together.

"What am I to do? Death demands a bargain. But what can we afford to bargain with?"

"We could offer the creature a sharp blow to the head," Hendrek suggested, hefting his cursed warclub, which no man could own but could only rent. It was the weapon called Headbasher, that stole the memories from men.

"A sharp blow to the head?" Norei frowned. "No, I don't think that was the sort of thing Wuntvor had in mind."

Hendrek nodded thoughtfully. "How about two sharp blows to the head?"

"You try my patience!" Death shrieked behind me. "You know what I desire. Make me an offer!"

"How about a little song and dance?" another voice boomed theatrically.

The earth shook as Damsel and Dragon bounded into the clearing.

As serious as our situation was, I couldn't help glancing at Alea with her long blond hair and scanty vaudevillian attire.

Anything?

But I had no time for errant thoughts. Death was waving its bony arms in the air. It was becoming more agitated with every passing minute.

"We've come up with a special song for this occasion," Alea said brightly, tossing her long blond hair so that it shone even beneath the clouds.

Anything?

"Hit it, Hubert!" Alea called out.

"I will not allow this!" Death screamed. "I am here for negotiation, not vaudeville!"

But Damsel and Dragon had already started to shuffle back and forth. I knew a song could not be far behind.

Unfortunately, I was correct:

"There's something in the air that's pretty scary,
The sun is gone, the wind's contrary!
It's quite exciting, we must confeth;
It must be time for a date with Death!"

"Say, Damsel," Hubert remarked. "Have you been introduced to Death?"

"Not officially," Alea replied jovially, "but I am dying to meet him!"

They launched into another verse:

"I must admit I'm feeling old,
My youth is gone, the world is cold,
All around me is such a meth,
It must be time for a date with Death!"

"Say, Dragon," Alea interjected. "I've heard that Death is rather a cold character."

Hubert slapped a scaly knee before replying: "Well, Damsel, you've heard Dead Wrong!"

"No more!" Death pleaded. "Please, no more!" The specter turned to me. "Make me an offer, please!"

"Death wants an offer?" Hubert chortled triumphantly. "See, Damsel, I knew we could win him over! We simply have to face it. No one can resist our flashing feet and snappy patter!"

"No, no!" Death insisted. "I was speaking to the Eternal Apprentice!"

"Oh, trying to be hard-nosed about this, so we won't charge an arm and a leg?" Hubert laughed again. "You forget, Mr. Death, that we've had to face negotiators much worse than you. After all, we work in the arts!"

"But I guess he's seen right through us, Hubie," Alea added. "Let's face it, we need new worlds to conquer. We've already mastered the world above with our song and dance. And now we've almost finished this gig as official entertainment for Wuntvor's quest. Hubie and I have decided it's time to look for limited engagements elsewhere."

"Nothing fancy, mind you," Hubert continued. "One-night stands, mostly; perhaps a longer engagement in your population centers. If you have population centers." The dragon sighed happily. "Just think, the first song-and-dance act ever to tour the Kingdom of the Dead."

Death stared at me even more intently. "A bargain! Quickly!"

"I have an idea!" Snarks interjected. "You return the wizard to us, and we'll make sure the dragon and the woman never bother you again."

Death hesitated before it replied.

"Tempting," it said at last. "But not enough."

"Is this creature bothering you?" a magnificently modulated voice spoke close by my ear. I did not even have to turn my head to know that the unicorn had arrived.

"No, no, we were only talking."

The unicorn sighed. "Yes, I know; you will talk to creatures like this. But will you spare a few moments for me? It is enough to try even my perfect patience. Won't you ever find time for some"—the beast paused meaningfully—"significant conversation?"

"It is time we got serious," Death interrupted hastily, as if afraid of being drowned out by the ever-increasing group of companions.

"So, you're having a party," yet another gruff voice commented loudly. "And you didn't wait for me?"

It was Jeffrey the wolf. "Hey. Never mind. I'm here now. It's amazing how a quest can come alive when there's a talking wolf along!"

"Or you will never see your master again!" Death shouted over the wolf.

"Doom," Hendrek added.

"Ho hey, ho hey! And after work we play!" a number of voices rang out in song. To my surprise, it was the Seven Other Dwarves.

"Hey!" the Brownie called. "You guys sing, too?"

"Do we sing, too?" one of the dwarves, whose name was Nasty, mimicked. "Of course we do, tiny. It's in our contract!"

"That is correct," sniffed another dwarve named Snooty. "It is one of the privileges most cherished by the Dwarve Union. Not that you'd know anything about that!"

"Yes, yes, most certainly." Smarmy, the leader of the dwarves, stepped forward. "Singing happy work songs is a tradition greatly cherished by dwarvedom. Unfortunately, we are a bit out of practice, for Mother Duck never much liked it. But with her off fighting the Netherhells, we thought it was high time we got in a few verses."

"You guys ever think about going into vaudeville?" Hubert queried. "We're always looking for opening acts."

"Will someone listen to me?" Death demanded.

Norei clutched my hand. "Yes, Wuntvor," she said bravely. "We must come up with a bargain for Death."

"Bargains?" Death laughed bitterly, its patience at an end. "I am tired of bargains! You know what I desire!"

"Did I hear someone mention bargains?" A demon wearing a loud, checkered coat appeared before us, a large sack in one hand, a lit cigar in the other. He lifted the sack, waving it in Death's direction. "Well, you need look no further than my extensive stock of previously owned weapons!"

"No more!" Death screamed. "I will have my due! We will talk *now!*"

But suddenly another, much larger, much uglier demon stood among us. With a single, disdainful glance toward Death, the large demon cleared his throat and began to declaim:

> "Guxx Unfufadoo, noble demon,
> Wishes to announce this presence—"

"Too much!" Death shrieked. "I will deal with all of you!" The creature lifted its hands above its head, spreading its bonelike fingers wide. And through the space between the fingers came the wind.

It began as a gale. Leaves were torn from the trees surrounding the clearing, then the smaller branches began to rip free. My companions tried to hold their ground, but they were forced to cover their faces so they would not choke on the dust that filled the air. The wind increased, and the larger tree branches groaned as they bent in two. My smaller fellows lost their footing, and had to huddle on the ground so as not to be blown away. One by one, the others also fell to the ground as the enchanted gale redoubled again, becoming so powerful that even Hubert had to strain against its force.

Death smiled at me through the gale, as if we shared a joke. And perhaps we did, for I did not feel the wind at all.

"Good," Death remarked, its voice soft and clear despite the wind around us. "Now we may conclude our business."

"Indeed," I replied, and my voice, too, sounded louder than the wind. There would be no more stalling. I would have to make Death an offer at last. I looked at the huddled form of Norei to one side, the mass of overlarge robes that hid Snarks on the other side. There was no way I could talk to any of my fellows!

Death laughed, the sound of plants being ripped up by their roots in the gale. "They cannot help you now. My power has put us beyond them. It is just you and I: the Eternal Apprentice and his Death."

The specter wriggled his fingers. The wind grew even stronger.

"Their advice was worthless, anyway. Surprised that I should know?" Death paused an instant in its wind production to smooth its rotting robes. "You shouldn't be. I knew everything they've said, and everything they were going to say. Pitiful mortals. Do you think you can keep any secrets from Death? I am everywhere. I am in all of you, and make my presence known a little bit more every day. I know all of you intimately, and, although you may deny it, all of you know me, too."

Death laughed again, the sound of trees felled by lightning. "Now, though, you will come to know me so much better. For I have taken the two of us beyond the others. Prepare for your demise, Eternal Apprentice. No one can help you now."

There was a crashing sound behind me. Perhaps the wind was actually tearing apart the trees. Death stared beyond me, as if astonished by its handiwork.

"Oops!"

A giant foot crashed between us, a foot that belonged to Richard the giant.

"Excuse me, fellows," Richard rumbled. "There seem to be some tricky winds down close to the ground. It's making walking a little difficult. Uh—you didn't want that part of the forest back there, anyways, did you?"

"I don't believe this!" Death screamed.

And then the wind was gone.

TWO

"Music hath charms to soothe the savage beast," or so the sages say. And I agree that, if you can hum a little ditty or two, you will have nothing to fear from the savage breast whatsoever. Unfortunately, 'tis another matter entirely with savage fingers, savage claws, savage teeth and savage fangs, all of which will gladly shred and bite to their heart's content as you provide the musical accompaniment.

—From *Wizardry in the Wild:*
A Sorceror's Guide to Outdoor Survival, fourth edition,
by Ebenezum, greatest wizard in the Western Kingdoms

Death had disappeared. But something was still wrong with the forest.

My companions stood, one by one, in the aftermath of the gale, each groaning, stretching, exclaiming or complaining according to his or her nature. I looked around the edges of the forest that boarded the clearing, to see if the specter might be playing some trick on us. But I saw no sign of its skeletal countenance. My large number of allies had managed to overwhelm it once again. Death had had to flee when faced by too much life.

Why didn't I feel happier about my victory? Was it simply that my master was still a prisoner of Death, and our first meeting with the specter had been so chaotic that I had had no opportunity to discover any further hint of Ebenezum's whereabouts? Or was there something more? Had there been a change in the forest, beyond the fact that it was a mass of splintered trees and squashed bushes where the giant passed through?

"Oops," Richard interrupted. "Could someone tell me what is going on?"

"Doom," Hendrek answered.

"Do you think this means Death isn't interested in new entertainment attractions for his kingdom?" Hubert wondered.

I asked my companions to calm down for a moment. There was something out beyond the clearing. If I listened for it, perhaps I could discover what it was.

After a muttered comment or two, my allies quieted. I stared out over the demolished corner of the forest, and listened. Perhaps, I realized, the wind had not vanished entirely. Though far less violent than before, it was still out there, blowing about the splintered wood, whispering through the uprooted leaves.

Whispering? As soon as the thought entered my head, I realized how apt an analogy I had found. For the wind did not blow mindlessly through the newly dead wood beyond the clearing. Rather, there was a pattern to the ebb and flow of the breeze, as if it blew against the leaves and branches to make specific sounds; words perhaps, phrases, even parts of sentences. I strained to hear what the wind was saying.

". . . not . . ." said the breeze through the branches. And then: ". . . not gone . . ."

"Doom," Hendrek murmured, but I waved him to silence.

"I am not . . ." the breeze whispered. "I am still . . . your answer . . . waiting for your answer."

"Death!" I whispered in reply. For I was sure it was the specter, speaking to me through the broken trees.

". . . cannot escape . . . everywhere . . . Death is . . ."

This was too strange. I had to investigate, even though it was surely one of Death's tricks. But I knew I would have to face Death's tricks and more if I was to rescue my master. I stepped forward and drew my sword.

"What do you want *now?*" Cuthbert, my enchanted blade, yelped. "There isn't going to be blood, is there?"

I looked out at the dead forest. Now that I had walked closer to the ruined wood, I noticed that the forest floor was covered by wisps of fog that seemed to be moving in anything but a random pattern, as if they were following some predetermined design.

"No," I answered quite honestly. "I don't believe there will be blood."

"Oh, no," Cuthbert moaned. "I know what that tone of voice means. There might not be any blood, but there's going to be plenty of ichor!"

I nodded grimly, for I could make no other answer. The sword was probably right. Any moment now, there would be ichor and more.

"Oops?" Richard called from where he stood, high above us all. "Pardon me, but is there something going on down there? It's so difficult to see anything clearly from my vantage point."

"Indeed," I replied. "It is difficult for us to see as well. We will have to investigate."

"Doom."

I glanced to my side, and saw Hendrek pacing me, step for step, his cursed warclub, Headbasher, swinging in his very large hand.

"Hendrek's right, even if he does refuse to lose weight," the annoyingly correct voice of Snarks came from my other side. His scaly green hands held a stout oak staff. "If we're going to fight this, we have to fight together."

"Don't you think it would be a good idea if you took someone with a knowledge of spells along?" Norei called as she caught up to the rest of us.

I gave my beloved a welcoming smile, then looked forward again into the dead forest. The fog was thickening as it lifted from the ground, a whorling gray mass that rose and fell violently, as if it were a great, gray blanket hiding an army of fiends beneath.

There was a small explosion by my feet. It was Tap the Brownie. He pointed at the roiling fog.

"Pretty creepy, huh? This looks like a job for Brownie Power!"

I stood still for a moment while the little fellow hopped into my pocket.

"Begin!" a huge voice spoke behind me.

Brax the salesdemon began to beat out a regular rhythm on a small drum he carried with him for this very purpose, while his fellow demon, Guxx Unfufadoo, declaimed:

> "Guxx Unfufadoo, soldier demon,
> Marches bravely into battle,
> With no thought of his own peril,
> Does it all for his friend Wuntvor!"

There was a moment's silence, followed by Guxx Unfufadoo's curt demand:

"Ask me!"

"Hmm?" Brax replied. "Oh, sorry, I forgot, I was putting away my dru—"

"The question!" Guxx insisted.

"Oh, yes!" Brax groveled. "Most certainly, Grand Hoohah." I heard the rustle of parchment. Brax cleared his throat. "Tell me, Guxx," he read in a monotone. "Why are you making this noble sacrifice?"

"Sacrifice? I see." Guxx paused a moment to consider, then commanded:

"Resume!"

Brax resumed beating the drum.

> "Guxx Unfufadoo, abused demon,
> Wrongly thrown from power below us;
> Knows if he helps lad in trouble,
> Wuntvor will return the favor!"

Return the favor? Did that mean Guxx expected me to go back down to the Netherhells with him and help him regain his power? Was that why he was aiding me? Perhaps, I thought, in all fairness, I should let the large demon know that another visit to the slime pools below was not in my immediate plans.

"Indeed—" I began.

"Wait a minute, Damsel!" Hubert yelled enthusiastically. "Guxx's declaiming puts me in the mood for a little song!"

Our march had brought us almost to the edge of the ruined wood, and I could see the first fingers of fog perhaps two dozen paces ahead. Some of them curled together as we approached, as if beckoning us to hurry. It was no longer the time for song, or declamation.

"Ind—" I tried to interject.

"Continue!" Guxx roared over my objection.

> "Guxx Unfufadoo, angered demon,
> Does not speak for entertainment,
> Lifts his voice for but one purpose,
> To put some fear in those he fights with!"

"Indeed—" I began again, but my heart was no longer in the conversation. I could not risk turning around while the wisps of fog gathered about me.

"No need to thank us!" Hubert assured me. "If simple declamation can keep Death's minions at bay, think what we might accomplish with a little song and dance."

"That's right, Dragon," Alea echoed Hubert's enthusiasm, "especially if we come up with something appropriate. Say, 612?"

"A wonderful choice!" Hubert agreed. "Shall we?"

The two of them sang together:

"It's getting scary out here in the big, wide world,
With creatures that jump and go boo!
But no matter what horrible monster we meet,
I'm not at all scared about you."

"Recommence!" Guxx screamed forcefully. Brax beat the drum more quickly.

"Guxx Unfufadoo, music critic,
Has had enough of this pair's singing!
Is ready to perform a service;
Perhaps some vocal cords need pruning?"

The demon flexed his claws meaningfully as he blew his nose. I realized he had come very close to making a true rhyme.

"Well, you know how we feel about that!" Hubert replied. "Take it, Damsel!"

Alea took it:

"It's so frightening that we want to hide,
For whatever else can we do?
Something really nasty—"

They both paused to point at Guxx.

"—might be by our side!
But I'm not at all scared about you!"

Guxx Unfufadoo began to jump up and down, his clawed fists punching invisible enemies before him, a fearsome grimace spread upon his countenance. All in all, the demon seemed even more angry than usual.

"Override!" he shrieked.

Brax drummed even more loudly than before.

"Doom." Hendrek, oblivious to the drama taking place between our more theatrical companions, used Headbasher to point into the shattered forest before us.

Oddly enough, the fog did seem to be retreated. Could whatever was waiting for us out there be a music critic as well? Perhaps the fog just didn't care for noise. Whichever the reason, the forest floor before us was fog-free for a hundred paces.

"This could be a trap," Hendrek grumbled.

"And I could have relatives living in the Netherhells," Snarks added. "You have an amazing talent, dear Hendrek, for stating the obvious."

Hendrek solemnly nodded in agreement. "It is a gift."

The drumming redoubled behind us, twice as loud. I was amazed that so much noise could come from one tiny drum. Once agin, the demon declaimed behind us:

> "Guxx Unfufadoo, angered demon,
> Has had enough of caterwauling!
> Seems you should have used your heads which
> From your necks will soon be falli—"

The demon's declamation dissolved in a fearsome bout of sneezing.

"Such a waste," Brax sighed behind us. "What a magnificent rhyming talent!"

Even I had to admit, it was a pity. Guxx Unfufadoo, the dread rhyming demon, had been defeated by a counterspell performed by my master which caused the creature, once strengthened by his rhymes, to sneeze violently whenever rhymed poetry was present in his speech. Now—even though Guxx had once been our sworn enemy—still I found it sad to see him reduced to a mere sneezing shadow of his former demonic nastiness.

"What's this?" Hubert exclaimed. "Guxx has given up?"

" 'Tis a pity," Alea agreed. "You might say he's lost by a nose."

"Gee, Damsel!" the dragon enthused. "That sounds like a cue for another verse!"

"Oops!" a voice rumbled from above. "No, it doesn't."

"It doesn't?" Damsel and Dragon asked in unison.

The ground shook behind me, the sound, I guessed, of Richard putting his foot down.

"It doesn't," the giant repeated. "There is something strange going on out there."

"Oh," Hubert replied meekly, "I guess it doesn't. Oh, well. The rest of the verses weren't all that good, anyway. In fact, the seventh and fifteenth stanzas were a trifle redundant—" The dragon's voice trailed off. "Something strange?"

Snarks laughed. "I never knew it could be so useful to have a giant along." But then he turned to look out at the dead wood before us. "Oh" was his only comment.

"Doom." Hendrek pointed again with his club. In the sudden silence, the fog had begun to creep back across the debris-strewn ground. "Whatever is out there is coming back for us."

"Indeed," I replied, doubt creeping into my voice. Should I encourage the vaudevillian duo's singing, after all? It was, at best, a difficult decision. Aloud, I mused: "What sort of trap advances on its prey?"

"Ah," a magnificently modulated voice spoke immediately behind me, "but whatever is out there will realize soon that *it* is what has been trapped, once it has been pierced by my glorious golden horn."

"Hey!" Jeffrey added from somewhere nearby. "And don't they know that no trap is complete unless you have a talking wolf along?"

I realized the Seven Other Dwarves were with us as well, as I heard them singing quietly in the background:

> "Ho hee, ho hee,
> No trap will bother we!"

I wished I had the dwarves' confidence. Couldn't they see what was happening? The fog's turbulence was increasing with every second it roiled toward us. And as it grew closer, I could see that it was not all a uniform gray, but actually showed spots of dully gleaming color here and there that swam within the mist. And the colors grew in intensity here, and faded there, like the flicker of sickly strings of lights, as if whatever was hiding within the mist was rising to the surface.

The voices within the fog were louder, too. For I realized that there was more than one calling out to me. Now that there was no more singing or declaiming, I could hear them much more clearly:

"Wuntvor—"

"—business is not finished—"

"Eternal Apprentice—"

"—come to us, Wuntvor—"

"—over so quickly—"

"Why don't you put down your sword?"

"—an end to eternity—"

"Wuntvor—"

"Let us caress you—"

"We will cover you so comfortably—"

"—over so quickly—"

"Wouldn't you like to rest—forever?"

"You heard what they said?" Cuthbert wailed. "About putting down your sword?"

"Indeed," I answered.

"Isn't that a good idea?" the sword pleaded hopefully. "Letting me rest someplace dry, say back behind us, away from the fog?"

I grunted in reply. "The way this fog moves, I have the feeling there is no place it could not cover, and no way we might escape it. I suppose I might give you a choice: Would you like to be stuck flat upon the ground, inanimate, while the clammy fog encloses you? Or would you like to be held in my hands, fighting your way to freedom?"

"That's a choice?" The sword shivered, and spoke in a resigned tone: "Very well. Ichor is my destiny."

"Indeed," I replied, and advanced upon the fog.

THREE

"Don't quote me. No comment."

—Statement of Ebenezum,
greatest wizard in the Western Kingdoms,
when first approached about Wizardgate

"Wuntvor—" the fog called out to me. Or perhaps it was something hiding in the fog. Or any number of things hiding in the fog.

"—come to us, Wuntvor—"

I looked to my companions. We were all together, a tight-kit group.

"—bring your friends—"

Hendrek and Snarks flanked me on either side, their weapons drawn. They were moving more cautiously than before. We had slowed our headlong rush to meet our destiny. The surrounding mist was far too strange. None of us could guess what might emerge from the dense grayness at any instant, and we all realized that we had to adjust our moves accordingly.

"We've been waiting—" the fog voices whispered.

"Doom," Hendrek said, his voice softer than before, as if the fog that reached to encircle us was a greater threat than even his pessimism could comprehend.

The fog voices answered in a jumble:

"—Eternal Apprentice—"

"—ever so long—"

"We are so comforting—"

"—Wuntvor—"

"This is all a little depressing," Snarks remarked with a lot less venom than usual.

This situation, apparently, was affecting all of us. I looked about. Norei was right behind me, flanked by the unicorn and the talking wolf. Guxx and Brax were next, the salesdemon grasping his drum, ready to beat at a moment's notice. The Seven Other Dwarves followed them, while Hubert took up the rear with Alea perched upon his scaly bluish-purple neck.

We had been quite spread out when we had begun our march toward the fog, but now the rear guard seemed to be catching up with the front ranks, so that we were all in a bunch, threatening to trod on each other's feet at a moment's notice. Perhaps it was that those of us in front had been slowing our pace. Or perhaps those in the rear had quickened theirs to keep away from the tendrils of mist that curled about their heels.

"—Wuntvor—"

I took an even smaller step toward the fog. What did the mist want from me?

"—that's the way—"

"—almost—"

"—only a moment—"

"—over so peacefully—"

Indeed, I thought. But for some reason, I could not bring myself to say even that single word. In fact, I couldn't bring myself to do much of anything. Somehow, my steps had slowed so much that I had trouble pushing my foot forward to take another. What was wrong here?

I turned to ask my companions. They had all stopped walking as well. In fact, they seemed to have stopped moving entirely. All of them stared forward, into the fog. Hubert blinked, slowly. I looked down into the pocket of my jerkin. The Brownie appeared wedged inside, hands covering his tiny cap, as if he never wanted to look up into the light of day again.

"Doo—" Hendrek began, but was unable to finish the word.

Something awful was happening!

"—Wuntvor—" The fog called my name instead.

"—over so quickly—"

"—and ever so final."

The Seven Other Dwarves sang listlessly:

"Hi hor, hi hor,
Why bother anymore?"

Then all eight of them began to snore.

Indeed, I thought. Why bother? The fog encircled us. In a matter of minutes, it would cover us as well. It was easier this way. No bother at all.

Norei forced her eyes open, as if she had to fight from falling asleep as well. "Oh, no!" she gasped, stifling a yawn. "Can't you see, Wunt—" Her eyes closed, and she slept.

"Norei?" I managed, but could not muster my thoughts sufficiently to frame a further question. And yet my beloved was trying to tell me something. I watched the tendrils of mist encircle her ankles.

The fog! It was the fog that was doing this! That's what Norei had tried to tell me. This gray mass about us was more than a physical presence. It affected our emotions as well, draining our will to resist.

Well, it wouldn't work on me! Why bother? I had asked myself a moment before while under the influence of the dreadful mist. I had to bother, no matter what the fog told me. My master's life depended on it! And the lives of my companions as well! Death would have to try harder still to defeat Wuntvor, the Eternal Apprentice. Not even something as insidious as a cursed fog could defeat me!

Or could it?

I blinked; a movement that took all my concentration. I knew what was troubling us at last, but I also knew I had no energy left to defeat it. I had used up all my reserves in one last burst of defiant thought, leaving me filled with the lethargy of death. And it looked like my other companions, Norei included, were in a worse state still. All of them, Brownie, unicorn, dragon, wolf, dwarves, demons and maiden —all of them were lost in deadly sleep.

My eyelids were too heavy. I felt them close, and my chin loll forward against my chest. But it couldn't end like this! Somewhere, deep within me, defiance still lived. Somehow, I had to reach it, to coax it to the surface, to fill me with its power and give me strength. I could feel it now, like a hot coal burning deep within my brain. I had to use that coal to set fire to my mind, and find some way to overcome the mist that surrounded us.

My eyes fluttered open for an instant. Using every shred of defiance I had left in me, I only had the strength for one more word:

"Help!"

"Oops!" came a reply from on high. And then there came a wind. Death's wind, I thought, as I drifted toward sleep. This time, even the giant would not escape the grip of Death.

"Wait—" the fog whispered.

"—fair at all—"

"—heard the last—"

"—stupid giant—"

Then the voices were lost to the ever-increasing gale. The wind stopped a moment later, and my eyes fluttered open. The fog was gone. We were surrounded by brilliant sunlight.

"Oops," Richard called. "Did I blow too hard?"

My companions let out a ragged cheer. Apparently, they were every bit as awake as I.

"Not at all!" I shouted aloft. "You have saved us from a dire fate!"

"Doom," Hendrek agreed.

"Gone?" my sword cried in disbelief. "It's gone?"

"But it wasn't me at all," Richard replied. "I was acting on your direction."

"I don't have to *do* anything?" the sword rejoined. "I don't have to *cut* anyone?" There seemed to be an edge of hysteria in its voice.

"Nonsense, big fellow!" Jeffrey objected to the giant's humility. "It was a wonderful rescue. Even a talking wolf couldn't have done any better!"

"No blood?" Cuthbert shrilled. "No ichor? No slicing? No dici—" I slid the sword back into its scabbard. It obviously needed a rest.

The large fellow blushed, his face as crimson as the setting sun. "Well, gee," he murmured. "It's so difficult to see what's going on down there. There was all this fog, and nobody seemed to be doing much of anything. And then the apprentice yelled. What was I to do? I simply felt it was time to make a giant effort."

"He's good on his rescues," Snarks remarked. "His speeches could use work."

"Oops," Richard responded. "But that's one of my problems. Being a giant is a lonely job." He sighed. "Think of it. Whenever you hear one of my kind mentioned, it's almost always in the singular. You know, 'There's a giant tearing up such-and-such a place!' or 'A giant's laying waste to so-and-so's domain!' My kind doesn't like to get together in bunches. A crowd of giants is even too big for us! You know, it's a wonder my father and mother met at all. Lucky for me, they were terrorizing neighboring kingdoms. Otherwise, I never would have been born!"

"Indeed," I replied, trying to think of a nice way to quiet the giant down. Not that I wasn't grateful for our rescue by the big fellow; in fact, I planned to thank him all over again once we had reached safer territory.

Right now, however, we were anything but safe, for I was sure Death still lurked about. We had driven the specter away in its skeletal state, and we had blown away its killer fog. But I had no reason to believe that we had seen the last of it.

"And another thing," Richard continued. "It's hard to get close to people. Let's face it, I could crush any of you without even thinking!"

"Doom," Hendrek murmured close to my ear. "I think I should take a look around."

Richard sighed more deeply still. The few trees left in the vicinity bent under the weight of the breeze. "Being a giant isn't easy. There's not a lot of us around. It's very difficult to socialize."

"Good idea," I replied to the large warrior. "I fear Death is near us still. Take some of the others with you."

Hendrek left my side, motioning for Jeffrey, Snarks and Norei to accompany him.

"I suppose that's why I fell in with Mother Duck," the giant went on. "She was very good at giving orders. And I found myself very comfortable taking them."

Hendrek strode forward into the dead forest, the other three forming a tight-knit group behind him. They were a formidable unit. Between Hendrek's club, Jeffrey's teeth and claws, Norei's spells and Snarks's sharp tongue, they should be able to defeat almost anything thrown against them.

"Still, I found myself increasingly disturbed over Mother Duck's need to control everybody," the giant went on, "especially after she got hold of all of you. It took my heart out of gianting." Richard sighed even more prodigiously. Small branches ripped free of nearby tree trunks.

"Methinks," he added, " 'tis time to go into another line of work."

There was a moment's silence. Richard was done at last.

"Have you considered vaudeville?" Hubert suggested.

"Doom!" The intensity of Hendrek's statement cut short Richard's answer. We all turned to see what had upset the warrior so.

Hendrek pointed with his warclub at the forest floor.

"The branches," he intoned. "They are moving of their own accord."

Now that the warrior mentioned it, I did think I saw pieces of dead wood twisting like snakes through the debris.

"Will they attack us?" Jeffrey whispered.

"Not unless they plan to attack us with words," Snarks replied. "They're forming themselves into letters."

"Stay close!" Norei warned. "This could be a trick."

"The perceptiveness of you humans never ceases to astound me," Snarks commented.

"Doom! They are forming words!"

"Oh, yeah!" Jeffrey frowned as he read, "Sur-ren-der, Wuntvo—" He looked up at the others. "That's all it says, so far."

"Watch out!" Norei yelled.

The animate branches must have finished their spelling, for they rose quickly into the air, heading straight for my four companions.

"Back, foul wood!" Hendrek exclaimed, lifting his club behind his head.

"Urk!" Jeffrey the wolf, who had been standing too close behind the large warrior, replied. Headbasher had done its hellish work again.

But Norei was busy as well. She made three quick passes in the air. The flying branches fell to the ground.

"There!" she said with some satisfaction. "Death will have to do better than that!"

"Who?" Jeffrey queried. "What?" The wolf's voice shifted down a register.

"Indeed," he said rather more calmly. "Wuntvor, listen quickly."

I would recognize that voice anywhere.

"Master!" I cried.

"Indeed," the wolf replied. "Death is distracted for the moment by your resourcefulness. But we must make plans for my escape. Death is keeping me prisoner in his king—"

Jeffrey's mouth snapped shut, but opened a moment later.

"Indeed?" a much drier voice remarked, the sound of sand wearing grooves into granite. "What a clever wizard your Ebenezum is, contacting you behind my back. But no one is cleverer than Death." The specter laughed, the sound of fish drowning in the open air. The wolf stared with hate-filled eyes, and silence surrounded us, as if all the world was waiting for the words of death.

The wolf looked away from us. "I have had enough nonsense! I think it is time I made my final offer. Listen carefully, if you ever expect to see your wizard again!"

FOUR

The sages say that "running is good for the health," and, for once, I agree with the sages, especially in those cases when one is being chased by anything carrying weapons, claws, legal summons, fire-breathing capability or any combination of the above.

—From *The Teachings of Ebenezum,*
Volume XXXIV.

"Ebenezum is dead," the wolf said with the specter's voice, "unless you intervene." Jeffrey paused to grin. "No, no. 'Intervene' is not the proper word. The correct word is 'sacrifice.' "

"Indeed?" I responded, my voice strong despite the queasy feeling that threatened to rise from my stomach. Death wanted to talk again. This time I would have to get the information I wanted.

"I should take you now!" the wolf growled. "But no. Coming to me has to be your decision, made with your own free will. Oh, how the fates conspire against me! Otherwise you will continue to be the Eternal Apprentice"—the wolf shuddered— "forever. But, should you choose thusly"—Jeffrey allowed himself a deadly smile— "your master will remain with me, forever. Yes, you heard what the clever wizard said. I have already taken him to the Kingdom of the Dead, and the only way he will ever leave is if you replace him."

"Indeed," I commented again, doing my best to think fast. "Then you wish me to come with you now, with no argument, no elaboration, nothing whatsoever?"

"Well, yes," the wolf replied, the slightest doubt entering his spectral voice, "that's the general idea. Otherwise, you know, your master—"

"Yes, yes, I know all about my master," I interrupted hastily. "But it does seem rather dull and boring, unimaginative even, for you to simply whisk me away from the land of the living."

"Dull? Boring? Unimaginative?" Jeffrey gnashed his teeth. "Death is anything but that! I know more interesting ways to die than—"

"I'm certain you do," I interjected again. "And I'll be glad to try any of them that you like."

"You will?" The wolf's mouth opened in surprise. "Any of them?"

"Certainly," I replied. "You can try three or four of them in a row on me if you like."

"You mean I can kill the Eternal Apprentice three or four times in a row?" Jeffrey clapped his forepaws. "You're too good to me. When can we start?"

"Not quite yet," I answered. "I think we have time to play a little game first."

"Game?" The wolf paused, scowling at me. "I am the master of games!"

"Indeed." I allowed myself the slightest of smiles. This was working better than I had hoped. "Then you will not object to playing one with someone as unskilled in gamesmanship as myself. Of course, to keep the game interesting, there will have to be a prize for the winner."

"A prize?" the Death-wolf retorted vitriolically. "Like the time I arm-wrestled your master, and he tricked me out of an entire kingdom? You must think Death a fool! I will not be swindled like that again!"

"Indeed? Well, if that's the way you feel about it"—I paused to yawn— "I suppose we have nothing else to talk about."

"But you'll never see your master again!" Death declared.

"My master?" I replied quizzically, as if I could barely be bothered to make conversation. "Oh, yes, the wizard. 'Tis a pity if he has to die, but let's be realistic. He was rather old already, wasn't he? How many years would he have left, even if you didn't take him now?"

"But—" Death was so astonished that it took the creature a moment to collect its spectral thoughts. Finally, the wolf blurted: "You must save your master!"

"Must I?" I blew casually upon my knuckles. "I don't see why. Without a game, it hardly seems worth it."

"Without a game?" The wolf took a deep breath, then laughed, the sound of small plants shriveling beneath a winter's frost. "Why am I worried? I am the master of games; you have said so yourself. I was defeated once, but it was by your master, a wily old wizard. You are

naught but a young and awkward apprentice, even if you are eternal."
Jeffrey once again allowed himself a smile. "Besides, you have made
promises to me. You, the Eternal Apprentice. You *will* die three or
four times?"

"If I lose the game?" I shrugged. "I suppose I will have to."

Death's laughter redoubled. "You will experience half a dozen
deaths before I am through, each one more lingering and unpleasant
than the one before! That is our bargain!"

"Indeed?" I replied, still appearing only mildly interested. "I suppose it might be, if—when I win—you return my master to the land of
the living unharmed, and take no one else in his stead."

"Oh, I might as well." Death chuckled. "Half a dozen deaths!"
Jeffrey's eyes stared into my own.

"So what is the game?" he demanded.

"Indeed," I replied. This was all going a bit too well. And more
than a little too quickly. I allowed myself a world-weary sigh before I
spoke again. "Why do we have to rush these matters so? We have just
struck the bargain. You must give me some little time to think, so that
I might come up with something worthy of your talents."

"Really?" Death paused for a moment to consider my request.
"Well, I suppose there is no harm in allowing you to reflect on your
impossible situation for a little while longer. Besides, it will give me a
few more hours to gloat. Half a dozen deaths! And they will be quite
imaginative deaths, I assure you. Very well. I shall return at midnight." The wolf winked broadly at me and my assembled companions. "It's the time of day that suits me best, don't you think?"

Death laughed again as we were surrounded by a moment of intense
wind. And then the gale was gone, as quickly as it had arrived.

Jeffrey blinked. "Hey!" he yelled at Hendrek. "You should watch
where you throw that warclub." The wolf rubbed the hirsute lump
atop his head. "Why is everybody staring at me?"

"Doom," the warrior replied. "You were the vessel for Death."

Jeffrey took a step away. "That doesn't mean you're going to hit me
again, does it? Can't you take a little constructive criticism?"

"No, he can't," Snarks replied for the warrior, "though Netherhells
knows I've tried."

"But Hendrek isn't going to attack you again," I interjected. "He
was trying to tell you that when his dread warclub robbed you of your
memory, Death stepped in to speak through your temporarily vacated
brain, using your mouth and body to give us his ultimatum!"

"Really? Death spoke through me?" The wolf rolled his tongue over his very large incisors. "So that's why my mouth tastes like rotting leaves." Jeffrey wrinkled his snout. "Fauugghh! Maybe I should eat something else to clear the pallet. How long has it been since I've had a square meal, anyway? And to think I came to Mother Duck's kingdom because it had a reputation for fine cuisine."

"Fine cuisine?" Norei replied with some trepidation.

"Doom," Hendrek added.

"Delicacies," Jeffrey explained. "You know, pigs, small girls dressed in red, grandmothers. The talking wolf's diet is surprisingly varied."

Snarks waved at Jeffrey with his staff. "Well, why don't you be good talking wolf and go out looking for them? I'm sure there's a grandmother out there somewhere. In the meantime, we have to make plans."

"Doom," Hendrek agreed.

"Your friends are right," Norei remarked forcefully. "We must plan quickly, but we are only able to plan through your efforts, Wuntvor. You were magnificent, in the way you handled Death."

Norei took my hand as she spoke, and I could not help but smile when I heard such a compliment from my beloved. Still, as flattering as Norei's words were, I felt that I did not truly deserve them. Instead, I told my companions I owed it all to my master. I had thought about how Ebenezum had dealt with Death when we had first met the specter, then done nothing more than follow the wizard's example.

"You are too modest—" Norei began.

"That's almost as good as Brownie Power!" Tap added.

"I always knew he had greatness in him," the unicorn interjected. "What an apprentice! What a lap!"

The dwarves cheered as one:

"Ho hi, ho hi,
He's our kind of guy!"

"So what is your plan?" Snarks interrupted.

I told them I didn't have one.

"Doom," Hendrek remarked.

I explained that my experience with the wizard only went so far. Ebenezum had taught me how to find Death's weaknesses. However, now that I had found them, I wasn't too sure what to do with them. My master had used a combination of arm wrestling and sneezing to defeat the specter before. But Death would be ready for similar tricks. If I wanted to defeat Death and regain my master, I would have to devise something entirely new.

"So you have absolutely no plan whatsoever?" Snarks clarified.

"Indeed," I replied.

"Doom," Hendrek chorused.

The Seven Other Dwarves stepped forward.

> "Hi haid, hi haid,
> Wuntvor needs our aid!"

Smarmy took an extra step forward. He held forth a large glass sphere.

"Beg pardon," the self-effacing dwarve remarked. "But, worthless though we may be, we thought we might be able to make some small, pitiful contribution to the continuation of your noble quest. In that spirit, we have made some efforts, minuscule though they may be, to procure something that, even in some insubstantial way, you might use to—"

"Shut up and give him the thing!" Nasty called.

"Oh, my," Smarmy replied. "Oh, yes."

I took the glass globe from his outstretched hands.

"It's a crystal ball," Norei said, a bit of wonder in her voice. "Isn't it?"

"Oh, my," Smarmy answered. "Oh—yes, it is. Not much of a crystal ball, perhaps, but it was the best we poor, insignificant—"

"It looks like a very nice crystal ball to me," Norei interrupted. "Doesn't it, Wuntvor?"

"Indeed," I answered. "I am quite flattered. Wherever—"

"We stole it from Mother Duck!" Nasty brayed. "She has tons of this stuff. Claims she needs it for her fairy stories!"

"I hope it's all right." Smarmy sighed. "It was so hard finding something appropriate. You already had an enchanted weapon and any number of magical companions. I mean, what do you give to the apprentice who has everything?"

"Indeed," I replied heartily. "How does it work?"

Smarmy hit his forehead with both of his wringing hands. "Oh! How forgetful can I be? There's a rhyme that goes with it!" He pulled a crumpled piece of parchment from his pocket and handed it to me.

"The Incantation," the parchment read. "Be sure to state quickly and in a loud voice:

> "Secret sphere, seashore seer,
> Surely showing sunshine seeking.
> Simply said, the shaft is shed,
> Spouting spells that send us shrieking!"

"It should be clear enough," Smarmy prompted. "Just recite the incantation, and the crystal will show you whatever you wish. What could be simpler? And once you get the hang of it, it will show you anything, or anyone, you want."

"Indeed?" I asked, genuinely intrigued. "Including my master?"

"Oops!" the giant interrupted from on high.

All conversation ceased down below. Considering what had transpired before, when Richard said "Oops," we listened.

"What is the matter?" I called aloft.

The giant scraped a foot along the ground. The one tree still standing in his vicinity was reduced to splinters.

"I would like to ask a boon," Richard said meekly.

"Indeed," I answered. "If it is in my power, you shall have it."

The giant smiled. "Good. What should I do next?"

"Beg pardon?" I asked, for I did not quite understand his request.

"Well, that is, you see, I told you about Mother Duck's need to control everything? Including me?"

"Indeed?"

Richard shook his head unhappily. "I got used to it. Without her to boss me around, I'm not quite sure what to do."

The Seven Other Dwarves nodded sympathetically.

"We know exactly what the giant's talking about!" Smarmy exclaimed. "Now that Mother Duck is gone, we have all the freedom we want. But what do we want to do with it?"

"Oh, wow," Spacey ventured.

"We could travel," Sickly coughed. "I wouldn't mind a better climate."

"Move somewhere that had a better class of creatures," Snooty mentioned.

"Sneak up behind people and scream," Noisy suggested.

"How about finding new and interesting things to drop?" Clumsy asked.

"You see?" Smarmy interjected. "It's so difficult to find a consensus!"

"Oops," Richard agreed. "But you haven't answered my question. What am I supposed to do? What is my function in the story? I need direction. I need motivation."

"Indeed," I murmured. "That's a big problem."

"Exactly," the giant stated. "Free will can be frightening."

"Might I again suggest vaudeville?" Hubert interjected helpfully. "There's very little free will involved."

"But there is a lot of dancing," Alea said.

"Dancing?" The giant looked doubtfully down to his feet.

"And snappy patter!" Hubert quickly added.

"Snappy patter?" Richard sounded interested. "That might be nice. Life gets tedious when all you can ever say is 'Time for Mother Duck's ovens.' A constant diet of threats is so limiting."

It seemed to me that I should add something to this conversation as well. It also seemed to me that there had to be other options beyond vaudeville.

"Indeed—" I began, but was distracted by a high-pitched sound that was rapidly approaching.

"Eep eep!" a tiny voice cried. "Eep eep!"

I would recognize those eeps anywhere. It was my magic ferret, back from doing whatever magic ferrets do.

"I think he's trying to tell you something!"

There was an intensity to the ferret's cries that I had not heard before. Could it be an eep of warning?

"Oops," Richard called down to us. "I think my hours of indecision are over."

"What is the matter?" Norei shouted her concern.

The giant frowned down at her. "Remember that Netherhells battle taking place two valleys over? Well, they're not fighting anymore."

"Indeed," I shouted to him, wishing for some further explanation. "Is everybody gone?"

"No, not everybody." Richard sighed. "Well, I guess it was time to get back to work, anyway. It was fun having freedom while it lasted."

"Doom," Hendrek interjected, as the Seven Other Dwarves explained the giant's behavior in song:

> "Ho hack, ho hack,
> Mother Duck is back!"

So that was what my ferret was trying to tell me! Beloved pet that he was, he had left us to watch Mother Duck, so that he might warn us if she had won the battle.

"Good ferret!" I enthused. "Excellent ferret!"

"Eep eep!" the ferret answered happily. "Eep eep eep!"

"Then we are surely doomed to a life of fairy tales!" Smarmy wailed.

"Indeed," I replied calmly. "I think not."

"Doom," Hendrek remarked, shifting his deadly warclub from hand to hand. "Then it is not too late to fight?"

"Not at all. Rather, it is not too late to run." I pointed at the nearby warning signs. "We are already on the edge of the Eastern Kingdoms. I suggest we begin traveling out of them, as of now."

And travel we did. After all, I had learned more than a few simple spells from the greatest wizard in the Western Kingdoms.

I had learned all about escape routes as well.

FIVE

Giants (see figure 346B) are your friends. Anything that large is your friend. Trust me. And if you find out I'm wrong, you can always will this book to your next of kin.

—From *Ebenezum's Handy Guide to Woodland Creatures*
(with accompanying illustrations), fourth edition,
by Ebenezum,
greatest wizard in the Western Kingdoms

I scooped up the crystal ball as I ran from the clearing into the woods. In the distance, I could hear a woman's voice.

"Richard, I see you! Come back here, you coward!"

"Oops!" Richard answered. A great cloud appeared over me and my companions. I didn't realize until it fell to earth a quarter mile in front of us that it was the giant's foot. Richard was running with us.

"Wuntvor!" Norei called from my side. "Where are we going?"

"Back toward Vushta!" I replied. "At least for the time being."

"Doom," Hendrek interjected room where he lumbered at Norei's side. "The time being?"

I nodded. "Until we can think of a better way to rescue Ebenezum."

"Make way!" a magnificent voice shouted as a brilliant blur of white galloped past, twisting suddenly to avoid a tight copse of trees. "It is best that a beast with a beautiful and deadly horn should lead the way."

"Sounds good to me," Snarks sneered from my other side. "That way, none of us will have to listen while the creature preens."

The two other demons were right on our heels, for I could hear the larger of them going on, with drum accompaniment, about "Guxx Unfufadoo, running demon."

"You'll pardon us if we fly on ahead," Hubert called over his flapping wings, "but this retreat seems a bit overcrowded."

"We'll meet you up ahead," Alea added. "In the Central Kingdoms. That way, we'll get a little time alone to practice some new material."

"Wait for that indispensable talking wolf!" shouted a voice some distance behind us. And I could hear other voices, even more distant.

> "Hi hort, hi hort,
> To bad our legs are short!"

Fainter even than the song of the Seven Other Dwarves was a faraway, out-of-breath eeping. It sounded as if my ferret, after rushing to warn me of Mother Duck, was now too exhausted to escape!

I jiggled the pocket of my jerkin with my free hand.

"Tap!" I called. "It's time for Brownie Power!"

"Now?" The little fellow grabbed the top of the pocket and glared out at me. "Are you sure?"

Tap did not look at all well. He appeared to be shivering—either that, or it was the movement of my pocket bouncing up and down as I jogged. He was entirely the wrong color as well, altogether too green for a Brownie. Of course, that also might be attributable to my jouncing pocket. I frowned at the wee man. Apparently, our recent scrape with Death, combined, perhaps, with the Brownie's current mode of transportation, had had a negative effect on the small fellow.

"That's telling him!" Snarks exclaimed, smiling at Tap's shivering form. "As far as we're concerned, it's never time for Brownie Power!"

"What? Huh?" Tap stood tall, his head clearing the top of my pocket by an inch or more. "No, His Brownieship would never let me back in if I think like that." He took a deep breath. "A Brownie must be ever alert, ever vigilant and ever ready to make shoes. That's part of the Brownie Creed! Where do you need Brownie Power? I'm ready now!"

"How noble!" Norei remarked with her beautiful smile.

"Doom!" Hendrek rumbled. "What self-sacrifice!"

"How sickening!" Snarks added.

I ignored all of them as I quickly told the Brownie my plan. There were members of our company who were lagging behind, who might soon be overtaken and once again subjugated by Mother Duck. There was only one way to save them: through the magic of Brownie transportation.

"A difficult job," Tap agreed. "But Brownie Power is up to it! Brownie Power is up to anything!"

"I've personally had Brownie Power up to here," Snarks remarked, but Tap was already gone, vanished with one of those smoke-producing-tiny-explosions he had.

"Richard!" Mother Duck's voice called again. She sounded as if she was drawing closer. How could someone of her advanced years move that quickly?

"Oops!" Richard shouted from some distance up ahead. "Goodbye!" The giant began to run, his first two steps sending tremors that threatened to knock us from our feet. Then he jumped over a low mountain range and disappeared from sight.

"Richard?" Mother Duck's voice protested shrilly. "What am I going to do without a giant? I mean, Jack-the-Very-Tall-Person-Killer simply doesn't sound right. Richard!"

But the giant was gone. And suddenly Mother Duck did not sound quite so close as before. Perhaps she had stopped her pursuit. It was then that I realized that the intervening woods prevented the woman from seeing the rest of us. Maybe she would stop now, exhausted from her earlier battle, and never realize her former victims were within easy recapture. If, somehow, we could increase slightly the distance between us; if, perhaps, we could remain quiet but for a few more moments—

There was a moderate explosion in our midst.

"Eep eep!" the ferret remarked.

"What a way for talking wolves to travel!" Jeffrey complained.

"Hey!" Noisy added enthusiastically. "That was great!"

"No," Tap groaned, falling to his knees. "That was Brownie Power! Eleven at one blow!" He fell face-first into the dirt.

"There's something in these woods, isn't there?" Mother Duck called from some distance behind us.

I quickly stuffed the Brownie back in my pocket.

"Indeed," I suggested. "I don't think we should be out here for long." I picked up the ferret as well, returning the small, furry creature to my pack.

"I hear you!" Mother Duck called somewhat more forcefully than before. "Don't think that you can escape me!"

"Doom," Hendrek rumbled as he glanced over his shoulder. "What should we do now?"

"Run even faster!" I replied, for I had seen a sign up ahead:

YOU ARE NOW ENTERING THE CENTRAL KINGDOMS
THANK YOUR LUCKY STARS!

I did not know if leaving Mother Duck's domain would actually help us. But it certainly wouldn't hurt.

We made it to the sign in a matter of moments, but not without some difficulty. The Seven Other Dwarves gasped behind me as one:

> "Ho heth, ho heth,
> We are quite out of breath!"

I paused to look behind us. It couldn't be! But it was. I could already see Mother Duck's figure darting rapidly through the trees.

"It's hopeless, you know!" she yelled for our benefit. "Once you visit Mother Duck, you visit her forever!"

The old woman seemed to be running at a speed five times as fast as a normal person. At this rate, she would overtake us in a couple minutes.

"How can she—" I began.

"In Mother Duck's kingdom"—Smarmy wheezed—"Mother Duck can do anything."

"Doom," Hendrek pointed out. "But we are no longer in Mother Duck's kingdom."

"Exactly," Norei stated, pulling back her sleeves to give her hands more room to conjure. "Allow me."

She made a rapid series of passes through the air, followed by a quick string of words of power. And the woods between us and Mother Duck started to grow.

Trees sprouted new branches pointing toward the ground, while bushes doubled their height in the blink of an eye. Dead leaves spread upon the ground turned green again and sent shoots into the soft earth, turning into a field of strong young saplings before us. Snarks yelled in surprise as his stout oak staff took root in the dirt between his feet, while the rest of us gasped in awe as the "You are now entering the Central Kingdoms" sign sprouted a hundred tiny branches, spreading from the square of wood like ripples from a pond, and completing, in concert with the trees and bushes, an impenetrable wall of vegetation.

"Not bad, huh?" Norei allowed.

"Indeed!" I enthused, looking at my beloved with renewed admiration. "What a wonderful spell!"

Norei blushed, the color on her cheeks making her even more beautiful than before. " 'Twas not all that special. Naught but a simple wild agricultural growth spell, slightly amended to allow for forest conditions."

"Doom," Hendrek interjected. "But will it stop Mother Duck?"

"I think it has a chance," Norei answered. "You see, if the spell has worked properly, it has not only formed the impenetrable forest wall that you see before you. In addition, the magic should continue to replicate itself upon the other side, causing the dense growth to push into the Eastern Kingdoms, straight for Mother Duck. She will have to stop that part of the spell first before she can hope to clear a path through this enchanted forest to reach us." My beloved paused, taking a deep breath. "I may not be able to stop Mother Duck, but I can certainly slow her down."

"Very impressive," Snarks commented. "Why didn't you do it before?"

But the demon's query didn't phase the beautiful witch in the least.

"Before," she replied, "we were in the Eastern Kingdoms, a locale that seems to increase Mother Duck's sorceries while dampening all other magicks. Now, however, we are beyond the influence of her spells. Outside of her kingdom, I imagine the two of us are more or less equals. And, this time, I had surprise on my side."

"Indeed," I beamed at my beloved. "Then what shall we do now?"

Norei smiled at me, dimpling prettily. "I suggest we resume running. My spell will not contain Mother Duck forever."

"Indeed!" I called to the others. "Let's go then, as quick as we can!"

We continued our flight at a brisk trot. The greater the distance we put between ourselves and Mother Duck, I reasoned, the more chance we had of escaping her altogether. Then, with any luck, we would catch up with Hubert and Alea, and perhaps even Richard the giant.

But what should we do after we rendezvoused with the others? Perhaps, as we continued to move quickly, I should try to contact my master.

I looked at the crystal ball, which I had been carrying all the while in my hand. But where had I put the incantation?

I excused myself as I reached into my pocket, but the Brownie was sound asleep, exhausted from his earlier exertions. I managed to find the parchment tucked behind him and, with some little difficulty, drew it forth. I shook the paper open with a flick of my wrist and once again read the magic words:

"Secret sphere, seashore seer,
Surely showing sunshine seeking . . ."

I had to read it "quickly and in a loud voice" according to the directions.

"Secret sphere," I began, "sheshore sheer—" No, that wasn't quite right, was it?

"Oh, dear," Snarks remarked solicitously. "Are you developing a stutter?"

"Doom," Hendrek replied forcefully. "He is using the crystal ball. Let him be."

Everyone around me quieted, waiting. The hush made me a little nervous. What if nothing happened?

I rushed through the incantation as best I could.

"Well?" Snarks asked at the conclusion of the rhyme.

"Doom," Hendrek rumbled again. "Give him time."

"Look!" Norei pointed to the crystal. "Something's happening!"

And it was. The globe, once transparent, was now filled with a gray mist, upon which I could see flashes of yellow light. But it was more than mere pyrotechnics, for the light formed itself into letters, and the letters into words.

"There is a message!" I announced, and proceeded to read aloud:

"We are," the message began, words swirling through the mist for an instant and then gone, "sorry, but we are unable . . . to complete your call . . . as spoken . . . Please release . . . the crystal . . . and try again."

"You call that a message?" Snarks asked.

"Doom," Hendrek began, but I waved them both to silence.

"Indeed," I remarked. "It is my own fault, for trying to conjure in flight. I fear I cannot run and read at the same time. I will use the crystal ball again when we stop to rest." Whenever that might be.

A loud voice hailed us from up ahead, where the forest ended at a towering cliff face.

"Hey, folks! It's us: the lady who wows all the males and the reptile with the winning scales!"

I would recognize that patter anywhere. It was Damsel and Dragon. I waved to the large purplish-blue reptile. Perhaps, when we reached them and regrouped, I would get a moment's respite to reuse the crystal.

"Oops!" an even louder voice remarked. Richard the giant peeked out from around the cliff face. "I was hiding."

"Indeed!" I shouted ahead. " 'Tis a pleasure to see you!" Now that we had left Mother Duck behind, having a giant on our side could be nothing but a boon.

"Once I jumped over the mountain, I circled around," the giant confided. "Mother Duck will never find me now!"

But another voice, clear yet distant, was carried by the breeze.

"Richard, you coward!" the woman screamed. "You won't escape me again!"

SIX

Always make the best use of your resources. Magic, escape routes, hungry demons, annoying in-laws: All can be used constructively by the creative wizard. And should you add, say, an irate client who is annoyed that an unforeseen side effect of your most recent spell has turned his wife into a chicken, well, I'm sure I don't have to tell you that the possibilities for combinations are almost limitless.

—From *No Bad Wizards:*
A Study of Sorcerers and How to Train Them, fourth edition,
by Ebenezum,
greatest wizard in the Western Kingdoms

"Oops," Richard remarked.

"Doom," Hendrek answered.

"Run!" I commanded. "If need be, to the Inland Sea!"

But then I had another thought as the rest of our party took off at a brisk trot. It had taken us a good two days to reach the Eastern Kingdoms from Vushta. There was no way we could run all the way back. I looked up at our very large companion.

"Richard, might you wait a minute?"

The giant paused mid-stride. "But Mother Duck—" he protested.

"Indeed," I replied. "I fear she might dog our footsteps forever, unless we devise a plan. She moved with astonishing speed when still in her kingdom. Even now, I imagine, she probably follows us with a pace and agility amazing for one of her advanced years. But how can any old lady, no matter how magically inclined, hope to catch up with a giant?"

"Oops," Richard responded. "I beg your pardon?"

"If you start now," I explained patiently, "you will easily outdistance Mother Duck. I imagine you could outdistance anyone, except for other giants."

Richard nodded, still dumbfounded.

I continued: "But Mother Duck is magical enough so that she might be able to overtake the rest of us, and once again subjugate us to her will."

"Doom," Hendrek interjected from some fifty paces ahead.

"And that would leave you without your newfound companions," I further explained, "who are here to help you find new direction in the world beyond the Eastern Kingdoms."

The giant nodded again, his forehead slowly uncreasing.

"I see you, Richard!" Mother Duck called again, this time louder, and closer, than before. "Wait until I get my spells on you!"

"Oops!" Richard commented with some consternation, frowning in the direction of the Eastern Kingdoms.

"Ignore her," I informed the giant. "If there was some way she could have affected you at this distance, she would have done so already."

"If you say so," the giant replied without much conviction in his voice.

"Indeed," I responded with my most reassuring tone. "As I was saying—if you are left alone, or we are left without you, we shall all surely once again fall prey to Mother Duck. But there is another way —a way we can combine your speed and our cunning—and that's if you pick us up and take us with you."

"Oops!" Richard smiled slowly, rather like a shadow creeping across the full moon. "What a good idea!" He began to pat various parts of his pants legs, producing sounds not unlike thunder echoing in the mountains.

"Indeed," I prompted. "Then my plan will work?"

"Oops," Richard answered. "It will if I have enough pockets." He gave up examining his pants and laid his hand, palm up, across half the field-size clearing. "Climb aboard."

I did as I was bade and, a moment later, found myself tucked in the giant's shirt pocket.

Richard took a tiny step forward so that he stood directly behind our fleeing company.

"Hey!" Snarks shouted with alarm. "Watch your feet!"

"Oops," Richard rumbled, but I cut him off, quickly explaining, in as loud a voice as I could muster, my plans to the others.

"Oh, my clever Wuntvor!" Norei enthused. Even though I was quite some distance away, I could still imagine the sweet smile upon her lovely face. I wondered for an instant if there was some way to discreetly ask Richard to place the young witch in the same pocket with me.

The dwarves cheered as well:

"Hi hicket, hi hicket,
That Wuntvor's just the ticket!"

Everyone else, with the possible exception of Guxx, seemed generally in favor of the plan. Even Hendrek's "Doom" sounded somewhat more cheerful than usual.

"Don't you go anywhere, Richard!" Mother Duck's ever-more-forceful voice called from somewhere not all that far to our rear.

"Commence!" Guxx commanded his drum-wielding cohort. Brax beat, but both were scooped up immediately by Richard, and any further drum beating and declamation was soon lost behind the thick fabric of the giant's britches.

Richard hurriedly picked up the remaining members of my retinue, stuffing them in various pockets upon his person. There was some grumbling among the companions, especially when Snarks found he was going to have to share pocket space with the unicorn, while Jeffrey exclaimed that someone with the stature of a talking wolf should surely be shown to a pocket above the belt. Still, only Hubert refused to be carried away, saying it would be better for all concerned if he and Alea flew on ahead.

"Indeed," I remarked as Richard pocketed the last of the dwarves in a small denim envelope slightly above his knee. "If we are all tucked firmly away—"

"If you know what's good for you, Richard," Mother Duck's very forceful voice interrupted, "you'll stand there until I get a little closer!"

"Oops!" Richard replied as he took off at an earthshaking pace.

We reached the Inland Sea in a little under three minutes. Richard stopped abruptly on the shore.

"Pardon me," he murmured, "but I'm a little afraid of water."

I assured the giant it was quite all right, and pointed to Vushta in the near distance. We were surrounded by silence, the only sounds the lapping of the waves by Richard's feet and the screams of gulls circling his brow. We had left Mother Duck far behind.

"Indeed," I said at last, reluctantly breaking into the first peaceful moment we had experienced since the heavens knew when. "It is perhaps time to place my companions and myself back on the ground. If we are all to proceed to Vushta, I believe it is advisable that I lead the way to provide the introductions."

"Oops," Richard nodded in understanding. "Unintroduced giants tend to bring out the worst in people."

The giant proceeded to unload us all from his various pockets.

"Begin!" Guxx screamed as he hit the ground. This time, he would not be denied.

> "Guxx Unfufadoo, dissheveled demon,
> Does not belong in giant's pocket;
> Has words to say to those who'l'l listen!
> 'Those that don't will feel his anger!' "

"The big fellow couldn't be the slightest bit annoyed?" Snarks ventured.

"And justifiably so!" Jeffrey snapped. "Here he is, the former ruler of the Netherhells, and he got a pocket even lower than mine."

"Indeed!" I said, hoping to halt this line of conversation before it became another full-fledged argument. Guxx Unfufadoo, the former Grand Hoohah (whatever that was) of all the Netherhells, was used to being obeyed, feared and fled from. He was not used to being ignored; and that was what my companions and I had been doing ever since Death arrived upon the scene. Still, there was no time to lose. Was there some way to assuage this demon's anger while we went about finding a way to save my master?

"Continue!" Guxx roared.

> "Guxx Unfufadoo, annoyed demon,
> Will stand no more of this abusive
> Treatment that's unfit for heroes,
> Wants a say in future ventures!"

Oh, dear. This was worse than I thought. Guxx wanted a say in our decision making? Somehow, I had to quiet the demon down now.

"Indeed," I began again. But now that he had gotten started, Guxx would let no one interrupt.

"Amplify!" he shrieked. Brax beat the drum even more vigorously.

"Guxx Unfufadoo, angered demon,
Has decided to speak loudly
Will decree that all shall listen,
Will stand alone as Wuntvor's partner!"

Stand alone? Wuntvor's partner? Guxx flexed his long, razor-sharp claws to punctuate his demands. His statements were becoming more outrageous with every declamation. But what could I do to stop them?

"There you are!" Hubert the dragon called from somewhere above. "It's taken us a minute to catch up with you. I must say, Richard, when you want to move, you move!"

"Oops," Richard agreed.

Hubert swooped down to land.

"Overwhelm!" the former Grand Hoohah bellowed.

"Guxx Unfufadoo, outraged demon—"

"Someone's declaiming?" Hubert remarked brightly as he landed. "Does that mean it's time for a little musical number?"

"Has no time for—
Musical number?"

Guxx's voice died in his throat.

"Indeed," I insisted to both demon and dragon. "No."

I looked about at my remaining companions. "There are obviously many issues that must be resolved concerning our quest. However, I should suggest that, rather than pausing to discuss our problems in the wild, it would be much better to debate them in the much safer confines of the College of Wizards in Vushta."

"Wuntvor?" Norei said softly. "Might I make a suggestion?"

I asked her to proceed.

"I was wondering," she remarked gently, "should we go to Vushta? There might be a few problems. The city might be full of wizards, but when we left them, they were all sneezing."

"Indeed," I replied, giving myself a moment to think, something that had been virtually impossible during our recent flight and subsequent demon declaiming. As usual, my beloved was all too correct. My master's malady had been passed on to the other wizards of Vushta, a malady that caused each and every wizard to sneeze violently when confronted by a mystic spell or a magical being. They had had enough trouble before, with unicorns and demons in their midsts. I shuddered now to think how the amassed noses of greater Vushta would react if we brought a giant among them.

Worse still, I had been sent by these amassed wizards to the Eastern Kingdoms to enlist the aid of Mother Duck in our fight against the Netherhells and, if possible, to see if she might know of a cure for the wizards' affliction. How would the magicians feel now if I returned to them empty-handed?

It was a quandary. I glanced about at my fellows, wondering if any of them could offer the advice I needed. But the one man whose wisdom was sorely needed was not among us. I sighed.

What would my master do?

I thought about the dwarves' gift, now safely tucked away in my pack. Mother Duck was miles behind, and Death seemed unlikely to make an appearance so close to a place teaming with life as the City of a Thousand Forbidden Delights. Perhaps it was time once again to consult the crystal ball.

"Indeed," I said to the others. "You have brought up weighty matters. It is time, perhaps, to consult powers greater than my own."

I opened the pack and, after pausing briefly to pet the ferret, extracted the globe. I reached into my pocket and nudged past the still-sleeping Brownie to retrieve the folded piece of parchment. I silently reread the incantation:

> Secret sphere, seashore seer,
> Surely showing sunshine seeking.
> Simply said, the shaft is shed,
> Spouting spells that send us shrieking.

I took a deep breath. It was now or never. But I would say the words more carefully than before, cautious to avoid the strange message I received when I first attempted to use the mystic crystal. Perhaps it wouldn't be as quickly spoken as the incantation instructions urged, but I would manage somehow.

And manage I did, on only the third try. I peered, deep within the magic ball.

There was something happening! In fact, I could hear voices! I brought the milky globe close to my ear so that I might better discern the words. The one speaking now had a high and brittle tone, like that of a woman of advanced years. Yes! I understood her quite clearly now:

"Then I said to the swami, 'If you call that fortunetelling, I've got some swampland I could sell—' Hey, who's that?"

So the mystic globe discerned my presence! But how should I address this magic ball? Politely, I decided after a moment, but directly.

"Indeed," I replied deferentially. "I am Wuntvor the apprentice. I'm trying to reach my master, the great wizard Ebenezum."

"He is Wuntvor the apprentice, trying to reach the great wizard," the voice mimicked. "Hey, don't you know this is a party crystal? What do you mean, eavesdropping on my conversation?"

"Party crystal?" I replied. "Eavesdropping?" But I could concoct no coherent reply. I could only think of one thing: that this woman would keep me from reaching my master!

"But madam!" I pleaded. "It is a matter of life or death!"

"Life, smife," the voice snorted. "That's what they all say. Well, I'll have you know that Mabel and I haven't had a good conversation in over a week!"

"But Vushta—" I sputtered. "Sneezing wizards! Imminent demon attacks from the Netherhells! My master, trapped in the Kingdom of the Dead!"

"What is this, a nuisance call?" The voice in the crystal was getting annoyed. "There's no need to get uppity. And there's no reason for you to feel put out. If you can't stand to wait your turn, you should have gotten yourself a private ball. Now, go away! I have a conversation to finish. —So, anyways, the Swami says to me, 'How dare you! A curse upon your firstborn!' Well, Mabel, I just had to laugh. You know how my eldest is, always taking his mother for granted. Maybe, I thought, if he has a curse on him, he'll write to me for a change—"

It was hopeless. I placed the glass globe back in my sack. What should I do?

The wind was picking up. Sand whipped up from the beach, stinging my face. I worried about this sudden change in the weather.

Death often announced itself with the wind. Did I hear some sounds carried by this stiffening breeze, sounds like boulders being ground to dust? No, that wasn't quite it. There was something else there instead, something faint, a woman's voice calling a single name.

Richard.

I shivered. It seemed as if Death was near, and Mother Duck wasn't far behind.

"Sounds pretty bad," Snarks agreed as he stepped forward from my companions. "That crazy old lady is coming for the giant, and it looks like we might get another visit from the death of the party. There's no way we can go back to Vushta, 'cause we flubbed the quest. And let's face it, it wasn't even much of a quest in the first place. And then there's that wizard of yours, but I guess, if you feel you've got to save him, you've got to save him."

I nodded. The demon had, in his own inimitable way, summarized our situation.

"You agree?" Snarks continued. "Very well. I think it's time you listened to me."

"Indeed?" I replied.

The demon nodded in turn, showing his mottled gray teeth in a fiendish smile.

"I have a plan."

SEVEN

There is absolutely no truth to the rumors of impropriety. And those seven women leaving my room in quick succession was simply a coincidence. If you'll excuse me—you're blocking my escape route.

—Further testimony from Ebenezum,
greatest wizard in the Western Kingdoms,
concerning Wizardgate

"Indeed?"

"It has to do with my extensive religious background," the demon confided.

I stared at the small green figure. We had first met the demon when he was part of a small hermetic order that somehow had bent the rules sufficiently so that they not only spoke to other people but charged them to stay overnight at their elaborate hovel. And that order had had a close, personal relationship with a very minor deity.

"Do you mean?" I blurted.

"Yes," Snarks confirmed. "Death believes it has us trapped, for, so long as we are upon this mortal plain, it can surround us at any moment. Even worse, while we are avoiding Death, we might run directly into the extremely annoying Mother Duck. And Vushta cannot save us, for the city is filled with sneezing wizards. There is only one hope. We must appeal to a higher authority. We must contact Plaugg, the moderately glorious!"

"Indeed?" I replied, stunned by the audacity of the demon's suggestion. "But isn't that going to be rather difficult?" I remembered how long it took Plaugg to pay attention the last time.

"Unfortunately correct," Snarks agreed. "Plaugg, praise his just barely illustrious name, might be a semiomnipotent deity, but he isn't a very attentive one. I have a feeling it has something to do with an unhappy homelife. But now is not the time for idle ecclesiastical speculation. It is, rather, time to contact Plaugg."

The demon sidled even closer to me, speaking in a voice barely above a whisper. "We who worship the intermittently influential gods have a saying: If you can't get the deity to come to you, you'd better go to the deity. Besides, you are in constant danger when on this mortal coil. I suggest, therefore, that you leave this coil for a friendlier clime. And where could you go? You've already gone down once. Now it's time to go up."

"Up?" I queried, even more flabbergasted than before. "You mean up in the heavens, among the deities?"

Snarks waved away my objections with a flick of a sickly green claw. "Well, surely, that's not such a big deal. Plaugg, bless his modestly exalted being, is pretty low on the ladder up there, I assure you. We should be able to sneak in without any trouble whatsoever."

"We?" I said. "Sneak in?"

"Simply leave all the fine points to me," Snarks assured me. "And I'm afraid I have to go along. After all, I'm the one with the history of Plaugg worship, praise his reasonably adequate name."

"Indeed," I commented. I felt I needed a moment to consider this radical suggestion. I folded my arms across my chest in an attempt to protect myself from the increasingly chill breeze.

My beloved stroked my cheek, a gesture I instantly wished she would repeat any number of times. She whispered my name, so common-sounding when spoken by others, but music when it issued from her lips.

"Indeed?" I queried, my throat suddenly dry.

"As surprising as Snark's suggestion may be," Norei ventured gently, "I fear it may be our only hope." She pointed at the shifting sands: "Look."

I followed her pointing finger and saw the words etched across the beach:

"Wuntvor. You cannot escape."

They were Death's words, formed by his control of the elements. Death was again carried by the wind.

"Doom," Hendrek muttered darkly. "Will this never end?"

But the breeze also carried other things, like the ever-strengthening voice of Mother Duck:

"Richard! Don't you dare move again!"

"Oops," Richard moaned. "Won't I ever get away?"

"Indeed!" I called to the others. "We must act quickly!" But what, I thought, should we do?

"We will need the assistance of the others," Snarks resumed hastily. "Hubert, for one."

"Me?" the dragon said. "This little green person, who cannot even appreciate the fine points of vaudeville, actually wants help from me?"

"Certainly," Snarks replied, for once not answering the large reptile's sarcasm. "We need someone to fly us to heaven."

"To heaven?" Alea questioned nervously. "Are you sure that can be done?"

Snarks smiled. "Trust me."

"Heaven?" Hubert shook his great wings and spouted a gout of flame. "Why not? It's worth a try. Think of the publicity value if it works!"

"And we'll get a brand-new audience besides!" Alea added, convinced by the demon, and dragon.

"Alas," Snarks quickly clarified. "I'm afraid that the damsel will have to stay behind."

"What?" Hubert protested. "And break up the act?"

"There's no room," Snarks explained.

"I could hold on to Wuntie's waist," Alea ventured. "You'd hardly know I was there!"

Snarks shook his sickly green head. "Too much weight."

"Too much weight?" Alea exploded. "Why, you undersized excuse for a—"

"Sorry," the demon interrupted, "but once we go, we have to go in a hurry. We want to get beyond Death's domain as quickly as possible."

"Beyond Death's domain?" Hubert said doubtfully. "I don't think I can fly that fast."

"Oh, I've thought of that, too." Snarks looked up at the giant. "Richard?"

"Oops," the giant replied.

"How are you at tossing things?" the demon asked.

"Well," the giant considered. "My aim's not too good. But I can toss a pretty fair distance."

"The very answer I was looking for. We're going to need you to toss the dragon, with Wuntvor and me strapped on his back, straight up in the air."

"Straight up?" The giant looked doubtfully into the sky. "I'll try."

"Interject!" a gruff voice screamed, accompanied by rapid drum-beats.

"Guxx Unfufadoo, confused demon,
Wants to know just what is happening;
Wants to know how he fits into
Wuntvor's plan to save his master!"

"Indeed!" I spoke quickly, for I knew that, with Death and Mother Duck nearby, there was no time to waste. "You will have a most important role, Guxx. For, when Hubert, Snarks and I are sent aloft, we will need others down below to lead the rest of my companions to safety. I have decided to appoint Norei the witch as your leader, for her magic might be needed to save you all. However, we will need more than magic to see us through. I therefore pronounce you, Guxx Unfufadoo, as Chief Protector and Keeper of the Claws for my companions. It is now your duty to see that no one comes to harm!"

"Comment!" Guxx commanded.

Brax beat a rapid rhythm.

"Guxx Unfufadoo, honored demon,
Likes to be called the protector;
Enjoys the chance to do some shredding;
Thinks the job's right up his alley!"

"Indeed, I replied, glad that I had at least temporarily satisfied the large demon. I turned to my beloved. "Once we are aloft, I think that Death will no longer bother you. For the time being, at least, he wants only me. Therefore, you need only avoid Mother Duck. I believe the best way to accomplish this is to take the remains of our party back into Vushta, and inform the wizards there as to the—uh—direction my quest has taken. Even in their impaired state, I think that the magic of those wizards, combined with whatever spells you might muster, will easily keep Mother Duck at bay."

"Wuntvor!" Norei enthused. "What a good plan!"

"I like a man who can take control!" Alea agreed.

The Seven Other Dwarves chimed in:

"Hi hense, hi hense,
He makes a lot of sense."

"Doom," Hendrek remarked. "I shall use my mighty warclub Headbasher to smash our way to Vushta if I must, wading waist-deep through the broken, bloody bodies of our foes!"

"And if that doesn't work," Brax interjected, "I have a small but sophisticated selection of previously owned weapons, available at ridiculously marked-down prices to any here who need them. I mean, I'm practically giving them away!"

"And I shall lead them into Vushta as quickly as I can," Norei said as she leaned close to me. Her lips brushed against my nose. "Now go! Get up on that dragon and fly!"

I remembered to breathe. My lungs had stopped all of their own accord when my beloved's lips had touched my face. I nodded dumbly and staggered over toward the dragon. My nose tingled where Norei had kissed it. Snarks was right behind me, pushing me a bit here and there when I wandered away from the proper path.

"I'll add my services, too," Jeffery the wolf assured me as I climbed upon Hubert's back. "I'm not averse to eating a foe in the line of duty. And who knows, maybe some of the foes will be pigs—or grandmothers!"

The unicorn trotted up beside Jeffrey as Snarks clambered up behind me. The beast gave a single shake of its blinding white mane.

"I shall use my magnificent golden horn in our defense as well." The unicorn sighed. "It all goes so quickly. Maybe when you get back we might find a quiet corner where you might"—the beast paused meaningfully for a second— "sit—and I might"—it paused again— "lay my—heavy head for a moment upon your—" It paused one more time, almost too overcome to continue. The last word came out as a whisper: "—lap?"

"Indeed," I answered, taken aback by the beast's pitiful sincerity. "Perhaps someday—"

"Leaving so soon?" asked a voice as dry as decaying leaves. Death's voice.

"Go!" Norei demanded. "We'll come up with a way to distract the specter—somehow!"

Death laughed, and I turned to see the skeletal figure standing on the beach, beckoning.

"You do want to see your master again, don't you, Wuntvor? You do want to save your master? Perhaps I should take you now. Perhaps I should take you all now."

"Oh, no, you don't!" exclaimed the imperious tones of Mother Duck. "I saw them first!"

I turned my head the other way. There was Mother Duck, rapidly striding toward us across the sand.

"Indeed," I said to the demon behind me. "I think now would be a good time to take our leave."

"Richard," Snarks called out to the giant, "if you would?"

"Oops," the giant replied, picking Hubert up with both hands. "Here you go!"

Richard grunted as he tossed up in the air with all his might. Hubert shrieked, a mixture of surprise and fright:

"Dragons aren't supposed to go this fast!"

I craned my neck to look behind. Richard and my other companions disappeared in the distance before I could blink.

"Oh, boy!" Snarks cheered. "We're really flying now! Nobody can stop us anymore!"

I clutched the dragon's scales for dear life. I was all too afraid that the demon was right.

EIGHT

What do you mean, wizards cannot foretell the future? While it may be true that some of us are not as skilled at prophesying as certain other mythological professionals who make that sort of thing their life's work, still your average mage is quite adept at looking into times to come. An example? If you insist. I see through the power of my mystic might that you shall grow older, and so shall I. We shall have our good days, and not so good days. You want something more specific? Very well. I see something happening to you any minute now, something that you cannot avoid.

You will soon have a wizard collecting his fee.

—From *Wizardhood*
(Wizard's Digest Condensed Edition), fourth edition,
by Ebenezum,
greatest wizard in the Western Kingdoms

I had remarked before that things sometimes seemed to go too fast for me. This was the first time, however, that I feared they were going too fast for everyone.

"Weehah!" Snarks whooped behind me. "This is the way to travel! You know, you'd have to spend good money to go on a ride like this down in the Netherhells!"

I might have been better able to appreciate the demon's point of view if the dragon who carried us hadn't been screaming so much. Getting away from the twin threats of Death and Mother Duck had seemed of paramount importance but an instant before, and, the heavens knew, Richard's muscular toss had certainly gotten us on our way. However, having one's mode of transportation constantly subject to shrieking fits did tend to put a damper on one's confidence. I did my best to hang on, hoping that things would calm down eventually.

And slow down we did, after what seemed to be an eternity.

"Oh, thank goodness!" Hubert exclaimed as he unfolded his wings and flapped them gently to stabilize our flight. "Wind resistance has brought us under control."

"Do we have to slow down?" Snarks whined. "This is the most fun I've had since skinny-dipping in the slime pits!"

"Indeed," I interjected, trying to put the whole thing into perspective. "I feel it was for the best that we got away from the situation down below as quickly as possible. Now, however, that we have achieved some distance from our initial danger, perhaps it is time to fly at a more reasonable, controlled speed, so that we might modify our direction to better meet our goal."

"Awww!" Snarks complained.

"A brilliant speech!" Hubert commented. "Have you ever thought of going into politics? Or perhaps the even more difficult field of theater management?"

"His explanations are certainly long-winded enough!" the demon agreed.

"But your recent declaration brings up a small problem," Hubert continued, choosing to ignore Snarks.

"Indeed?" I replied. "Well, whatever it is, I'm sure we can work it out among us."

"That's right!" Snarks enthused. "I'm the Plaugg worshipper around here, praise his ever so vaguely noble name."

"Well," the dragon went on a bit sheepishly. "You mentioned direction? You mentioned control?"

"Indeed?" I prompted.

"Well, both of them are good and noble goals," the dragon went on. "But neither is much use if you don't know where you're going." Hubert cleared his throat, producing a fair quantity of smoke. "Uh, where exactly is heaven, anyways?"

I glanced back at my small green companion.

"That is not the sort of question you should ask a demon," Snarks answered a bit huffily.

"Weren't you the one who was supposed to be the expert on Plaugg?" I reminded the demon.

Snarks nodded. "Praise his marginally magnificent name. I always assumed that heaven was—you know—up. But I'm not the expert here. Hubert's the one who's put in all the flying time."

"Hey," the dragon interjected. "I'm in entertainment, not tourism.

If you wanted a travel itinerary, you should have consulted my brother Morty."

"Morty?" Snarks asked.

"What's the matter with Morty?" Hubert bristled. "It's a perfectly good dragon name. Perhaps not as distinctive as Hubert, but then, how many names are?"

"I refuse to answer that question at this great a height," Snarks responded.

"Indeed," I interjected once again. "I'm afraid this line of discourse is getting us nowhere near our goal. There must be some way we can find heaven!"

"I can't fly up forever," Hubert agreed. "My wings will get tired."

"So what do you want?" Snarks remarked derisively. "A crystal ball?"

"Indeed?" I remarked, with renewed enthusiasm. "I *have* a crystal ball! Snarks?" I pointed to the pack on my back. "If you would?"

"You call *that* thing a crystal ball?" the demon replied. "Well, I suppose, if I must."

I heard the rustle of fabric as Snarks opened my pack.

"Eep eep! Eep eep eep!"

"Yowp!" Snarks exclaimed. "This thing is booby-trapped!"

I apologized to the demon. I had forgotten about my watch-ferret. I suggested that perhaps it would be better if Snarks pulled the pack from my back and handed it to me.

"Gladly," the demon answered as he gingerly handed the pack, once again closed, over my shoulder so that I could get a firm grip on it.

"Tell me," Snarks added. "Do you always keep small animals tucked amidst your clothing?"

"Indeed," I replied, opening the pack for myself. "You never know when they'll come in handy."

"Eep!" the ferret responded. I petted the small furry creature for a moment, then retrieved the magic crystal.

"Here goes nothing," I murmured rhetorically as I reached in my pocket for the incantation.

"You can say that again," Snarks murmured back.

There was a lump in my pocket. I had quite forgotten, in my haste to get away, that I had a sleeping Brownie upon my person; and did, in fact, still have a sleeping Brownie nestled in my pocket. I pulled the direction from behind the fellow's inert form. Tap muttered something about shoes.

I held the crystal ball with my right hand, the incantation with my left. But now that I once again had the magic sphere, what should I do with it? Should I attempt to contact Plaugg? But what if a crystal of this sort could not speak with a deity, no matter how minor? I had had enough trouble with this mystic device already to discourage me from further experimentation. No, I should use this glass globe for its original purpose, to contact my master in the Kingdom of the Dead. Ebenezum would know the way to heaven. My master knew almost everything.

"Now, no talking, please," I warned the demon. "I must concentrate so that the spell will work correctly."

Snarks, seemingly on the verge of adding a comment or two, only nodded.

Very well. I read the incantation once more:

> "Secret sphere, seashore seer,
> Surely showing sunshine seeking.
> Simply said, the shaft is shed,
> Spouting spells that send us shrieking."

I gazed deep within the crystal ball. Ebenezum, I thought, let me contact Ebenezum.

There were no voices this time warning me away, nor messages that had misspoken the spell. This time I would get through! I gazed intently at the globe, which was suddenly filled with a dense smoke. From somewhere, I heard a distant ringing, then an audible click.

After a moment's silence, the ringing began again, fainter than the first time. Then another click, and nothing. I thought I might have heard even fainter voices through the silence, but their conversation was not loud enough for me to make out the words. At last, the ball clicked again, followed by a ringing so quiet that it was barely discernible. I realized how far the powers of this globe had to reach to contact the Kingdom of the Dead. I began to feel that the crystal's search for my master might take forever.

There was another click, another moment of silence, and then a voice began to speak, faint but discernible. It was not my master's voice, but that of a stranger! What could this mean? It spoke quickly, in clipped, impersonal tones, and I listened carefully, fearful of what it might tell me about Ebenezum:

"All mystic circuits are busy at the present time. Please put down your crystal and try again later."

"Oof!" Hubert remarked. Snarks and I were jostled forcibly as the dragon's feet connected with something solid. The crystal ball flew from my hands, and was lost almost instantly in the cloud bank that surrounded us. Apparently, we had landed somewhere.

"My ball!" I shouted after the recently disappeared device.

"No great loss," Snarks replied.

To my surprise, I found that I agreed with the demon.

Hubert swiveled his head about to regard the two of us.

"Excuse me, fellows, but I simply had to take a breather."

"Indeed," I said, looking at our cloud-shrouded surroundings. "Do you have any idea where we are?"

"Of course," Hubert replied confidently. "Up here is dragon territory. I brought us to the second highest peak in the world, and someplace that we might get some information."

"Indeed?" I answered, doing my best to discern anything in our vicinity save the never-ending grayness. "There are habitations hereabouts?"

"There are more than simple habitations," the dragon sniffed dramatically. "We are near the home of the Three Fates. They can tell us everything we need to know"—he paused for effect—"and perhaps a few things we might wish to stay ignorant of."

"Doom," Snarks intoned. I glanced back at the small green demon.

"Hey," he shrugged. "Hendrek may be stuck down below, but he's with us in spirit."

"Indeed," I replied. "Hubert, if you will lead us to the fates?"

"No need," the dragon answered. "The fates shall find us."

And with that, as if the fates had been listening, the weather changed dramatically. The fog burned away in an instant, and we found ourselves upon a sun-drenched, windswept mountainside, a hundred yards away from an imposing building made of shining black stone.

"The Temple of the Fates," Hubert explained.

"Who seeks the wisdom of the fates?" a woman's voice called.

"Three humble travelers," I shouted back, "searching for the way to heaven!"

"A worthy goal!" the woman replied. "You may approach the temple!"

"Indeed," I whispered to the others. "Perhaps Snarks and I should dismount. I don't know if riding into a temple like this on a dragon would be considered proper etiquette."

Neither of my companions disagreed, so the demon and I slid from the dragon's back and walked up the gentle mountain slope to the imposing edifice. We mounted the building's first step.

"You may enter!" the voice cried from within. "And we will answer three questions—no more, no less—although we do apologize for being a little short-handed at the moment."

I took the final two steps quickly, and entered the building through a great, round portal. The walls within were of the deepest black, yet somehow glistened with an eerie light. I heard Snarks at my heels, as our two sets of feet thumped across the marble-hard floors.

"Turn," two voices spoke as one, "and face the fates."

I did as I was told, and saw from the corner of my eye that Hubert had stuck his head into the portal behind us. What I saw next, though, caused me to stop all movement whatsoever, save the opening of my mouth.

Two women stood on adjoining pedestals, if women they truly were. For they wore long robes, perhaps of gray, or perhaps of white or black, or perhaps of every color at once or no color at all. They were tall and lithe, with long-fingered hands and delicate feet, and long hair cascading across their shoulders, although the tresses also resisted any categorization as to color or texture.

But I could accept their hair and clothing readily enough. What really surprised me were their faces—if that was what you could call the orbs that sat atop their shoulders. Not that their heads did not have eyes, noses, ears and mouths, but that they had too many. But that did not explain it, either, for at any moment one of their faces would only hold two eyes, one nose, one mouth. It was just that one instant the eyes would be small and blue, and then change to a pair that was large and black, and then transform again to green and almond-shaped. The mouth, the nose, the cheeks, the chin, every part of the face, would likewise re-form, so that one visage would be replaced by another totally new, completely different. And it happened so quickly, one likeness, then another, and a fourth, a fifth, an eighth, a tenth; the features fled across their faces like clouds across the sun. It was as if their faces were the face of every woman in the world, perhaps every woman who had ever lived or would ever live. But after a moment I realized that even that was too simple, for the faces were too many and varied; there were men there as well, and children; everyone young and old, every shape and size and color.

These, I thought, were the fates.

The one on the left inclined her head.

"I am Victoria."

The one on the right bowed slightly.

"And I am Mary Jane. We are the Two Fates."

"Normally," Victoria added, "we are the Three Fates. Unfortunately, our sister, Hortense, is not with us at the moment. She is—" The fate hesitated, unable to continue.

"On vacation," her sister fate finished for her. "She complained of overwork."

"Being a fate can be trying at times," Victoria admitted. "Still—"

"Oh, come, now," Mary Jane chided. "Hortense was becoming really frazzled. She needed a break—"

"The fates watch over all eternity!" Victoria exclaimed. "How can you take a break from that?"

"It's all a matter of attitude," Mary Jane insisted. "I'm sure Hortense went somewhere warm and sunny and quiet. Although I do wish she'd drop us a line."

"But we are making our petitioners wait!" Victoria reminded her sister. She waved graciously at me and my companions. "Our petty little squabbles should not affect you. At least, I hope they don't affect you very much."

"What else can we do?" Mary Jane asked. "We'd best get on with it."

"Very well." Victoria sighed. "Remember, we shall answer three questions—no more, no less! So ask, mortals, and the fates shall reply." She looked to Mary Jane, who nodded in response. The Two Fates climbed onto adjoining platforms, leaving a third pedestal empty.

"Indeed," I answered, for I wanted to make sure it was I who asked the questions. I thought for an instant what I should ask first, but that answer was obvious. I had to ask the fates what the crystal ball had failed to tell me.

"How shall I find my master, the great wizard Ebenezum?"

"Here is the answer!" Victoria and Mary Jane shouted in unison.

"If ye shall seek the land of Death," Victoria began.

"And carefully ye save your breath—" Mary Jane continued.

This was followed by silence. The fates looked at us expectantly.

"That's it?" Snarks demanded.

"Is that your second question?" the fates asked in unison.

"Indeed, no!" I hastily interjected. "Snarks was but remarking on the nature of your prophecy, for it seemed somehow incomplete."

"I'm afraid so," Victoria agreed. "Usually, there is a third line that completes the prophecy, but with Hortense gone—"

"Quite right," Mary Jane continued. "There's no one here to finish our prediction!"

"Indeed!" I said. "But couldn't one of you recite the third line?"

"Indeed not!" Mary Jane chided.

"Entirely out of the question!" Victoria sniffed. "There is a precise division of labor here, and we don't want to step on any toes. Each fate recites one third of the prophesy—no more, no less."

"That's how we've always done it," Mary Jane agreed, "and it's how we always will do it. After all, we fates have to live with one another throughout eternity!"

"Indeed." I pondered this new problem. "Let me ask you this—not officially, mind you—what if I were to ask you that same question a second time? Could one of you then deliver the missing portion of the prophecy?"

"Oh, my, no," Mary Jane murmured. "What an absurd idea."

"I'm afraid not," Victoria added more solemnly. "Prophecy is a tricky thing, you see. It's all based on the inspiration of the moment. If we don't get it the first time, it's lost forever."

"So that's all we get?" Snarks demanded. "Two thirds of a prophecy?"

"Well," Mary Jane huffed. "You needn't take that attitude!"

"I should say so!" Victoria added. "What you received is certainly better than no prophecy at all!"

"It is?" Snarks replied, not at all convinced.

"Why, of course!" Victoria insisted.

"Prophecies are always stated in the form of rhyming riddles, anyway," Mary Jane added.

"Quite correct," Victoria added. "So this riddle is simply a bit more difficult than those we usually speak. But the problem shouldn't be insurmountable."

"Exactly!" Mary Jane enthused. "Especially with the rhyme scheme of the first two lines. Now, let's see, my prediction was 'And carefully ye save your breath—' "

"And mine was 'If ye shall seek the land of Death,' " Victoria added.

"So discovering the third line should be simplicity itself!" Mary Jane smiled with her many mouths. "Simply think of something that rhymes with breath and death!"

But Victoria frowned. "Actually, there isn't all that much that rhymes with breath and death."

The fate was quite correct in that assumption. I could think of no rhymes at all.

"It could be breath or death again," Mary Jane added uncertainly. "Rhyming's tricky that way."

"Indeed!" I remarked, trying hard to keep despair from my voice. "Is there no other rhyme?"

"Of course there is!" Hubert rumbled from where his head rested on the portal. "Shibboleth!"

"Shibboleth?" Snarks asked.

"A legitimate word," Victoria responded.

"Quite possibly the answer," Mary Jane added. "Let's see:

"If ye shall seek the land of Death,
And carefully ye save your breath,
Da da da da da shibboleth!"

She nodded, quite pleased with herself. "I don't see why not."

"I came upon the word in my experience in the legitimate theater," the dragon explained proudly. "You learn a great deal when you trod the boards with true thespians!"

"Indeed," I queried, "what does the word mean?"

"Mean? Shibboleth?" The dragon puffed a pensive plume of smoke. "The theater is a hectic place. I barely have time to learn my lines. You can't expect me to understand them as well!"

"Don't look at me," Snarks added. "We didn't have any shibboleths at all in the Netherhells—unless there were some hiding in the slime pits."

I turned to the fates.

"Do you perchance know the meaning of the word?"

"Is that your second question?" the Two Fates replied as one.

"No, no, certainly not!" I insisted. "The second question is something entirely different." I studied the two women for a moment. "Before I ask that second question, however, I do have the slightest procedural inquiry. I gather, from our earlier discussion, that that sort of question is allowed?"

The fates glanced at each other, their flickering faces twin masks of thought.

Victoria turned to look at me first. "Well, in this case, I suppose so."

Mary Jane nodded. "With Hortense gone, we do have to bend the rules a little."

"Very well," I replied, pointing at the pedestals on which they stood. "It appears that what part of the prophecy you speak is dependent on your positions on those platforms?"

"Very astute," Victoria remarked. "We always foretell left to right."

"Indeed," I answered. "Therefore, since the two of you are standing on the left-hand and central pillars, you will be able to tell me the first two thirds of my prophecy!"

"You're very good at this!" Mary Jane said brightly. "You know, with a mind like that, you could apply yourself and guess that riddle!"

"Indeed," I said. "Perhaps in a few minutes. First, I need to ask a boon."

"A boon?" Victoria frowned.

"We usually don't do those," Mary Jane explained. "We tend to specialize in questions."

"I realize that," I replied, maintaining my patience as I had seen my master maintain his a hundred times before. "But this is a small boon, and would cause you little trouble. I simply ask, if you please, if Mary Jane would move from the central pedestal to that on the right? Then, when I ask a question, I should be able to get both the beginning and the end of your prophecy."

The fates looked at each other again.

"I suppose so—"

"Do you think Hortense would—"

"Why would she care? She's off sunning herself someplace!"

"Very well, mortal," the two of them answered in unison. " 'Tis the least we can do."

Mary Jane stepped over to the right-hand pillar. Victoria waited a moment while her sister smoothed her robes. Then both turned to face me and my companions. Mary Jane spoke next:

"Now we shall answer two questions—no more, no less. Ask mortals, and the fates shall reply!"

"Indeed," I said again. But what should I ask? Perhaps, if I phrased the substance of my first question differently, their reply would give me different clues, allowing me to solve the riddles of both their prophecies. It was certainly worth a try.

"*Where* shall I find my master, the great wizard Ebenezum?"

"Here is the answer!" the Two Fates shouted together.

"Ye shall ever higher go—" Victoria began.

There was a moment of silence.

"And then directions they will show!" Mary Jane concluded triumphantly.

The fates glanced at each other.

"Doesn't work much better, does it?" Victoria admitted.

Mary Jane nodded. "That bit missing in the middle does seem important."

"Still," Victoria volunteered, "go and show have a lot better rhymes than shibboleth. Blow, flow, snow—"

"Flambeau, undertow, outgrow—" Mary Jane added helpfully.

"Mistletoe, overthrow—" Victoria mentioned. "Why, the possibilities are virtually endless!" But her enthusiasm deflated almost immediately. "Oh, dear, that could be even more of a problem, couldn't it?"

"Indeed—" I began.

"No, no!" Victoria interrupted. "There's no need for you to even mention it! These prophecies of ours do tend to build. I'll move over to the central pillar of my own accord. That way, next time you ask a question, you'll get the most important part of our foretelling!"

The fate stepped over to the next pedestal. "It's too bad about Hortense. I don't suppose any of you have any prediction experience? No, you don't look like the type."

"It is a shame," Mary Jane added. "If only we had something or someone to fill in on the third platform. Even a crystal ball would do!"

I felt a sudden urge to clear my throat.

"Indeed," Snarks remarked.

The fates looked at me with concern. "You'd better watch out there," Victoria cautioned. "It's very easy to catch cold in the mountain air."

I assured the fates that I was as well as could be expected under the circumstances. Perhaps, I suggested, it was time to get on with the prophecies.

"Very well," Victoria replied. "Now we shall answer one question— no more, no less. Ask mortal, and let the fates reply!"

"Indeed," I said for what—I must admit—I was glad was the final time. I had gotten nowhere asking about my master. Perhaps, then, I should ask about my other pressing concern, and hope there was something—anything—in the answer that I might find useful. I spoke again:

"How might I defeat Death, and keep him from taking me prisoner?"

"Here is the answer!" the Two Fates cried with finality.

There was a moment of silence.

"You will do just as you please," Victoria announced.

"And manage all of Death's decrees!" Mary Jane concluded.

"That was even worse than the other ones!" Snarks exclaimed.

"Oh, come on, now," Hubert chided the demon. "Give them credit. It's always hard when you break up an act. And yet they go on with the show! What troopers!"

"No," Mary Jane interjected. "The small obnoxious fellow was right. If anything, that prophecy was even more incomplete than the first two."

Victoria looked uncomfortably at her sister fate. "Well, maybe we can come up with something. It is their last prophecy, after all. What rhymes with please and decrees?"

"Almost everything," Mary Jane replied miserably.

"Well," Victoria admitted, "we've never done this before, but maybe, if we really, *really* try, we can eke out some glimmer of that first third of the riddle."

"It's worth a try," Mary Jane agreed. "They did come a long way, after all, with no idea that Hortense would be off somewhere gallivanting about when they arrived. Let's see, what do we have so far?"

"—you will do just as you please, and manage all of Death's decrees!" Victoria replied.

"Exactly!" Mary Jane paused to ponder. "I've heard that sort of prophecy before. It's one of those where the first line usually begins with 'if.' "

"Almost always!" Victoria cheered. "Actually, those prophecies usually begin with a phrase: 'If you should—' "

"That's right!" Mary Jane smiled out at me. "See, we're halfway there already. If you should—uh—da da da da da. Well, it's certainly worth a try."

"I should say so!" Victoria replied. "Both of us will close our eyes and say whatever comes into our heads."

"With luck," Mary Jane added, "one of them will be the prophecy." She turned to her fellow fate. "Are you ready?"

"Whenever you are."

The two fates closed their eyes and swayed back and forth upon their pedestals.

Victoria spoke first:

"If you should shout cacophonies?"

Mary Jane answered a moment later:

"If you should tap him on the knees?"

Victoria moaned and spoke again:

"If you should do a full striptease?"

"If you should eat some cottage cheese?" Mary Jane added immediately.

Both fates opened their eyes and made more or less the same horrible sequence of faces.

"That was pretty terrible," Victoria allowed.

Mary Jane agreed. "When the muse leaves me, I'm worthless."

I thanked them both, and said that it was time we took our leave. My master was in dire distress in the land of Death, and for all I knew that danger might be growing with every passing minute. We would have to try and contact Plaugg, and rely on his ever so sightly godlike powers to come to our aid.

"Bless his minimal resplendence," Snarks added reverentially.

In the meantime, I added, I would consider their prophecies, and surely find some helpful clues therein.

It was only then that I remembered.

"Oh, no!" I exclaimed. In my concern for my master, I had completely forgotten to ask them the directions to heaven. I sheepishly explained my omission.

"Oh, dear," Mary Jane replied.

"Quite a shame," Victoria added.

"Do you think it would have done you any good, anyway?" Snarks demanded. "Do you understand anything these two have told you?"

"If only we could—" Mary Jane began.

"Now, now," Victoria reprimanded. "You know the rules. Three questions—"

"—no more, no less," Mary Jane agreed miserably.

"And they've all been used up," Victoria concluded. "However, that's in our official role. Perhaps we might be able to advise them unofficially?"

I looked hopefully at the two immortals. Could they actually help us, after all, even after my bumbling mistake?

"Oh, do you think we might?" Mary Jane asked, a bit of cheer returned to her voice.

"Oh, why not?" Victoria replied. "It's the least we can do with Hortense gone. Listen, mortals, to what the fates suggest." She pointed above her. "Heaven, to the best of our knowledge, is somewhere up there."

"Up," Mary Jane agreed. "Definitely up."

"Exactly *where* up there I'm afraid we're a little vague on," Victoria added.

"They never invite us to any of their parties," Mary Jane explained.

"Yes," Victoria sighed. "Something like that would certainly brighten up a Saturday night!"

"Well, never mind about our social lives—if you could call them that," Mary Jane hastily amended. "Rather, shall we say—" She glanced at her sister.

The Two Fates smiled as one. "We hope we've helped you with your quest."

I thanked the immortal sisters and we took our leave, passing back through the portal and back to the mountainside, the fates' final words carried to us through the thin, high air:

"I do wish Hortense would send us a card!"

"Well, that was certainly educational," Snarks remarked when we had gotten some distance from the temple. "I now know where not to come when I'm looking for answers."

" 'Twas nobody's fault," I amended. " 'Tis but one more difficulty on our road."

"Our road is nothing but difficulties!" Snarks complained.

"Indeed," Hubert the dragon rumbled. "And because this journey failed, I now have another difficulty which I cannot avoid."

"What do you mean?" I asked the morose-looking reptile.

Hubert sighed mightily, his nostrils emitting a prodigious amount of steam. "I must go somewhere where I swore I would never go again. But it is a place where we will surely get the answers to your questions. I must do it, for since I have met you and the wizard, that meeting has opened up my life. I owe the wizard this journey out of gratitude. Let us hope I survive the experience. If you would climb on my back?"

Snarks and I did as Hubert bade.

"Hang on!" the dragon announced. And we were airborne once again.

NINE

When pleading for your life with demons, dragons or the various monsters one encounters within the sorcerous arts, it is generally not wise to place too much of the argument for the continuation of one's existence on the needs of one's family and other relations, for, let us face it, demons, dragons and various monsters also have families and other relations, and, thinking of their own maiden aunts and mothers-in-law, may eat you as an act of mercy.

—From *The Teachings of Ebenezum,*
Volume XLI.

"Indeed," I asked the dragon once we were safely aloft, "would it be too much trouble to tell us where you are taking us?"

"No, I suppose not," Hubert replied miserably. "I just want to get this over with." His scales shook beneath us. Had the giant reptile shivered?

"We'd like to get this over with, too!" Snarks exclaimed. "So tell us, already!"

"Very well," Hubert answered, gloom still pervading his tones. "We have to go to the home of the dragons."

"Indeed?" I said, somewhat surprised.

"That's it?" Snarks stated rather more baldly. "What's wrong with that?"

"Plenty, I assure you," the dragon continued morosely. "But it's worse than that." Hubert sighed. "We have to go see Morty."

"Morty?" Snarks asked.

"Is there a problem with Morty?" I suggested.

"Is there a problem?" Hubert shot forth a plume of fire. "How can I make you, who are not dragons, and not subject to the dictates of strict dragon society—how can I *possibly* make you understand?"

"Indeed," I gently prompted. "I imagine we have already been together far longer, and gotten to know each other far better, than any human, demon and dragon ever have before! Why not tell us your problem, and we will attempt to comprehend?"

"Yes, why not?" the dragon agreed not too enthusiastically. "It will at least help pass the time until we get"—he shivered again—"there."

Hubert paused, billows of smoke cascading from his nostrils. I held my breath as the fumes passed me by, fearful that if I coughed I might break the reptile's concentration.

"Where can I begin?" Hubert began.

"This is going to be long-winded, isn't it?" Snarks whispered fatalistically.

"I guess you could say I've always been a different sort of dragon," Hubert continued, already swept up in the drama of his narrative. "Not that I wasn't given plenty of chances to fit in. I could have gone into one of the acceptable dragon occupations: world conquest, gold hoarding, damsel-napping, distant and ethereal flight patterns. But no, I had to strike out on my own. The theater had found its way into my ice-cold reptile blood!

"You see, it all started in my apprenticeship days. One of the older dragons—my Uncle Spike, actually—had taken me down to the world of men for some of my elementary lessons—uh, Panic and Mayhem 101, I believe. So here I was, supposed to stomp and snort and scare the population into fleeing willy-nilly—that was the general purpose of the lesson, you see. But my uncle had made the mistake of setting us down in the middle of this large community on market day.

"Uncle Spike then went off to scare a few humans in my direction; you know, to get the ball rolling, as it were. But he had unwittingly left me in a spot that would change my very life!" The dragon emitted a long, nostalgic sigh. "For, not fifty yards distant from where I landed, stood a Punch and Judy show!"

"A Punch and Judy show?" Snarks commented. "Sounds pretty impressive to me!"

"Yes," Hubert replied happily, too far lost in memory to note the demon's sarcasm. "Punch and Judy and all the rest. How I loved those little puppets!"

"This isn't only going to be long-winded," Snarks despaired. "This is going to be maudlin!"

Hubert laughed a sad little laugh. "Oh, I was lost within a minute of setting my eyes on that tiny stage. You see, there was not only a Punch puppet, and a Judy puppet, and a policeman puppet—there was a dragon puppet, too!"

"Oh, that explains everything!" Snarks remarked.

I thought of cautioning the demon to silence, but Hubert was oblivious to all but the story of his life.

"Yes," the dragon continued. "There it was, before me, all of life on that tiny stage. Punch hit Judy, Judy hit Punch, the policeman hit both of them, they hit the policeman back. Then the dragon came in, and things got *really* interesting!"

Hubert stopped talking suddenly. I looked past his head and saw we were approaching another distant mountain.

"Oh, dear," the dragon moaned.

This, I guessed, was Hubert's ancestral home.

We flew on through the clouds, and I got a better look at our destination. It was not your typical mountain. Oh, it was high enough, and it had crags and rocky outcroppings to spare. But it was totally lacking a peak. What should be the final quarter or so of the mountain (if it had followed the rules generally used for this sort of thing) was missing, replaced instead by a broad plateau; a space, I realized as we approached, of some size.

"The home of the dragons," Hubert noted morosely, his enthusiasm fled. We neared our destination with excruciating slowness. Had Hubert deliberately reduced his speed?

"Indeed," I said. Obviously, the dragon did not look forward to this homecoming. I had a feeling he might be overdramatizing his problems. But then, I have never visited the home of the dragons. Perhaps, I thought, it was best to get Hubert's mind off of what was to come. And I could think of but one way to do this.

"Hubert," I reminded him gently, "you never finished telling us your story."

"What?" the dragon asked, his moping temporarily disturbed. "Oh, you mean about that town and Uncle Spike and Punch and Judy. All that?"

"That's all right," Snarks reassured him. "You don't have to tell us."

"No, no," Hubert insisted. "What's the use of starting a story if you're not willing to get to the point? It's not fair to your audience!"

"Indeed," I interjected before the demon could comment further. "So why don't you finish?"

Hubert nodded grimly. "The show must go on, even if I do have to see Morty. Now, where was I? Oh, that's right. Punch and Judy, and then the dragon puppet. Well, let me tell you, I was lost! Uncle Spike kept sending harried villagers my way, and I didn't fry a single one of them! I didn't even know they were there! I didn't pay any attention to the audience of the puppet show, either, though I vaguely remember some children screaming and fleeing in panic. I was totally absorbed in the action on the tiny stage—Punch hit the dragon, Judy hit the dragon, the dragon hit Judy, the dragon hit Punch. And then the policeman showed up!"

"You did have to encourage him, didn't you?" Snarks muttered.

"I don't need to tell you, I was excited. Here was the Punch and Judy show, with all the audience and miscellaneous other citizenry fled. It was a show performed only for me! And I began to think, if an audience applauded a dragon puppet, then consider what their reaction to the real thing would be!"

"Indeed," I agreed. " 'Tis a thought to ponder."

"Rather than talk about," Snarks added, "especially at great length."

"Well," I stated, "it certainly was an inspirational story."

"Unfortunately," Hubert admitted, "it was more flammable than inspirational. As I became more involved in the puppet show, I waddled closer and closer to that tiny stage. Then the puppet dragon got the upper hand!" Hubert coughed delicately. "At that tender age, you don't have quite the control over your flame that you might. In my enthusiasm, I'm afraid I burned the booth to the ground. The puppeteer got away unharmed, but I fear I singed Punch and Judy beyond recognition. Which was fortunate, because, when Uncle Spike arrived, I could at least show him a little mayhem."

"Did he buy it?" Snarks asked, interested despite himself.

"I got a passing grade," Hubert acknowledged. "But my exams no longer mattered. From that moment onward I had but one goal—the theater!"

The dragon sighed. "But that doesn't matter anymore. In a few minutes, we will be—*there* again!"

"But can it be that bad?" I asked.

"That bad," Hubert agreed miserably. "And worse! Dragons will never appreciate show business!"

"At last, someone I can relate to," Snarks stated with new enthusiasm. "Sounds like dragons are my kind of creature!"

"They are if you like burning and conquering and devouring and hoarding," Hubert said glumly. "Dragons are very good at that!" He blew a despairing puff of smoke. "Hubert—they'd ask me—Hubert, don't you like to rend and tear and destroy? Don't you like amassing gold? You want to do what? Act? But aren't burning and destroying and hoarding all acts? Oh, they would never understand. And Morty!"

"Morty?" Snarks asked.

"Yes, Morty was always the worst—my older brother, excelling at all those things for which I had no aptitude—basic mayhem, applied burning, advanced treasure collection—he passed them all with honors!"

"Morty?" Snarks said again.

"And now I have to go back and face all that one more time!" Hubert concluded.

"Indeed," I said reassuringly. "Perhaps it will not be as bad as you imagine."

But Hubert laughed bitterly. "Oh, no. It will be as bad as that and worse. Believe me, you do not know the depths that dragons will sink to! But I will be strong, for your master! I will persevere, for your master. I will even see Morty, for your master. And we will find the way to heaven, after all!"

"Morty?" Snarks interjected again.

"We are almost there," Hubert remarked. "I'm going to angle in for a landing. Hang on! And once we get there, let me do the talking."

"Must we?" Snarks asked, his words almost lost to the increasing wind. But then he and I both were forced to lean down against the reptile and clutch his scales.

Hubert landed smoothly in a clearing on the edge of the plateau. A single, dark gray dragon, almost indistinguishable from the surrounding rock, watched our descent.

Hubert came to a full stop and looked at the other reptile. "I think I know that dragon."

"I can't hear you!" the other dragon called. "I have carrots in my ears!"

"I beg your pardon?" Hubert replied.

"It is you, isn't it?" the other dragon cheered. "You wouldn't know about this, would you? You've been away. Well, I can tell you, nephew, it's all your fault!"

"Oh, dear," Hubert whispered. "It's my Uncle Spike."

"Nice to see you again!" Uncle Spike continued as he trotted towards us. "We've heard how well you've been doing down below. You can't imagine the furor that's caused!" The dragon chuckled, sending sparks flying out from between his teeth. "And what's that on your back? A gift or two for your Uncle Spike? Perhaps a few munchies?"

"Certainly not!" Hubert said hastily. "These are my companions on a very important quest. I'm afraid I didn't have time to bring gifts, uncle. This is not a pleasure visit, but rather a necessary stop on a mission that could change the course of destiny!"

"Ah, nephew, it's easy to see how you can wow them down on the surface world. What a sense of style!"

"Thank you, I'm sure," Hubert replied softly, taken aback by the compliment. "I never expected to hear something like that in the land of the dragons."

"A lot has changed around here," Spike agreed. "And it's all because of you!"

"Maybe," Snarks piped up hopefully, "they've outlawed musical comedy."

"Oho!" Uncle Spike cried, looking at the demon for the first time. "Who is this tidbit?"

"Are you demeaning my size?" Snarks demanded. "I am a full-grown demon!"

"Oh, dear, no," Spike replied with a shake of his massive head. "On the contrary, I am complimenting your taste."

"Really?" Snarks responded, surprised. He self-consciously fingered his heavy woolen attire. "Oh, it's nothing, really. These are just some old robes from my religious order."

"Oh, no, no," Spike chided. "You misunderstand. Not taste as in selection of wardrobe. More like taste as in the opportunity to become a light snack. And may I say, you certainly look yummy!"

"I'm sorry," Snarks replied. "I was supposed to let Hubert do the talking."

"Yes, uncle," Hubert interjected. "These two on my back are under my protection. They are crucial to the completion of my task. I would appreciate it, therefore, if you would stop considering them as light meals."

"Oho!" Spike guffawed. "That's a good one! Under an *actor's* protection?" Flame shot twenty feet in the air as he roared with laughter. "Wait until I tell the others about that one! I tell you, Hubert, you can certainly see that you're a professional!"

"I suppose so, uncle," Hubert replied doubtfully. "But, enjoyable as it is to talk to you, I'm afraid we have a mission to complete. I therefore must see my brother Morty as quickly as possible."

"Morty?" Spike responded, still amused. "His horde is just over here in the next crag. You haven't been here in a while, have you? Well, I'll be glad to show you the way." He looked speculatively at Snarks and myself. "A reptile can certainly get hungry this time of day, it being between meals and all. I could really stand a little pick-me-up. Do you really need two—"

"Yes, Uncle Spike," Hubert replied firmly.

"Simply asking! No need to get upset." Spike's tongue darted from his mouth to taste the air in our vicinity. "And let me know if you change your mind."

"Morty, Uncle Spike?"

"Surely," the large reptile nodded as he turned to lead the way. "I'm simply putting in my request now, before all the other dragons see your tasty—um—companions. Remember, my boy, you should always spare a kindly thought for your elders."

Spike walked toward the interior of the plateau, and Hubert followed.

"Indeed," I whispered to the latter dragon as we strode across the barren rock. "Is this what you were so worried about?"

"Yes and no," Hubert whispered back. "Uncle Spike has been more pleasant than I ever thought he could be. But there is something strange going on here."

"You mean his constant desire to eat us?" I suggested.

"No, no," Hubert disagreed. "That's perfectly natural for a dragon. I meant some of the comments he's been making. 'I can't hear you—I have carrots in my ears?' There seem to have been some fundamental changes in dragon society."

"But couldn't that be for the good?" I reasoned.

"Nothing in dragon society is ever for the good," Hubert replied morosely. "I am more worried now than I was before we came here."

"Great," Snarks replied. "Well, it's been nice knowing you. Or at least as nice as it can be knowing a human and a dragon."

If I had been surprised by the fatalism of Snarks's remark, I was even more surprised when Hubert nodded his agreement.

"It will get worse. We still have to see Morty."

TEN

Q: Are dragons hungry?
A: Is the sky blue?
Q: Are dragons fast?
A: Should a tax collector be avoided whenever possible?
Q: Do dragons eat wizards?
A: Have you forgotten to remind the reptiles of your facility with indigestion spells?

—From *Ask Mr. Magic:*
A Wizard's Guide to 364 of Today's Most Pressing
Sorcerous Problems, scholastic edition,
by Ebenezum
greatest wizard in the Western Kingdoms

Uncle Spike led us to the entrance of a very large cave.

"This is the place," the older dragon chuckled. "Allow me to introduce us." He yelled into the cave:

"Let your pages do the walking through the yellow fingers!"

"It's no wonder, with prices like that!" another voice roared in response.

Spike and the voice inside the cave laughed heartily.

"I'm beginning to see a pattern here," Hubert muttered darkly. "A pattern I don't like at all."

"Come on," Spike waved for us to follow. "Let's go in and see Morty."

"Morty?" Snarks, obviously unable to help himself, said again.

Hubert reluctantly followed.

"Hey, Morty!" Spike called. "Guess who's here? It's your brother Huey!"

"Huey?" Snarks asked.

"I told you I didn't want to come back here," Hubert replied.

"What?" Morty's voice called. "The smokeless wonder is back again? Well, come on in!"

"I suppose I have to," Hubert murmured, walking forward as if every step was an effort.

"The smokeless won—" Snarks began before a particularly sharp look from me silenced him. I figured that Hubert was in enough distress without a demonic chorus.

The dragon carried us into a truly massive cavern, larger even than the great hall at the wizard's college. But what really took my breath away were the huge tapestries covering every available foot of walls and ceiling, each great hanging sporting a sewn-in message.

SEE THE SOUTHERN KINGDOMS!
MOTHER DUCK'S REALM—A FAIRYLAND
FOR MERE PIECES OF GOLD!
THE WESTERN KINGDOMS—THERE'S MORE
THERE THAN MEETS THE EYE!
THE LAND OF THE DRAGONS—YOUR VACATION
IN THE CLOUDS!

Each of the tapestries also featured elaborate illustrations. The one concerning the Southern Kingdoms showed a large picture of the sun, while the Mother Duck hanging prominently displayed a large castle. Only the tapestry for the Western Kingdoms was fairly nondescript.

And in the midst of the tapestries squatted the largest dragon I had ever seen, half again the size of Hubert and bright red besides.

"Huey!" the huge reptile rumbled. "And how's my pip-squeak brother?"

"I'm glad to see you, too, Morty," Hubert managed miserably.

"Hear you've done pretty well down among the humans," Morty went on cheerily. "Who would've thought it?"

"Morty," Hubert said, barely managing his temper, "I'm here for a reason."

"Really?" his brother remarked heartily. "You want another flame-shooting contest? Or maybe we can compare our gold hordes?"

"It's no time for games, Morty," Hubert replied. "Besides, you always win."

"And you always were a spoilsport, Huey," Morty chuckled. "But maybe I can do something for you, anyway."

"I understand you've got a successful travel business—" Hubert continued doggedly.

"You see it all around you!" Morty cheered, tossing his massive head back and forth at the various tapestries that crowded the room. "At last, I've found a way to satisfy a dragon's wanderlust! Yes, you could say Morty's Travel is a roaring success. What else would you expect from your older brother? But you said you needed help."

There was a commotion at the mouth of the cave.

"That was no lady," a voice called, "that was my wife!"

"The joke's on him," another voice added. "The mouse is a ventriloquist."

"Sorry," Morty yelled back. "You can't get in here without a tie!"

Morty and Spike laughed along with the two new voices. Hubert shivered quietly.

"My worst fears have been realized," he whispered.

The floor shook as two other dragons, one a dull orange, the other sort of a red-brick tone, trundled into the back of the cave.

"Dewey!" Morty greeted the newcomers. "Ferdie!"

"Dewey?" Snarks repeated. "Ferdie?"

"Oh, my," the dull-orange dragon remarked as he glanced our way. "Hors-devours."

"I've done it again, haven't I?" Snarks whispered in horror. I nodded. The demon did have a way of attracting the attention of others. Very large others. It was interesting, I reflected, how ineffectual one seemed in the presence of giant reptiles. I might have a magic sword and a magic ferret, but what use was either of them against fire-breathing lizards? I thought again of the Brownie, but realized that even shoe magic would be ineffectual against creatures of this size; creatures who seemed to be showing all too much interest in Snarks and me.

"No, no, Ferdie!" Hubert interjected. "These are friends."

"Very appetizing friends," Ferdie agreed. "But we shouldn't eat before we are properly introduced, should we?"

"Always know your food," Dewey agreed. "That's a dragon's guide to happy digestion."

"So!" Morty boomed. "What brings you fellows here? Need a few travel tips?"

"We always get our travel tips from you," Ferdie said.

"Wouldn't go anyplace else than Morty's Travel," Dewey amplified.

"That's why we're number one!" Morty exclaimed cheerily. "Of course, with me in charge, what else could we be?"

"Still, there are improvements that could be made," Ferdie continued, eyeing Snarks and me with far too much interest.

"Most certainly," Dewey added, saliva dripping from his huge incisors. "Like the introduction of a snack tray for hungry customers."

"Yes!" Uncle Spike agreed from the far side of the room. "The very idea that I suggested earlier!"

"It doesn't have to be anything out of the ordinary," Dewey explained further. "Simply some of your dragon staples. Say, like these fellows here. Nice, bite-size creatures from down below. So round, so soft, so succulent!"

"Yes, soft is a must," Ferdie concurred. "None of those exotic things with exoskeletons, please! They hurt my teeth."

"Never eat an unknown species," Spike added sagely.

"Another tip for happy dragon digestion," Dewey concluded. "But how do we split them up?"

"They are a little on the small side," Ferdie agreed.

"Oh, everyone will get their share," Uncle Spike assured them. "Anybody got a knife?"

"Wait a second!" Hubert roared. "Hasn't anybody been listening? My friends are not for eating!"

"Not even a bite?" Ferdie frowned.

"Look at all the arms and legs they have," Dewey demanded. "Surely they wouldn't miss one or two?"

"Out of the question!" Hubert replied adamantly.

"Huey never was one to share his playthings," Morty remarked.

"Share them?" Hubert retorted. "If you saw them, you took them!"

"Now, now, boys," Uncle Spike chided. "We shouldn't let old family grudges spoil this fine reunion, should we? Let's put all thoughts of eating and generously sharing our food aside for a moment, and officially welcome Hubert back to his homeland!"

Dewey and Ferdie cheered.

"So you really are a song-and-dance dragon?" Ferdie asked enthusiastically.

"We've got all your clippings," Dewey added. "At least all of those we could find on your trips through the lowlands."

"It's sort of a sideline while we're pillaging and burning," Ferdie explained.

"Yes, yes," Morty interrupted. "I'm sure we're all glad to see Huey again. But isn't it time to talk travel?"

"That's right," Dewey harmonized. "We always come to Morty's travel. After all, isn't Morty Hubert's brother?"

"His brother? B-but that's beside the point when Morty's gives you such great travel services!" Morty insisted.

"Yes," Ferdie appended. "We figured if we came here often enough, we were bound to meet the famous member of the family."

"*Another* side benefit of Morty's Travel!" the large red dragon stressed. "Although a very minor one."

"Of course, when we were waiting around for you to show, we had to do some business with Morty," Dewey elucidated. "I tell you, being a fan can be so expensive!"

"So what business do you want to do *now?*" Morty emphasized. "We have deals you wouldn't believe!"

"I'm sure you do," Ferdie replied. "But for the moment, we would like to talk to your brother."

"Yes," Dewey enthused. "You must tell us all about your experiences on the stage!"

"You really want to know about my experiences?" Hubert answered in disbelief.

"These deals won't last forever!" Morty ventured. No one seemed to notice.

"Are you kidding?" Spike laughed. "Every dragon here wants to know about your experiences. Your success has had a profound effect upon the entirety of dragon culture!"

"So that's what that was all about!" Hubert marveled.

"These offers are for a limited time only!" Morty remarked rather more loudly than was necessary. He was ignored by the others.

"The punch lines," Hubert went on. "When I heard you exchange them, I was afraid you were mocking everything I stood for."

"The punch lines?" Snarks asked.

"Quiet, appetizers," Dewey admonished. "We'll deal with you presently."

Snarks quieted.

"On the contrary—" Ferdie began. "You should consider the custom an honor—"

"Mockery was the furthest thing from our minds," Dewey further assured. "When we heard of your success telling jokes, it opened up whole new vistas for dragonkind."

"That's right!" Uncle Spike agreed. "And soon we all began to tell jokes!"

"As a way of greeting—" Ferdie added.

"It became the 'in' thing to do—" Dewey expounded.

"This could be," Morty cried hoarsely, "a once-in-a-lifetime opportunity!" The others continued talking as if he wasn't even there.

"Of course, telling a complete joke every time you greet someone can be very time-consuming," Spike maintained.

"So, over time, we shortened the form," Ferdie clarified.

"I see," the dragon upon which we sat interposed. "And now you simply say the best part, like—" Hubert paused.

"Oh, oh," Ferdie hollered. "Would you—could you—if it wouldn't be asking too much—do a punch line?"

"Yes, yes," Dewey huzzahed. "Do one for us, Huey. Please?"

"Oh, very well. If I must." Hubert considered for a moment, before speaking again:

"Because his pink ones were in the wash."

All the dragons save Morty guffawed heartily.

"He's already a master!" Dewey marveled.

"Why hadn't we seen his genius before?" Ferdie queried.

"You may *never* see bargains like this again!" Morty screamed. No one even bothered to glance at him.

"Well, we certainly see it now," Uncle Spike asserted. "Huey, you will have to tell us all your secrets."

"Secrets?" Hubert responded doubtfully.

"Yes," Ferdie explicated, "you know, how you entice humans and others into seeing your act."

"How?" Hubert ruminated. "Well, you know, publicity, word of mouth. . . ."

"I'm sure we'll learn about the preparation soon enough," Dewey chirruped. "We want to hear how you put audiences under your reptile spell!"

"Really?" Hubert responded dubiously. "Well, I guess you could call it that. I do have a partner, you know. We start out with a little song, a little dance, then really hook them with some snappy patter."

"And then you eat them!" Uncle Spike suggested.

"Pardon?" Hubert replied, somewhat aghast.

"I thought that would naturally be what happens next," Spike expounded.

"Most certainly not!" Hubert contradicted. "Once you have the audience with you, you milk their emotions for all it's worth. You know, a sensitive song of lost love, followed by a specialty dance number and a rousing, patriotic finale!"

"Oh, I see," Spike answered with sudden comprehension. "And *then* you eat them!"

"Uh"—Hubert hesitated—"no. Then it's time for the audience to applaud wildly, so that you can come back for your encore."

"Obviously," Ferdie interjected, "we don't understand any of the finer points of your newly chosen profession."

"Quite right," Dewey assented. "But tell us, Huey old dragon. When exactly *do* you eat them?"

"Oh, my." Hubert looked at the others. "I'm afraid I don't."

"You don't eat them?" Spike erupted incredulously.

"You don't eat *anybody?*" Ferdie echoed.

"It all seems rather pointless, doesn't it?" Dewey agreed with the others. "How do you survive?"

"Well," Hubert replied a bit defensively, "I do get paid a bit."

"Paid?" Uncle Spike chuckled. "You sly reptile!"

"What a horde of gold you must have!" Ferdie marveled.

The other dragons—save Morty, who was sulking in a corner—all smoked heartily.

"Well, it's been quite nice to visit with all of you again," Hubert puffed. "But I must speak with my brother."

The red dragon in the corner raised his head.

"Morty's the one to go for travel," Dewey agreed.

"Of course," Ferdie interjected, "we can travel anytime. But it's not every day we get to talk to a star!"

"Thanks again," Hubert replied modestly. "But if I might be able to talk to my brother alone?"

"Fair enough," Spike piped up as he eyed Snarks and me speculatively. "Would you like me to watch your snacks?"

"On second thought," Hubert amended hastily, "I believe it would be in everybody's interest if my two companions also consulted with Morty."

"Doesn't sound very interesting to me," Spike remarked. He glanced at Dewey and Ferdie. "What do you fellows think?"

"We'll do anything," Ferdie enthused, "if you'll put on a show!"

"Well, I don't know—" Hubert hesitated.

"No show, no go!" Ferdie insisted.

"And, you know," Dewey added ominously as he breathed a thin line of smoke in our direction, "all this talking has made me hungry."

"Oh, all right!" Hubert relented. "I'll do a show. But just a little one!"

Dewey and Ferdie both applauded.

"We knew we could twist your tail!" Dewey exclaimed.

"We'll have to go out and tell the others!" Ferdie added.

"Yep," Uncle Spike agreed. "I'll have to get out of here right now to tell your Aunt Louise."

"Louise?" Snarks piped up before his demon hands covered his mouth.

"My, this one certainly is a talkative tidbit," Spike remarked, moving his smoking snout rather closer to us than was comfortable.

"Now, uncle," Hubert cautioned.

"Oh, we understand, Huey," Spike assured him. "There's no reason to be ashamed. I'm sure a traveler like you never knows where he might spend the night. It's always wise to bring an extra food supply."

"In fact," Dewey added, "it's a cornerstone of dragon digestion."

"Life on the road must certainly be tough," Ferdie continued. "Far be it from us to force you to share what might be your only sustenance."

"But—" Hubert responded.

"Say no more," Spike interrupted. "We understand. But maybe, after the performance, we can trade you a real meal for those tidbits!"

"But—" Hubert tried again.

"No need to thank us!" Ferdie assured him.

"But—" Hubert insisted.

"We have to go tell the others about the show!" Dewey called as he left with Ferdie and Spike.

"But—" Hubert began again. But the three dragons were gone.

"Oh, dear," Snarks whispered.

"Indeed," I agreed. "We will have to be careful in our dealings with dragons. Otherwise, we will end our days as somebody's lunch."

Hubert sighed. " 'Tis the nature of dragons. They always look at the world through their stomachs."

" 'Tis rather the nature of an adventurous life," I assured the dragon. "I have been threatened with digestion by many other species in the course of my travels. It's the sort of thing you come to count on in the apprenticeship business."

"I suppose you're going to say it's my fault that the dragons noticed us so much," Snarks said defensively. "And I suppose it is."

The demon groaned. "There's something about dragon names," Snarks despaired. "I can't help myself."

"Oh, well," Hubert allowed. "I can understand that with Spike."

"You can?" Snarks replied uncomprehendingly.

"Certainly," the dragon explained. " 'Spike' is only my uncle's nickname. His real name is Bruce."

"Bruce?" Snarks repeated, unable to do otherwise.

"I agree entirely," Hubert consented. "What kind of name is that for a dragon?"

He looked over at his brother, who still moped in the corner. "But I must speak with Morty if we are to complete our mission."

Morty straightened as we approached. "And what do *you* want?"

"I need your help," Hubert explained. "That's why I'm here."

"You need *my* help?" Morty ventured incredulously. "Hubert, the star, condescends to ask something from his humble travel-agent brother, so lowly a dragon that others only use his services because of his famous relations?"

"He's taking this a little hard, isn't he?" Snarks commented.

"Drama runs in the family," Hubert explained.

It seemed to me that this drama had run far enough. Now that we were not in immediate danger of being eaten for a chance remark, perhaps there was something I could do to remedy this situation.

"Indeed," I interjected. "And I am sure he would be very good at it, had he chosen drama as his profession. In fact, he might have been even better than you, Hubert."

The other dragon's ears perked up. "I might?"

"Certainly," I hurriedly added. "But he chose an even more noble dragon profession, that of guiding his fellows through the skies!"

"I did?" Morty replied. He took a moment to dust off his wings. "I did!"

"I see what you're saying," Hubert continued, picking up on my cue. "Look, Morty, what does it matter what others think? We know who's the older brother around here, don't we?"

"Yes," Morty said uncertainly, "I guess that hasn't changed." He absently flexed his wing muscles. "Want to try a little flying contest?"

"Why bother?" Hubert conceded. "We both know you'd win. Plus, we don't have much time. We need your help now."

Morty snorted a tentative bit of smoke. "Oh, well, if you put it that way, I suppose we could work out something, if only because you're my brother."

"Morty, I knew I could count on you!" Hubert enthused. "Now, can you tell me the way to heaven?"

"Heaven?" Morty frowned. "I always thought it was—you know—up." He looked distractedly about the room. "But maybe I can find better directions."

He strolled over to the Western Kingdoms tapestry. "I keep all my odd maps and information back here. So few dragons want to go to the Western Kingdoms—such a dreary place!—that I have plenty of room." He sat back on his haunches and pushed the tapestry aside with his snout.

"Let's see," he ruminated. "Ah. The very file." He ruffled through a pile of parchment. "This could be a bit of a problem. Heaven appears to be awfully large."

"Indeed!" I called helpfully. "We seek the whereabouts of a minor deity, a Plaugg?"

"The inconsequentially majestic!" Snarks added.

"Ah." Morty nodded, brightening considerably. "The lowest level possible, huh? Well, that should make things a little easier." He pulled a piece of parchment from the bottom of the pile. "Here we go." He handed the document to Hubert. "You have to travel up, and a little to the left."

Hubert glanced over the directions. "Seems simple enough."

"Of course it is!" the other dragon insisted. "Morty's Travel has the best directions available!"

"This should do nicely," Hubert agreed. "What do we owe you?"

Morty considered. "Well, you do have those two succulent—but no, you want to hold on to them for some reason. Let us just say that I should be happiest when you're gone. I ask, therefore, for your speediest exit possible."

"Then, brother, I am gone," Hubert assured him, backing out of the cave with his two passengers still intact.

"Oh, no, you're not!" Dewey and Ferdie echoed from the cave mouth. "It's showtime!"

ELEVEN

"There is no business like show business. There is also no business like certified public accounting, but that doesn't rhyme as well."

—From *Wake Up and Conjure:*
A Wizard's Guide to Everyday Life, fourth edition,
by Ebenezum,
greatest wizard in the Western Kingdoms

"But—" Hubert began.

"The beer that made Mel Famey walk us!" Ferdie declared.

"I've come for the man who show my paw!" Dewey added.

"No one's going to make a gosh darn canoe out of me!" Hubert replied after a moment's consideration.

The dragons laughed at some length.

"That's the spirit!" Ferdie said encouragingly.

"Nothing special," Hubert stated. "Just show biz in the blood."

"That's exactly what we're looking for!" Dewey trumpeted. "And we're all ready for you. Everybody's gathered back at the landing plateau!"

"That's awfully nice, fellows," Hubert began, "but—"

"And they're calling for you!" Ferdie cried.

"They are?" Hubert smiled. "Well, let's not keep them waiting!"

"But Hubert!" I whispered in the dragon's ear. Hadn't he promised his brother to leave quickly? And hadn't we wasted enough time here in our search for my master?

Hubert made a shushing sound as he walked to meet the other dragons.

"Oho," Ferdie pointed out. "So now the other tidbit is bothering you!"

"Yes, they do seem like such an annoyance," Dewey agreed. "I'm sure you'll feel much better once you're rid of them."

"But—" Hubert began.

"You've held out on us for long enough!" Dewey insisted. "It's time for a snack."

"It's time for escape," Snarks whispered in my ear.

But Hubert shook his head vehemently.

"No, it is not," our dragon allowed. "Not with these fellows."

I silently repressed a cheer. Hubert would not let us down!

"Why not?" Ferdie demanded.

"Give us one good reason!" Dewey chorused.

"Um. A good reason?" Hubert replied uncertainly.

"Dragon's dinner, here we come," Snarks whispered. But Hubert brightened, shouting: "Because they're part of the show!"

"Part of the show?" the two reptiles said in unison, the disappointment plain upon their dragon faces.

"I guess we'll have to wait, then," Dewey spoke reluctantly.

"At least until after the performance," Ferdie agreed.

"Very good," Hubert remarked with the proper note of imperiousness. "Now stand aside, so that my assistants and I might prepare for the show."

The other dragons deferentially made way for Hubert and his retinue.

"In show business," Hubert explained when we had reached a sufficient distance from the others, "it sometimes pays to be difficult."

"If that's the case," Snarks rejoined, "you should be incredibly wealthy."

I ignored the demon's remark, for I had other things on my mind.

"Indeed," I asked Hubert, "we're now part of the performance?"

"Don't worry," the dragon assured me. "We'll fake it."

"Fake it?" Snarks replied miserably. "Maybe I should have been a dragon's dinner, after all."

"You may still have a chance," Hubert remarked, "if the performance doesn't go well."

"Indeed?" I asked somewhat reluctantly.

Hubert nodded. "Dragons, as a rule, do not constitute a forgiving audience." He reached up and took off his top hat. "But here. You need to learn your lines." He pulled two sheaves of parchment from inside the hat brim, and handed them to me. I passed one of the two on to Snarks.

"You actually keep your music in your hat?" the demon asked incredulously.

"What—" The dragon chuckled, twirling the hat back atop his head. "Do you think I wear this thing just for show?"

I looked down at the piece of parchment in my hands. It was a song about dragons, with stanzas clearly marked with a number 1, 2 or 3.

"I thought this was a particularly appropriate little ditty, with three parts, of course. I shall be number one—that part carries much of the weight of the song. Wuntvor shall be number two, and Snarks number three. Simply follow my lead, and everything shall be fine. Any questions?"

"Yeah," Snarks piped up. "Do we have to do this?"

"I am afraid so," Hubert responded. "I am not a solo act. My numbers require a partner. In addition, we need an excuse to keep the two of you off my fellow dragons' dinner tables."

Snarks swallowed hard.

"So it's sing . . . or be eaten?"

"That's about it," the dragon replied. "What shall it be?"

"I'm thinking!" the demon answered. "I'm thinking!"

Then Hubert rounded a bend and there were dragons everywhere.

"People who live in grass houses shouldn't stow thrones!" a delicate pink reptile called.

"I wouldn't send a knight out on a dog like this!" a large blue-green lizard added.

"Well, you wouldn't eat a fine pig like that all at once!" a bright yellow dragon chimed in.

"So I bit him!" a very large bluish-purple dragon rumbled.

And so it went, a hundred dragons shouting a hundred punch lines all at once, so that all you could hear were occasional references to dogs, chickens and salesmen, followed quickly by an overwhelming wave of laughter, then silence.

All the dragons were waiting for Hubert's response.

The showdragon cleared his throat.

"How he got into my pajamas, I'll never know."

Well, if there had been a house there, he would have brought it down. As it was, the audience's laughter seemed to shake the whole plateau. But then the laughter died down as well, and more than a hundred dragons looked at us expectantly.

"Is it my imagination," Snarks whispered, "or do these guys look like they haven't eaten in a week?"

"Quick!" Hubert instructed us. "Get down on either side of me. It's showtime!"

"But—" Snarks began.

But it was already too late. Hubert was singing:

> "Dragons are different, dragons are swell,
> Dragons can burn you with their sense of smell!"

He glanced over at me. That meant it was my turn! I quickly sang the words of my stanza, trying to repeat the tune Hubert had begun:

> "Dragons are different, it's useful to know,
> 'Cause one can crush you with his little toe."

"Isn't this song going to give these guys ideas?" Snarks whispered.

"Your turn!" I whispered back.

Snarks looked out at the assembled dragons and froze.

"Dinnertime!" I added.

Snarks cleared his throat and sang:

> "Dragons are different, it can't be revoked;
> They prefer their dinners thoroughly smoked."

"All together now!" Hubert declared. Snarks and I did our best to join the dragon in the chorus:

> "They're kings of all reptiles;
> Their manners divine,
> 'Cause all these dragons—
> Why, they're friends of mine!"

Snarks glanced at me, the edge of hysteria in his whispered plea: "Why do I get the eating lines?"

It was then I noticed that Ferdie and Dewey had positioned themselves on Snarks's side of the performance, and were in addition watching the demon with more than routine interest.

"Here we go again!" Hubert prompted the two of us. He sang:

> "Dragons are different, they like to fly
> And pillage and burn—they're not at all shy!"

The audience had begun to clap along. Hubert had picked a real crowd pleaser. But it was my turn:

> "Dragons are different, both young and old;
> They take what they want, as long as it's gold!"

The crowd kept the rhythm up, even though Snarks was late coming in again. I glanced at the demon.

"I can't say this!" he whispered back.

"Dinner—" Hubert whispered from overhead.

Snarks sang:

> "Dragons are different, you can be sure,
> When it comes to eating, they're not demure!"

Dewey and Ferdie seemed to like those lines. They had started to drool.

"All together once again!" Hubert called down to us. It was time for the chorus:

> "They're some lucky lizards
> With scales so sublime,
> And all these dragons—
> Why, they're friends of mine!"

Then Hubert started to dance. Both Snarks and I scurried away to give him room. He stomped up and down while flapping his wings and shooting great gouts of flame into the air. The crowd couldn't get enough of him.

It took him a full five minutes to slow down, winded at last. He looked down at the two of us.

"Take it—uh—partners!" he wheezed.

"Take it?" Snarks whispered hysterically. "Take it where?"

"I think Hubert wants us to dance," I suggested.

"No self-respecting demon—" Snarks noticed that Ferdie and Dewey were leaning closer still.

The demon danced. My way, as I was dancing his way. Our feet managed to land in the same place at the same time. We tripped and fell. I tried to roll over and rise, but had somehow gotten my arms and scabbard stuck amidst the demon's robes. It took us a full minute to extricate ourselves from our predicament. We turned to face the crowd.

The audience loved it.

"What now?" Snarks whispered. "I don't have another food verse, do I?"

"The final chorus!" Hubert called. He and I sang while Snarks backed away from certain overzealous members of the audience.

> "So call up a dragon
> If you want to dine;
> And all these dragons—
> Why, they're friends of mine!"

Hubert waved to the crowd as he spoke to the two of us in a stage whisper.

"Get on my back, quick!"

We did as the dragon asked. Once we were firmly in place, Hubert backed away from the throng. "Thank you! Thank you!" he called. "You're a beautiful audience!"

Most of the crowd were calling for encores, save for Dewey and Ferdie, who seemed to be saying things like "That would hit the spot!" and "My compliments to the chef!" I noticed Uncle Spike again as well, leading a lavender dragon who I assumed was Aunt Louise. Both Spike and Louise were watching me all too intently.

"Bye!" Hubert called to the throng. "Until we see you again!" He turned to us. "Always leave them wanting more."

The crowd called to us in a frenzy:

"Sure enough. The black horse was two inches taller than the white horse!"

"Yeah, but we need the eggs!"

"Oh, nothing. Worms can't talk!"

"Wrapping paper!"

"Oh, sure. Just after I got it all tired out!"

"Oh, my God! I shot a nun!"

Hubert paused in his flight to survey the upturned faces of the crowd below him.

"Gee," he called below, "do you think I should have said Joe DiMaggio?"

Then he turned again, and we rose, with a great flapping of wings.

We were on our way to heaven.

TWELVE

The concept of heaven is many different things to many different species. To a troll, it would be edible. To a giant, it might be a short distance overhead, right up that beanstalk over there. And to a unicorn, heaven consists of wherever that particular beast happens to be at that particular moment. And where is heaven for wizards? Well, that's a concept many of my fellows are still working on, but I assure you that that little tax-exempt retirement home overlooking the pleasure district of Vushta is at least on the proper road.

—From *The Teachings of Ebenezum,*
Special Weekly Update, Number 306

"Now, let's see," Hubert mused. "It's got to be around here someplace." The reptile exhaled. "At least it better be. There's not much strength left in these old wings."

We had flown up, and a little to the left, for quite some time. The home of the dragons had receded into the distance, now no more than a speck on the great curve of the globe beneath us. For the world below now looked like nothing so much as a giant sphere, and all the rivers and oceans and mountains therein looked like no more than insignificant lines and blotches and tiny spots scratched upon that great surface.

We must be nearing the home of the gods.

The air around us had changed of late, as Hubert flew even higher. When we had left the mountaintop of the dragon's home behind, we had left the clouds as well, and had flown through a vast expanse of open air. Now, however, we approached another cloudy region, although this vaporous shroud seemed far different from the fog and storm clouds below. Indeed, this new vista before us was incredibly

white and fluffy, although very dense as well, as if something might be
hidden on the other side.

"Look!" Hubert called excitedly. He pointed to a dark speck among
the clouds overhead.

"Indeed," I replied. "What are we looking at?"

"Directions!" Hubert shouted.

And I saw, as we flew closer, that the speck was a sign, somehow
attached to the bottom of a cloud. I squinted in an attempt to read the
words.

"ALL DELIVERIES TO REAR DOOR."

Beneath those words was an arrow, pointing left. The dragon
changed his course slightly to follow these new directions.

"Indeed!" I yelled forward toward Hubert's ear. "Is this the way we
should be going? We're not exactly delivering anything!"

"But certainly we are!" Snarks objected. "We are delivering our
fondest wishes to Plaugg, the slightly splendiferous!"

"Besides," the dragon reminded me, "it's not as if we were invited
up here. Who knows how the keepers of the heavenly gates are going
to react to our arrival? If we have any hopes of getting in here at all, I
think the service entrance is by far our best bet."

"Indeed," I said, impressed by the remarkably thoughtful consideration my companions were giving to our present situation. I supposed
that approaching heaven might bring that out in one. "I don't want to
incur anybody's wrath, either," I added.

It seemed to me that was the sort of reaction you got from gods—
wrath, floods, retribution, that sort of thing.

"I think we're getting close," Hubert called back again. "Thank
goodness—these wings are weary!"

And, in fact, the nature of the clouds above us was changing, for
while they were still as fleecy as before, they seemed to be graying as
we passed beneath them, getting definitely dingy in spots, as though
they had been smudged here and there. It was as if this area of cloud
cover was used rather more than the rest, and not nearly as frequently
washed.

"Another sign," Hubert rumbled.

Sure enough, there was a flat, brown area on the cloud immediately
overhead, as if someone had set a door in the midst of the vapor. And
on this door were large red letters: "R AR DOO"

"Rar doo?" Sparks inquired.

It puzzled me for a second as well.

"Indeed," I said after a moment's reflection. "If you added two letters, the sign would become 'REAR DOOR.' "

"You can tell why this fellow's our leader!" Hubert enthused. "If this is the rear door, then this is where we must go? Shall I knock?"

I told him I didn't see any reason why not. Hubert did as he was bade.

He waited a moment. There was no answer.

"There has to be somebody home!" Snarks insisted. "I mean, this is heaven, isn't it?"

"Indeed," I replied. "Hubert, why don't you knock a little louder?"

"Anything you say," Hubert agreed. "It's time for a real dragon knock!" He clenched his forepaw into a fist and drew it back as far as it would go.

"Yoo-hoo!" he called as he sent his fist crashing forward.

The door burst open.

"Oh, dear," Hubert remarked. "Do you think I broke it?"

"Should things even break in heaven?" Snarks asked. "Somehow, it would seem to be against the rules."

"Broken or not," I interjected, "I suggest we fly inside."

"True enough," Hubert answered as he fluttered his wings for one final effort. "We can worry about the niceties once we are on the other side."

We flew through the open trapdoor, into a very bright light.

The first thing I noticed was the sound of a choir, a thousand soprano voices singing at the top of their range. The next thing I saw, and it was very well lit up here, was a road of golden brick that wound its way through the clouds.

"Oof!"

Hubert landed, rather less gracefully than usual, at the beginning of the road, which, upon closer inspection, seemed to be made of regular bricks painted gold. I could tell because the paint had flaked off here and there, especially on the end of the road nearest the door. And in that small space between the road and the door was another sign, hand-lettered and slightly faded: "Please close door when you are finished."

"Hubert," I said, pointing to the sign. "Do you think we should?"

The dragon nodded. "It's only polite." He reached over and swung the door shut.

"Congratulations!" a voice boomed over the constant singing. *"You have passed the test!"*

When the three of us were done jumping and cowering, I noticed a small fellow, dressed in a rather colorless tunic, standing on the far side of the now closed door.

"Pardon," I asked, "but are you speaking to us?"

The small fellow smiled. "Don't see anybody else around here, do you?"

"Meaning no disrespect," I added hastily, "but no, we don't."

"Then I must be talking to you," the fellow concluded.

"Indeed," I replied. This fellow didn't seem to be very direct. I wondered how far I could question him without incurring his wrath, if indeed he was a god.

"Pardon me," I began again, "but would you mind telling us who you are?"

"Not at all!" the fellow answered. "As you see, this is the delivery entrance. And I am, of course, Devino, the god of delivery entrances. That's the way things work up here."

"And we have passed the test?" I ventured.

"I just said that, didn't I?" the god of delivery entrances replied with a grin. "You can't let just anybody into heaven. However, seeing you close the door behind you, I know you're the right sort."

"Seems like an awfully simple test," Snarks muttered.

Devino sighed and nodded. "Actually, when you're the god of delivery entrances, there aren't too many tests you can perform. But you're here now, and you may enter heaven."

I thanked the deity, and asked him if he might be able to direct us to the home of Plaugg.

"The overwhelmingly adequate," Snarks added reverentially.

"You're in luck," the delivery deity said. He pointed down the road. "Plaugg lives just past that cloud. First mansion on the right."

We thanked the deity and began our walk down the heavenly road. Hubert remarked on how happy he was to be able to move his feet for a change.

The clouds bordered the bricks on either side, looking like nothing so much as snow-covered hills, as if this landscape was as substantial as the world we had come from down below. And who knew, perhaps it was, for we were in a special place with special rules. I had been across large parts of the earth below, and had even ventured beneath the ground to the fearsome realms of the Netherhells. But never had I found myself in a place so wondrously strange as this, the home of all the gods.

Still, I could do no less than venture here, for the sake of Ebenezum. It was all so different, and so unreal. But we were mere steps from our goal! And with Plaugg's assistance, perhaps I would be able to save my master at last!

"Watch where you're walking!" a voice bellowed.

Hubert, Snarks and I stopped abruptly. Sound certainly had a way of carrying up here.

Ahead of us stood another fellow, a little larger than the god of delivery entrances, and a little pudgier. He also wore a tunic, although his garment seemed to have gold threads worked into the colorless fabric, which made the cloth somehow simultaneously drab and glistening. This new deity pointed to a sign by his side.

Caution!
DEITIES AT WORK
Road legally closed.

"And we mean it!" the fellow added. "Oh, sorry. I didn't intend to bellow in your ears. It's simply all this stress I've been under lately."

"Indeed?" I asked, seeking to learn the nature of this god.

"I should say so," the deity replied. "They don't realize what a full-time job this is, especially with people wanting to use these roads all the time!"

"Then you work on the roads?"

"What else have I got time to do?" the deity laughed bitterly. "Oh, sorry. I should probably introduce myself. I am Devano, the god of brick roads painted with gold flake. With a job like that, I'm obviously stuck in the lower reaches of heaven!"

"Indeed," I commented, "and you're working on this particular road?"

"You read the sign?" Devano replied moodily. "This gold flake takes constant upkeep! It's not like those real gold roads uptown."

"Uptown?" Snarks asked.

"Yeah, you know, the posh neighborhoods—Pantheon Heights, Olympus Manor, places like that. But do you think they could be bothered to put in those gold roads down here?"

"I'm sure it is quite a problem," I agreed. "However, we must travel farther up this road for a very important meeting with a deity. Is there any possibility we might be able to get through?"

Devano frowned. "The paint job's pretty new. You two small fellows could probably get through without causing too much damage, but if I'm not mistaken, one of you is a dragon."

"That's quite correct," Hubert rumbled.

"Of course I'm correct," Devano said brusquely. "I'm a deity."

"Indeed," I interjected again. "We intend no disrespect—"

"I should hope not!" Devano insisted. "We don't want any wraths incurred around here, do we?"

"What kind of wrath could a gold-flake painter have?" Snarks asked before I could stop him.

"Would you like to be bronzed?" Devano muttered darkly. "Or perhaps gilding would suit you better? It can be arranged."

"I fear we do not desire either bronzing or gilding," I replied. "What we need is to travel up this road until we find Plaugg."

"The tolerably resplendent," Snarks added.

"Sorry," Devano asserted. "The reptile makes one step on that road, and it's wrathtime!"

"Maybe I could walk around," Hubert suggested, nodding toward the surrounding cloud hills.

The deity shook his head. "They'd never take his weight. It's a problem living someplace as insubstantial as this. And it's a long way down."

"And my wings are in no shape for that kind of exercise," Hubert moaned.

"Unfortunately, we must go on ahead," I stated. "We must see Plaugg—"

"The reasonably radiant," Snarks interjected.

"—for the sake of my master!" I concluded.

"Well, what will become of me?" Hubert asked, a hint of trepidation in his voice.

"You'll have to stay behind," Snarks said bluntly, "with the gold-flake god here."

"It won't be so bad," Devano assured him. "I haven't had anyone to discuss brick painting technique with in ever so long."

"Brick painting technique?" Hubert asked. "I'm sure it would be fascinating, but on second thought, my wings have gotten all sorts of rest in the last few minutes. Up, up, and—uh—away!"

And with that, Hubert raised himself a half dozen paces above the road.

"Don't land before the intersection up ahead!" Devano called. "Or it's wrath city!"

"Yes, sir, Your Deityship, sir," Hubert groaned. He flew on ahead, his face wrinkled in a very unpleasant expression.

"May we go as well?" I asked the god.

"Certainly," Devano answered. "As long as you keep over to the left. That's the side I painted first."

I thanked the god of painting gold flake on brick roads, and we resumed our journey in silence, the only sounds those distant, ethereal, never-ending voices. We caught up with Hubert a few moments later. The dragon was breathing heavily, collapsed on the spot where the golden road branched in three directions.

"I don't use—those wing muscles—enough anymore!" Hubert gasped. "As of now—for the foreseeable future—flying is right out!"

"Indeed," I reassured the reptile, even though I wondered: Without Hubert's flying help, how would we get out of here once we were done with Plaugg?

I asked the other question that was on my mind instead.

"Which way is it to Plaugg's?"

"The spectacularly so-so," Snarks added.

"Pardon?" another voice boomed all around.

After the three of us had managed to quiet our jumping hearts, we looked for the owner of the overwhelming voice. No matter how many times it happened, this call-out-of-nowhere business had never ceased to be disconcerting. A tunicked figure waved from the middle road.

"Heard you had a little trouble!" the newcomer called. This time, we only cowered for a moment. "Oh, sorry. Booming voices come with the territory. It's the only way we can hear each other over the stupid music you always hear playing." The high, soprano voices hummed happily in the background. "And if you think it's bad around here, you should go over to the shopping mall."

"Pardon?" I asked. I had heard of these "shopping malls." Wasn't that something they had in the Netherhells?

"But that's beside the point," the newcomer continued. "I have come here to help you find your way."

"Indeed?" I inquired.

"Exactly. I am Devoono, god of showing wanderers the way through the byways of the lower reaches of heaven."

"That's all?" Snarks asked.

Devoono nodded. "It is a rather specialized calling, I grant you, but it has its rewards."

"Like what?" Snarks demanded.

"Well, for one thing, I don't have to paint bricks," Devoono answered. "But I heard that you travelers have lost your way?"

"Indeed," I replied, glad that this fellow was in a much better mood than the last deity we had come across. "We need to locate Plaugg."

"The incredibly inconsequential," Snarks chimed in.

"Easy enough." Devoono pointed down the far right road. "Walk down there. It's the first mansion, well, the first swelling, you'll come to."

"That close?" I mused. "How can we possibly thank you?"

But the deity just nodded pleasantly. "Think nothing of it. It's better than sitting around a delivery entrance all day!"

Then he disappeared without a sound.

"It's a little disconcerting around here," Hubert remarked.

"Are you kidding?" Snarks sneered. "It's a *lot* disconcerting around here. Give me the molten slime pits of the Netherhells any day. At least there you know when something's going to come out and grab you!"

"Indeed," I interjected. "I believe it is time we went and grabbed Plaugg."

"The incredibly indifferent," Snarks added.

"If you will follow me?" I suggested, turning down the right-hand golden road.

The dwelling came in sight almost immediately, and I could see why the deity we had spoken with most recently had hesitated calling it a mansion. For, while it was reasonably large, it was not without its problems. To put it charitably, it needed a little work. The massive pillars to either side of the door were slightly askew, there were cracks here and there in the numerous statues, and there seemed to be piles of orange, spongy stuff littering the front walk.

It was a wondrous place, gone ever so slightly to seed. I had never seen a building at once so ordinary and so magnificent. Even if Devoono hadn't shown us the way, there would have been no mistaking it.

It had to be the mansion of Plaugg.

THIRTEEN

Eiquette is as important to wizards as it is to anyone else. Say, for example, that one of your numerous visiting in-laws criticizes the upkeep of the home. You, of course, should smile graciously at this remark, and pleasantly reply that you will be more than glad to turn them into a broom.

—From *Ask Ebenezum:*
A Handy Compendium of Wizards' Do's and Don'ts,
fourth edition,
by Ebenezum,
greatest wizard in the Western Kingdoms

We walked up to the front door, which appeared to be a bit loose on its hinges.

"Shall I?" Hubert asked, his massive forepaw ready to knock.

"Actually," I remarked, "I believe the honor of announcing our presence should go to Snarks. After all, he's the member of our company who worships Plaugg."

"The ineptly unequaled," Snarks whispered, awed by his surroundings. "Who thought I would ever be here, at the tumbledown mansion of *Him?*"

"So are you going to knock?" Hubert prompted.

The demon blinked and stared at the large reptile. "That's the problem with dragons. No sense of the true proprieties. I shall knock when I am spiritually prepared."

Snarks took a deep breath and knocked.

A woman's voice answered.

"We don't want any!"

Snarks took a step away. "Are you sure this is the right place?"

"Indeed," I replied. "At least that last deity said so."

"That must mean that Plaugg does not live in solitude!" Snarks shivered with the thought. "The theological implications alone are staggering."

"We're still not inside," Hubert reminded the demon. "We still have to see this guy."

"This guy?" Snarks exploded. "You refer to *Him* as 'this guy'? I'll have you know that Plaugg, bless His magnificently mediocre name, is the *Ultimate* Guy!"

"Indeed," I said soothingly. "Perhaps you should knock again."

Snarks smoothed his robes, calming himself with an effort.

"You are right, of course," the demon said at last. "I am ever so slightly overwrought, being so close—"

He stopped talking and knocked.

"We gave at the office!" the voice shouted.

"No, madam!" I called back. "You misunderstand. We are here seeking the wisdom of Plaugg!"

"Seeking his *what?*" the woman yelled. "Now I *know* you're at the wrong house." I heard the sound of feet scuffling across flagstone. "Oh, very well. I suppose I have to humor the old deity. Wait a moment and I'll lift the latch."

The door made a creaking sound and swung wide. There was no one on the other side.

"Come on in if you're coming!" the woman's voice called. "You can't keep deities waiting all day!"

Snarks and I stepped gingerly inside, crossing a cracked marble foyer into a very large room in severe need of cleaning.

"Plaugg!" the voice shouted. "Believe it or not, there's somebody here to see you."

"What?" a somewhat confused-sounding male voice called back. "Oh, very well. I'll be there in a minute."

Snarks looked wonderingly about the rather dingy but immense room we found ourselves in. "You know who that was," he whispered. "Plaugg!"

"The miraculously tardy," the disembodied woman's voice added. "He's bad enough as it is. You should be careful not to encourage him."

"Here I come! Here I come!" A fellow who was even shorter and more nondescript than the last couple deities we had met brushed aside a large cobweb and stepped into the room from one of the many surrounding alcoves. "Give me a minute now to adjust my robes." He fumbled with his tunic, which seemed rather grayer than those of others we had seen. He tugged his clothes three inches along one shoulder, frowned, then tugged them back the other way.

"There," he said at last, although I could see no difference. "That will have to do. Now, what seems to be the problem?"

Snarks fell to his knees. Even I remembered this remarkably nondescript deity from that day, so long ago, when he saved us from the Netherhells. It was Plaugg.

"Oh, Your Nondescriptness," Snarks groveled. "This is such an honor, Your Unremarkableness. How do I begin—"

"Pardon me," Plaugg interrupted, "but aren't you a demon?"

"Why, yes, Your Insipidness," Snarks stammered, "here to—um—"

"I thought as much," Plaugg replied proudly. "I'm a deity, you know. Things like this rarely escape my notice."

"Really?" the woman's voice remarked. "Then why don't you notice things around the house?"

"Now, dearest," Plaugg said with a frown. "I'm sure these nice pilgrims don't want to hear about—"

"Well, I don't want to hear about it, either!" the other voice exclaimed. "But how else am I going to get you to listen—"

"Dearest," Plaugg replied firmly. "Now is not the time or place. And why don't you manifest yourself for these nice people? It's not very polite, hanging around the room like that and making declarations from the ether."

"Oh, I suppose you're right," the woman agreed. "For once."

A light gray cloud coalesced at the center of the room. Plaugg turned back to Snarks.

"We don't get many demons up here."

"We don't get much of anybody up here!" declared the woman's voice, now attached to a form which, besides being female, was of much the same stature and shape as Plaugg. "I mean, who would want to come to a place like this?"

"Now, Devuna," Plaugg cautioned.

But, once started, the goddess was not so easily stopped. "Why don't you look at this dump? Everything in this place needs to be cleaned up and repaired. And the outside? Hah! You can barely call our home a mansion anymore, it needs so much work."

"You're becoming overwrought, dear—" Plaugg began.

"Overwrought?" Devuna laughed caustically. "Tell me this! When's the last time you swept the manna off the sidewalk?"

"Oh, my, is it piling up again?" Plaugg said distractedly. "That's one of the problems with living in a place where foodstuffs fall from the void." The god glanced at Snarks and myself. "You folks wouldn't want any, would you? It's quite tasty. Nutritious, too."

"Indeed," I replied, for it seemed time for someone to take action so that this conversation did not wander aimlessly forever. "Perhaps we will try a bit later, but now we must ask for your assistance."

"Yes, Your Prosaicness," Snarks piped up. " 'Tis the very thing that I, as Your worshipper, have been trying to put into words, if only I could find . . ." The demon's voice trailed off.

"See?" Plaugg pointed out to his spouse. "They need my assistance!"

The goddess snorted. "Good luck with them getting it!"

Plaugg turned apologetically back to Snarks and myself. "You'll have to excuse my wife, Devuna. I'm afraid, when a couple lives together throughout eternity, these little problems can creep up."

"Little?" Devuna exploded. "You call that constant drip, drip, drip in the sink a *little* problem?"

"Well, perhaps not, but you know the trouble I have there," Plaugg defended himself. "I have to find the time to study the problem, so that I might discover exactly the right motion for deific repair of that sort. After all, if I make the gesture in the proper direction, the leak is gone. However, should I inadvertently reverse the move, the waters of the heavens descend upon us." He spread his hands in a gesture of helplessness. "You can see my problem, can't you?"

Devuna grunted in dismissal. I, however, could certainly sympathize with the deity, having been in many similar situations myself.

Plaugg sighed, nodding sadly. "Sometimes, being a deity is more problem than it's worth."

"We appreciate Your concerns, Your So-soness," Snarks spoke up, "but, if we might, we could use a moment of Your reasonably valuable time."

Plaugg smiled at the demon. "Anything for my worshippers. By the way, that's a dragon looking through the doorway, isn't it?"

"Pleased to meet you!" Hubert called.

"We don't get many dragons up here," Plaugg admitted.

"We're never going to have anybody up here ever again," his wife insisted, "if you don't do some work around the place." She glared at her god-husband. "And that *anybody* includes good-for-nothing deities!"

"Indeed," I spoke to the goddess, seeking to distract her so that Snarks might properly petition Plaugg. "You are Devuna?"

"And proud of it!" Devuna sniffed. "I am the goddess of put-upon wives whose names begin with *P, Q* and *R.*"

"Indeed?" I replied.

"Exactly," she answered. "The job had so many worshippers, we had to divide up the duties."

"I had no idea," I continued, "that the deity business was so specialized."

"It's the modern way." She shot another incriminating look at her husband. "Everyone's got a specialty, except Plaugg!"

"Someone's got to be a general practitioner!" Plaugg shot back. "It's a tradition up here in the Elysian fields."

"Tradition—smadition!" His wife carped. She glanced back at me. "The simple truth is that Plaugg is incapable of making decisions."

"I can too make decisions!" Plaugg exclaimed. "At least, I think I can."

"Oh, Your Nothing-Specialness!" Snarks interjected. "Please hear us out, for, with every passing moment, our situation is getting worse!"

"Quite right," Plaugg agreed. "Devuna and I have all eternity to argue, a fact I sometimes attempt to forget. Tell me now, petitioners: What is your problem?"

Together, Snarks and I briefly outlined what had happened so far: how Death had decided that I was the Eternal Apprentice; how Death coveted my soul which—because I was the Eternal Apprentice—until now had been unobtainable; how I had thus far managed to avoid the fiend in that selfsame quest for my soul; how my master had been spirited to the land of Death by that treacherous specter, so that I would be expected to exchange my own life for that of the wizard; and how I had to find a way to rescue Ebenezum without sacrificing myself.

"Oh, of course!" Plaugg stated. "I knew that. Being a deity, I am somewhat omnipotent, you know."

"Then, might You help us, Your Adequateness?" Snarks implored.

Plaugg considered for a second. "Anything for a worshipper—"

He paused again as Snarks and I exchanged grins.

"—within limits," he concluded.

"What did I tell you?" Devuna interposed. "Nothing but talk, talk, talk."

"Now, now, dearest," Plaugg chided. "There's actually quite a lot I can do. It will simply take me a little time to do it." He glanced distractedly at Snarks and me. "Somehow, we need to get you into the Kingdom Death. I am, unfortunately, not properly informed on methods to transport worshippers into totally different spheres of existence." He smiled apologetically. "I'm afraid I have enough trouble getting around myself."

"He never leaves the house," Devuna agreed. "Can't even get him to run a simple errand."

"Now, now," Plaugg contradicted. "That's not precisely true. It's simply that I have to watch my movements. Should I walk one way, I can go down to the corner and pick up some groceries. However, should my movements inadvertently change mid-errand, I could alter the very fabric of the cosmos." He shrugged exhaustedly. "No one truly appreciates the problems of a deity."

"Excuses, always excuses," Devuna muttered.

"Least of all my wife," Plaugg concluded. "Now, how soon must you rescue this wizard?" He stared into space for an instant, his lips moving silently, then returned his gaze to Snarks and myself. "Would two weeks from Wednesday be sufficient?"

"B-but, Your Unexceptionalness!" Snarks stammered. "That cannot —" His voice died, the demon unable to contradict his deity.

"Indeed," I added helpfully. "It may already be too late—"

Plaugg's laughter held a touch of embarrassment. "Oh, that's right, you did say it was urgent. It's just that, when you're a deity, why, you tend to have simply *everything* on your mind! An immediate solution, hmm?"

"Unfortunately true, Your Passableness!" Snarks replied. "We must reach the Kingdom Death with all speed."

Plaugg sighed. "Speed, huh? I don't know if I can help you there."

"You can say that again!" Devuna interjected.

"Of course," Plaugg added uncertainly, "you could take a tour bus—"

"Indeed," I said. "A tour bus?" I was unfamiliar with the heavenly term.

"What an idea!" Devuna exclaimed, new admiration in her voice. "A tour bus would get them down there in no time at all. Every once in a while, you remind me why I married you."

"Think nothing of it," Plaugg remarked self-deprecatingly.

"I usually don't," Devuna answered with a smile.

"Dearest," Plaugg prompted, "you wouldn't happen to have a schedule?"

The goddess frowned. "You're right. I do have one around here someplace." She furrowed her brow, and a piece of parchment materialized in her hand. She studied the newfound paper for an instant. "We're in luck. The Kingdom of Death Express leaves in seventeen minutes!"

"Indeed," I said again, totally confused. "A tour bus?"

"Don't worry," Plaugg assured me. "I'll take care of everything. Which gate does it leave from, dearest?"

"Oh, that's right," Devuna nodded in sudden understanding. "Pearly is closed down for construction." She looked down to the bottom of her parchment. "All tours are temporarily leaving from Celestial."

"Celestial it is." Plaugg smiled. "I'll have you there in a jiffy." He paused to wave at the dragon in the doorway. "All three of you. And if you need anything else, all you have to do is ask. That's what I'm here for. I can hear most anything, which can be a bit of a problem sometimes, let me tell you. However, since I know you'll be calling, I'll be listening. Now, let's see—" He bit his lower lip in concentration.

"Does this mean you're going to be making house calls again?" his wife demanded.

"In a minute, dearest." Plaugg frowned.

"He can make house calls," Devuna muttered distractedly, "but can he sweep the steps? Sometimes—"

"I've got it!" Plaugg cried triumphantly. "Have a nice tour! Don't forget to write!"

The deity's voice faded as Snarks and I were surrounded by smoke. My companions and I were to be sent to the "tour bus," whatever that was.

But one thing was certain. We were going at last to rescue my master! My joy would have been complete, save for one thought:

Once we got to the Kingdom of Death, what would we do next?

FOURTEEN

I am reminded of an amusing incident that occurred early in my career. A certain spell had been intended to increase a king's knowledge, but through a small error on my part, had instead doubled the size of everyone's nose within the kingdom. I attempted to apologize to the angry throng when the king, whose nose had been none too small to begin with, rushed upon the scene with the royal executioner in tow, and demanded a satisfactory conclusion of our business, or else.

The angry mob, however, who couldn't have cared less about royalty getting their money's worth, revolted, storming the castle and grabbing me away from the executioner's blade. After a couple more minor errors, I managed to set things right with the majority of the population, especially with regards to nose size, although I did neglect to extend the antidote spell to the monarch.

And so I left that particular land, but—and I think this proves I am a fair wizard—not before I had written an anonymous note, advising the king that, if he were to properly weight his crown in the back, it would aid in balancing his head so that his chin was not constantly resting on his chest.

Now, what is the point of this little tale? Consider this: How else might I get rescued by an angry mob an instant before being murdered by a vengeful king? I think the moral is obvious. It always pays to advertise.

—From *Wake Up and Conjure!:*
The Collected Speeches of Ebenezum,
Greatest Wizard in the Western Kingdoms,
Volume CCCXII,
The Year of the Demon,
the first three weeks of summer

"Watch your step!"

The smoke had cleared abruptly. I was standing at the foot of a subtly vibrating stairway.

"Hurry it up, would you, please?" said a fellow standing by my side. He wore a gray robe and matching cap. "I've got a schedule to keep. And I need that ticket."

Ticket? Oh, I realized, the fellow must be referring to the square of parchment I held in my hand. I passed it to him.

"Good enough," the gray fellow said as he pointed up the stairs. "Sit wherever you like on the bus."

I carefully ascended the barely jiggling stairway as the fellow spoke to Snarks.

"Ticket? Say, you're a demon, aren't you?"

Snarks complimented the fellow's perceptiveness.

"We don't get many demons on this tour. Actually, we don't get much of anybody on this tour. It's a popular misconception that a tour of the Kingdom of the Dead might be downright depressing! Well, let me tell you right now, with me behind the wheel, it's anything but! Hop on the bus, now!"

I heard Snarks's feet behind me as I reached the top of the stairs.

"Wait a second, mac," declared the fellow who was apparently our guide. "This may be a heavenly bus, but there's no way we can fit a dragon in here!"

I looked back down the stairs past Snarks. Hubert tipped his top hat and showed the fellow his ticket.

"Okay, okay," the guide said with a frown. He pointed overhead. "I guess you can ride on top."

"The proper place for a dragon," Hubert rumbled as he clambered on top of whatever this thing was that I now stood inside.

"That's it, then?" the guide called, looking hopefully about the cloud fields that surrounded this "bus." "This is your last chance!" he added.

He was answered by silence.

"Everybody in their seats, then!" he called up to us. "It's time for the tour!"

Snarks joined me at the top of the stairs. I turned to look down a long aisle, bordered on either side by padded benches. The rest of this "bus" was empty—we had been the first to climb within it. I sat on the second bench from the front, next to a large, covered window. Snarks sat on my other side.

"A tour bus?" the demon whispered in wonder. "Surely, this is one of the mystic engines of the gods."

The guide jumped up the steps two at a time and sat at a small bench at the very front of the enclosed interior. He did something with his hands. We were surrounded by a rumbling, like distant thunder.

"Welcome!" the guide's voice boomed even though he faced away from us. "On a heavenly tour you will never forget!"

There was a tapping at my window. I turned, and saw Hubert's upside-down face grinning at me.

"I hope everyone is quite comfortable in their seats," the guide continued, "because here we go!"

There was a whooshing sound, like we were surrounded by a great wind, and we were no longer in heaven. We were surrounded by blue sky, far above the world.

"I'm Devorno, your divine driver," our guide continued. "And I'll be showing you some of the sights on our trip beyond the realm of the living! That's right! I guess you could say there's any number of things I'll be dying to tell you! Ha, ha, ha!"

Snarks blanched where he sat by my side. "Does this guy know Hubert?" he whispered.

I knew instantly what the demon meant. There was a certain awfulness about the driver's humor that was immediately recognizable.

"But this bus does more than fly through the air," Devorno continued. "Now, when I pull this cord here, this magic carriage will send us sailing through a dozen different realms of existence, straight to our goal, the Kingdom of Death. Look carefully, now. On a trip like this, you never know what you might see!"

The driver pulled the cord.

The light changed again, going from deep red to brilliant yellow to blinding white, as if we were flying into the heart of the sun. Then, as quickly as the light flared, it was gone, replaced by a soft golden glow. And in that glow stood at least a hundred women. What's more, all of them were staring at me. Wasn't that Alea in the corner? The women all opened their mouths to speak at the same time, and said a single word in unison. Could that be Norei that we just passed? I realized with a start what that single word had been. All the women had spoken my name.

"There they are," the driver interjected, "all the women that you might ever love. A part of each of them waits for you in this realm of possibilities, as you wait for them elsewhere. Just think, your life could be spent with any one of these beauties. Now, that's what I call living!"

So it was an image of Norei I saw! And Alea as well. But all those women? After I had already discovered my own true love? Surely it was some mistake. I turned to ask Snarks his opinion, but found him staring out the window, openmouthed.

"I've never seen so many female demons in one place!" he whispered.

"Female demons?" I replied. "Indeed." Apparently, on this edge of heaven, each of us saw only that which pertained to him specifically. I wondered if the same held true for the dragon who rode on top. But then I heard Hubert's tail thumping on the roof overhead.

"But we have to say goodbye to our lovely ladies," the driver's voice broke into my thoughts, "for we are passing into another place altogether."

The lighting changed from golden to palest blue. But that was not all that differed, for the landscape was now crowded with people: thousands upon thousands, men, women and children of all sizes, types and ages; so many that the very ground upon which they stood seemed to sag beneath their numbers. And among them, again, were those that I recognized, including a giant and a dragon.

"This place is almost empty," Snarks complained as he stared out the window beside me.

"Yes, gentlemen," the driver continued, "in this place are arrayed your life's companions. All those with whom you might form a bond, as indeed, in other realms, you wait as a companion for others."

But there were thousands of them out there!

"Six?" Snarks whispered. "That's all I'm ever going to get is—six companions? Plus, I know half of them already. You're out there; I'd recognize that terrible posture anywhere. And that fellow wearing the breastplate that should house two or three—well, that was to be Hendrek. But wait—there's someone else moving out there, someone so small I almost missed him. So small?" A look of horror overtook the demon's countenance. "It could not be! He couldn't be a companion of mine! Not—the Brownie!"

"I'm bringing the laces now—" Tap mumbled from where he rested, deep within my pocket. The words were followed by a soft snoring.

"Indeed," I replied, for what now happened here gave me much to think about. I saw thousands from the window, while Snarks perhaps saw seven. What could account for this dicrepancy? Perhaps I was truly the Eternal apprentice, after all. Why else would I have so many and the demon so few?

"The Brownie?" Snarks whispered again. "Is there any way to send companions back?"

Well, it was either that I was the Eternal apprentice, I further conjectured, or Snarks's nature was such that he annoyed almost everyone he met, thus keeping his companions to the barest minimum. Perhaps this quandary was unsolvable.

Hubert was making some consistent noise on the roof above us. After a moment's conjecture, I decided it was a soft shoe.

"But we leave this realm behind as well," the guide's voice boomed, "as we move into a more dangerous corner of the cosmos."

The light changed again, this time shifting to an angry red glow. I saw others, arrayed across the celestial countryside we passed, although this time they did not look so friendly. In fact, they looked rather more like monsters and demons of the most unsavory kind.

"We pass now," the guide continued, "and very quickly, may I add, through the region of danger and fear. All your problems wait out there for you, gentlemen, and would be only too happy to get a chance at you now, rather than waiting until their proper time. Lucky for us, though, this bus is beyond their reach. It's a little feature we have called climate control."

I could not take my eyes off the fiends that we passed. I realized I had faced some of them before, both with my sword, Cuthbert, and with my stout oak staff. That must mean that I might have to face the many others sometime in the future.

Or perhaps I would not have to face any more of them, save one, for in the very center of the friends stood Death, laughing.

"But that's enough of that," our guide interjected. "And now, as the heavenly shores recede farther into the distance, we pass through a few realms that are not so personal. Sit back and relax, as you see things not quite of the world below or this world above."

The guide's voice was replaced by that high choir music we had heard all over heaven.

The colors outside the bus changed again, then yet again, as if the vehicle was speeding us through many places on our way to our destination. Sights flashed by our window at lightning speed, at first portraying scenes of knights and heroes, as you might see on tapestries, then changing to more fantastic themes, as if we had once again returned to the fairy tales of the Eastern Kingdoms. And then the sights grew stranger still. A group of men wearing helmets and immense amounts of padding fought in the mud over a small brown ovoid. A second group of men holding sticks chased a small round stone around the ice. What was the meaning of these strange activities? A third group of very tall men wearing only their underwear bounced this large ball, occasionally crashing into each other as one of them tossed the ball into the air. Then the scene shifted again, and two very large men faced each other in a roped-off square, both leaping and grabbing, each man trying to get an advantage over the other.

Ah, but I knew what happened now! This was wrestling, the most popular sport in all of the Western Kingdoms! Then were those other, much stranger activities sports as well? But how could any other sport have the honesty and true excitement of the art of grappling? I was destined never to know, for the lighting shifted again.

This seemed to be a quieter realm, mostly made up of strangely garbed people engaged in earnest conversation, although, for some odd reason, the colors had become more intense than in any realm we had seen before. But there were flashes of other things as well: large containers of what appeared to be food and drink, and conveyances smaller than the bus we now rode in, but somehow related—these vehicles were almost always painted red, and seemed to come with a fair damsel seated within as these little buses moved all too fast down twisting roads.

The faces grew larger as I watched people cough and sneeze. My interest increased, for I hoped I might catch a glimpse of my master, but I saw naught but pictures of strange bottles and boxes, covered by pitures and lettering that were stranger still.

A giant head appeared from nowhere, accompanied by a voice so loud that it penetrated the window that separated us:

"I had a headache *this* big—"

"Whoops!" the guide called back to us. "We've gotten a little off course here. But don't worry, folks, I just have to make a slight correction, and we'll be in the Kingdom of Death in no time!"

The guide pulled another pair of cords. The bus shook. I heard a faint squealing sound from somewhere. All of the intense colors vanished, to be replaced by a world of gray.

I didn't need the guide to tell us where we were now.

We had arrived in the Kingdom of Death.

FIFTEEN

I have always sworn by the wisdom of traveling with companions. In dangerous situations, the more companions you have, the more secure you will feel. Thus, should you be faced with a sudden attack by some fearsome beast of the forest, you will be better able to defend yourself if you have a companion or two by your side, rather than having to face the danger alone. Similarly, should you be the victim of a surprise attack by the Netherhells, a dozen weapon-wielding companions are more than welcome by your side.

And what about companions for that moment when you enter the Kingdom of Death? Well, let me put it to you this way: have you ever wanted the entire city of Vushta to be your friend?

—From *Some Thoughts on Apprenticeship,*
by Wuntvor, assistant to Ebenezum,
greatest wizard in the Western Kingdoms
(a work in progress)

"Doesn't look too lively around here, does it?" the guide's cheer attempted, but failed, to penetrate the surrounding gloom. "And little wonder, 'cause this is a dead town if I've ever seen one! Ha, ha! Just kidding, folks. Yes, we've reached our destination, land of the big D! But the tour has only begun! In the next few minutes, we'll hit all the points of interest in this realm, and maybe, if we're lucky, get a glimpse of the head specter itself!"

So we would see Death? I supposed there was no avoiding a confrontation, now that we had entered his realm. Still, I wished there was some way I might contact my master before I grappled with the bony fiend.

I looked out the window, but there was no sign of Death yet. In fact, there was not much sign of anything at all. The landscape about us was colorless, and almost featureless, as if the whole of the space around was coated with a thin fog above a layer of gray snow. It was hard to make out anything in the dim light, but I thought I saw figures moving slowly through the distance, at that point where objects went from indistinct to invisible.

"We are traveling now through the Region of Unrelieved Grayness!" our guide explained. "At least that's what they call it hereabouts. With a name like that, it's no wonder property values around here are so low!"

"It's too bad we need this guy to take us to your master," Snarks whispered in my ear. "Otherwise, we could strangle him."

I softly replied that Snarks should contain himself. Any moment now, it would be time to leave this bus and guide behind. That's when the real danger would begin.

"But the Region of Unrelieved Grayness does not go on forever!" the guide announced happily. "No, we will pass beyond it in a moment to other parts of Death's kingdom. For the land of the dead is as varied as the souls that reside here, as varied as all the worlds the dead have come from, if not more so."

It became brighter outside as the guide spoke. The air was slowly clearing, and I could see hints of color through the haze, a faint blue here, a bit of pink there, a swatch of green close by the ground. Then, as if someone—or something—had snapped his fingers, the air cleared completely, and the view outside was as bright as noon on a summer's day, except, oddly enough, that I could see no sign of the sun. We had entered a place full of green grass and blue sky, and were approaching a pavilion of tents, each a different color, and each one somehow, impossibly, brighter than the one before.

"You will see, over on your left, one of Death's gaming areas," our guide continued. "We'll tour another of these later on, for they litter this realm. As some of you may know, Death is very fond of games."

I could not suppress a shudder. I was all too aware of Death's fondness for games. Up to this point, I had spent all my energy finding a way to reach my master. Now I would have to find a way to confront Death. What game would I have to play to rescue Ebenezum?

"There are places here that are not so different from the world you know, gentlemen," the guide's booming voice remarked. "In fact, we are now passing that part of Death's domain that most resembles the Western Kingdoms. As you can see, we are surrounded by unrelieved greenery. It's almost as dull as the real thing, isn't it, folks?"

Western Kingdoms? Dull? Maybe I should reconsider Snarks's offer
to strangle this fellow.

"Why are these places here?" the guide continued rhetorically.
"What is the reason for gray areas next door to regions of endless
light? Who can truly fathom the world of the dead?" The bus divinity
paused dramatically. "We may never know the answers to these questions. But perhaps we'll get some inklings about those secrets at our
first stop, just ahead. And, as an extra bonus, you can get any of a
number of mouth-watering refreshments as well!"

The bus turned sharply and stopped. We had pulled up next to a
small wooden structure with a festively painted sign hung across the
roof:

LAND OF THE DEAD
SOUVENIR SHOP
and Snack Bar
(Tourist Tips, Too)
"All the Dead Stop Here"

Other, smaller signs covered the window below:

PETRIFIED WOOD INSIDE!

We can supply all your ash and dust needs!
420 varieties!

Inert Objects of Every Kind!
If it doesn't move, we've got it!

"Everybody out!" the guide announced. "And don't dawdle. The
tour resumes in fifteen minutes." And with that, Devorno climbed
down the steps and out of the bus.

"Shall we?" I asked the demon.

"I'll do anything to get away from here," Snarks replied.

I led the way out of the strange vehicle.

"It's quite something, isn't it?" Hubert rumbled from the top of the
bus.

"Indeed," I said. "Then your journey was satisfactory?" I had to
admit to myself that, in the heat of the tour, I had all but forgotten

about Hubert crouching overhead. If I had not been so concerned for
my master, I might have worried more for the dragon's safety.

"More than satisfactory!" the dragon enthused. "Once I got used to
the sudden changes in scenery, it became inspirational!"

"Inspirational?" Snarks replied with a bit of trepidation. The demon
climbed down to my side.

"Yes!" the dragon replied rapturously. "Just think of the song-and-
dance routines that can come out of an experience like this. Something
like—" Hubert cleared his throat and sang:

> "You haven't lived until you've seen
> The Kingdom of the Dead.
> It's the sort of place to excite your spleen!
> You heard what I said!
> So go to the place that's really keen
> Once your skin is shed
> Don't waste time! Come on! Careen
> To that Kingdom of the Dead!"

His jaw snapped shut as he looked to us for approval.

"Indeed," I remarked.

"Or something like that," he added. "After all, it's only a first
draft."

"Indeed," I said again, digging my heels into the ground, which
seemed as real as the earth beneath one's feet in the Western Kingdoms. "Should we go inside?"

"I think we have to," Snarks answered dryly. "At least, we do if we
want to get our money's worth."

"If it's all right with you fellows," Hubert said, "I think I'll simply
stay out here and *experience!*"

I nodded, and told Snarks to follow me, for I realized that there was
another reason to go inside as well. Now that we had reached the
Kingdom of Death, we had to find my master. What better place to
start than an information center like this?

As I opened the door to the strange structure, I felt the Brownie stir
in my pocket and mutter something about shining the buckles in a
minute. Perhaps, I considered, now was the time to wake the sleeping
Tap.

The door made a noise as I opened it: a sound halfway between a squeaking hinge and Death's dark laughter. It took me a second to realize that the specter wasn't waiting for me on the other side.

"That got your attention, didn't it?" Devorno shouted from across the room. "I tell you, Death is a marketing genius!"

Snarks frowned as he looked around the room, which seemed filled with piles of stones and dust. Signs stuck from the pile tops:

Dirt Cheap!
Everything Must Go!
Rock-bottom Prices!

"This is marketing genius?" the demon asked.

"Well," Devorno said, "perhaps this place is not the best example. But it is only one small piece of Death's handiwork. Who do you think came up with the idea of war, anyway?"

"Indeed," I interjected. "You mentioned the possibility of refreshments?" It had occurred to me that, if we were going to wander through the Kingdom of Death for who knew how long in search of my master, perhaps it would be better to eat first.

"Most certainly," our guide replied. "The food counter is in the back over there." He pointed to the rear of the building. I saw a small table, over which hung a placard which listed prices for "Rigor Mortis Burgers" and "Death Shakes." What kind of food was this?

"Uh," I added, for it occurred to me that I had seen no one but Devorno and Snarks within this building, "is there no one here to serve us?"

"Well, there may not be any*one* in particular," our guide explained a bit apologetically, "but there is definitely some*thing.*" He pointed at the table in the back. "Simply put your money there, and state what it is that you desire. The item will appear almost instantaneously. It's a little disconcerting, I'll grant you. But around here, it's a lot more pleasant than many of the other possibilities. Trust me."

"Indeed," I replied. Now that I thought of it, I was wondering if I could trust the food. For one thing, there was something about the name "Rigor Mortis Burger" that did nothing for the appetite. And a second point to consider was Death's love for games. If the specter knew I was here, would it playfully add something to the burger that would ensure I would stay in Death's kingdom forever?"

"On second thought," I stated, "I'm not hungry."

"Probably wise," Devorno admitted. "This place is worse than Slime-o-Rama."

"Home of the Slime Burgers?" Snarks responded. "That isn't possible!"

But the bus deity no longer heard the demon. Instead, he stared at the door through which we had entered, his face twisted in fright.

"I shouldn't have said that, should I?" he whimpered. "I know I'm under contract. Please, if you're going to—make it quick, and painless?"

A great shadow fell across the room. I wanted to turn around, to confront the newcomer, but fear kept me rooted to the spot. Snarks, full of demonic bravery, wheeled about. His jaw opened in astonishment.

"It cannot be!"

A hand fell on my shoulder.

"Excuse me," said a voice both gentle and powerful. It was a voice I knew.

The newcomer spoke again:

"You wouldn't happen to know where I might find a wild pig?"

It was the Dealer of Death.

SIXTEEN

You can't go home again, and why would you want to, anyways?

—From *The Demon wise Guide to the Netherhells,
or Why I'm Glad You're Going and I'm Not,*
by Snarks, most honest demon ever come from down
below
(another tome still awaiting publication)

Snarks said what I could only think.

"What are *you* doing here?"

The Dealer of Death sighed. "That means you don't have any wild pigs, doesn't it?"

"Indeed," I replied. "I'm afraid we didn't think to bring any. But then we weren't expecting to encounter you, either."

The Dealer nodded. "You are no more surprised than I. One minute, I was facing up to that Netherhells committee, which was threatening to boil my blood. The next thing I knew, here I was—wherever this is."

I briefly answered that when I had last seen the Dealer, it had been in Vushta, after the demon committee had indeed boiled his blood, sending him into a near-death coma.

"Then he's dead?" Snarks asked in disbelief. "He doesn't look very dead to me."

"Nor do I feel it." The Dealer absently flexed his shoulder muscles as he considered my most recent statement. "And your explanation makes a great deal of sense to me, for it explains why I am different from the others here."

The large fellow cracked his knuckles, ten small, simultaneous explosions. "For although I am in this place, I do not seem subject to its rules in the same way as those I have met. Perhaps it is because my earthly body still straddles that line between life and death. From what I understand, Death usually takes a more active interest in cases like me who have halfway entered his kingdom. However, from what I have also heard, the specter has become obsessed with something lately, and has no time for the likes of me, instead spending its days muttering 'Eternal, eternal.' Whatever that means."

"Indeed," I said grimly. "I may have some idea."

The Dealer nodded happily. "I figured that you might. I've noticed that things always seem to happen around you, and decided that that was exactly what I needed. I mean, it's perfectly nice around here, except that perhaps it's a bit low-key. And I haven't strangled a single wild pig since I've gotten here!" He sighed again. "I mean, how can you strangle something when it's already dead?"

The Dealer's hands closed around an imaginary neck as he continued. "I shouldn't have hoped, I guess. It's simply when I saw you had a dragon outside, I thought . . ." His voice trailed off, leaving his fondest dream unsaid.

"Indeed?" I asked. "So you are here to help us?"

"Of course," the Dealer answered. "You're the sort of fellow who inspires that sort of thing."

I could do nothing but nod in return, for that very talent of mine was one of the reasons Death wanted me for its own. But I would not despair, for my master's life was in danger.

"Indeed," I began after I took a deep breath. "Then you will help me find the wizard Ebenezum?"

"Most certainly, if that is what you wish," the Dealer agreed. "It feels good to have a direction again. After all, an assassin in the land of the dead is a bit purposeless."

"Then lead on!" I pointed to the door. "Into the Kingdom of the Dead!"

"Wait a second!" Devorno interrupted. "What about the tour?"

"I am sorry, good guide," I responded, "but the tour will have to wait. We have a wizard to rescue and a world to save!"

"Hey, if you didn't like the tour, just say so!" the guide replied defensively. "Excuses, excuses, nothing but excuses."

"No, really!" I retorted, trying not to hurt the divinity's feelings. "We have to leave here, for reasons having nothing to do with you—"

"Sure, sure," the guide answered despondently. "Dig the knife in a little deeper. Why don't you tell me right out—"

"Okay," Snarks interrupted before I could further explain. "You found us out. I've never heard a more boring guide in my life. We didn't want to go on your tour, anyway! But now that we've left it, maybe we'll be able to wake ourselves up!"

"What?" Devorno replied in outrage. "Well, if that's the way you feel about it!"

The guide stormed past us out of the shop. A second later, I heard the strange sound that the bus made when it moved; then that sound, too, retreated into the distance.

Snarks nodded in satisfaction. "Cruel but fair. It's the demon way. Otherwise it would have taken us forever to get rid of him."

"Indeed," I said, wondering if there might have been some other way. But perhaps the demon was right for once, for now we were free to find my master.

I turned to the others, and told them there was no time to delay. Only, where could we begin?

"Leave that to me," the dealer remarked quietly as he motioned us to follow him from the shop. "I have had time to explore, and I have found the perfect starting point."

Snarks and I accompanied the dealer outside the dwelling, where we found a somewhat disgruntled dragon.

"All I have to say," the reptile remarked sternly, "is, if you want the top of your bus back, you only have to ask." He paused to brush some imaginary dust from his tail. "Here I was, one minute basking in the glow of whatever it is the light around here comes from, and the next—whamo!—the bus has vanished and I am deposited on whatever passes for the ground around here, which is quite substantial, let me assure you." The dragon winced as he tried to sit. "What did you do to that deity? You guys didn't somehow incur his wrath or anything?"

I told the dragon I would explain everything as we moved. At the moment, the most important thing was to locate my master.

Hubert stared at the Dealer of Death.

"Say. Aren't you—"

The Dealer nodded.

"It doesn't surprise me," the dragon replied laconically. "Nothing surprises me anymore." He paused, then added hopefully: "I wonder if there's a song in there somewhere."

"Indeed," I added. "If only we had time to explore the possibilities. Unfortunately, we must follow the Dealer."

And we did just that, walking after the well-muscled assassin into that nearby forest that looked an awful lot like the Western Woods.

The Dealer frowned. "I know it's around here somewhere." He turned left, crossing a stream and passing a twisted oak that somehow seemed very familiar.

"Yes, yes!" the Dealer exclaimed with new excitement. "This is the way!"

I followed the assassin uneasily, almost overwhelmed by déjà vu. This was not simply the Western Woods; this was the corner of the woods directly behind Ebenezum's cottage.

"Ah!" the Dealer chortled. "As I suspected. Here we are."

And we were. We stepped out of the forest halfway between the cottage and the well from which I used to fetch water. But how would this be? We weren't in the Western Woods, we were in the Kingdom of Death.

"This is not the real thing," the Dealer assured me, "but an incredible simulation."

"But how would you know about this place?" I asked. "And how could you know that this looked like my master's cottage?"

"You forget," the Dealer replied, "that I am a member of the Urracht sect, the most fanatically devoted order of assassins that the world has ever known. When I was first hired by King Urfoo the Vengeful to kill your master and his companions, I, of course, spent a few days learning everything I could about the wizard. And that included all I could discover about the wizard's dwelling, should I have to kill him there. Now, certainly, that we are in the Kingdom of Death, all this killing business becomes academic. But still, it was important at the time."

"Indeed," I commented, impressed by this man's fanatical devotion. Thank goodness his mission to kill us was far in the past, or perhaps far in the future.

"So are we going to stand around here and admire the simulation," Snarks prompted, "or what?"

"Indeed, no," I replied. "But perhaps this place holds some clue to my master's whereabouts."

"It holds more than that." The dealer pointed at the steps that led into the cottage. "Look."

If I had been surprised before, now I was downright astonished, for on the top step was a very familiar pile of books and mystical instruments, a pile that had once resided in my pack, until I had been snatched aloft by a giant bird who wasn't too concerned about what happened to my possessions. And as I approached, I saw there were other things upon the pile as well: my stout oak staff, a hefty wizardry do-it-yourself book and the crystal ball.

"What is all this doing here?" I asked.

The Dealer considered. "These are all things that you lost, are they not?"

I nodded in wonder.

"Well," the Dealer continued, "here's where they are to be found. Perhaps all lost objects end in the Kingdom of the Dead, I don't know. Or perhaps this is a special case. Look around at this exact reproduction of your home in the Western Woods. I told you before that I had studied you and your master. I have a feeling that someone, or something, else has become even more obsessed than I with where you and the wizard come from, so obsessed that it was forced to re-create all this, in hopes that it would give some clue as to your background, something that it could use to overcome its obsession. Am I correct?"

I nodded again. "The specter has done this, then, to seek out my weakness."

The Dealer nodded in return. "Only time will tell if it has succeeded."

"Indeed," I replied. "Then it is doubly important that I contact my master, for this strange place has given me the means to do so."

I climbed the step and picked up the crystal ball, then paused a moment while I fished the incantation from my pocket. Would that Brownie never wake up? But I had no time to think of Tap now. I only had the time and energy to contact my master.

"Secret sphere, seashore seer—" I began, rapidly reading through the rhyme without a hitch. The crystal ball clouded obediently, without errant noises or spoken messages. This time, it would work for sure!

"I must—" I began, barely able to speak for the excitement rising with my breast. "I must speak with my master, the great wizard Ebenezum!"

To my astonishment, I was answered by a very familiar voice: "Yes, Wuntvor?"

But I could see nothing in the crystal! I feared the clouds would keep me from fully contacting my master. I shook the sphere, trying to conquer the mystic forces therein.

"Master?" I called. "Ebenezum? Where are you?"
Someone tapped me on the shoulder. I glanced around.
"Indeed," a voice intoned.
It was my master.

SEVENTEEN

"You ask if I have any comment about those six attractive and scantily clad women that were seen leaving my study the other day. And perhaps, because of that visit, it is true that I am not quite the wizard that you had thought me to be. Happily, however, the young women who visited me also had entirely different thoughts. Next question?"

—Ebenezum,
during the conference in which he claimed "that everything about
Wizardgate will be revealed"

"Indeed?" I cried, quite beside myself.

"Yes," my master replied. "Here I am. Death didn't know what else to do with me."

"Hey, that's great!" Hubert enthused. "Now that we've found the wizard, we can get out of here!" The dragon paused. "Uh, we *can* get out of here, can't we?"

"Indeed," my master said as he thoughtfully tugged on his beard. "How did you manage to find me in the first place? I imagine we could simply reverse the process."

"Oops," Snarks remarked as I glanced his way. "Hey, how could I know that boring tour guide might actually become important?"

I briefly described how we had enlisted Plaugg's aid to reach this place, but then had to somehow rid ourselves of the bus of the gods.

"I see," Ebenezum said when I was done. " 'Tis a shame, but it can't be helped. I am glad to see you, anyway, Wuntvor. Working together, we have a much better chance against the specter than I had by myself."

"So you can use magic around here?" Hubert asked.

"I suppose so. I don't seem to have the reaction to it I once had: sneezing and all that. However, there is a problem using magic in

Death's domain. This house you see, these woods, the sky above us, the ground below, all are creations of the specter's imagination; of its own very powerful magic, if you will. Therefore, any spells you try here exist within that greater sorcery—Death's sorcery, perhaps the greatest magic ever known—which might give your own magic some unexpected results."

"Indeed," I replied, marveling at how well my master grasped the situation. It was good to be able to rely on his wisdom again.

"So, Wuntvor," the wizard asked, "what shall we do next?"

"In-indeed?" I stammered, rather taken aback. My master was here, and whenever I was with my master, he automatically took charge. At least that had happened until now. This time, however, he was asking for my advice!

I took a deep breath. Very well. My master's request had been a surprise, but I would not let it get the better of me. Ebenezum had been trapped in Death's kingdom for some time now, and perhaps felt his facilities were somewhat hampered by being so long in these surroundings. What more natural, then, but to ask advice of someone who was new on the scene, and not yet under the spell of the Kingdom of the Dead? It made perfect sense.

"Indeed," I repeated. "I had not given it much thought. I was so concerned with finding you that I had not spent much time planning what would happen thereafter. I do have a couple ideas, however."

"Indeed," the wizard mused, an odd glint in his eye. "You must share them with me."

"In a minute?" Snarks interjected. "First, the apprentice and I must have a conference."

"Really?" Ebenezum chuckled dryly. "I hardly think that is necessary."

"Indeed," I began, turning to the demon. "If there is some problem, cannot we all—"

"The necessity of our talk can only be determined as we confer," Snarks insisted. "Besides, it will only take a moment. You surely have a moment, after being here all this time."

"If you put it that way," I said, "I suppose—"

"Wuntvor!" my master barked, suddenly severe. "We are back together after all this time. Surely you don't need to leave now to talk to a demon?"

"Indeed," I replied. The wizard hardly sounded like himself. I guessed that the long days of being trapped in Death's domain had taken their toll. "Still, I don't think a minute—"

"Do not dispute me!" Ebenezum rumbled, his eyes dark with fury. "You will come with me now."

"But is that the wisest course?" I counseled the wizard. "I know that you must be anxious to leave this place, but until we fully consider the options—"

The wizard pointed at me with one long-fingered hand. "You will come with me now, or not at all."

"Very well," I answered, trying to calm my master down. "But are you sure this is the best way—"

"I know what the best course is for the Eternal Apprentice!" the mage exclaimed. "Wuntvor, take my hand!"

His longer fingers reached for me, fingers that seemed bonier than I remembered. Had Death been starving my master as well? I glanced at Snarks, who was vehemently shaking his head. What did the demon know that he could not tell me? Surely, taking the wizard's hand could not harm me.

But I looked at that hand again, at those five bony, white fingers. Perhaps it would harm me, after all.

I took a step away.

"You will not get away that easily!" the mage declared as he made a quick grab for me. I stepped aside, but his fingers gripped the flap of my pack, tearing it open.

"Eep eep!" cried the angry ferret as it erupted in the wizard's face.

"A ferret?" the mage shrieked. "Keep it away from me! You know how I feel about ferrets!"

Now I was sure something was wrong.

My master didn't feel one way or another about ferrets. The last time I had produced scores of them from my magic hat, he had taken them perfectly in stride. But I remembered something else that had an aversion to the small, rapidly reproducing creatures.

The mage brushed the animal aside and recomposed himself, staring at me with ever more hollow eyes.

"You will come with me now!" the wizard demanded, but somehow, silently, the Dealer had moved so that he stood between the mage and myself.

"Perhaps it is time to calm yourself," the Dealer said reasonably.

"Calm?" the wizard screamed. "How can I have any calm when *he* is here!" The mage's hand shook as he pointed at me. "I will have you yet!"

And with those words his robes changed, losing their silver moons and stars and becoming garments of darkest black. His hands turned bonier still, and the beard fell away, revealing a skull-like grin. Death's grin.

Death laughed, the sound of insects drowning in the incoming tide. "Why should I get upset? You are in my domain now. There is no way to escape." It spent a moment smoothing its robes; a moment, I suspect, used to gain the calm the specter already professed. "You have won our first little game. But there will be more; many more."

The death's-head smile seemed to widen. "I had wondered where you had gotten to. Heaven, was it? How very clever. But I should have expected something of the sort from the Eternal Apprentice! I was actually caught off my guard when you arrived, for at least half a minute." It laughed again, the sound of lemmings plunging to their doom. "Now, however, that we have been properly reintroduced, we shall play by my rules. You have no choice, if you ever want to see your master again!"

Death's laughter echoed about us, but the specter had vanished from our midst.

"Indeed," I said to Snarks, when I once again remembered to breathe. "Was that what you wished to tell me?"

"Something of the sort," the demon said. "It's a talent I picked up in the Netherhells. When you're surrounded by liars, cheats and confidence fiends from the day you are born, you tend to readily recognize the type. I wasn't exactly sure who that was at first. I was only certain that it was not your master. Then, I'll admit, when I guessed that it was really Death"—the demon shivered— "I was afraid if I went and told you about it the wrong way, we'd all get zapped."

"I had no idea Death was such a great actor," Hubert added with new respect. "Imagine the career the specter could have if it wasn't so intent on killing people."

"We are in Death's kingdom," the Dealer reminded us quietly. "Here, the specter can do almost anything. Because we are still alive, it has no direct control over us. However, since this is its domain, I'm sure Death could devise any number of means to make us no longer alive."

"But if this being is so powerful," Snarks objected, "why are we still breathing?"

The Dealer nodded. "There is another factor we have not considered. Death seems to have an emotional problem when it comes to the Eternal apprentice—the mention of the name alone is enough to get the specter to lose its coldly rational head. When the Eternal Apprentice confronts it directly—well, then, death has *real* problems. And in those problems is the hope for our salvation."

"Indeed," I interjected, trying to comprehend the gist of what the Dealer had just told us. "I am quite impressed with your understanding of this situation."

"It is only natural, when you think about it," the Dealer replied humbly. "After all, as an assassin, death has been my life."

"Indeed," I said again. "But what you have told me is disquieting as well. Death controls this kingdom so completely that it can make us see or feel anything it wishes."

"Within the limits I have already described," the Dealer agreed. "You can depend on nothing in this kingdom, except your wits."

"Indeed," I replied after a moment's consideration. "My wits?"

"His wits?" Snarks exclaimed. "Oh, no, we've lost for sure."

"No, not simply *his* wits," the dealer reprimanded the demon. "Although you do make light of someone who is the Eternal Apprentice. But, besides his wits, we also have those of myself and the dragon. Not to mention *your* wits."

"Oh," Snarks said, a bit humbled. "My wits? In that case, we can't lose!"

"Indeed, we have more than those," I added. "For we also have the wits of the ferret, small as they may be, and two more intelligences as well."

I drew forth Cuthbert by way of demonstration.

"What? Huh?" the sword began. "I thought you were going to leave me in there forever! Oh, I know, sometimes I ask you to do things like that, but I don't really mean it. That is, I don't mean it as long as there's no blood to be spilled anywhere. There isn't, is there? Or ichor?"

I assured the talking blade that the immediate region was battle-free.

"Ah," Cuthbert sighed. "Then it's simply a chance to get free of my scabbard and see the sights. That's more like it! It's nice around here, too. Very bright and cheerful. Would anyone mind telling me where we are?"

I told the sword we were in the Kingdom of Death.

"The Kingdom of *what*?" Cuthbert squawked. "That does not sound at all positive. What are you going to want me to cut up around here? Trust you to find a place where there's something worse than ichor!"

"Alas," the Dealer of Death remarked. "Such is the lot of heroes."

"Oh-oh," the sword shuddered. "I remember *this* guy! when he was wielding me, it was blood city! Hack and slash, slash and hack, morning, noon and night. Then, for a change of pace, we did gorings and decapitations! This guy never paused for breath!"

"On the contrary," the Dealer interposed, "I find decapitations quite restful."

"Indeed," I tried to calm the sword, for I, too, remembered when the Dealer had used Cuthbert to hack and slash his way across the Netherhells. "I imagine there will be scant need for killing, since everybody else around here is already dead. And, for similar reasons, I can't see any reason why I would have to lend you to someone."

"That's the ticket!" Cuthbert cheered. "I'm your sword, and don't you forget it! Now, would you mind putting me back in my scabbard until we're someplace normal?"

I did as the sword requested.

"I'm not worried at all now," Snarks remarked. "That weapon is going to be a whole bunch of help!"

"But didn't you say there were *two* who could help us?" Hubert rumbled.

"That's true," I replied. "And I think it's time to wake the second one." I patted my pocket.

"The second one?" Snarks asked with a shudder. "In there?"

I nodded.

"You didn't bring—" the demon was unable to name the object of his fear.

I nodded again.

The demon looked up to the heavens, if there were indeed heavens in this realm.

"Is there no escape?" he whispered.

"Indeed," I said. "Not in this life." I tapped my pocket.

"Wha—" the Brownie mumbled. "Who?" The little fellow yawned and stretched, standing so that he could peer over the pocket top. "Sorry. I seem to have taken a little nap, there. Too much Brownie Power, I guess. Where are we? What time is it?"

A spectral laugh swallowed whatever answer I might have made. Death was once again in our midst.

"It is time for the games to begin," it intoned dryly.

I saw then that Death was not alone. It had brought a man-size cage along, and in that cage was my master, the wizard Ebenezum!

"These games will be different from those we've played before," Death continued summarily. "We are in my kingdom, so we will play by my rules. It goes without saying, of course, that I also get to choose the games we play."

"Indeed—" I began.

"An interesting point," Death conceded before I could go any further. "In the sake of fairness, therefore, for I may be more experienced at one or two of these pastimes, I suggest we play best out of three. Any objections?"

"Indeed—" I tried again.

"Excellent," the specter replied. "As in any true game, there is of course a prize for winning, and a forfeit for losing. The prize, you will be happy to learn, is the wizard Ebenezum, as well as freedom for you and your companions. That was what you were going to ask, wasn't it?"

"Indeed," I answered, "but—"

"Oh, yes," Death hurriedly added, "if you win and are returned to the world you know, you will of course be allowed to live out the rest of your natural lives." The specter grinned at each of us. "However long or short those lives may be."

"Indeed!" I interjected once more. "However—"

"Oh, the forfeit!" Death chuckled, the sound of a fish flopping about in a bucket as it drowns in the open air. "Well, you know what that is, don't you? If you lose two, none of you get to leave. And the Eternal Apprentice is mine forever!"

I was silent this time.

"Do you accept?" Death demanded.

What could I do? I looked over at my master. He solemnly nodded back at me. Did that mean I should accept Death's challenge? What other way could I possibly have of rescuing the wizard and escaping the specter's clutches?

There was only one answer.

"Indeed," I replied.

"Excellent!" Death said heartily. The specter swept back its robes and surveyed me and all my companions before it spoke again. "I have thought upon this moment long and hard, and I have decided that for our first game, we should have something steeped in tradition. A game of skill, and a game of champions. And only one game could truly suit all these criteria."

Death raised his hand, palm up, before him, and in that hand appeared a sphere not unlike my crystal ball, save that this new globe was jet-black.

"The game, gentlemen"—Death spoke slowly, drawing out the suspense—"is bowling."

EIGHTEEN

There are rumors that I have heard that wizards are not "good sports." Nothing could be further from the truth. Most mages I know will be glad to turn you into any number of lower animals and other life-forms. What? You don't want to be turned into a tadpole or tree fungus? Well, who's being a good sport now? No answer, huh? Oh, I forgot, tree fungi can't talk. Can they?

—Introductory chapter to the great wizard Ebenezum's
newest self-help course,
How to Make Friends and Influence People by Threatening to Turn Them Into Toads,
never released to the general public,
due to some problems among test groups with getting
tree fungi to continue paying for lessons

"B-bowling?" I sputtered. "But we have never heard of such a thing!"

Death waved away my objections with a bony hand. "You will pick it up soon enough. If not"—it paused to stare at me with its blank eye sockets—"perhaps we can give you all of eternity to practice."

The specter waved both hands. "But I said this was a game of champions." The hands pointed to his right. "Therefore, let my champion appear."

A puff of orange smoke appeared where Death had indicated, and there stood a man, average-looking, a couple inches shorter than myself, fairly well muscled, but no match for a specimen like the Dealer of Death. All in all, the fellow looked absolutely too ordinary to be a champion, save for one thing: his bright orange and green shirt. I looked more closely at this strange new garment, and saw that over the pocket was written a single word: "Ernie."

"This is my champion," Death announced as it waved its hands again. "And this is our field of battle."

A long wooden aisle appeared before us, at the end of which stood ten clublike objects.

"Ernie?" Death said to his champion. "If you would explain?"

"Gladly." The champion nodded pleasantly to the rest of us. "How you doin', fellas?" He picked up the black sphere, which had reappeared by the wooden aisle. "This is a bowling ball. That"—he nodded at the aisle—"is the lane, down which you roll the ball. The object of the game is to hit those pins"—he pointed at the club things at the other end—"and knock them over. Every time it's your turn, you get two tries to knock the pins down. The more pins you knock down, the better you do. Like this."

Ernie took three steps forward and launched the ball down the wooden lane. The ball curved slightly, then swung back in again, knocking all ten pins over with a solid crash.

"That, gentlemen," Ernie continued, "is the best you can do. It's known as a strike. If you take both your turns to knock down all the pins, it's known as a spare. You'll get extra points—"

"Enough explanations!" Death interrupted. "They can ask questions as they go along. I've waited too long for this to delay another instant! They must choose their champion now!"

"Indeed," I replied. "If you—"

"Ah," Death answered before I could go further. "You would like some privacy? Of course."

I didn't feel any movement, nor did I see Death, his champion and the caged Ebenezum move, yet, somehow, there were now a hundred yards between us. It was all a bit disconcerting. Still, it was no more disconcerting than Death answering me before I had spoken. I would have to deal with it somehow. But why didn't I feel more positive about that thought?

"Indeed," I said to my companions. "We need a champion."

"For bowling?" Snarks despaired.

"If you could distract those guys," Hubert offered, "I might be able to knock the pins down with my tail."

"And I might be able to influence the ball with Brownie Power," Tap piped up. "However, it would be much better if the game had shoes in it."

"No," I replied, "I have the feeling that if we tried to influence the game through magical means, Death would simply influence it the other way. We will play honestly, unless Death does otherwise. And I think there is only one here with the skill and accuracy necessary to become our champion, to stand up in the face of Death and overcome any challenge—"

"I'm touched by this show of faith—" Hubert began.

"No, no," I gently told the dragon. "Your expertise lies in other, more theatrical areas. For the sport of bowling, I'm afraid we must turn to the Dealer."

"I shall do my best," the assassin replied humbly. "Perhaps I can imagine that the ball is a wild pig."

I clapped the well-muscled fellow on the shoulder, hurting my hand slightly. "I'm sure you will do admirably," I said as I flexed my hand behind my back.

"You are decided?" Death asked, suddenly at our side once more. "Good! Let the competition begin!" The specter coughed delicately. "I, of course, will act as commentator."

Somehow, the light around us dimmed, so that the only truly bright spot was in the vicinity of the bowling lane. I heard the soft murmur of a crowd. Death apparently had seen fit to bring some of its ghosts along.

"Your champion should go first," the Dealer declared. "I need to study his form."

"Very good," Death repeated in a strangely hushed tone. "The challenger has elected for our Bowling for Souls champion to start. Ernie waits for the pins to set. He takes careful aim. One, two, three steps, and a perfect release! The ball's rolling, rolling. It looks good! Yes, it's a strike!"

The ball had hit the first pin ever so slightly to one side, which helped knock over the pins behind it, and they the pins behind them. All ten were down. It was an impressive performance. Was there any way the Dealer could match it?

The assassin looked girmly down the lane as the pins magically righted themselves.

"I will do my best," he whispered to me. "No less could be expected from one of the Urracht!"

He held the ball as he saw the champion hold it, and took the same steps, one, two, three.

"Now the challenger has the ball," Death's soft voice intoned. "He steps forward cautiously."

Something squealed out in the audience.

"The challenger releases the ball," Death announced. "Uh-oh, it's curving the wrong way. It looks like a gutter ball!"

The Dealer stared out into the audience. "Is that a wild pig?"

"The challenger receives a second ball," Death droned on.

"I could have sworn I heard a wild pig," the Dealer insisted.

"The challenger must release the ball, or forfeit his turn," Death replied with no change of tone.

"That's the way it's going to be, then?" the assassin remarked grimly. "So be it."

"The challenger gets the ball, and prepares himself again," Death returned to describing the action. "Here comes the approach."

This time the squeal was even louder. The Dealer barely flinched.

"There goes the ball. It looks like a better shot this time. He'll at least get a couple pins. No! It's curving in! Give five, no, six pins to the challenger."

His turn completed, the dealer silently returned to my side. He whispered in my ear:

"You do not toy with the Urracht!"

"The champion once again has the ball," Death commented.

Ernie glanced nervously at the specter.

"Isn't it getting a little noisy in here?"

The champion was right. Not only were there wild-pig noises out there, but the crowd was getting louder as well. Another ploy, I imagined, to undermine the Dealer's confidence. Now, however, that the assassin knew about these tricks, I felt Death might be in for a surprise.

"The champion is being a bit temperamental," Death replied. "He has obviously forgotten what happens in this kingdom to temperamental champions. But no, now he is steeling himself, reaching inside for that special something shared by all great athletes. He moves forward with the ball. There it goes. It looks good—maybe just a little off. Oh, too bad! Five pins down. The shot was a bit too much to the right side."

Ernie waited for the ball to come back to him. He had begun to sweat, even though the air wasn't appreciably warm. I wondered exactly *what* it was that they did to temperamental champions down here.

"Here he goes again," Death whispered. "Yes, he's got it! The other five are down! That's Ernie for you! He always gives a hundred and ten percent. What a competitor!"

It was the Dealer's turn again, but this time he approached with a determination that went beyond anything I had ever seen before, a fanaticism based on the total destruction of ten pins at the far end of the lane.

The assassin felled all ten with the first ball, despite the three wild-pig bleats from the audience.

"An impressive move," Death muttered, "but it won't phase the champion."

Ernie, however, looked completely phased. His hair was matted now with sweat, and he jumped every time something made a sound like a wild pig.

"I-I am not used to w-working under these conditions!" he stammered.

"Some champions may get used to not working at all," Death replied. The threat did little good. Ernie got two pins with his first ball, and only one with his second.

The Dealer got another strike, despite a full score of wild pigs crying their hearts out.

He nodded grimly to me upon his return.

"Before, it was just a ball and ten pins. Now it is a weapon against ten wild pigs!"

We would win this one. The Dealer of Death was in his element.

"Okay, okay!" Death remarked in a more normal tone. "I know when I'm beaten. I forfeit. You win the first of the three challenges."

Hubert cheered as Ernie disappeared.

"But perhaps it was a bit unfair," Death continued generously, "presenting you with a sport that you had never witnessed before as your first game. I think the next contest shall be a bit simpler—say, a guessing game?"

"A contest of wits?" Snarks demanded. "Let's have at it, then. I am ready."

"As I knew you would be. But we are not quite prepared. Give me a moment while I call up an impartial third party."

There was a puff of blue smoke by Death's left side, quickly replaced by a tall, frail fellow with stooped shoulders and squinting eyes.

"Our judge," Death introduced the newcomer.

"I'm as impartial as they get in this kingdom," the frail fellow agreed.

"And I have appointed our judge as keeper of the rules," the specter added. "I trust that is satisfactory?"

"Indeed," I replied, not wishing to quibble over a minor point. "And what rules must we follow?"

The judge unfolded a crumpled sheet of parchment. His voice quavered slightly as he read:

"The first rule is that no one is to ask about the rules. The penalty is an immediate forfeit."

"What?" Snarks demanded. "How can we forfeit a game we don't even know about?"

"It is a little severe, so early in the game," Death agreed. "Why don't we give them another chance?"

"You're the boss," the frail fellow replied. "The game goes on."

"I should say so!" Snarks exclaimed. "Who ever heard of those kinds of rules!"

The judge further unfolded the parchment before him, and again read aloud:

"The second rule is that no one is to complain about the rules. The penalty is immediate forfeit."

"Wait a second!" Snarks demanded. "That rule is all tied up with the first one. This is no fair at all!"

"I'm sorry," the judge replied, "but it says here—"

"Now, now," Death interrupted. "Even I will admit that these rules are a bit arbitrary. Why not give our guests one more chance? That way, no one could possibly accuse us of any bias."

The judge shrugged. "If you say so." He nodded to the rest of us. "You guys are getting off easy here. The game goes on again. Well?" He tapped his foot impatiently. "It's your move!"

Snarks turned to me. "What do we do?"

"Indeed," I replied, for I had given the matter some thought. "We do nothing."

"Nothing?" the demon replied.

"Exactly. For what has happened the last two times we attempted to start the game?"

"We immediately lost." Snarks's face brightened as he saw my point. "Oh, I see! You're saying that the game is so constructed that if you attempt to play it—"

"You lose," I finished the thought for him. "So the only thing we can do—the only way we can win—is if we refuse to play."

"Brilliant!" Snarks admitted. "And coming from a human, too! My hat would be off to you, if I wore one."

"So," the judge called to us. "What is the delay? The game must continue!"

I cautioned my companions to silence with a single glance.

"No response?" the judge frowned. "I see." He further unfolded his parchment and read:

"The third rule is that, should anyone refuse to continue playing the game, they will automatically lose. In other words, immediate forfeit."

This time Death shrugged. "What else can we do? I think the judge and I have been more than fair."

"The game is over," the judge agreed.

Death tsked. "Unfortunately, you have brought this upon yourselves, gentle beings, and you have lost. We now stand tied with one contest apiece."

The judge popped out of existence, and the specter paused a moment to stare at each of us in turn.

"I think we should all take a few minutes," Death said slowly, "and consider the importance of our last contest, which will be far more trying than either of those which have gone before. After all, the third game decides whether the wizard goes back with you, or you come to me, for all eternity."

Death's laugh was so cold that it seemed to freeze my heart.

And his laughter went on forever.

NINETEEN

Sometimes, being in the magic business can be a little difficult. Then again, sometimes it can be downright dangerous. In fact, in certain situations, this kind of work can become outright deadly. And then there's times when it gets really bad—

—Unfinished chapter from *Some Thoughts on Apprenticeship,*
by Wuntvor, apprentice to Ebenezum,
greatest wizard in the Western Kingdoms
(a work in progress)

"The time is come!"

Death once again stood at arm's reach.

I shook my head. Before this last contest began, there was one more deceit that needed to be taken care of.

"Indeed!" I called to the specter, for I would not lose this battle without a fight. "Before we begin our last contest, I need a promise."

"A promise?" The fiend nodded its bony head. "Very well. As you know, Death always keeps its promises."

"Good," I replied. "Then show us the real Ebenezum."

The specter chuckled. "Oh, you want to see the *real* wizard! I suppose, if you insist—"

Death waved its hands, and the mage within the cage changed subtly. The revised wizard pulled at his robes as he looked about.

"Why, Wuntvor," my master remarked. "What are you doing here?"

"I have come to save you!" I replied.

"Indeed?" The mage tugged reflectively at his beard. "I am a little hazy on exactly where I am. However, your mission sounds like a laudable goal, at the very least."

Snarks tugged at my shirt. "How did you know?"

"Indeed," I answered. "Once you had alerted me to Death's initial deception, it was simplicity itself. Until a moment ago, the magician in the cage had been too still, too silent. In short, he had not acted at all like my master. It was another of Death's ploys, designed, I am sure, like the wild-pig squeals during the first contest, to hurt us through surprise."

"You are too clever for me, Eternal Apprentice!" Death hissed. "but it will not matter, for our last battle is not one of wits, but of wills."

The specter stepped even closer to me. "Gaze into my eyes, you who are called Wuntvor—in this life. For our last test shall be a staring contest! It is simplicity itself—whoever looks away first, loses. And the contest begins now!"

I looked up and found myself gazing into the twin eye sockets of Death, two pools of blackness so deep that you might fall into them forever. I wanted to look away, before I lost my soul somewhere in those deep recesses. But I could not, no matter how my instincts screamed for escape for, the moment my gaze shifted, then truly would I be lost for eternity. I was forced to gaze into the void, deeper and deeper into a darkness that was never-ending. And, somehow, I had to stare into Death's gaze long enough to overcome this supernatural being. I had to do it for my soul, for my companions, for my master!

"Stare," Death prompted with a laugh, the sound of small beetles roasting to death beneath the desert sun. "Stare deep, Eternal Apprentice."

I was surrounded by blackness, a total absence of light that went on forever, before me and to either side and, I was sure, behind me as well. I was surrounded by Death's darkness. I felt panic rise within me. What was happening? Was I trapped within the specter's stare? Would I be lost in it as well?

Then Death spoke again:

"Stare forever, Eternal Apprentice."

And its voice broke the spell. For why did Death want me? Because I *was* the Eternal Apprentice? And did not Death desire my soul because it had been—until this moment—forever beyond the specter's grasp? Death was not my master! In a way, if what the specter said about me was true, we were equals, the fiend always taking life, while I returned to it over and over again. And if we were equals, there was no reason to panic, no reason, indeed, to doubt that I might be able to win this contest

"Indeed," I replied to the specter, and as soon as I had spoken, my perspective changed, and I was no longer lost deep within the fiend's gaze, but was instead staring once again at the skull-face of Death.

The specter's never-ending smile twitched unpleasantly.

"You fight me, apprentice. Don't you know that you have already lost? Don't you know that, sooner or later, everybody loses to Death?"

This time, I laughed. Death had tried to intimidate me with the force of its presence. Well, perhaps two could travel that road.

"Is that so?" I answered. "Then how do you explain my existence?"

"Then you admit it!" Death screamed triumphantly. "You admit you are the Eternal Apprentice! Oh, how sweet the victory will be, now that I know you are truly the one I seek!"

Oh, dear, I thought. This was not necessarily the result I was looking for. Death's smile reasserted itself, as if the specter was ready now to squander even the last ounce of its energy to defeat me.

"You will look away, Eternal Apprentice," Death whispered, "and you will lose."

It was then that I heard the ghosts. Faintly at first, but stronger with every passing second—the clank of armor, the shouts of men, the tread of mailed boots across packed earth. The noise grew louder still, until it was almost deafening. And it came from everywhere, as if we were being surrounded by an army that went on forever.

"Wuntvor!" Hubert called. "We are being attacked!"

"Indeed!" I yelled back at the dragon, for I could not look away. "You must hold them off, for the sake of my master, and all our souls!"

I heard the clank of ghostly swords and shields, but then I heard more: the roar and crackle of Hubert's flame, the sharp thwack of Snarks's staff, the near-silent blows of the Dealer and the rapidly dancing feet of the Brownie. They would keep my back and flanks safe from these marauding spirits. Together, my companions would hold them until we had won!

But even as I stared at those bottomless eye sockets before me, I could see other things moving in the corners of my vision. I realized then, with a grim certainty, that the ghosts were not content to merely attack my fellows, but were advancing around Death as well, a legion headed straight for me. I caught a glimpse of a spectral sword. Another of the haunted horde flashed a red dagger that I hoped was covered with ghostly blood.

Could I be harmed by ghosts? I feared the answer, and I would know all too soon, for they would be upon me in an instant. Still, they were not unstoppable. From what I heard, my fellows were taking care of any number of the ghostly warriors. But how could I fend them off without looking away from Death?

And then it occurred to me: Perhaps I could not, but my weapon could.

I drew my trusty sword.

"Eek!" Cuthbert shrieked. "What's going on here? This doesn't look at all good! Listen! I take back what I said about getting out of my scabbard from time to—"

"Indeed," I said, interrupting the sword's hysteria. "I am sorry, but you must fight, perhaps harder than you ever have before."

"This is sounding worse with every passing minute!" Cuthbert complained. "Don't I have any say in this matter?"

"Indeed," I answered. "You could completely refuse to do my bidding."

"Really?" the sword replied, calming a bit. "Say, that's awfully nice of you."

"Of course," I continued, "then I would most likely be murdered by these marauding ghosts."

"Gee," Cuthbert remarked uncertainly. "Do you think so?"

"I can't see it going any other way." I paused for a second, then mused, "Of course, there's nothing for you to worry about. No matter what happens to me, there's no chance at all of you being abandoned. The moment I am dead, I'm sure the Dealer will scoop you up and get to work."

"The Dealer? You mean old hack-and-slash?" the sword asked distastefully. "Do you really think so?"

"Well," I replied, "look at it this way: Who's going to stop him?"

"Oh—er—who ever said I didn't want to fight? I'm your sword forever!" Cuthbert cheered. "Onward, into the fray!"

The sword had made its decision not a moment too soon, for the fray, as it were, was coming to us, the legion of ghosts moaning forward to the attack.

"You have to defend yourself, Eternal Apprentice," Death leered. "You have to look away!"

I laughed with a bravado that I almost felt, for Cuthbert guided my hand as I continued to stare deep within Death's dark orbs. I heard the ghostly clang of my sword against whatever it was it fought.

"I think not," I answered the specter. "It takes more than a few pitiful ghosts to defeat the likes of me!"

"Few?" Death sputtered. "Pitiful?" The specter almost glanced away to look at its legions. Almost, but not quite. For the first time, I realized I had a real chance of defeating this creature. The Dealer had said Death had a problem with me. Perhaps I could make that problem the specter's undoing.

"Hah!" my sword cried triumphantly. "Got you!"

I heard another sound, half slice, half gush, like an axe cutting through week-old snow.

"Oh, no!" Cuthbert moaned. "There is something worse than ichor! Ectoplasm!"

"I've gone altogether too easy on you, so far!" Death screamed at me, far more overwrought than the situation warranted. "We'll see how eternal you are, after you've faced my berserker legion!"

"Berserker legion?" Cuthbert asked uncertainly. "I do not like the sound of that!"

I didn't like the sound of what came next, either, for the ghostly moaning about us rose, becoming an unearthly shriek that seemed to have no end.

"Good," the Dealer stated calmly from somewhere nearby. "At last I will have a challenge."

"Look at these guys!" Snarks wailed, and for once, I was glad I could not.

The shrieking was joined by a rhythmic clanking, as if spectral swords clanged against ghostly shields, first ten, then a hundred, then five hundred strong.

"I think it's time for reinforcements!" Snarks screamed.

"Do you mean—" I called back.

"Plaugg!" Snarks replied. "O most unexceptional of deities, we beseech you! We need your barely tolerable aid, and we need it now!"

There was nothing for a moment, but then there was a voice, very faint but somehow still clearly understandable despite the wailing ghosts.

"I hear you, my worshipper."

"Oh, Your Adequateness!" Snarks yelled. "We need you here at once!"

"Oh, dear," the deity's faint voice replied. "How can I put this? You see"—Plaugg coughed distantly—"I'm afraid that is impossible."

"Impossible?" the demon wailed. "But why, Your Pretty-Goodness?"

"The driver refuses to go on that route again," Plaugg explained, his voice fainter with every word. "Something about a bus full of insulting travelers—"

And then Plaugg's voice was gone.

"Oh, no," Snarks murmured. "Have I doomed us all?"

But I could not believe this was the end. I was so close to saving my master. There had to be a way!

"Wuntvor!" a voice called to me above the ghostly chaos. My master's voice!

"Indeed?" I called back, my eyes still fixed on the specter.

"If you allow Death to attack you over and over again, you will lose!" the wizard exclaimed. "You must form a counterattack!"

"Silence, pitiful mage!" Death barked. "You are still under my control!"

"Is he?" I shot back at the specter. "I do not think he will be for long."

For a thought had occurred to me. My master had said we needed a weapon for a counterattack. But what better weapon was there than my master, the great wizard Ebenezum?

At first, I had thought our magic was useless in death's domain. But Snarks had somehow managed to call Plaugg. And the Brownie seemed to be holding his own against the ghostly warriors, for I was sure, could I but turn my head, that I would see shoes raining from nowhere upon our enemy. Therefore, Brownie magic worked here. And who had told us that it wouldn't? Not Ebenezum, but Death, disguised as the wizard.

Ah, but that specter was clever. And I had to be more clever still, if the Eternal Apprentice was to win the day.

"Snarks!" I called to the demon. "I need your help!"

"I've been—telling you that—ever since we've met!" Snarks yelled back between blows of his stout oak staff.

"Indeed," I answered. "I need you to get something out of my pack."

"I'd be—glad to," Snarks replied. "Soon as I—can get away."

"Tap! Hubert! Dealer!" I called to the others. "I need your aid as well. You must form a semicircle behind me, to protect Snarks while he does my bidding."

"Brownie Power to the rescue!" Tap announced.

Hubert assured me: "My most dramatic flame is in your service."

"I find any strategic move fascinating," the Dealer added.

"Okay, boss man!" Snarks interjected. "The demon wit is at your service!"

"Look inside my pack," I instructed him. "There you will find a book—a Home Study Course."

I heard a rustling at my back.

"Eep! Eep eep eep!"

Snarks yelped. "Can't you do *something* about that ferret?"

"Sorry," I apologized. "But my guess is that the ferret can take care of itself."

"A ferret?" Death screamed his distance. "You dare to bring a ferret into this battle?"

The specter wavered, almost looking away again. If *I* made him nervous, my ferrets made him doubly so.

"Magic for the Millions?" Snarks read as he retrieved the book.

"That's the one," I assured him. "Now, look in the back, under multiplication spells."

I heard the sound of pages turning.

"Don't you dare let that ferret get near me!" Death warned. But the specter calmed itself as soon as it spoke. "But what am I saying? I am Death. And Death always wins." The fiend chuckled aridly. "No mere ferret can save you now!"

"Multiplication spells?" Snarks mused. "Oh, there's a lot of them. In fact, there may be a few too many! Would you mind telling me what you'd like to multiply?"

"Shoes," I replied. "At least at first."

The Brownie cheered as Snarks asked if I was kidding.

"Indeed, no," I replied. "We need to quickly reproduce something to keep these ghosts away. Thanks to the Brownie, we already have a rain of footwear. Why not increase it?"

"And do it soon, would you?" Cuthbert pleaded. "The ghosts are everywhere. There's a whole lot of cutting going on here."

"I think a general multiplication spell is best," I further informed the demon, "for we will have to use it on something else later."

"One general spell coming up!" I once again heard Snarks flipping pages.

"Blechh! Blechh! Bllecchh!" the sword screamed. "Ectoplasm is cold! Ectoplasm is slimy! Ectoplasm is everywhere!"

"Ah, here we go!" the demon said triumphantly. "A multiplication spell, short and simple. How do you want to do it?"

"Indeed," I answered, careful to keep my gaze locked on that of Death while my sword hand leaped about under Cuthbert's guidance. "I fear that spell casting is beyond me at the moment. I'm afraid that the honor of making magic must pass to you."

"Me?" Snarks squealed in disbelief. "But I'm a demon. Wizards are supposed to cast spells on demons, not the other way around. I mean, there are certain proprieties—"

"And if we follow them, we shall be killed," I interrupted. "Still, I can see your point. I suppose if a demon isn't good enough to perform magic—"

"N-not good enough—I never said anything of the kind!" Snarks retorted. "Demons may come from the bottom, but they rate way on top! I will perform magic that will put Brownie Power to shame! Now, if the rest of you will look the other way, while I make a fool of myself trying to get this spell to work—"

The rest of us were too busy fighting off our ghosts to reply.

"You make such foolish plans," Death chuckled. "Why not surrender now, before I make you look ridiculous throughout eternity?"

"Indeed," I said sharply as I heard Snarks snuffling through the spell behind me. "The Eternal Apprentice is free to be ridiculous anytime he chooses! If I have my way, you will never have any control over that!"

Snarks called out strings of arcane words while clapping his hands and whistling. He hooted like an owl three times, yelled loudly and did something complicated with his feet upon the packed ground.

"The shoes!" Tap called. "The shoes are coming!"

A chorus of ghostly cries rose around us. I heard an "Ouch!" here, a "Yelp!" there, an "Oh, no, not high heels!" somewhere else.

"They are falling back!" the Dealer announced. "Your plan worked."

"Of course it did," Snarks agreed. "Wasn't there a demon involved —ow!"

I felt it, too. The shoes were not only falling on the ghosts. Now they were dropping on us as well. It began as an occasional soft-soled sandal, but I could hear boots dropping in my vicinity. Soon, the rain of shoes would make us helpless as well.

There was only one person I knew that could stop this sort of thing. Now that the ghosts had retreated, it was time to free him.

"Hubert!" I shouted over the ever-increasing thump-thump-thump of cascading footwear. "Dealer! We have to get Ebenezum out of this cage!"

Death laughed, still only flinching slightly beneath the shoe rain.

"Free your master? Whatever makes you think I will allow that?"

"You will have no choice!" I replied. "Snarks, now that you have mastered the spell to multiply shoes, it is time to turn it to other purposes. It is time to multiply ferrets!"

"Ferrets?" Snarks quavered. "He wanted me, a demon, to cast a spell. Well, I'm adaptable, especially in situations of life and death. And then he wanted the spell to produce shoes! Now, now, I calmed myself, it is life and death, after all, and it will probably be the most distasteful task you ever will have to perform. I mean, what could be worse than shoes? And then he tells me!" The demon choked, the next word lodged in his throat. "F-f-ferrets!"

This was too much. There was no longer any time for Snarks's objections. But could I trust the shoes to continue to keep the ghosts at bay? Careful not to take my eyes away from Death, I ran quickly to the demon's side. There was but one thing to do.

"Here," I said, handing the demon my sword.

"Huh?" Snarks replied.

"What?" Cuthbert yelped.

"If you don't want to cast, you've got to cut!" I answered the demon. "Now, quickly, repeat the spell to me, and I shall perform it!"

"What?" Cuthbert yelped again.

I managed to pat the sword's hilt as I finally released it into the demon's grip. "Now, now," I said reassuringly for Cuthbert's benefit. "You'll just keep on doing that fine job." My now free hand waved absently in the direction of the Dealer of Death. "Unless, of course, you'd rather I gave you to somebody else."

"I'm cutting!" Cuthbert shrieked. "I'm cutting!"

"Indeed," I murmured. "Now, Snarks, repeat the directions for the spell."

"Do I have to?" the demon whined.

"You could cast it yourself," I suggested.

"You convinced me," Snarks said. "You want me to start now?"

"In a moment," I replied, making sure that my gaze was firmly interlocked with that of Death. I had managed for some time to meet the specter's stare, and, apart from a slight watering in the corners of my eyes, was none the worse for wear. If I could simply concentrate on the spell while continuing to stare at Death, I could not help but succeed. And what problems could I have? Snarks, a rank beginner at the art of magic, had managed the multiplication spell to perfection. It should therefore be no problem at all for one with my experience. So why was I worried? Nothing could stop us now!

I took a deep breath.

"Begin."

"If that's the way you want it," Snarks agreed, and began to relay the spell to me.

"You will not stop me with your ferrets!" Death screamed, although there seemed to be a bit of panic in the specter's tone.

I told Snarks to ignore the fiend. In turn, the demon told me to clap, and I clapped. He told me to whistle, and I whistled. He told me to give three owl hoots, and I did that as well.

"Uh-oh," Snarks mumbled mid-spell. "Here come the ghosts."

"One ferret or a hundred ferrets!" Death proclaimed, cheered by its advancing army. "It makes no difference. I will not be stopped by those small, insignificant creatures, no matter how lively they may be." Still, if the specter was so sure of itself, why did its voice crack?

"Now here—comes the—difficult part," Snarks managed, fending off renewed attacks from the ghostly horde. "You must step left, jump, shuffle, step right, shuffle and jump. Quickly now!"

I did as the demon instructed, stepping, then jumping.

"It will never work, Eternal Apprentice," Death insisted. "I no longer feel any fear of your little helpers!"

Perhaps it was Death's repeated taunts that unnerved me. Or perhaps it was merely trying to concentrate simultaneously on Death's stare and my dancing feet. Whatever, when I attempted my second shuffle, I slipped and almost fell, barely managing to keep my gaze locked with that of the specter. It was more difficult than I realized to shuffle when you could not glance at your feet. But I had to finish the spell, and trust that my slight misstep would not change the outcome.

I stepped and jumped and shuffled. Come, ferrets! I thought. Perhaps they would not turn the tide for good, as Death had claimed, but at the very least they would distract the specter long enough for me to think of something else.

"Eep!" my ferret cried. I took the small animal's cry as a good sign. The spell must be working.

"Snarks!" I called. "Are the ferrets multiplying?"

"*Eep!*" The ferret screamed somewhat more insistently.

"Well," Snarks admitted, an odd tone to his voice, "not exactly."
And at that moment, the ground I stood upon was shaken by a thunderous cry:

"EEEP!"

"What?" Death whispered. "It cannot be!"

"EEEP!" the deafening sound came again, whatever made it saying, "Yes, it very well *can* be."

"No, not that large," Death groaned. "I could deal with anything—anything but something like that—anything but a fifty-foot ferret!"

And then the ground shook of its own accord. The ferret was coming.

"EEEP!"

"No," Death whispered. "I won't allow it! Not in *my* kingdom!"

It was too much for the specter, too much eeping life for it to even comprehend. It hugged its robes close by its sides, trying to shrink away from the approaching behemoth, the stupendous gray form moving inexorably toward it through the falling shoes.

"No!" Death shrieked. "Anything but *that* ferret!"

And then a great, furry shadow fell across the specter.

"EEEP!"

Death shrieked, looking up and away, searching for some escape from the rapidly descending ferret.

Death had looked away. I had won.

"Indeed," Ebenezum remarked from close by my side. "This might be a good time for a change of scene."

TWENTY

"Very well. If I must, I will fully explain everything. Let me begin with a demonstration. What am I doing? Only a very simple spell of forgetfulness. What spell of forgetfulness, you ask? Does anyone remember what I was talking about? What are you all doing here, anyways?"

—Ebenezum's final comments on Wizardgate,
whatever that was

"Indeed, yes," I replied. "Do you have any idea how we might leave?"

"No problem at all," my master assured me. "This sojourn in the Kingdom of Death seems to have completely cured my malady. My guess is that, in a place like this, one goes beyond sneezing."

"You're not going anywhere!" Death screamed hysterically as it rapidly retreated. "I'll deal with you, as soon as I'm finished with this —animal!"

"I'm afraid not," I replied to the specter as my master assumed standard conjuring position. "After all, I won."

"Won?" Death hyperventilated, upset perhaps by how easily the huge ferret galloped after it. "Well, I suppose you did, technically. However, I'm quite certain ferrets are against the rules!"

"Rules?" Snarks asked. "What rules?"

"Indeed," Ebenezum interrupted. "If you fellows would gather around me, we'll be leaving now."

"All right, so you've won!" Death screamed as it ran from the monstrous rodent. "Enjoy the rest of your lives, as pitifully short as they will be! I'll be seeing you!"

"Indeed," I replied. "Will you?"

The specter's unearthly shriek was caught short by my master's spell.

All was darkness, then all was light.

I opened my eyes when someone said "Doom." We were back in Vushta, surrounded by wizards and companions. The wizards, as usual, were sneezing.

"Over?" Cuthbert shrieked, still a bit hysterical. "It's really over?" The sword whistled with relief. "Say, would anybody know anything about getting rid of dried ectoplasm stains?"

"Later," I said to the sword as I reclaimed and resheathed it.

"Indeed," Ebenezum called to the others. "Were you expecting us?"

"Doom, no," Hendrek answered. "We were expecting what you landed on top of."

"EEEP!" the fifty-foot ferret who had returned with us remarked.

"What? Who?" an old woman's voice called from beneath the great furry mass. "What is all this? Where am I?"

A gray head popped up behind the huge ferret's form. It was Mother Duck. She frowned.

"This looks an awful lot like Vushta. Why would I come to Vushta?"

Nobody answered her, save for those few wizards still sneezing.

"Smelly place," Mother Duck grumped. "Noisy, too. It's no wonder everybody has a cold. Does anyone know the way to the Eastern Kingdoms?"

Everyone who was capable of it pointed east.

"What am I doing, wandering around like this? I hope I'm not getting too old. And *Vushta?*" She made a face. "Next thing you know, I'll wind up straying into those dreadful Western Kingdoms." She waved vaguely at the crowd around her. "Excuse me, but there's no place like home." And with that, she wandered back in the general direction of her domain.

"Doom," Hendrek remarked when the old lady had passed out of sight. "She was about to attack us, and make Vushta part of her kingdom."

"Then," Norei added from Hendrek's side, "as she was calling forth all the sorcery at her command, you showed up."

"Indeed?" Ebenezum replied. "It's no wonder, then. Instead of the sorceries she desired, she was overcome by an enchanted ferret. And what an enchanted ferret! An overload of that sort would undo anyone in the magical arts."

"Oops!" Richard the giant added in wonder. "So she's gone?"

"It would appear so," the wizard agreed.

The Seven Other Dwarves cheered along.

> "Hi hun, hi hun,
> Then that must mean we've won!"

"That's right!" Tap pulled at my pants leg. "That means His Brownieship is bound to take me back! Doesn't it?"

"Indeed," my master answered. "At least Mother Duck is no longer a threat. But what of the Netherhells?"

I took a moment to explain what Mother Duck had done to the demon's Conquest by Committee.

"Really?" the wizard replied, a certain admiration in his voice. "Then perhaps we will; have a chance to fix the damage done to Vushta before the Netherhells can regroup."

A gruff voice came from the crowd, accompanied by rapid drumbeats.

"Interject!"

The former Grand Hoohah stepped forward. Brax the salesdemon was only half a pace behind.

> "Guxx Unfufadoo, relieved demon,
> Glad he is that you've defeated
> Mother Duck, and says those demons
> Down below are ripe for conquest!"

"That's right!" Brax added. "Guxx and I are going back to the Netherhells to take over again!"

"Doom," Hendrek remarked. "All by yourselves?"

"Contradict!" Guxx exclaimed. Brax beat his rhythm.

> "Guxx Unfufadoo, vengeful demon,
> Has no claws so right for tearing;
> Has the muscles strong for rending;
> Thinks that these will do quite nicely!"

No one disagreed with the demon, who only sneezed slightly at his rhyme.

"So I guess we'll be on our way!" Brax called to the rest of us. "Now there's one thing I want you all to consider carefully: This is your last chance to buy a really high-quality used weapon, just in case, shall we say, that we end up on opposite sides."

There were no takers here, either.

"Conquer!" Guxx announced. He marched off with Brax beating the drum behind him.

"Indeed," Ebenezum mused with a tug of his beard. "Things seem simpler hereabouts since the last time I was in the neighborhood. Perhaps now we can get around to curing the wizards."

"And get everything back to normal?" I asked.

"Yes, Wuntvor," Norei said as she approached me. "I'm glad to have you back."

"So everything's all right?" Hubert cheered, releasing a substantial quantity of smoke. "Alea! Let's do a snappy musical number in celebration."

The damsel stepped forward from the crowd, but she was frowning. "Musical number? Look, Hubie, I've been meaning to talk to you in private—" her voice died, her hands fluttering at her sides. She paused, then sighed. "Well, I suppose I could do it, if it's okay with my new partner."

"New partner?" the dragon yelped in astonishment.

The damsel looked down at her dancing-slippered feet. "Well, you know, you were gone for an awful long time. And I wasn't sure you were ever coming back. I mean, a girl's got to eat!"

"But Alea!" Hubert protested. "Who could take the place of a dragon?"

"Oops," Richard commented.

Alea smiled encouragingly up at the giant. "Take it, Richard! Let's show them our stuff!"

And the giant and Alea sang together:

"Hey, we've got something
You can really dig;
When we do a big show,
It's really big!
All of Vushta is in a whirl
For a giant and a girl!"

Alea pirouetted prettily as Richard stomped half a dozen foothills behind her.

"I thought Damsel and Dragon was as bad as this sort of thing could get," Snarks whispered. "I was wrong."

"Doom," Hendrek agreed in an equally hushed tone, glancing up at the rampaging giant. "But who's going to criticize them?"

Snorphosio the wizard ran into our midst.

"The Dealer of Death!" he cried with uncharacteristic abruptness. "He has revived!"

And the Dealer was right behind him. The well-muscled assassin smiled.

"Not only revived," he murmured pleasantly, "but ready to strangle. Show me those wild pigs!"

"How could she?" Hubert moaned overhead. "I do admit their act has a certain novelty value when considered on a very large scale, but still, what's a dragon to do?"

A furry fellow in a green hat tugged at the dragon's tail. "I say, big guy. Have you ever considered how unique your act might be with the assistance of a talented talking wolf?"

And I heard another, magnificently modulated voice from the rear of the crowd:

"My lap has returned." The unicorn sighed musically. "I am content."

"And Wuntie?" Alea fluttered her eyelashes prettily. "When you have a chance, we have all sorts of catching up to do!"

Norei squeezed my arm, somehow managing to drag me in her direction. "I guess you are right, Wuntvor. Everything is back to normal."

"Indeed," my master added. "and we must get back to work."

Arm in arm, Norei and I followed my master, the great wizard Ebenezum, back toward the university library. The sun was bright overhead, and the air had the crisp edge of early fall. I felt a spring in my step, brought about by being back among those whom I loved best, and on the verge of solving all our problems.

"EEEP!" the fifty-foot-high ferret called as it happily trundled after us.

I squeezed Norei's hand. I mean, what could possibly go wrong now?